Acclaim for **MARTYN BEDFORD**'s

THE HOUDINI GIRL

"An erotic mystery. . . . Magic, trickery, disappearance and the nature of both honesty and deception are elaborately developed metaphors in the book, worked out on a dizzying number of levels."   —*Newsday*

"Well-executed. . . . Bedford's performance . . . shows diligence and craft."   —*The Boston Globe*

"Bedford is a writer to watch."
                —*Seattle Post-Intelligencer*

"Bedford adroitly weaves magic . . . and detective work into a fast-paced story that ends up being surprisingly poignant."   —*Detroit Free Press*

"Bedford is a clever, provocative writer and *The Houdini Girl* is a great success, delivering what he always promised: writing that is interesting, nerve-wracking, bold, unusual, stylish, never complacent and always intelligent."   —*The Times* (London)

"Few authors have plumbed the metaphor that love is magic as thoroughly as Martyn Bedford does. . . . [An] intricately structured, cleverly compelling novel."
                —*Publishers Weekly*

Also by MARTYN BEDFORD

Acts of Revision

MARTYN BEDFORD

THE HOUDINI GIRL

Martyn Bedford is the author of *Acts of Revision*,
which won the *Yorkshire Post* First Novel Award.
He lives with his wife in England.

THE
HOUDINI
GIRL

MARTYN BEDFORD

VINTAGE CRIME/BLACK LIZARD

Vintage Books

A Division of Random House, Inc.

New York

To my dad, Peter Bedford

FIRST VINTAGE CRIME/BLACK LIZARD EDITION, JUNE 2000

Copyright © 1998 by Martyn Bedford

The Library of Congress has cataloged the Pantheon as follows:
Bedford, Martyn.
The Houdini girl / Martyn Bedford.
p. cm.
ISBN 0-375-40527-5
I. Title.
PR6052.31112H68 1999
823'.914—dc21 98-35826
CIP

Vintage ISBN: 0-375-70476-0

Author photograph © Bellworth Photography Ltd., Sheffield

www.vintagebooks.com

Printed in the United States of America
10 9 8 7 6 5 4 3 2 1

The magician is supremely honest. He tells you he is going to deceive you, then lives up to his word.

– *Ricky Jay, magician*

THE HOUDINI GIRL

Prologue

Truth is, I tricked her into falling for me. Rosa Kelly: dark hair, blue eyes – wicked combination. And, though she could've had her pick, she fell for me. OK, maybe 'tricked' has inappropriate connotations. How about this: she wasn't tricked so much as beguiled? Yes. Altogether more apt. *Beguiled*. Comparable to 'bewitched', with its suggestions of sensuality and enchantment. Certainly, the illusion with which I beguiled her depended, for effect and execution, on intimacy of touch and a semblance of the supernatural. We were in a pub in Oxford, the Eagle and Child; wood panelling, nooks and crannies. We were strangers. I was with my friends, she was with hers. Someone in my group knew someone in hers and, following the complicated rearrangement of tables and chairs, there were thirteen of us seated together. An inauspicious assembly if you're inclined to superstition, which I am not. I'd noticed Rosa even before the two parties had become one, though I made sure to give no indication of paying her more, or less, attention than the other newcomers in our smoky, boozy alcove. The positioning of the chairs – I swear I had nothing to do with it, occupied as I was with the transfer of drinks – brought us directly opposite one another. She was smoking Marlboro and drinking Belgian lager straight from the bottle. Her eyeshadow was pale green, to match her lipstick. She wore a ring on every finger and on both thumbs.

'Watch that one, Rosa, he's a magician,' said one of my friends as the introductions were completed.

Rosa, drawing deeply on a cigarette, exhaled across the table. 'There,' she said, 'I've made him disappear in a puff of smoke.'

Everyone roared at that. Brilliant timing, impeccable delivery. I might've reached over and produced a cheese-and-onion crisp from behind her ear, but when you've just been upstaged in public the least embarrassing recourse is to play the supporting role with good grace. Besides, a *crisp*? So I laughed along with the rest of them. Rosa's voice was slightly husky, her accent a curious concoction of Irish and London; her eyes and mouth smiled in perfect synchronization, as though she enjoyed nothing more than being made to laugh. She turned to the guy on her left, asking him to pass an ashtray. They fell into conversation, her long black hair snagging now and then on his shoulder as she leaned close to hear him. Me, I drank and talked to my friends and went to the bar and to the toilet. And, with discretion, I observed her hands – all those rings, the emerald nails, the way she held her drink, lit a cigarette. She had long bony fingers and thin wrists engulfed in bracelets and friendship bands and the cuffs of a multicoloured woollen sweater several sizes too big for her. Every fresh bottle of beer, she shredded the label clean off with her thumbnail.

I have magician's hands. By that, I don't mean they are the perfect size or shape for my work, because such perfection of design is rare. It helps to have hands large enough to facilitate, say, the concealment of a playing card; but large hands have large fingers, less well suited to the more nimble manipulations. The trick is to adapt. Most anatomical deficiencies of the hand can, within reason, be compensated for by rigorous practice or by appropriate props. (If you've got small hands, use a smaller pack of cards.) My hands are neither too large nor too small; what they are is well trained. I have taught myself dexterity and ambidexterity. A speciality in my repertoire of sleights is 'acquitment' – the showing of a hand as empty while actually it contains something. Done ineptly, this is known in the profession as 'hand-washing'. Two tips: one, rehearse in front of a mirror until your movements appear entirely natural; two, never look at your hands while effecting a sleight, because the one place the audience is sure to look is where you're looking.

Rosa's hands weren't magical; for all their conscious disguise of adornment and manipulation, they revealed rather than concealed. I longed to hold them. We'd all been drinking for a while when a familiar appeal issued from the hubbub of overlapping chatter. *Hey, Red, show us a trick.* Even my oldest friends do this. You get used to it.

'I'm playing the Crucible, in Sheffield, next Friday, if you want to come along.'

'Fuck off and show us a trick.'

'Fuck off yourself.'

'What's this, the Illusion of the Cantankerous Git?'

After a moment or two of this, you give in. And you always involve someone else in the illusion, because they love all that. *I'll need the help of an assistant from the audience; come on, don't be shy . . .* That evening, I made eye contact across the table. Blue irises, green eyeshadow. With no perceptible alteration, Rosa's expression said *Don't even think about it.* But the enthusiastic coercion of others as they edged their chairs closer to our table made it more awkward for her to decline than to agree.

'Go on, then.' Defiance. Her eyes, her tone of voice, the set of her shoulders said she was prepared to be unimpressed; nothing I could do could possibly surprise or interest her or escape her detection. And if I tried to make her appear foolish I'd fail because she didn't give a shite what anyone thought of her, least of all me. She smiled. 'If you're good, I'll let you make me a giraffe out of balloons.'

I instructed her to hold out her hands, palms downwards. She did this. I took them in mine and drew them over the centre of the table. Her skin was cool and dry. Releasing her hands, I told her to make fists. She made fists. Everyone was quiet now, watching and listening with rapt attention.

'You're a Roman Catholic, right?' I asked.

'And there's you guessing that, with me talking like a Kerrywoman.'

One or two people giggled.

'Do you believe in the stigmata?'

'The what?'

'That we can be marked with the sign of Christ's suffering on the cross?'

'Oh, sure.'

I dipped the tip of my right middle finger into the ashtray, piled with the accumulated tappings from her own cigarettes. Displaying the silvery-grey stain at the end of the finger, I declared, 'By rubbing this into the back of your clenched fist, I shall cause the ash to pass through the hand and appear like a stigma in the centre of your palm.'

Her eyes said *Oh, yeah*. I kept my face a blank of composed concentration. Placing my fingertip on the back of her right hand, I began massaging the ash gently into the pale skin with a small, circular movement. The bracelets on her wrist clicked against one another as she responded involuntarily to the pressure of my touch. All eyes were focused on the point of contact, where a charcoal smear now blemished the skin. Rosa glanced up at me, then down again at the back of her hand.

'Now, Rosa, please unclench your fist and display your hand palm upwards.'

She did as instructed. Her palm was unmarked. Silence gave way to stifled laughs, a groan, a jeer. Rosa caught my eye again, smirking slightly, and I feigned an expression of alarmed incomprehension. She was about to recline in her seat.

'Are you left-handed?' I asked suddenly.

She nodded.

'You are?'

'Yeah.'

'In that case, would you unclench your left hand for me?'

It was her turn for puzzlement. Her smile became uncertain. The onlookers had fallen quiet once more, switching attention to her other fist. Rosa uncurled the fingers and, slowly, hesitantly, revolved the palm upwards. In its centre was an unmistakable dab of cigarette ash.

PART ONE

Oxford

Let us begin by committing ourselves to the truth – to see it like it is and to tell it like it is – to find the truth, to speak the truth and live with the truth.

– *Richard Nixon*
nomination acceptance speech,
Miami, 8 August 1968

Four men push a cabinet on stage. Houdini leads an elephant into the cabinet. Houdini shows the cabinet empty. *Twenty* men push the cabinet off stage. Where did the elephant go?

– *attributed to*
Walter Gibson (1897–1985)
magician, journalist, writer

Red

Ask away, I won't tell you how it's done. I never divulge the methodology of a specific effect. 'Exposure' – that is, deliberate revelation of the secret means by which magic is accomplished, as opposed to '*dis*closure' by accident or incompetence – is discreditable. This isn't mere adherence on my part to a tenet of the Magic Circle, nor stubborn respect for the traditions of our profession (although it's true we've endeavoured to guard our secrets for four thousand years). No, my reason for keeping schtum is pure self-interest. Methods are seldom as interesting as the feats performed by their means; if I tell the audience how it's done, I diminish their respect for me. Simple as that. Exposure, especially in the immediate aftermath of an effect, can't be anything but anticlimactic. Besides, divulging the 'trick' might satisfy an onlooker's curiosity, but magic isn't about tricks. To trick someone suggests you have (to your benefit and their disadvantage) cheated, swindled or deceived them in some under-hand way. Trickery implies a perpetrator and a victim.

I am not a trickster, I am a magician. That is, I perform feats of conjuring and illusion for the purposes of entertainment. *Performance* is the key. In truth, tricks are incidental; if magic consists of mere trickery, then acting requires nothing but cos-tume and make-up. I used to be an actor. To be exact, I was a member of an undergraduate drama society at Oxford (Poly, as was, not the University). I still live in Oxford; I still act. When I'm on stage, I'm an actor playing the part of a magician. Spectators, for all this, remain fixated on secrets, on trickery. They witness the performance – the *performance* – of a stunning magical feat, and barely has their initial amazement subsided than they are asking (I hear them, I see it in their faces): *How the fuck did he do that?*

As I say, magic, as an art form, isn't the mere presentation of puzzles to confound the onlooker; it isn't about tricks, it's about *illusion*. And being privy to the mechanics of a magical feat destroys any sense of illusion. I am an illusionist. Without illusion I am nothing. I believe Rosa appreciated this from the very beginning.

When our friends in the pub that evening – mine and Rosa's – implored me to divulge how the ash stain came to appear in her left palm, I declined. When they proposed various theories and hypotheses, I smiled non-committally. And when they urged me to repeat the illusion, I said no. Another of my golden rules: never perform the same feat twice before the same audience; once the element of surprise is gone, the illusion is devalued as a spectacle and the method becomes easier to detect. Rosa, who had more reasons than most for wanting to know the trick, didn't add her voice to the collective plea for disillusion. She sat quietly, frowning, holding her palm in front of her face as if to assure herself that the 'stigma' was there. Then she licked it off. Looking me full in the face across the table, her tongue streaked with ash, she said, 'How come they call you Red? You a fucking communist or something?'

Later that night, when I asked why she'd decided to sleep with me, she said a) I didn't cough when she made me vanish in a cloud of smoke; and b) my hands, as I guided hers into position for the stigmata illusion, weren't clammy.

'No other reason?'

'Nah.'

'It wasn't because you fancied me?'

'I shagged you, didn't I?'

She told me she was twenty-four going on twenty-five, four years younger than me, though there were occasions when I felt juvenile in her presence. For instance, I couldn't refrain from asking whether she was friends with the guy she'd been flirting with in the Eagle and Child. Rosa said she'd never met him before.

'Anyway, I wasn't *flirting* with him.'

'Come off it.'

'You were the one I was flirting with.'

'You didn't speak to me all evening. You didn't even *look* at me.'

'Exactly.'

I reflected on this, running over the sequence of events that culminated in our introduction. I visualized her, assisting in the rearrangement of tables and chairs. I asked, 'Did you engineer it so we wound up sitting opposite each other?'

She smiled, shaking her head. 'Now, that would be telling.'

I asked Rosa about herself, and she told me. She was born in Killarney, County Kerry, and emigrated to London with her parents at the age of nine. An only child, *despite what they say about Catholics*. Something to do with a difficult labour. *Daddy fucked her putting me in there, and I fucked her coming out.* Seeing my expression, she shrugged off my unease at her remark. When Rosa spoke, whatever she said, you could like it or lump it. Mammy (*Mary, natch*) was a school dinner-lady; Daddy was a postman. Postman Patrick. They died in a car crash when she was fourteen. *Mangled. You should've seen the car.* She was put into care – children's homes, foster parents. She left school, examless, and moved into a bedsit before she was seventeen. Kensal Rise. And, by the way, she wasn't RC any more. Not a proper one; she'd lapsed.

'How is it you've retained your Irish accent?'

'*Retained*, is it?'

'No, seriously.'

Another shrug. 'I work with a bunch of Micks.'

'Doing what?'

'Dogsbody.' She stubbed out a cigarette. I'd no idea how many she'd smoked since we'd walked home from the pub. 'You heard of *Erin*?' I shook my head. 'Newspaper for Irish ex-pats. "Editorial assistant", that's me. Carting bits of paper from one gobshite journalist to another, answering the phone and making tea. Oh, and I get to sort the fucking post.'

'You enjoy it, then?'

'You should see the office – like a public convenience, with computers instead of sinks.'

The second syllable of 'convenience' was elasticated to

accommodate several 'e's between the 'v' and the 'n'. It must've been three in the morning. We were sitting cross-legged on my bed, facing one another, naked, smoking and listening to music. We'd fucked, twice. I don't know how we came to leave the pub together, it just happened. One minute, thirteen people were saying beery cheerios in St Giles; the next, the two of us were strolling through town towards Osney. A clear, cool night in early spring. Rosa wanted a burger from the cabin by the station, so we had one each with chips and ate from greaseproof bags as we walked. Her mouth tasted of minced beef and ketchup when we stopped to kiss outside my house. In the glare of the security light, her hair hung in black swathes that framed a face made spectral by the harsh magnesium-white. The green strokes of make-up were rendered luminous.

In my bedroom she asked two questions before we undressed.

'D'you have condoms?'

'Yes.'

'Are you shagging someone else?'

'No.'

She held my gaze for a moment before beginning to unbutton my shirt. In bed, I was a puppet – hands, mouth, cock manoeuvred about her body by the tug of invisible strings. Rosa *fucked* me. And she used me to fuck herself. I told her, truthfully, I'd never had such a good shag in my entire life; she said she was glad about that. As we lay there afterwards, however, I found myself wondering about someone who would fuck a stranger less than four hours after they'd first met. It didn't occur to me that I'd behaved no differently to her. At least, it didn't strike me to make a comparison. Not at the time, though it does now. Besides, it wasn't just the fact that we'd fucked, it was the way we'd done it. I was at once exhilarated and excited and unfathomably afraid of the implications of a woman who could fuck so well.

'You a fucking communist or something?'

I drained my pint. Raising my voice above the noise of the pub, I replied, 'Red was the name of a horse.' My throat was raw from the smoke. 'Red Alligator, '68 Grand National. Dad won so much money he treated himself and Mum to a holiday. That was when I was conceived, so they reckon.'

Rosa said, 'Your old feller named you "Red" after a horse?'

'No, he called me Fletcher, after the winning jockey. Fletcher Brandon is my actual name. People call me Red because . . . I suppose, as nicknames go, it's more interesting than "Fletch".' I elaborated. 'What it was, a friend of mine called me Red one time and it just sort of caught on.'

'Fletcher Brandon.' She rolled the name in her mouth like a boiled sweet.

'Dad was hoping I'd grow up to be a jockey. Wrong build, as it turned out.'

'What if the horse hadn't won?'

'Yeah, I used to wonder – suppose his big win had come up at that year's Derby. Sir Ivor. I'd have been christened Piggott instead of Fletcher.' Rosa, noting my empty glass, offered me a slug of her lager. The side of the bottle was tacky where the label had been pared off. 'That would've meant me being conceived in June, though, rather than April.'

'So?'

'Different egg, different sperm, different me. I'd have been made to vanish even before I was born. The greatest disappearing act of all!'

Rosa reclaimed her drink. 'Anyone ever told you you talk a load of shite?'

I could've expanded on the subject of my name. My *names*. But someone interrupted to ask what I was drinking (*My fucking beer* – Rosa) and anyway, her previous remark – for all it'd been dressed in a smile – had had a deflating effect. In the months to follow, the accusation that I was talking shite would become a familiar refrain. So I didn't tell her Brandon wasn't the name I was born with. I chose it for myself. My original surname was Clarke, but I changed it, legally, when I was nineteen, when Dad fucked and then fucked off with a woman who was only two years older than me. Why 'Brandon'? At that time, I was starting to take my 'hobby' more seriously – no longer content to practise magic without an appreciation of its theory, its art,

13

its history. Among the books, I came across a reference to the principal juggler and conjuror in the court of Henry VIII. Brandon: the first British illusionist on record. His wasn't the most pleasant repertoire, but as an anarchic mathematics under-graduate he appealed to me. One of his feats – performed before the king – was to cause a pigeon to drop dead from its perch while the magician, uttering incantations, repeatedly stabbed a picture of the bird. The illusion was accomplished by Brandon having previously dosed the pigeon with nux vomica, timing the climax of his performance to coincide with the requisite number of minutes (established by experiment) for the poison to take effect. This is one secret method I don't mind exposing, my namesake's 'trick' being seldom scripted into modern conjuring routines.

No further mention of names, then. And, in all honesty, I forget what we did talk about, Rosa and I, as the fuss engendered by my small act of illusion evaporated, people returned to their places, and my fee – a fresh pint – was set in front of me. I recall that she showed no interest whatsoever in eliciting from me the secret of the stigmata; I recall, also, being impressed by that. A sucker for unpredictability, me. A sucker for Rosa, to tell the truth.

Even so, our initial meeting happened almost a year ago, and I find that some details of our time together in the intervening months are uncertain or elusive, while others are etched in my memory with all the definition of the present. In the light of what has taken place, I'd willingly re-create each minute of each day we shared and expand every one of those moments to last an hour. But this is a feat beyond the power of magic. Although, as I go over events in my mind, I appear to be doing just that – reviving and magnifying spent time. Another illusion, self-inflicted. What began as a commitment to memory, a preservation of the past before it slipped like sand through my fingers, has assumed the nature of a quest. A quest for truth. My obsession has been the scrutiny of moments and details in the belief that contained within them are the secrets of understanding. I under-stand this, at least: the clearest, most vivid recollection I have –

my abiding and unalterable memory of Rosa Kelly – is of how *vibrant* she was that first night. I have never met anyone who was so alive.

It's the same old shite, whichever way you look at it. This business with the ash. Very clever, sure, but the same old shite they always give you. I've heard it all before. They think if they tart it up you'll . . . But they can't ever tart it up enough so you don't see the shite of it. What he's really saying (what's that line?) . . . yeah, 'Pick a card, any card.' So you either pick a card or you don't pick one. You can say fuck off with your cards and stick them in your hole, ya bollix. Or you can pick a card. When you pick one, it doesn't mean he's not a bollix, it just means you've picked a card. I pick one. By letting him do the thing with the ash, I pick a card. But it's not any card, like he says. It's the card he wants you to pick. They can do that, they can choose the card for you and make like it's you what chose it. And it's always a heart, the jack or the king or something. You pick his card, and it says 'Love'. You can go for that. You can say yeah, OK I'll have that. Or you can say fuck that, show me the card I'm really picking. Only, he won't. They don't, ever. What you see is what you get, until it isn't any more. But by that time you've made your choice. What they want is a ride. What you are, to them, is a ride. Sometimes you want a ride too, and that's fine. That's OK with me. But if you want something else . . . What I'm saying is, if he shows you the jack of hearts and it's the jack of hearts you're after, you're not going to look up his sleeve for the jack of spades. Are you? You ought to, if you've any fucking sense, but you don't. So he does the stuff with the ash, and I let him. And I say yeah, I'll go for that. But in my head it's 'this might be the usual shite or it might not.' Only, you don't know for sure. Except it's mostly shite they give you sooner or later.

The morning after was a Sunday, we stayed in bed until mid-afternoon. We ate breakfast and lunch off trays like a pair of bedridden invalids. We dozed, on and off, and we fucked. At four o'clock, Rosa got up without a word and began to dress. I asked where she was going and she said she was away home to collect her things.

'I thought I could move in, if you like.'

I sat up. She was finger-combing her hair in the mirror above the chest of drawers, applying make-up. Seeing her in reflection, I noticed something about her mouth. Her lips. Full and sensual, set in something between a pout and a blown kiss, her lips seemed permanently to be slightly parted. I was reminded of those models in ads for telephone sex. But Rosa wasn't posing, not even conscious of being observed. She reached inside her T-shirt and doused each underarm with my deodorant.

'Rosa.'

'Seen my woolly anywhere?'

'Over there.' I pointed to a corner of the room, where her patchwork-quilt-patterned jumper was spilling from the rim of a wastepaper basket. She retrieved it and pulled it on. The upper portion of her bright green leggings disappeared.

'You never see a girl get dressed before?'

'Have you thought this through?' I asked.

'Not much.'

I reached over to the bedside table for cigarettes, lit one and offered the pack. She took a drag on mine instead, releasing a plume of smoke towards the ceiling.

'Yes or no?' she demanded.

'How long for?'

She shrugged.

'What if we fuck up?' I said.

'Write to Marje Proops.'

'Marje Proops is dead.'

'Write to her anyway.'

I laughed. 'Rosa, I don't even *know* you.'

'And me, I s'pose I could choose "The Life and Works of Fletcher Brandon" as my specialist subject?'

I filled my lungs with smoke and exhaled through my nose. There was a half-finished mug of tea beside the bed, stone cold and scummy. Rosa and I had been in one another's company for twenty hours and eleven minutes, give or take.

'How come you've a tan this time of year?' she asked.

'Sunbed.'

'Why?'

'I need to look good on stage.'

'You have a sunbed here, or what?'

'Look, I'm not getting this.'

She went across to open the curtains, bleaching the room with daylight. The bedding reeked of our bodies and beer and stale tobacco. Rosa opened a window.

'I like you,' she said. 'I like shagging you. We could see how it goes.'

'What about where you're living now?'

'I'm sharing with friends. I could always move back there . . . afterwards, like.'

'Don't you have to give notice?'

'They won't mind.'

I studied her from the rear as she stared out of the window. 'I don't know.'

'I'm leaving now, so.' She turned. 'I'll come back, or I won't. It's up to you.'

Rosa fetched her belongings. She declined my offer of transport or help with carrying her things, returning an hour and a half later in a taxi with a large suitcase, a backpack, a holdall, dresses on hangers, a full-length cheval mirror, a bicycle, half a dozen heavily pregnant carrier bags and wearing four hats on her head. She said she'd pay the same in rent as she gave her friends and we'd split bills fifty-fifty. I explained to her that I was often away for days on end, doing shows in different parts of the country; she said that was fine because we'd have less time to learn to hate each other. On the Monday, she came home with a black kitten from an animal rescue centre.

'Every feller's dream,' she said, 'two females at once.'

'I don't like cats.'

'Your furniture could do with a good scratching, if you ask me.'

The kitten, it transpired, was male, though Rosa persisted in referring to him as 'she'. That was in March. Almost a year later, they were still living at my place, and I hadn't once resorted to necromantic contact with Mrs Proops. Then, three things occurred to reduce my life to what it is now. The first, I don't want to think about for the moment. The second, I have to; I haven't been able to think of anything else.

I was performing in Bradford. St George's Hall, for one night, the first show of a four-day tour of West Yorkshire that was to include Halifax, Huddersfield and Leeds. St George's is handy for the station, and for Stakis, where I stay when I play Bradford. The hotel is next to an NCP car-park and, from the outside, the two buildings are almost indistinguishable. By leaning out of my bedroom window I could see the front of the theatre, bedecked with billboards advertising my show:

Peter Prestige the Prodigious Prestidigitator

Corny and excessively alliterative, I know, but it's grown on me. Peter was my maternal grandfather's name, while Prestige has appropriate etymological roots in the Latin *praestigiae*, or 'conjuror's tricks', akin to *praestringere* – to tie up, to blindfold. The stage name was chosen for my public début in the students' union bar at Oxford Poly, with the aid of my friend, fellow student and, subsequently, theatrical agent, Paul Fievre (pronounced 'fever'). It would help keep my feet on the ground, he said, no matter how successful I became. *A constant reminder that 'prestige'*

– being held in high regard – is, by definition, an illusion. Rosa considered Paul to be even more full of shite than I was.

I was due on in Bradford at nine. I'd spent the afternoon at the theatre with my stage assistant – The Lovely Kim – preparing for the show. Back at the hotel, I ate a light meal and called Rosa from my room; the answering machine played my own voice to me. Half six. She'd probably gone for a drink after work with her colleagues at the newspaper. I left a message and decided to try again after the show.

The act went down a storm, from opener to finale. Kim, typically, played her part to perfection. In two years' working together we've developed a rapport which, according to Paul, produces a sexual *frisson* that audiences find irresistible. *It's as though they're voyeurs watching two attractive people indulging in sophisticated foreplay.* Certainly, Kim is no mere 'box-jumper'. She possesses that indefinable, unteachable quality: stage presence. A girlfriend – the one prior to Rosa – effectively undermined our relationship by her failure to believe that the on-stage aura, the *frisson*, was nothing more than an act, or to accept my repeated assurances as to the innocence of the time Kim and I, of professional necessity, spent together in rehearsal or away on tour. She tormented herself with the notion of my betrayal. Rosa, in contrast, seemed entirely immune to jealousy or mistrust with regard to Kim, or anyone else. *You're good together,* she said, the first time she saw my show. And that was that. I thought they might strike up a friendship, but Rosa – shaking her head emphatically on an occasion when I expressed surprise that they hadn't – replied, 'We're too alike.' As for Kim, she was barely able to mask her dislike of the new woman in my life.

I closed the show at St George's Hall with the Zigzag Girl illusion. One of my favourites – visually appealing, entirely angle-proof and suitable to be performed under almost any conditions. The illusion begins with a narrow cabinet standing centre-stage into which Kim is shut so that only her face, hands and one foot are visible. I drive two large blades horizontally into the front of the cabinet, dividing it into three. I then slide the central section sideways, completely out of alignment with the top and bottom. An empty space now exists where Kim's middle should be. Her face, hands and foot can still be seen in the upper, middle and lower sections respectively, although her body appears to have been trisected. She is smiling. The cabinet is then brought back into alignment, the blades are removed and the door is opened to allow The Lovely Kim to step out, whole and unharmed. Applause, bow, curtain; thank you, Bradford, and good-night. Of course, these are but the mechanics of procedure; it is originality of performance – the showmanship, the rapport between illusionist and assistant, the patter, the sheer *panache* with which the effect is executed – that elevates this illusion (or any illusion) from trickery to magic. We made repeat curtain-calls before retiring to our dressing rooms.

I was removing my stage make-up when there was a knock at the door. I shouted for whoever it was to come in. Two constables – one male, one female – both in uniform. I broke off from what I was doing and dropped a discoloured cotton-wool swab into the bin beside my dressing-table. I sat on my stool, half-turned to face them; I didn't say anything. The WPC took off her hat; I'd have given anything for her to keep her hat on, but she took it off. I'd have given anything for her face to be formed into a different expression. She introduced herself and her colleague. Her accent was broad Bradford. She asked if I was Mr Fletcher Brandon; I said I was. She named my address in Oxford and asked me to confirm that I resided there with a Miss Rosa Marie Bernadette Kelly. I said yes; I said Rosa was my girlfriend. The WPC was pressing her hat in and out of shape between her hands as she spoke. I kept my eyes on the hat. West Yorkshire police had been contacted, she said, by their colleagues in the Thames Valley. There had been an incident. Those were her words: *an incident*. She said she was very sorry. And then she told me Miss Kelly was dead.

The kitten, like me, had two names. Rosa called *her* Kerrygold, not out of patriotic nostalgia but because of the creature's addiction to licking butter. To distract him from spoiling ours – removed from the security of the fridge now and then for spreadability's sake – we left a pat of 'K' each morning in his food dish. For all that this made Rosa's preferred name apt, I insisted on christening him after the sorcerer of Arthurian legend: Merlin. Not that it mattered what we called the kitten, because under no circumstances would he respond to, or even register, anything we said. At first I thought he was deaf, until I discovered that the rattling of a spoon against the inside of a newly emptied Whiskas tin would bring him hurtling to the kitchen step from the obscurest corners of the garden. Merlin was absolutely black, from his ears to his tail to his toes.

In the days after Rosa's death he was unbearable to watch. The little affection he'd displayed had been reserved for her: hers was the lap he sat on, if inclined to sit on a lap; hers were the calves he brushed against during the preparations for feeding; she was the one in the crook of whose legs he slept at night; it was she he woke each morning with a rasping face-lick. Me, I received feline indifference or an occasional, unprovoked, swipe that left the back of my hand scratched and mottled with allergic reaction. With Rosa gone, Merlin had taken to patrolling the house room by room as though he might find her hidden away in some dark corner. Any item of hers he came across – a pair of shoes, a magazine, a discarded piece of clothing, a tube of lipstick – he would sniff investigatively, or lick with all the fastidious attention he applied to the ritual cleaning of his fur. He never left the house. If anyone came to the door Merlin would dart into the hall and scrutinize the caller from somewhere between my feet before slinking away on establishing it wasn't her. By the third day he'd ceased searching and had settled himself instead on a pile of Rosa's jumpers in the bottom of the wardrobe. I found him there that night when I went to hang up my clothes before going to bed. I spoke his name; then I spoke hers, and Merlin raised his head from her patchwork-quilt woolly, peering up at me through the motley garments of Rosa's that overhung him in draped suspension like the tresses of a weeping willow.

Paul Fievre, my friend and agent, phoned the people who needed to know, cancelled bookings, fielded calls, acted as chauffeur, cook, home help, counsellor. Funeral plans and the formal registration of Rosa's death were on hold pending notification from the coroner's office; there would have to be an inquest. I wanted to see her, I said, following my return on the first available train the morning after the Bradford show. Paul made the arrangements. And it was Paul who let the police officer into my house that same afternoon. I was in the living room. I heard them in the hall, the awkward formality of pleasantries, the officer asking *How's he taking it?*, Paul replying *He doesn't really know what day of the week it is.* The policeman was in plain clothes.

'DC Fuller,' he declared, shaking my hand. 'Thames Valley CID.'

He expressed condolences and said that he would be accompanying me to the district mortuary. First, a few questions, if I wouldn't mind. He sat on the sofa while Paul and I occupied the armchairs. About my age, but already thin on top; he'd nicked himself shaving, his chin blemished with dried blood. I was the only one smoking.

'I've seen your show,' he said. 'Police benevolent fund cabaret, last year.' He smiled. 'You were very good.' When I didn't reply, he produced a notepad and pen and, looking at Paul and then back at me, cleared his throat twice in rapid succession. 'I understand you lived here with Miss Kelly, is that correct?'

I nodded.

'Are you the owner of the property?'

'Yes.'

'And how long had Miss Kelly resided with you at this address?'

'About a year. March last year, she moved in.'

'Had you known each other long? When she moved in, I mean?'

I hesitated. 'Not long, no.'

He smiled again. 'Bit of a whirlwind romance, was it?'

I nodded.

'And you were lovers?'

I looked at him.

'I'm trying to establish your relationship to the . . . to Miss Kelly.'

'We were lovers, partners – whatever you want to call it. Yes.'

'OK, fine.' He laid the pad and pen beside him on the sofa and ran a hand through his receding hair, breaking off eye contact for a moment. 'How much do you know of the circumstances of Miss Kelly's death?'

I took a drag on my cigarette. 'They told me she fell off a train.'

Gaze still averted, he elaborated. Rosa had *descended* on to the track from a slow-moving train as it approached Reading station, landing in the path of an express travelling in the opposite direction. It wasn't clear, at this stage, whether or not her departure from the train was accidental.

'You mean she might've been *pushed*?'

'There's nothing to suggest the death was suspicious but, as I say, inquiries are ongoing, and we can't discount that possibility just yet.' He paused. 'Of course, it's also possible she may have . . . jumped.'

'Suicide? You think Rosa killed herself?'

Paul interjected, 'Red, they're *not sure*. That's all he's saying.'

I stubbed out my cigarette. Addressing the detective constable, I said, 'Don't you fucking come here telling me she killed herself.'

The three of us shared an uneasy silence. Then, clearing his throat again and reaching for the notebook and pen, the officer resumed. 'The incident occurred at approximately two fifteen. I was hoping you could shed some light on why Miss Kelly was travelling from Oxford to Reading at that time on a Friday afternoon.'

I shook my head. 'I assumed she was at work. Have you asked them?'

He consulted an earlier page in the pad. '*Erin*, is that right?'

'Their office is in Hythe Bridge Street. She was an editorial assistant.'

'According to my notes, Miss Kelly worked there part-time.'

'You've got that wrong, then. She was full-time.'

'Three days a week,' he said, studying his notes again. 'Monday to Wednesday. Friday was one of her days off.'

'Listen, we've lived in the same house together for a year – I ought to know what days she goes out to work.'

'Her boss, the editor . . . here it is, Mr Riordan – I spoke to him yesterday – he informed me that Miss Kelly only worked a three-day week. Mondays, Tuesdays and Wednesdays.' DC Fuller shrugged. 'That's what he told me.'

I lit another cigarette. 'Well, you must've got it wrong.'

'All right, let's leave that for the moment.' He coughed. ''Scuse me. Now, when did you last see Miss Kelly?'

'Yesterday morning. We had breakfast, then she left for work.'

'What time was that?'

'About quarter to nine.'

'You hadn't set off for Bradford at this point?'

'I left half an hour after she did. I went on the train.'

'Did anyone travel with you?'

'My stage assistant.'

'And her name is . . . ?'

'Kim Preece.'

The constable frowned, tapping the end of the biro between his teeth then using it as a pointer in my direction. 'The Lovely Kim.' He grinned. 'I remember *her*.'

He began to recount one of the illusions which had particularly impressed him at the police cabaret show, only to halt himself. His face resumed an expression more suited to the nature of the interview.

'Miss Kelly had no reason to go to Reading, as far as you're aware? She didn't know anyone there?'

'No, like I say . . .'

'And when she left yesterday morning, was there anything out of the ordinary about her behaviour? Her mood, I mean. Or was she perfectly normal?'

'Rosa was *never* perfectly normal.' I smiled as I said this, then my eyes filled up. When I could speak again, I said, 'No, there was nothing unusual.'

'I'm sorry, Mr Brandon, but I have to ask these questions.'

'Sure.'

Paul, who had remained unobtrusive in his armchair, offered to brew a pot of tea. I nodded. He went off to attend to it, leaving me alone with DC Fuller.

'She didn't indicate where she was going or what she was doing?'

'She was going to *work*. We kissed goodbye, and that was it.'

'She made no mention of having to go to Reading for any reason?'

'I told you, no. I haven't got a fucking clue why she was on that train.'

He spent a moment scribbling notes. Looking up from the pad, he asked, 'Had Miss Kelly been depressed at all recently, would you say? Upset or, I don't know, not her usual self?'

I reiterated. 'Rosa wasn't about to kill herself.'

'OK, OK, fine.' The shaving nick on his chin had begun to weep where he'd inadvertently scratched it. He removed a paper handkerchief from his jacket pocket and dabbed at the pinprick of blood. Inspecting the tissue, he said, 'And there'd been nothing between you – in your relationship, I mean – that might . . .'

'No. Absolutely not.'

'Money worries? Under pressure at work? Family troubles?'

'She didn't have any family.'

'Ah, I was going to ask . . .' He turned to a fresh page. 'No next of kin, then?'

'Her parents died in a car crash when she was fourteen. She was an only child.'

'What about grandparents, or aunts and uncles?'

'Maybe, back in Ireland. But she never mentioned them the whole time I knew her, and she never received letters or phone calls from any family. Not even birthday or Christmas cards. Rosa had been living over here for years.'

He nodded, made another note. 'I know you've only been back home a few hours, Mr Brandon, but have you had a chance to establish whether any of Miss Kelly's belongings are missing?'

'How d'you mean?'

'Clothes, toiletries, credit card . . . that sort of thing. Had she packed a bag?'

'I don't think so, no. She had a leather shoulder-bag with her when she left the house. She nearly always carried that around.' I paused. 'I haven't had a proper look, to be honest. There's nothing obviously missing, anyway.'

'And she didn't leave a note or message of any description?'

'No.'

Paul returned with a tea tray and set it down on the low wooden table in the centre of the room. He gave my shoulder a squeeze. The police officer waited for me to compose myself. At that moment the front door was opened, followed by footsteps in the hall. I was half-way out of my seat when Mrs Blake, a neighbour from two doors along, appeared in the living-room doorway. She looked startled.

'I'm sorry, Mr Brandon, I'd no idea you were back.'

'What is it, Peggy?'

Holding up the spare key with which she'd let herself in, she said, 'Your young lady called round yesterday morning and asked if I wouldn't mind popping in to feed the cat for a few days while you were both away.'

We're standing at the traffic lights, waiting for the green man, and a hearse goes by so I take my hat off, the woolly one Auntie Niamh knitted with my name in it. I bow my head. And she tugs my hand, Auntie does, and says, 'You're not at home now, Rosa.' Uncle Michael says, 'Probably not even one of ours.' I go to a new school. Class 3g. First day, Miss Carlyle gets me to stand up at the front and tell everyone my name and how old I am and where I come from. At playtime the other children call me Houlihan the Hooligan. 'Oym noyne,' they go. 'Oym noyne.' They say I live in Ballyfuckawful. Anyway, I say, my name's Kelly now. Rosa Kelly. I live at 27 Chissett Road, Kensal Rise, London NW6. And I'll be ten soon.

I've a room to myself, because Liam and Declan are grown up and don't live here any more and Mairead is in the United States of America and Julia has the other bedroom. She's fifteen. I didn't have any brothers and sisters, and now I have four. I like my room. It used to be Liam and Declan's room and it's got two beds. I always sleep in the one by the window. I have pictures on my walls and I have my own wardrobe and a chest of drawers and a desk Uncle Michael made. I've to keep my room tidy, only Auntie won't let me use the Hoover. I don't like school. I like Miss Carlyle. She says I'm good at painting. I have a friend called Nicola, who's ten. But when I play with her some of the boys call me 'nigger lover'. I have a pair of roller-skates Auntie bought me for Christmas.

When I go to bed, Auntie Niamh comes in and kisses me good-night and tucks me in. She doesn't tell me a story. Mammy used to tell me a story, but Auntie Niamh doesn't. I cry sometimes when I think about Mammy. Mammy had a headache and died and went to heaven to live with Our Lady. When I get a headache I ask Auntie if I'll die too and she says it wasn't that sort of headache. And anyway, I'm not to say such a thing. Auntie Niamh is Mammy's sister. She says I'm too big for bedtime stories. Uncle Michael says I'm a big girl. He buys me ice-creams, he lets me help mend his car. I wear Liam's old overalls. They're blue and they're too big, so I've to roll up the sleeves and trouser legs. Uncle Michael teaches me songs and shows me the waltz with me standing on his feet. Auntie Niamh says we're a right pair. She looks at me and says I'm my mother's daughter. Sometimes Uncle Michael comes in to say good-night after Auntie. If I'm already asleep he wakes me up. He says big girls don't cry. I tell Julia and she says if I make up lies about her daddy she'll kill me. She says nobody will believe me because my own daddy's a murdering bastard.

The Face

I didn't ring my mother. She never met Rosa, she never knew of her existence. Mum emigrated to Vancouver with her second husband, a Canadian teacher she met when he was on an exchange at the school where she worked. I haven't seen them in two years; we write every few months. Mum hasn't said as much, but I suspect I remind her of Dad. I didn't tell him about Rosa's death, either. He lives alone in Glasgow, awaiting early retirement from the post (senior environmental health officer) he took to escape Oxford when his marginally post-pubescent mistress, having married him, ditched him. Sporadically, he calls up drunk in the middle of the night, or leaves effusive messages on the answering machine. Rosa picked up the phone one time and, on hearing her voice, he demanded to know who she was. She replied *Never mind me, who the fuck are you?* Dad claims he taught me magic. He didn't, he taught me card tricks. Who I did ring was my brother, Taaffe. We spoke about Rosa for two hours.

There was a time when 'magic' implied the setting aside of the laws of nature and science, or that which defied rational explanation or comprehension. A magician was a practitioner of the occult and a possessor of supernatural powers, one who deployed the ritual ceremonies of sorcery. As a consequence, those conjurors and illusionists who plied their trade in an era when popular belief in such 'black' magic remained strong trod a dangerous path. That seemingly paranormal quality of their feats exposed them, literally, to diabolical misconstruction. They were doers of evil. Their only defence was that great anathema, the divulging of their methods. So grave was their dilemma that in 1584 a man named Scot wrote a book, *The Discoverie of Witchcraft*, explaining the techniques of legerdemain so that conjurors would be protected from false accusations of satanic practices. And even he subsequently expressed regret at having made public some of the mysteries of magic.

I'm not a magician in the original sense. The magical effects – the illusions – I perform operate in apparent rather than actual defiance of natural laws. I am not a miracle-worker. The miraculous *appearance* of my feats is due to the skilful screening from observation of the means of their achievement. Any magician claiming, seriously, to possess paranormal powers is a charlatan. Don't fall for it. Paul, English graduate and *grade-A gobshite*, asserts that, in the terminology of literary theory, today's magic is modernist rather than post-modernist because it challenges the way we see things rather than the nature of things themselves.

Here's a general definition of a magical feat: *Someone or something is caused to pass mysteriously from one place or condition to another.*

With me stuck overnight in Bradford, Paul had agreed to a police request to perform the identification. Subsequently, when I inquired after her condition, he simply looked away. When I demanded to see her for myself, he reflected for a moment, then said, 'You want to be sure about this.'

'I've seen a dead body before. I saw my grandfather.'

'This . . . Red, this is different.'

'Would you see her, if you were me?'

Paul didn't reply straight away. At last, he said, 'When my mum died, they said I could go in and see her. I was twenty-two. I said no. I couldn't face it.'

I didn't say anything.

He shook his head. 'It's like I never said goodbye to her. I've never regretted anything so much in my entire life.'

DC Fuller and a coroner's officer went in with me. I had been advised to prepare myself. The coroner's officer explained the process by which I would be allowed to *view* the body. There would be a covering; this would be withdrawn to expose her face. Due to the extent of her injuries, I would not be permitted to see more than that (even then, I was warned of damage to the head which I might find distressing). With the circumstances of her death still under investigation and a full post-mortem yet to be completed, I could not touch her nor be left alone with her. Within reason I could spend as much time with her as I wished.

The form beneath the sheet did not resemble with any exactness the outline of a human body. At the time, its component parts were unmistakable: there were the feet, the legs, the arms, the torso; there was the head. You can't help the thoughts that come, unbidden. And the thought that occurred to me as I stood beside Rosa's cloaked remains was of a 'jimmy' – the collapsible wire frame we magicians use to give an audience the impression that a person remains concealed beneath a large cloth. I would've given anything for the coroner's officer to whisk away the sheet with a theatrical flourish to reveal a bare table and for Rosa, in sequinned costume, to emerge, stage left, with beaming radiance. As I drew nearer, I saw that it wasn't a table but a trolley, its wheels locked in position. The room was cool; spartan and clinical, and reeking of hygienic vigilance. I was asked if I was ready. I said I was. The sheet was drawn back from the head. The first shock was the absence of make-up – Rosa wouldn't venture out of the house without vivid matching eyeshadow and lipstick (green, purple, turquoise, pink), as well as blusher and heavy kohl-black eyeliner. I'd only ever seen her face stripped of cosmetics last thing at night, or at breakfast, or when she'd just come out of the shower. Her hair, I noticed, was too short. This was the second shock: Rosa's black swathes had been reduced to little more than a crew cut, the contrast being sufficiently stark to make her appear almost bald. I assumed this was the result of preparations for the post-mortem, that she'd been shaved for reasons I didn't care to imagine. The third shock was the right-hand side of her head, where the upper part of her ear was missing and the stubbly flesh above it had been torn away in a great fold to expose a raw area of scalp. This bloodied membrane was embedded with unidentifiable greyish-white chips the size of thumbnails. In response to my question, the coroner's officer informed me they were impacted fragments of stone and gravel from the railway track. I went over to a wash-basin and retched into it.

DC Fuller fetched a glass of water. 'You don't have to be here,' he said.

'I know.'

I stood at the sink a while longer, alternating deep breaths with mouthfuls of water. The water tasted of metal. When I was ready, I returned to the trolley. Apart from the obvious injury and two or three less significant abrasions, her head was remarkably undamaged; her face bore no evidence at all of her violent death. I asked if they'd removed her make-up and was told no, she hadn't been wearing any when she was brought into the mortuary. I said Rosa never went out without it; I said she'd been made-up when she left the house that morning. *Succulent Peach*, I remembered her seeking my opinion. The coroner's officer shrugged, offering no explanation for the discrepancy. DC Fuller made a note. Then we stopped talking and I took a step closer, close enough to have reached out and touched her. I stared at her face. Her skin was like moulded plastic. Her eyes were closed and her lips were, as ever, slightly parted, though colourless now and drained of their familiar sensuality; her jaw had relaxed so that her chin sagged. She might've been about to snore, only there was no mistaking hers for the face of someone asleep. I wanted to kiss her forehead, I wanted to trace the strong black arcs of her eyebrows with my fingertips, I wanted to place my face above hers and inhale. I couldn't believe that if I spoke to her she wouldn't hear, that if I touched her she wouldn't respond; I couldn't believe that Rosa would not, at any moment, open her eyes and smile and sit up and begin laughing and talking and swearing like a Kerrywoman. It was her. It was still her.

For weeks I couldn't erase that image of her face. It visited me day and night, so that I couldn't visualize her as she'd been when she was alive without the features transforming into a mask of inanimation. I began to doubt that I'd done the right thing in seeing her. But I suspect that this image – the cold, factual finality of seeing her dead – is all that prevents me from becoming stalled in those cruel and self-deceiving moments of fleeting euphoria when I think she might not be gone.

Rosa's last words to me, that Friday morning, were *Seeya*. That's all: *Seeya*. Two words conflated into one, accompanied by an indolent wave as she set off down the road without troubling to shut the gate behind her. Mine to her, as recorded by my answerphone nearly ten hours later, were 'Hi, s'only me. You're obviously out boozing . . . So, anyway, I got to Bradford OK and we're all set up. Um, right, I'll give you a buzz later. Bye. And, hey, Merlin, don't you delete this message, you hear?' Our little joke. I complained one time to Rosa that whenever *she* went away – to visit friends in London, or wherever – she never rang to leave a message for me. She swore she'd left loads, only Kerrygold must've learned how to press the erase button. *You know she gets jealous if I show you too much affection.* So there it was, the last sentence I ever spoke to Rosa was directed at the cat. Not that Rosa got to hear it.

The police were puzzled. No personal belongings were recovered from the railway track and the only item of unclaimed baggage found on board the Oxford–Reading train was a small canvas holdall containing Rosa's toiletry bag and two or three changes of clothing. The holdall was mine. Printed indelibly inside it was my name and address, enabling the police – circuitously – to put a name to the body and to trace me to a hotel in West Yorkshire. What had not been found was the shoulder-bag Rosa always carried with her and in which she kept her purse, cigarettes, lighter, keys and other essentials. It wasn't in the house; I checked after DC Fuller's visit. Also missing was her cash card and the Irish passport she kept in a drawer in the bedside table. The passport – green, with a golden harp on the cover – had been issued when she was eighteen; now and then she'd get it out so we could hoot at her Sinéad O'Connor hairstyle in the photograph. According to the police, Rosa had withdrawn £500 from her bank and building-society accounts in separate transactions between 11:52 and 12:15 at cashpoints in Oxford city centre.

The cash was not on her, nor was it in the holdall. The train had continued into Reading station, its crew unaware of the accident a few hundred yards back down the line, and the passengers had disembarked before the express driver's alarm call had been relayed to platform staff. It was possible, suggested DC Fuller, that the shoulder-bag (complete with money and passport) had been lifted from Rosa's vacated seat by an opportunist thief, while the holdall remained neglected on an overhead luggage shelf.

Paul and I discussed this. He asked me, 'Would you draw out that much money, pack a bag with enough clothes to last a few days – *and* your passport – and then commit suicide by throwing yourself off a train?'

I shook my head.

'And, suppose it was an accident – she goes off to the toilet or something and somehow a door flies open and she falls out – would *you* go walkabout on a train and leave a bag containing five hundred quid in cash unattended on your seat?'

'No,' I said, after a moment's thought. 'Not without good reason.'

What was also puzzling was Rosa's deliberate alteration of her appearance. The coroner's officer stated – because, by then, I was disconcerted enough to ask him – that her hair had not been cropped by anyone at the mortuary. If it had been cut, it must have happened prior to her death, he insisted; photographs taken at the scene supported this. As for the absence of make-up, when Paul tidied the house some days later, he came across several balls of peach-stained cotton wool in the waste basket next to the chest of drawers Rosa used as a makeshift dressing-table. The Rosa Kelly who left my place for the second time that morning was a markedly different-looking woman to the one who'd said goodbye to me at quarter to nine.

One of the maxims of magic is never to attempt in public anything you cannot perform with ease in private. As my dad says, *If something can fuck up on you, it will*; and he should know. Practice and rehearsal are as essential to the illusionist as they are to any other performance artist. The tedious part is perfecting the components of each effect, the monotonous repetition of sleights, blinds and moves. Only then can you combine them, going through the illusion from start to finish as it will be seen on stage. And this for each feat within the routine, leading up to full dress rehearsal. The pitfall thereafter is *over*rehearsing until you're somnambulant with familiarity. Quality, not quantity, is the key. Kim finds this excessive, but I script the entire show as though it were a play, and I insist that we, the actors, learn our parts. *Ease up, Red, this isn't the RSC.* But I told her, the actor who's mastered the mechanics of a role can devote his energy to its *performance.* Watch a substandard magician (actor, musician, whatever) at work and try to put your finger on what makes him bad. I'll tell you: it's the impression that his concentration is divided between technique and presentation.

I have a daytime let on a room above the Port Mahon pub, in St Clement's. Evenings, they have folk music. Kim and I rehearse there most weekday mornings; in the afternoons I work on solo elements of the act. Don, the landlord, also provides secure storage for props, costumes and apparatus. When I first broached the subject, he said, 'I don't want you sawing any women in half on my premises.'

'I have to practise somewhere, Don.'

'Any blood, you clean it up yourself.' He pulled us both a pint, and I saw by the gleam in his eye that the joke was on me.

I was at the pub, rehearsing an illusion called Assistant's Revenge, when Kim and Rosa met for the first time. It was the day after the adoption of Merlin from the rescue centre, two days after Rosa moved in. I hadn't mentioned her to Kim, though my assistant remarked that, the last two mornings, I'd looked like an advert for a grin factory. Neither of us was in stage gear. I wore tracksuit bottoms and a loose-fitting jacket adapted to provide the necessary pockets and compartments. Kim was in a plain white T-shirt, yellow-and-white-striped leggings. Her blonde hair, bleached by a winter holiday, was scrunchied into a pony-tail. Before joining my show she was a croupier and blackjack dealer at a casino. When I auditioned her, she said, 'They hired me as a hostess, but I was too bright for most of the punters' liking so the boss switched me to the tables.'

'What sort of hostess?' I asked.

From the expression on her face, I thought she was going to walk out of the interview there and then. Finally she replied, 'Any guy on his own at the bar, it was my job to go over and say hello.'

'Just talking, then?'

This time she reciprocated my smile. 'No, it was mostly listening.'

I've always worked with an assistant. I know it's hackneyed – the male magician and his pretty female sidekick – but Kim's good, and it's not my fault she looks the way she does. There are advantages in having a co-performer, not least of which being physical help in shifting equipment. She can also aid misdirection, subtly distracting an audience's attention at a vital moment. And she allows a broader repertoire of illusions. In fact, since Kim's arrival, effects requiring the participation of an assistant, rather than mere 'waitressing' of props, have evolved from an optional extra into being the focal point of my act. The primary disadvantage is financial: an assistant has to be paid wages and expenses and you've to supply her with costumes. However, Peter Prestige makes a tidy living thank you very much.

What happens in Assistant's Revenge is the magician is strapped to an upright frame by his assistant, who then walks a curtain right the way round him, momentarily disappearing from view behind the frame as she makes her way full circle to the front.

At the moment of her anticipated reappearance, however, it is not the assistant but the magician who emerges with the curtain in tow. Drawing it open, he reveals her strapped to the frame in his place. Correctly performed, the exchange is seamless. (Don't ask, because I won't tell you.) It was the timing with which Kim and I were having difficulty that morning in rehearsal. I suggested we run through it once more then break for lunch. So there I was spread-eagled on the rectangular frame, Kim tightening the last of the straps around my wrists and ankles, when our attention was diverted by a husky half-London, half-Irish voice:

'If you're after electrocuting him, I'm your woman for pressing the button.'

Rosa. I'd arranged to meet her downstairs for a sandwich, but the session had overrun. She was standing in the doorway, holding a bottle of her usual Belgian lager and a partially eaten roll. I apologized. I got Kim to untie me rather than release myself in front of Rosa. Introduced, the two women exchanged smiles but no words.

'When are you due back at work?' I asked.

'Forty minutes,' said Rosa. 'And I've to walk 'cos the bike's shagged.'

Rosa's bicycle was gearless, painted black, and older than she was, heavy as a motorbike, and you had to back-pedal to apply the brake. She'd already taken Merlin out for a ride, dismissing my concern that the kitten ought to be confined indoors until he'd settled in his new home. Of course, Merlin, riding in the basket, had loved it. I kissed Rosa self-consciously. She smelled of beer, raw onion and cheddar. As we descended the narrow staircase and went into the bar, I invited Kim to join us. She declined; shopping, she said. Kim was putting on her coat and rearranging her hair when Rosa, displaying an empty pack of Marlboros, asked if I had a cigarette. I couldn't resist. I produced a pack from one of my pockets and, holding it in front of me, caused a single cigarette to levitate from the box and rise to my lips. Rosa's eyes were on my mouth; when she lowered her gaze to the packet it had changed into a box of matches, one of which floated out, struck itself against the side of the box and rose to light the cigarette. I handed the cigarette to her. She took it, unsmiling, studying my face. Kim, trying not to laugh, placed a sympathetic hand on Rosa's shoulder and said, 'You'll get used to him.'

Rosa smiled then and took a deep draw on the cigarette. Kim said goodbye; she told Rosa how nice it was to meet her, and Rosa smiled again by way of reply.

Witness: Mr David Cunliffe (train driver)

WITNESS: The other train was alongside me, more or less stationary I'd say. Up ahead, I saw a door open and this woman jumped down.

CORONER: When you say 'jumped', what do you mean by that exactly?

WITNESS: She didn't look like she was falling or she'd been pushed or anything.

CORONER: How could you tell that?

WITNESS: She was sort of holding the door and stepping down like you would if you were getting on to a platform. Only there was quite a drop, so it was more like she jumped down. Like she was letting herself drop.

CORONER: Would it have been possible for the door to be opened manually?

WITNESS: It's mostly automatic doors these days, but not all of the older types of train have been phased out yet.

CORONER: And the action of opening the door and jumping down on to the track seemed deliberate on her part, would you say?

WITNESS: Yes.

CORONER: How far ahead of you did this take place?

WITNESS: No more than twenty yards. Twenty-five at the most.

CORONER: The train you were driving had just left Reading, had it?

WITNESS: It had. I was doing about forty. I braked as soon as I saw her, but there was . . . she was too close. I didn't have a chance of stopping.

CORONER: What did the woman do? Did she make any attempt to remove herself from the path of your train?

WITNESS: She sort of stumbled as she landed. When she landed, her knees sort of gave way and she fell forwards. Face first. Then . . .

CORONER: Please, take as much time as you need.

WITNESS: She didn't have time to pick herself up, never mind get out of the way.

CORONER: And you would say she stumbled? There was no question in your mind that she, perhaps, threw herself on to the track in front of you.

WITNESS: No, she stumbled. I don't think she even saw me coming.

Witness: Mr Terence Farr (passenger)

CORONER: Can you tell us, please, your recollection of the moments immediately prior to the incident in question?

WITNESS: Yes, I was getting my suitcase down from the luggage rack – I knew we were about to come into Reading, you see . . .

CORONER: Your suitcase was on the shelf above your seat, was it?

WITNESS: No, it was too big to go up there, so I'd put it in the, you know, those shelves at the end of the carriage.

CORONER: You were retrieving your case. What happened then?

WITNESS: A young woman wanted to get past. I'd got my case half-way down and I had to stop to let her get by.

CORONER: You now know that woman to be the deceased, Miss Kelly?

WITNESS: Yes.

CORONER: You say she was trying to get past. Was she in any way distressed or agitated, so far as you could tell? Or what was her manner?

WITNESS: I suppose you could say she was rather impatient.

She was quite young, and, at my age, you don't always manage to do things as quickly as other people might wish.

CORONER: She pushed past somewhat abruptly, then?

WITNESS: Oh, don't get me wrong, she wasn't rude, as such, just a little on the impatient side. Everyone seems to be in a hurry, these days.

CORONER: And she wasn't distressed?

WITNESS: No. Not so you'd notice.

CORONER: What happened after she'd pushed past you?

WITNESS: She went through the door into the, you know, the area between our carriage and the next one.

CORONER: Was anyone else in the area between the two carriages?

WITNESS: Not that I could see, no. A chap did squeeze by me just after the young woman, but that was afterwards – after the accident, I mean. As the accident happened, to be strictly accurate.

CORONER: Did you see how Miss Kelly came to leave the train?

WITNESS: Not as such. I was still manoeuvring my case into the aisle and I felt a sudden gust of fresh air – the door was open again, on account of this chap – and then there was an almighty bang.

CORONER: What did you do?'

WITNESS: I went to investigate. The window in the door – the outside door – was completely shattered and there were bits of broken glass everywhere.

CORONER: The door was shut, was it?

WITNESS: Yes. I imagine, knowing what I do now, that it must have been banged shut by the other train, or by the sidewind or something as it went past, and that was what blew all the glass out.

CORONER: There was no sign of the young woman?

WITNESS: No. At the time, I assumed she was in the WC or she'd carried on through to the next carriage. That is, I would have assumed something along those lines if I'd given it much thought. I didn't think for one moment that she'd, you know, jumped from the train.

CORONER: The other man, the one who passed you just after Miss Kelly, he was with you, in the area between the two carriages, was he?

WITNESS: Yes.

CORONER: Were any words exchanged between you?

WITNESS: I said something like 'What happened?' and he replied that he thought someone must have thrown something at the train. 'Kids,' he said.

CORONER: Can you recall where he would have been at the precise moment you heard the bang? Was he squeezing past you at that point or was he already in the area where Miss Kelly would have been?

WITNESS: He was just going through the door at the end of the carriage.

CORONER: So there is no possibility in your mind that this man could have pushed Miss Kelly out of the train or been in any way responsible for what happened, or that he could have prevented it from happening?

WITNESS: Oh, no – absolutely not.

Witness: PC Colin Hurlock (coroner's officer)

CORONER: The passenger described by Mr Farr and other witnesses today, have attempts been made to locate or identify him?

WITNESS: All the usual appeals for witnesses have been made, yes.

CORONER: But he has not responded?

WITNESS: No, sir, he has not.

CORONER: Is it likely, do you think, that he disembarked from the train at Reading and went about his business unaware that anything more than a broken window had occurred? And that news of the incident and of the appeal for witnesses has somehow escaped his attention?

WITNESS: It's quite possible, yes.

Witness: Dr Iain Sutherland (pathologist)

WITNESS: The deceased displayed transection injuries to the upper torso and upper and lower limbs consistent with having been struck, whilst prone, by the wheels of a moderately fast-moving train. A number of abrasions and contusions about the head, body and limbs, as well as various fractures, were, in my opinion, the result of propulsion along the track succeeding this initial, and certainly instantaneously fatal, impact.

CORONER: Transection injuries? You mean she was, literally, cut to pieces?

WITNESS: I hesitate to describe it in such terms, but . . . yes, that is the nub of it.

Rosa. Even now, I spy her on a busy street in a glimpse of dark hair or multicoloured clothing; I hear her voice in pubs; I see her riding a black bicycle. I smell her in my bed.

Over beer and sandwiches in the Port Mahon, Rosa said, 'How long is it since you and her stopped shagging?'

'Who, *Kim*?'

It was the first and last time Rosa referred to Kim in this context. The direct, matter-of-fact tone of her question betrayed no hint of jealousy or insecurity; she might have been discussing plans for our evening meal. My response – hasty, accompanied by a casual laugh – neither deflected nor deceived her.

'Red, I have eyes in my head.'

I took a long draught of beer, replacing the glass on its coaster with excessive concentration. 'You don't miss much, do you?'

'I'm just filling in the bits I can't work out for myself.'

I nodded, helped myself to another drink. 'It started not long after she joined the show and carried on for just over a year, on and off. She's living with a guy now.'

'This was while you were with . . .'

'Yeah. Yes it was.'

Rosa digested this information. At length, she said, 'OK, two

43

things: first, who you shagged before me is your own business; second' – she indicated the faked pack of cigarettes – 'you ever try and show me up again with one of your tricks, you'll be picking the pieces out your fucking hole.'

That night I was asleep when Rosa came to bed. She woke me without a word. As soon as I was hard she drew me on top and hooked her feet behind my back, not fucking me so much as using her legs to squeeze the ejaculation from me like juice from a lemon. She remained silent throughout. While I was still inside her, spent, she contracted the muscles in her vagina around my detumescent prick. Then she kissed me. Expelled from her mouth into mine was a gobbet of slight bitter-tasting warm fluid the consistency of watery glue. I'd never swallowed cum, but this was how I imagined it would be. I recoiled to see her smiling up at me in the semi-darkness. I laughed. It was all I could do to stop myself asking, 'How the fuck did you *do* that?'

You can always tell. Even after it's all over, there's something left behind in the way they are with each other and they don't even realize it's happening. I see it in them straight away; obvious as fuck. I'm standing in the doorway with a beer and a cheese 'n' onion roll and she's tying him to some great contraption. I watch her buckle this leather strap round his wrist. And it's something about the way she does it. I'm not saying she's being intimate, or there's anything still going on between them, it's just . . . what I mean is, if there'd never been anything between them, she'd do it different, that's all. I can't even see her face, the way she's looking at him or anything, I can just tell.

He hasn't seen me. I watch a bit longer, then I come out with some crack that makes him jump like she's poked a finger in his hole. She turns round. And I look at her and I think, if I was a feller I'd let her poke a finger anywhere she wanted; and she looks like she'd do it as well. She unties him and we do all the hello stuff, all that smiley bollix, and I think she's going to shake my hand or do pretend kisses for fuck sake; but she doesn't. We don't. Kim, her name is. There's a poster on the wall: 'Peter Prestige and The Lovely Kim.' His hair was long when the picture was taken; it makes me smile to see how different he looks. Carole-Ann reckons he reminds her of a French feller she used to know — not just the dark hair and the tan, but something to do with the shape of his face and the way he moves his hands when he's talking or smoking. She says Red's 'very edible'. I like his shirts, how they fit him. I told Carole-Anne this and she gave me one of her 'You're weird' looks.

Kim's very edible, I can see that. We're down in the bar now and she says she's not stopping. One half of my head is going 'Go on, then, fuck off,' and the other half is going 'Stay if you want, what do I care?' Then Red does this trick with a cigarette. Kim hasn't left yet and she's wetting herself, I can tell. Like, it's the funniest thing she's seen in her whole life, only she's just managing to keep from laughing. Cos the

45

Kims don't laugh, they smirk. I'm not sure, maybe it's . . . he's just showing off for the sake of it, because sometimes a feller is like a dog with a waggy tail and a hangy-out tongue. What I'm saying is I don't think he's making an arse of me for her benefit. But whatever, that's the way she chooses to take it, so he might as well be. Then she touches me. A woman-to-woman squeeze, some stupid gobshite remark. I keep my face absolutely blank, but there must be something in the way I look at her. She doesn't know what it is yet, but she's already sensed something about me that Red hasn't. And whatever it is has wiped that smirk right off her pretty face.

After the demise of the greatest illusionist of them all, Harry Houdini, no fewer than seven versions of how he died came into popular circulation. The jury at the inquest into Rosa's death were faced with a similar confusion of alternative truths. Summing up, the coroner enumerated them: accidental death, death by misadventure, unlawful killing, suicide or an open verdict. He reminded the jurors of the legal requirement of satisfaction beyond reasonable doubt. Then, effectively ruled out unlawful killing. *You have to ask yourselves, How, and by whom?* Suicide. *There was no note. She had not declared, to anyone who knew her, an intention to kill herself; her GP her partner, her friends, her colleagues, all testify that she had shown no symptoms of depression, no suicidal tendencies.* Accidental death. *You have heard expert evidence that there was no fault in the mechanism of the door which might have caused it to open unexpectedly; and, from the driver of the oncoming train, that Miss Kelly appeared to let herself out and jump, deliberately, on to the track.* The coroner's conclusion: *It is likely we shall never know the reason why this young woman – 'spontaneous, headstrong and unpredictable', as described by Mr Brandon, the man with whom she lived – why she left the train when she did. But it is reasonable to infer that she did so of her own volition.* Paul Fievre, sitting beside me in the courtroom, whispered, 'The bastard's trying to make them go for misadventure.' *There are matters which this inquest has been unable to resolve: Why was Miss Kelly travelling on this train? What became of the bag she, according to testimony, always carried with her? Why had she taken measures to alter her appearance?* ('What about the missing witness?' said Paul, under his breath.) *However, it is far from clear whether a solution to these mysteries might aid us further in the central purpose of our inquiry: how this unfortunate woman came about her death.* The jurors retired. When they returned, an hour later, from their deliberations, the forewoman delivered an open verdict. I thought Paul was going to leap from his seat and give the air a celebratory punch.

'How does that make a difference?' I asked him afterwards.

'It means the police can't dismiss this as some nutty woman getting off a train too soon.'

'What if it *was* misadventure, though?'

'Yeah, but what if it *wasn't*?'

In the car-park outside the coroner's court one or two of Rosa's colleagues from *Erin* offered comfort and shared sorrow. The newspaper's editor, Conal Riordan, pressed my hand between both of his. He had huge freckly hands. He was half a foot taller than me, his head electrified with ginger hair and beard. I asked how come Rosa had only worked three days a week when I was under the impression she'd been full-time? He became embarrassed. He couldn't explain that. He said he took it for granted I knew she had Thursdays and Fridays off. So where'd she been on those days when she left the house at the usual time, as though going to work? Two days a week, every week for eleven months. Nearly one hundred days unaccounted for, I said. What the fuck was she up to? He didn't know. He was sorry, he really didn't have any idea. I called him a lying bastard. Conal didn't hit me; he didn't even appear inclined to.

Magician and liar share so many common skills necessary to their success: the planning of a deceptive strategy; the facility to mislead in face-to-face confrontation; an inkling into the workings of your victim's mind; an aptitude for acting; a good memory. You make the real appear fake, the fake appear real. You conceal, you disguise, you divert attention; you plough the division between what seems to be happening and what is actually happening. I could go on drawing parallels. But I won't, because there is one overriding difference, a *paradox*: magic is founded in honesty; lying is founded in dishonesty. In lying there is no relationship of consent between deceiver and deceived. Whereas the spectators at a magic show, by their very attendance, have agreed to be misled; theirs is a collective suspension of disbelief.

If the stage illusionist is a liar, then so is the actor who creates a fiction in complicity with his audience.

I've been thinking a lot about lying, lately. *Bearing false witness*, to use a biblical phrase, one of those definitive, arbitrary 'Thou shalt nots'. God's last word on the subject, if you believe in him (which I don't). I described Houdini as the greatest illusionist of all but, truly speaking, he comes a distant fourth to Father, Son and Holy Ghost. But – lies. I've been thinking about the lie I told my girlfriend – the woman who preceded Rosa – when she accused me of having an affair with Kim. Then there's the lie I told Rosa herself; I don't want to dwell on that one, though it recurs unbidden in my thoughts. And what of *her* lies? The lie she lived each Thursday and Friday. All the others, which have spooled out like unravelled cassette tape as I've replayed the last fifteen months of my existence with and without Rosa. Of the two of us, it's hard to say who possessed the greater mastery of the art of deception.

I live close to the Thames. Also known as the Isis, for the duration of its serpentine passage through Oxford. Don't ask me why, I don't know. *Some snobby bollix of a reason*, Rosa suggested. We were walking along the tow-path towards Port Meadow. Sunday morning, a week to the day since she'd invited herself to share my home. Daffodils ornamented the verges of the track, and a benevolent breeze was weighted with the fragrance of wild garlic. There were ducks and coots on the river, a pair of shy moorhens, and two grebes describing a '22' silhoutted against the surface. We'd prepared a picnic, divided into our day-packs; each step was accompanied by the muffled chink of beer bottles. When I took Rosa's hand, she did not withdraw it, nor did she return the pressure of my fingers. We were smoking. She flicked her cigarette butt into the undergrowth. At a spot beyond the chandlery and the houseboat moorings, we spread a blanket over a patch of turf where the path yielded to the incline of the bank. Across the channel of almost imperceptibly drifting water lay the meadow, patterned with cattle. A father and son were having difficulty raising a bright red kite. I put the beer – eight bottles in all – in a large string bag that, Rosa said, reminded her of the vest her dad used to wear. I asked if she still missed her parents. She didn't answer for a moment, then moved her head in a gesture that was neither a shake nor a nod.

'Do you have pictures of them?'

'No.'

'None at all?'

She looked at me. 'Now, you're the mathematician . . . so, is there a difference – *numerically*, like – between no pictures and none at all?'

I let the subject drop. Going to the water's edge, I wedged the bag of bottles in the shallows to cool. I told Rosa I'd learned this from Hemingway – except it was wine instead of beer, and the river was somewhere in the Spanish mountains. I tried to inject a casual warmth into my voice, but the mood had been bruised by Rosa's last remark. She sat, unresponsive, pulling parcels of food out of the packs and arranging them haphazardly about her. I couldn't think of anything else to say. When I rejoined her, drying my hands on the blanket, she lit two cigarettes and handed me one.

'Friend of yours, is he, this Hemingway feller?'

I went to answer. Then I saw her smile, and my smile came too.

It rained on the day of the funeral, drenching mourners at the gardens of remembrance and battering the cortège of cars that conveyed us to the function room of the Port Mahon. In the information pack I received from the undertakers was a booklet: 'Bereavement and Beyond'. It said grieving was a natural process and had to be allowed to run its course; it said that though the experience was unique to the individual, there were similarities common to all bereaved people. There was a long list under the heading 'The Do's and Don't's of Grieving'. Nowhere did it say: Don't have nightmares; Don't let yourself be reduced to tears because you can't open a jar of marmalade or because the rubbish sack splits on the way to the dustbin; Don't clean her bike; Don't sit alone in a room all day with the curtains drawn;

Don't wake up before dawn every morning; Don't talk to her; Don't fill two bowls with cereal before you realize she isn't there to eat hers; Don't hear her footstep in every creak of the house; Don't sleep in her half of the bed; Don't answer the phone expecting to hear her voice; Don't ask *why*? Nowhere did it say I wasn't to ask why?

At the funeral reception – the wake – my brother, Taaffe, drew me aside and asked if I wanted to doss down with him and his family for a while. I said, 'Don't make any major life changes while you are still grieving.'

'Red, I'm not talking about adoption.'

Even my brother called me Red. I told him, 'I'm going to look after myself and eat well and get plenty of rest and I'm going to express my feelings as much as possible and I'm going to begin to make longer-term plans for the future so I've got something to look forward to and . . .' I raised my whisky glass '. . . I won't turn to drugs, cigarettes or alcohol and I'm going to make space in my life for grief rather than space in my grief for life, and no matter what I do – no matter *what* – I'm never ever going to see her again.'

When I'd finished saying all that, it wasn't me that was crying but Taaffe. I put my arm round him and told him he was the softest cunt I'd ever met.

I've referred to three occurrences that reduced my life to what it is now. I said I didn't want to talk about the first; I still don't. The second was Rosa's death. The third was the arrival of a parcel at my house a few days after the funeral. I was in my dressing-gown, unshaven and unshowered, when the knock came at the door. I signed for the delivery and went through to the kitchen. I cleared space on the table among the debris of the previous night's half-eaten take-away. The package was an irregular rectangle enclosed in brown paper and sealed with strips of thick tape. Bulky, fairly heavy. My name and address were inscribed in large capitals. The unfamiliar handwriting looked feminine. It required a sharp vegetable-knife to sever the tape so that I could rip away the double layer of paper. Inside was a black leather shoulder-bag, zipped shut and bulging. The bag was of a style available, no doubt, in most fashion boutiques and department stores, but I recognized it immediately.

The Memory Man

The plate, cutlery and glass stood stacked in the sink with the rest of the neglected washing-up; the dead beer-cans and a foil carton of solidified left-overs of rogan josh were crammed into the flip-top bin. Laid out on the kitchen table, in no particular order, were the contents of Rosa's shoulder-bag. The bag itself was empty, sagging by its strap from the back of a chair. There was nothing, at first glance, to indicate who'd sent the parcel, no note, anonymous or otherwise – nothing. Several of the items were so familiar, so redolent of Rosa, it was as though she herself was in the room rather than this assortment of inanimate possessions. Momentarily, I savoured the irrational idea that she'd faked her own death and sent the bag as a signal that she was still alive. But I'd seen her in the mortuary. And the handwriting wasn't hers. I retrieved the torn brown wrapping-paper and inspected the postmark; the parcel had been sent the previous day, within the Oxford postal district.

There was a plastic pack of ham-and-mustard sandwiches with an expired sell-by date. The bread was mottled with bluey-green mould. Her lunch for the journey, supplemented by crisps and a can of Diet Coke. Reading material: a glossy magazine, as well as a newspaper that had been published on the day of her death. She'd taken five packs of Marlboro – four unopened, one with twelve cigarettes remaining – and two disposable lighters. I found her address book, a biro, a bunch of keys, a personal safety alarm, an Oxford–Reading rail ticket and a make-up bag packed with items she'd chosen, for some reason, either not to apply to her face that final morning, or to remove. I also found a wig. Auburn, collar-length and curly, it was unexpectedly realistic in appearance and to the touch. I held the wig, turning it over in my hands. I tried to picture Rosa's pale face – blue eyes and strong, dark eyebrows – framed with these reddish-brown locks. But all I could see was that image revealed by the folding back of a sheet: ruptured charcoal stubble, the waxen features of lifelessness. Had she had her hair shorn to accommodate this wig? Why? And why hadn't she been wearing it when she died? I set it aside and resumed the inspection: cheque-book, cash card, purse. The purse was fat; I unzipped it. Two hundred and fifty pounds, and seven hundred guilders. The Dutch notes, colourful and gaily decorated, made the sterling appear drab by comparison. Her passport was there. I studied the photograph, gently rubbing my thumb over the clear laminate seal. The Sinéad O'Connor look we'd laughed over; she was grinning mischievously, as though she'd have been captured poking her tongue out at the camera if the flash had gone off a moment sooner. She looked so happy.

I had to stop for a while. I went over to the sink and poured myself a glass of water and drank it. I cupped my hands beneath the cold tap and douched my face. It was mid-morning and I hadn't had breakfast, but the idea of eating made me queasy. I stared out of the window for a long time before returning to the table. Between the pages of the passport was a ticket for the Reading–Heathrow shuttle bus and an air ticket to Amsterdam, one-way, made out in Rosa's name. There was also a slip of paper, torn from a spiral-bound pad, bearing the names Nikolaas and Lena and their telephone numbers; the configuration of numerals wasn't English. No surnames, no addresses. I recognized the handwriting as Rosa's – the looping 'k' and 'l', the circle instead of a dot above the 'i' and that characteristic reversed 'N' in 'Nikolaas' . . . Each word grabbed its space on the page. Four remaining items. Another passport: UK, one of the newer, burgundy, European Community type. I opened it. The photo was of a young light-skinned Afro-Caribbean woman: surname, Jackson; other names, Charity Ann Magdalena; nationality, British; date of birth, o8 Jan 8o; children, o; sex, F; place of birth, London; date of issue, 14 Mar 98. The space for contact names and addresses in the event of an emergency had been left blank, and none of the pages bore visas or other stamps – unsurprising, the passport was less than a month old. I looked again at the photograph. I didn't recognize her, I didn't recognize her name. She had long black hair, defined cheekbones, a mouth made lustrous with lipstick, and dark eyes that didn't gaze at the camera so much as confront it. Ear-rings glinted with reflected flash. Eighteen years old. I closed the passport and placed it back on the table with Rosa's. Lying beside it was a pack of playing cards. Over the months I'd taught Rosa some card tricks and she'd taken to carrying a deck with her at all times on the off chance of being able to impress friends and strangers. I took them out of the packet. Fifty-one. I didn't even have to count them to know that one card was missing. I fanned them. No queen of spades. I thought about this for a moment, but the significance or otherwise of the card's absence was unguessable. As well as the cards, there was a spiral-bound pad. The first sheet had been torn out. The following pages contained what I assumed to be the scores from two games of gin rummy, one in Rosa's hand, the other penned by someone else. I made another inspection of the address on the parcel – the style was identical to that of the names at the head of each column of scores. The card players were R O S A and VICKY. I couldn't recall Rosa ever mentioning or introducing me to a Vicky, nor could I find anyone of that name in her address book. Whoever Vicky was, she'd won both times at rummy, and she'd sent me the shoulder-bag Rosa always carried with her. If Rosa had abandoned the bag on the train the day she died then, as far as I could see, Vicky must've been on that train too.

There was something else in the bag – a sealed envelope bearing my name and address and a stamp. Rosa's writing. Perhaps she'd intended to post it from Reading, or the airport. I left it till last because I was afraid of its contents. Fucking petrified, to be honest. When I'd examined every other item spread out on that table, I sat cradling the letter in my hands for several minutes before opening it.

> Red,
> Ive gone. I dont have to tell you why. Dont touch my stuff as some one will come for them. You wont find me so dont try. Look after Kerrygold.
>
> Rosa
> ps Dont tell any one any thing about me.

Here's a mnemonic rhyme I taught Rosa:

> Eight kings threatened to save
> Ninety-five ladies for one sick knave.

Concealed in there are all thirteen card values (eight, king, three, ten, two, seven, nine, five, queen, four, ace, six, jack). Another mnemonic, CHaSeD, spells out the four suits in a sequence of clubs, hearts, spades, diamonds. With this one rhyme and the key word, you can train yourself to remember the order of all fifty-two cards in a stacked (i.e. prearranged) deck: eight of clubs, king of hearts, three of spades, ten of diamonds, two of clubs, seven of hearts . . . right through to the jack of clubs. Yet, if you fan the cards for examination by a member of the audience, they appear to be entirely random. Knowing the exact position of every card in a deck enables you to perform a number of different feats, though don't ask me to reveal what these are. It's not as complicated as it seems – Rosa picked it up in two or three evenings' practice; she said it was a *fickin hoot*. She even tried to devise a rhyme of her own, something along the lines of *Two sex queens ate one fucking jack's severed* . . .

'Fucking?' I said. 'Where d'you get "fucking" from?'

'Four-king!'

And the exercise dissolved in a haze of alcoholic mirth as we set about working the remaining card values into a mnemonic that became increasingly surreal.

Techniques of systematized memory are a useful tool for an illusionist, not just in card effects, but in various demonstrations of 'mental magic'. It's astonishing how much storage capacity the human brain has, when properly trained. Besides, most audiences will credit a performer with some miraculous psychic gift in preference to the mundane alternative – that he's gone to more time and trouble to learn something than seems imaginable. Committing a long list of names to memory is one thing, but remembering what Rosa looked like when she was alive is another matter. Or how her voice sounded. Or the way she walked. Or her smell, the taste of her mouth. Effective storage and retrieval of information is affected by stress, anxiety, depression, fatigue. I know all that. I also know you can enhance memory function by increasing the flow of oxygenated blood to the brain. Which is why, in the weeks after Rosa died, I took up cycling. The key to her bike lock was on the bunch I found in her returned possessions, so I began going for a spin every day on the old black boneshaker. Merlin, however, refused to ride in the basket, drawing blood from my hand the one time I tried to make him. I would pedal furiously, to work up a sweat and increase my breathing rate. Paul thought my behaviour unhealthy, obsessive, but I told him I was just making sure enough oxygen reached my brain – so I wouldn't forget. Only, what I remembered and what I forgot continued to seem arbitrary and beyond my control. Among the things I do recall, perfectly and without recourse to mnemonics, are the contents of Rosa's shoulder-bag and every single word of her letter.

For twenty-four hours, the delivery of the parcel was known only to me and to Vicky. Having Rosa's personal effects returned to me, I didn't want to be deprived of them again so soon. It was like having her home again. Also, I was curious, reluctant to notify the police until I'd fathomed why Vicky hadn't sent the bag to them in the first instance. If she'd wanted the true circumstances of Rosa's death – and the purpose of her journey to Amsterdam – to be uncovered, she should have presented the evidence to those best qualified to investigate. How did Vicky come to be in possession of the bag? Why had she held on to it for so long, until after the funeral and the inquest? Why had she sent it to *me*? And why hadn't she enclosed an explanatory letter, or come forward, if she could give an eye-witness account of those final hours and minutes of Rosa's life? The more I thought about it, the more I grew convinced the gin rummy scores had been an oversight on Vicky's part – she'd forgotten, I felt sure, that the notepad contained a clue to her identity. As far as she knew, there was no way of tracing the parcel to her.

By the following morning I'd moved no nearer to understanding her reason for bypassing the police. I was annoyed with her. I rang DC Fuller. He said he'd be with me right away. Returning to the kitchen, where Rosa's belongings were still strewn across the table, I was unsure whether to leave them like that or put them back in the bag for the detective to take away. I'd probably already made a mistake by handling them, disturbing any forensic evidence and obliterating other fingerprints with my own. I cast a final look over them, weighing up the implications of each item in turn and in combination. Hopeless. A jumble, a mess of disconnection. Maybe Rosa had been murdered, and maybe she hadn't; maybe she'd jumped down in front of that train, like the coroner said, and no one would ever know why. And maybe no one would ever know why she'd been travelling to Amsterdam. Whatever, this was for the police to sort out, not me. I just missed her. I missed her so fucking much. And I didn't want this. I didn't want my head filled with this. *Fuck you, Vicky. Whoever you are, fuck you for doing this to me.*

There was a time when that would've been that: wait for the police to arrive, hand over the bag and all its contents to them . . . let them get on with their job. Doing the right thing, the correct, conventional, citizenly thing. But Rosa had stormed my life for a year. She'd left her mark on me, and on the way my mind worked. Sometimes, in conversation with a friend or stranger, I would come out with a remark that was pure Rosa-speak; I'd have a thought that was pure Rosa-think. I liked that. Even when we were apart for a few hours, a few days, it was as though she was still around. I think I had a similar effect on her, though she never said so. If she'd lived long enough, we might've become the sort of couple that tell favourite anecdotes in tandem, tripping over one another to supply the punch-line. But she didn't. And all I had, that morning, were memories, Rosa-speak, and her last possessions, on the point of being repossessed.

I heard a car draw to a halt outside, I heard an engine being switched off and a door being opened and slammed shut. In the time it took DC Fuller to reach the front step I'd removed two objects from the table and hidden them. One was the piece of paper bearing the names 'Nikolaas' and 'Lena' and two telephone numbers; the other was Charity Ann Magdalena Jackson's passport.

There are two women, Amy and Jennifer. Amy is black. Jennifer has straight blonde hair half-way down her back; she doesn't say her name is Jenny, it's Jennifer. She's very pretty. I don't like her. I like Amy best; she reminds me of Nicola, my friend at school, only Amy is proper black and Nicola is brown. Jennifer puts a video camera on a sort of tripod thing and points it at me. She says they have to film the interview and is that OK? I don't say nothing. No one's made a film of me before. They're younger than Auntie Niamh and they're dressed like girls in our sixth form. Jennifer asks me some questions, stuff they already know, and all that I'm-your-friend shite. She asks how old I am and I say I'm fourteen. She looks at a piece of paper and says I'm thirteen aren't I, then says oh no she's got it wrong cos of when my birthday is. They ask me other stuff, about school and about living at Auntie Niamh and Uncle Michael's. Then Amy asks about what he does to me and I tell her.

'How old were you the first time this happened?'

'Nine. No, ten. I was ten.'

Jennifer asks a lot of stuff about how often he did this and how many years it went on for and did he ever hurt me and what other things did he do and did he get me to do things to him. And she asks when was the first time he had full sexual intercourse with me. That's what she calls it: 'full sexual intercourse'.

I have to think about this because I get mixed up. I say, 'I was twelve.'

I'm crying. I don't want to, not in front of them. I try to stop but I can't. Amy gets me a tissue and a drink of water. Jennifer waits a bit then starts the camera up again, and when I've finished saying how he fucked me they ask a lot more questions like did I ever tell anyone? Auntie, or my stepsisters and stepbrothers? I shake my head. Jennifer wants to know why not and I say I don't know and she writes something down. I say I told Nicola and Mrs Mountjoy. Mrs Mountjoy's my art teacher. Me telling Mrs Mountjoy is why I'm here. Jennifer goes, 'Rosa, I have to ask you this: did you ever hurt yourself and pretend it was your uncle who'd done it?'

'No.'

'Are you telling the truth, Rosa?'

I just look at her. In my head I'm saying fuckofffuckofffuckofffuckoff. Then she goes, 'We can't help you properly unless you tell us everything.'

I start crying again. I can feel my face and neck are all blotchy. I tell them I hurt myself sometimes.

'You realize it makes it harder for us to tell when you're doing it and when he's doing it?' I just shrug. She goes, 'If you make some things up, it gives him the chance to say you're making it all up.'

'I'm not making it up.'

'I'm not saying you are, I'm just pointing out the difficulties.'

I look at Amy. 'Will he go to prison?'

She says, 'We'd need you to testify in court. Would you be prepared to do that, Rosa? Or we could do it on film, like this.'

I tell her I don't want to go back there any more, to that house. Amy says I won't have to, even if he doesn't go to prison I won't have to go back ever again.

Find the Lady

There's a stage illusion called Find the Lady. Kim steps up on to one of three stools, then three giant playing cards are lowered (the stools stand well apart, their legs in view beneath the bottom edge of each card). When the card in front of Kim is raised, she's gone, reappearing on one of the other stools. After a few quickfire repetitions of this, all three cards are raised; Kim has vanished altogether. The illusion derives its name and general principle from a classic gambling game in which the victim tries to keep track of one of three playing cards – usually a queen – being exchanged at high speed by the card-sharp. The punter places a bet on the one he believes to be the queen; he is almost always wrong.

This was the gist of the monologue I'd launched into before Paul Fievre took advantage of a brief pause to say, 'Red, I know all this. Why are you *telling* me this?'

We were at his place. I'd phoned him after the detective constable left, asking if I could come straight round. He was working, the loft of his terraced house in Jericho having been converted into an office from which he ran his agency. Its solitary Velux window afforded a view over a section of the Oxford Canal – if you stood on tiptoe and poked your head out of the angled opening. The room, congested with the customary office gadgetry and furniture, was soporifically warm. Posters and publicity shots of his clients, including me, chequered the walls. Penny was at work, the twins were with a minder. Paul sat on the edge of his desk while I occupied the only chair. Between us, on the mousemat of his wordprocessor, lay the items I'd palmed from my kitchen table. I'd asked, as a favour, if he would keep Charity Jackson's passport and the piece of paper somewhere safe. It had been his response – *Why take these? Why not any of Rosa's other things?* – that prompted my spiel on Find the Lady.

'Look,' I resumed, 'suppose you're the punter – assuming the card-sharp is using pure sleight of hand rather than doctored cards – the one card you *don't* bet on is the one he's led you to think is the queen. Right?'

Paul shrugged. 'Sure.'

'You pick one of the other two – that way, at least, you've a fifty–fifty chance of being right. Like I say, assuming there's a queen there at all.'

'So, what're you saying?'

'The puzzle here is the lady: Rosa. What was she up to?' I raised a hand to prevent another interruption. 'What I've ignored are the personal items, *her* things, and what I'm gambling on are the only objects in her bag which seem to have nothing whatsoever to do with her.'

Paul signalled a grudging affirmation of my reasoning. He nodded again, after some hesitation, when I repeated my request for him to mind the borrowed items.

'You know you'd be making yourself an accomplice to withholding evidence?'

'It's fatherhood,' he replied, deadpan. 'What happens is you have this enhanced awareness of your social responsibilities.'

I thanked him. Then, I said, 'I'd also like to use your phone to ring Holland.'

Mostly, it was pubs and clubs and bed. In those early weeks our relationship seemed to be based almost entirely on a mutual predilection for smoking, drinking and fucking. Rosa liked to dance, too, but for me, clubbing was a means of continuing to booze after closing time. She told me I boogied like a tailor's dummy. The Irish were the only people who really *danced* because they didn't give a shite what anyone thought. *Let go, for fuck sake.* Rosa became a threshing machine – arms, legs and long hair flailing the air and creating a clearing in the midst of the busiest dance-floor. Raining sweat. She reckoned Es, whizz and poppers were designed to give English kids a taste of what it was like to be Irish. I never saw her do drugs. She drank and smoked, but that was all; she didn't even smoke dope. Offered anything, she'd just shake her head and the pusher would push off. I don't recall her being approached twice by the same person.

I once asked her, 'Have you ever experimented?'

She nodded. 'In biology, Mr Davidson got us to cut up a frog.'

Dancing was Rosa's fix; most weekends we'd walk home together through dormant streets, drunk, inadequately dressed against the 2 a.m. chill, ears resonant with spent sound. Exhilarated and exhausted. Never too tired to fuck, though. If anything, those post-club nights saw us chart new territories of sexual exploration, with Rosa as chief navigator. She was the more voracious, the more imaginative, the less inhibited. Then, one time, I made a miscalculation. Heady with the seeming limit-lessness of what was permissible, infected by her abandon, seeking, I suppose, to take the initiative for once . . . I poked a finger into her anus. Rosa bucked violently, swatting my hand away and spilling me backwards against the headboard. Then, with a grunt of ejected breath, she punched me so hard she smashed my nose.

'Jesus fucking christ!' I was stooped over the wash-basin, its glazed white bowl swirling pink with running water and snotty gobbets of red. 'Fuck. Jesus *fuck*, Rosa.'

She was standing naked behind me, watching me in the mirror. When I tried to straighten up, blood collected in my throat, making me gag. I braced myself against the basin, trailing a spaghetti of crimson saliva. Our eyes met in reflection, her image refracted in the blur of my involuntary tears. Without a word she turned and left the bathroom. By the time I'd cleaned up, Rosa was lying in her half of the bed with her back towards me and the duvet pulled up around her neck and shoulders. I thought she was feigning sleep, but when I slipped in beside her she said in a husky whisper, 'Can you breathe through your nose?'

'Yeah, I think so. Just about.'

'It doesn't need setting, then.'

She still had her back to me. We fell silent. When, at last, I placed a hand on her bare waist she didn't respond, nor did she withdraw or push me away; she simply lay there, her warm flesh rising and falling beneath my palm with each shallow breath.

I couldn't work for two weeks, cancelling all engagements until the swelling had disappeared and the bruising was sufficiently faded to be masked by stage make-up. My nose had kinked fractionally out of alignment, the bridge marked by a thin, faint indentation that even now, almost a year later, I habitually stroke with the tip of my index finger when I'm lost in thought. To explain away the injury to others – Paul, Kim, mutual friends – I decided against attributing it to an accident. Instead, I applied the 'honesty principle' – in magicianship, divulging the actual method by which an effect is achieved, on the assumption that the truth is so implausible to a lay audience that you won't be believed. I told people Rosa had hit me, I was a battered spouse. They laughed, accusing me of covering up some freakish act of clumsiness to which I was too embarrassed to confess.

Using Paul's phone, I dialled the two numbers. No answer on Lena's, nor when I tried again from a phone-box at various times over the following days. I got an answering machine on Nikolaas's number; the recording (a male voice) was surprisingly terse and – hazarding a guess at translation – didn't seem to give a name or consist of anything other than the briefest instruction to leave a message. I hesitated, uncertain of what to say and, in any case, reluctant to reveal my identity or phone number. I hung up. I rang twice more, from pay phones, with the same consequence.

Despite agreeing to help me, Paul counselled against withholding information from the police; he also queried what he termed the tactics of unnecessary subterfuge. *Why would they want to search your house, or monitor your calls?* The root of the problem, he suggested, was my fear of succumbing to grief. This . . . *preoccupation* with taking it upon myself to investigate Rosa's death was an unconscious attempt to blot out the pain of losing her.

'You're not grieving, you're trying to keep her alive.'

I shook my head. I told him it was me I was trying to keep alive. Not that I was suicidal or anything – I just wanted to fill the emptiness.

'When I wake up in the morning, there doesn't seem to be any reason to get out of bed,' I said. 'I can't be bothered to wash or eat or cook or do anything. Some days I don't even get dressed. I don't rehearse any more . . . I don't even want to *think* about performing.' I looked at him. 'You know what, Paul? I wish I could go into hibernation for six months and wake up and all this would be over.'

Even with hindsight, it's hard to say whose assessment was closest to the truth. What *is* true is that Paul turned out to be wrong about the police.

It wasn't DC Fuller who turned up but a detective inspector and a detective sergeant, in plain clothes, along with four men in blue overalls who resembled a team of car-exhaust fitters. The DS didn't say much. He had a crop of coppery hair and freckles and was apparently in need of a good night's sleep. The DI looked uncannily like my father, only sober. That same dark brown hair with meticulous off-centre parting, that same greying moustache. Younger, though – in his forties – and allergic to Merlin. To cats in general, he said, after a spectacular sneezing fit that left him red-eyed and wheezy and had the convenient side-effect of causing Merlin to bolt for the cat-flap. It was DI Strudwick who introduced them; they both displayed ID, the sergeant, DS Crookes, also showing me a warrant. The inspector, snuffling into a hanky, suggested we go into the back garden while the Kwik-Fit crew searched my house.

Outside, Strudwick, removing his jacket and declining my offer of beer, got straight down to business. He explained that the recovery of Rosa's bag had produced *one or two interesting developments*. Not least of which, it occurred to me, had been its effect in arousing police curiosity in an odd but hitherto unsuspicious death. They were especially keen to know more about Rosa. Her passport had been helpful, enabling them to obtain files from the office where the document had been issued. And it was from these records that the officers discovered her original surname was not Kelly and that she wasn't an orphan.

'You told DC Fuller her parents were both dead,' said the inspector.

'That's what she told me. They died in a car crash when she was fourteen, and she was taken into care, that's what she said.'

'Did she tell you anything more about them?'

'Mary and Patrick. Mum was a school dinner-lady and Dad was a postman.'

Strudwick shared a smile with his colleague. The sergeant's left eye was half-closed in the spring sunshine. We were sitting on white plastic chairs on the patio, separated by a table Rosa had stolen, complete with parasol, late one night from outside our local pub. The air smelled of new-mown grass from a neighbouring garden.

' "Mary" was right,' said the DI. 'Hotel barmaid in Killarney. Died of a brain haemorrhage when your Miss Kelly was nine years old. Her father – *Gerard* – was indeed a postman. Gerard Brendan Houlihan.'

I waited for him to continue.

'The name rang a very loud bell with one of our chief inspectors at St Aldate's – used to work in the anti-terrorist squad back in the seventies. In 1973 Mr Houlihan was sentenced to life imprisonment in the Republic of Ireland for providing a safe house for IRA activists and for storing and preparing bomb-making equipment, arms and ammunition. His wife was pregnant with Rosa at the time of his arrest.'

I went to speak, then had to stop myself and start again. This time my voice held. 'I didn't know any of this.'

DI Strudwick went on: 'After her mother died, Rosa Houlihan – as was – was formally adopted by her maternal aunt and uncle, Niamh and Michael Kelly, and moved to live with them in London. As I say, this was when she was nine. Her real father would've been up for parole before now, if he hadn't stabbed a prison warder.'

'Have you contacted them, her uncle and aunt?' I asked.

'Still trying to trace them. The young lady's whereabouts and activities, post-adoption and prior to Oxford . . .' He smiled. 'Well, they require a little unravelling.'

Then the information stopped and the questions began. Not a formal interview, as such, though the DS made occasional notes. We talked for more than an hour, my attention distracted by noises from the house as the forensic officers went about their work or by the piecemeal registering of this new childhood the inspector had grafted on to my previous notion of Rosa's past. They wanted to know everything I could tell them about her. They asked me about the contents of the bag and the circumstances of its return. Why Amsterdam? Had she been there before? Did she know anyone in Holland? Did I know she was going there? (Don't know, don't think so; don't know; no.) Who is Vicky? What about the wig? (Don't know. Haven't a clue.) They went through Rosa's address book, gathering any information I could supply on the names listed within it. Did she have Irish friends? Did any of them come to the house? (Yes. Sometimes.) Their names? (I gave them names.) Did she ever go to Ireland during the time I lived with her? (No, not to my knowledge.) What about London? (Sometimes. She had friends there.) Names?

I interjected. 'Are you saying she was a terrorist?'

'We're only . . .'

'Her dad was in the IRA, she's Irish, therefore – she's a terrorist.' I gestured at the house. 'Your boys hoping to find Semtex in her knicker drawer?'

'We're compiling a picture, Mr Brandon. That's all.'

At which point Merlin sprang on to Strudwick's lap. The officer froze, staring into the cat's eyes as though mesmerized with fright, then – delayed reaction – tipped him rudely on to the ground. A sneeze. He excused himself, and sneezed again.

Cycling

The questions were drawing to a conclusion; through the French windows I could see the officers in overalls carrying plastic sacks filled, I presumed, with Rosa's belongings. A cloud had passed in front of the sun so the copper-haired detective sergeant was no longer squinting. Yawning, now; he looked tired rather than bored. I thought, tell me about it. The backs of my thighs were numb with pins and needles from having sat so long in one position. I shifted my weight, half-listening as DI Strudwick explained how he wanted to discuss *more personal* matters. Me and Rosa. I fumbled for answers to his questions, then he reeled off another: 'Would you describe her as a secretive person?'

I considered this for a moment. 'How d'you mean, "secretive"?'

'Did she . . . did you ever get the feeling she was keeping things from you?'

'Like what?'

'Her job at the newspaper; you were under the impression she worked there full-time . . .'

'I only found that out afterwards.'

'All right, what about the unposted letter she wrote to you? The postscript.' The inspector consulted his notebook. 'Here we are: "Dont tell any one any thing about me." Why would she have written that?'

I shrugged.

'You don't think her PS was a way of marking your card – that she suspected people might come round asking questions about her?'

'I don't imagine she knew she was going to die.'

'Perhaps not, but she knew she was going away and wouldn't be coming back. Not to *you*, anyway.' A pause, as if to let this remark sink in. He tapped his notebook. 'Why was she leaving you, Mr Brandon?'

'I've no idea.'

'You've no idea.' A statement rather than a question. His expression disclosed nothing, but the tone of voice betrayed his scepticism.

'Look, the whole time we were together, I had this feeling she might up and leave whenever she wanted. You couldn't take anything for granted with Rosa. She moved in with me on a whim and, for all I know, she moved out on a whim.'

He glanced again at his notes. ' "Ive gone. I dont have to tell you why." Sounds like more than a whim to me.' He looked at me across the garden table. 'Also sounds as though she thought *you* knew the reason well enough.'

'No.' I shook my head. 'No, I read that as her saying not that she didn't *need* to tell me, but that she was under *no obligation* to.'

'You live together for a year – you're lovers – and she just clears off for no apparent reason. No explanation, nothing.'

'That's the sort of woman she was.'

'Enjoy that type of relationship, do you?'

Returning his unsmiling gaze, I said, 'It was the only type she was offering.'

They left soon after that. A few minutes later, the inspector's sidekick returned holding a dishevelled Merlin one-handed beneath the belly. The cat was peering down from this vantage point, at a loss to fathom why his outstretched feet wouldn't reach the ground. DS Crookes explained that *a forensic* had spotted something moving in one of the sacks they'd loaded into the van. He set Merlin down on the doorstep, the cat immediately darting through my legs and into the house.

'The cat belonged to her, did she?'

'It's a he. And you were lucky he didn't give you a swipe.'

The sergeant, straight-faced, nodded towards one of the police vehicles parked along the road. 'Inspector Strudwick reserved that privilege for himself, sir.'

★

I pedalled into the city centre, dismounted at Bonn Square and wheeled Rosa's bike to Carfax before remounting and continuing up the High. Rosa persistently ignored the no-cycling restriction in Queen Street, or any of Oxford's pedestrianized areas, no matter how often she was flagged down. Nor could she be bothered with lights after those that came with the bike were stolen one night while it was chained outside a pub. Remembering to detach the lights and carry them around with her (*in the pub for fuck sake!*) was more hassle than doing without. I cycled over Magdalen Bridge. Early picnickers had staked their claims along the stretch of grass beside the Cherwell, and on the river itself a few punts were already out. Five minutes later I was dismounting again, slightly out of breath and flushed from the ride. I fastened the bike to railings at the front of a red-brick terraced house just off Cowley Road.

Dympna must've been watching because, as I reached for the knocker, the door surprised me by opening inwards. She was trying a smile on for size, only it didn't fit too well. We exchanged hellos. I followed her along the hall to her bedsit. The walls, and the doors of the fitted wardrobe, were flyposted with Irish writers and musicians – a bespectacled Joyce cheek by jowl with Bono. The vivid design of the duvet cover and cushions combined with tangerine-and-crimson curtains and gaily patterned carpet to create a psychedelic ambience. Often we had sat in this room – me and Rosa, Dympna and her bloke John – smoking and boozing and jawing and singing along to music until dawn. Now, I felt like a stranger.

Dympna made tea and tipped biscuits on to plates – to keep herself occupied, it seemed, rather than from a genuine sense of hospitality – prolonging the moment when we would have to extend the scope of our conversation beyond the weather and milk-and-sugar requirements. We hadn't met since the funeral; we'd spoken once, when I phoned to ask if I could see her. I watched her from the only armchair, her haystack of gingery-blonde curls spilling from a blue headband, her dimpled elbows, her bare feet. She wore a baggy T-shirt and frayed jeans. Rosa's best mate. They'd flat-shared in London years before, lost touch after Rosa moved out, then revived their friendship after a chance meeting at an Irish rock festival. At that time Rosa was unemployed, and Dympna – in Oxford, working as a feature writer on *Erin* – was able to wangle her an editorial assistant's post and find her a room with a friend. So the story went.

'Is that too strong?'

'That's fine, thanks.'

I set the mug down on the broad arm of the chair along with a side plate of bourbons. Dympna sat on one of the upright chairs at the table, her freckled face made creamy by the light from the window. A radio was playing in one of the other bedsits. Breakfast things were stacked, gleaming, in a wire rack beside the sink; the room was pungent with pot-pourri and stale spliff.

'D'you miss her?' I hadn't planned that, the words just occurred to me and I let them out. It occurred to me, too, that we'd never before been in one another's company without Rosa or other people being present.

Dympna lowered her eyes. 'A lot,' she said, almost in a whisper.

I thought she was on the verge of asking me the same question, but she didn't, she simply looked at me and then towards the window. There followed a momentary awkwardness as we tried to out-polite each other with cigarettes. She conceded, and we smoked mine.

'I heard the police turned up at your offices,' I said.

'Yeah.' Dympna tucked a flop of curls back beneath the hairband. 'Bastards.'

'They were at my place, too.'

'I know.'

'They think she might've been mixed up with the IRA.'

She nodded. Dympna had separated two rectangles of biscuit and was nibbling like a squirrel at the thin layer of chocolate-cream filling.

I asked, 'Do they think someone at the paper was involved as well, or what?'

'Do *you*?'

I didn't answer. I didn't feel I had to, and I trusted my

expression conveyed as much. Dympna's antagonism visibly receded. She dunked the remains of her biscuit and ate it whole. With a wave of the hand, she said, 'The police haven't a fucking thought in their heads, if you want my opinion.'

Though no longer overtly hostile towards me, as we continued talking it was plainly stated in her manner that she was Rosa's friend, not mine. If I'd expected a cooperative intimacy – empathy, even – born of our mutual loss, I was mistaken. Every move, every facial gesture, every word, cloaked the unuttered demands *Why are you here? What do you want from me?*

'Rosa told you, didn't she?'

'Told me what?'

'Why she was leaving me.'

She exhaled. 'Red . . .'

'It's OK, Dymp, we don't have to talk about it.' I watched her extinguish a half-smoked B&H. I added, 'This isn't about me. Why she died, I mean . . . it's not about *me and her*, is it, it's about *her*.'

Dympna didn't reply, didn't even look at me, but her contempt was palpable. I could live with that. I dislodged ash from my own ill-attended cigarette and inhaled. As the smoke dispersed, I asked, 'Did you know what Rosa was up to every Thursday and Friday?' No reply. 'Did you know why she was going to Amsterdam?' No reply. 'Dymp, who's Charity Jackson?' A frown, no reply. 'OK, who's Vicky?' This time I sensed a distinct alteration in the quality of her silence.

She smiled, looked up. Her eyes were moist. She said, 'We used to sleep together sometimes, me and Rosa, when we were in London. Not sex, just sharing a bed. If one of us had a crisis – bloke-related, usually – we'd snuggle under the covers and talk till we fell asleep. She always reckoned I . . . smelled of vanilla ice-cream.'

I watched her cry.

'And this would do the trick would it?' Petty. I was irritated by the implication that not only had she known Rosa longer than I had but that theirs had been a relationship I, as a man, could only guess at. I was jealous, to be honest. 'A cuddle and a cosy woman-to-woman chat under the bedclothes and – hey presto! – the crisis is solved.'

She wiped the tears from her face. 'Who's talking about solutions?'

A memory of my own surfaced: Rosa, sucking her thumb, oblivious of being watched as she slept. In the morning, she laughed it off, but I could tell she was embarrassed at my seeing her in a state of such childlike defencelessness. I took a swig of tea. It was tepid and I'd hardly touched it.

'I lost her too, you know,' I said.

'Sure.'

'What is it, Dymp?' I asked, adopting a conciliatory tone. 'Did you give her your word you wouldn't say anything?'

Her voice was flat, cold. 'I didn't need to.'

'Not even to me? Not even with what's happened?'

She shook her head.

'All right, if you won't talk to me, at least tell me where I can find this Vicky.'

Dympna told me to leave. She said *I think you'd better go, Red.* Not angry so much as weary – like an invalid dismissing a visitor from her bedside after becoming overtired by their company. Her chair clunked against the table leg as she stood up. She went over to the sink and sluiced out the dregs of her tea.

'Did you *ever* like me?'

Turning to face me, she said, 'You were with Rosa. I trusted her judgement.' She hesitated, smiling despite herself. 'Fuck it, Red, 'course I liked you.'

'Were you the one she asked to collect her things from my place?'

The smile evaporated. She didn't answer for a long time, then she nodded.

'And she told you why?'

'No. She just said she was leaving.'

Dympna's asking me about Red, how I feel about him, and I don't know what to say because I don't know myself so I just sort of shrug. She's smoking a spliff. Her eyes are bloodshot and she's got this grin on her face like her mouth's fixed that way for good. I count up how many weeks I've been living with him. Seven. Fuck all. Seven weeks is fuck all when you think about it. Dympna says she was sure about John after seven days. I don't believe her. It's crap when people say stuff like that, they just say it cos it sounds good. Like, romantic. Or they make it happen that way in their memory and after a while they actually start believing that's the way it was. I tell her I'm pleased for her. She gives me a look like she knows I think it's shite, but she's spliffy so she lets it go.

'Must be something there or you wouldn't still be with him,' she says.

'I'm not saying I don't like the guy. I do. He's a gas ticket.'

She laughs. She says she hasn't heard that expression in years. Her room is reeking. I'm feeling spliffy myself and I'm not even smoking the stuff. What I've to do, she says, is draw up a personal mandala, whatever the fuck that is.

'Is that, like, as in Nelson Mandala?'

'No, listen . . .'

What it is, you get this sheet of paper and draw a big circle and in the circle you put all the things that are important to you: people, places, work, whatever. You can write them down or you can draw little pictures. The more important it is, the nearer it goes to the middle of the circle; the less important, the nearer to the outside. Things you don't give a shit about — you don't put them in the circle at all. Dympna says she does her personal mandala all the time, every couple of months, and it's always different. New things come into the circle, old things get left out, other things move nearer to the middle or further away.

'The thing is, you've got to be totally honest with yourself. And don't do it when you're angry or upset or anything.'

She's a bit of a fucking hippie, old Dymps. I ask what's the point of all this and she says it makes you think more clearly about yourself and what matters to you.

'The way to find out how much you care for Red is to see how you feel about him in relation to all the other aspects of your life.'

So anyway, she hands me this sheet of paper and a felt-tip pen and I give it a go. It's hard actually. You'd think it's easy, but it isn't. I think it's going to take about ten minutes but I'm still at it an hour later and Dympna has made a pot of tea and she's eating a slice of fruit cake as big as a brick. When I've finished I show her. She looks at it for a long time, smiling and nodding.

'I'm nearer the middle than he is,' she says.

'Yeah, but I'd sooner shag him than you.'

We have a laugh at that and I ask if I can cut myself some cake before it disappears down her gob. She looks at my mandala a bit longer then gives it back. The way she looks at me, like, 'Well?' Fuck sake, I don't know. I like him. We shag, we have a good craíc, and he hasn't done anything yet to make me hate him. And I've no notion to fuck off, which is something, for me, after seven weeks.

Misdirection

The most important skill in a magician's repertoire? Misdirection. Without it, even the most adept sleight of hand or ingenious mechanical device will not create the illusion of 'real' magic. Conversely, with its aid the simplest method can be used to concoct a semblance of the miraculous. There are two essential elements to misdirection: first, divert attention *away* from the methodology – the secret – of an illusion; second, divert attention *towards* some point or aspect which seems crucial but isn't. The purpose is to militate against the spectator's faculties of observation, not against his understanding. Most people are familiar with the concept of misdirection in magic. *Don't look at the hand that is active, watch the one apparently idle by the conjuror's side . . .* Even so, a good illusionist will not only 'manage' the audience's gaze, but use their knowledge against them in a subtle series of visual bluffs and double bluffs.

Misdirection is another tactic common to illusionist and liar. The adulterous wife, for instance, caught in the act of talking on the phone to her lover, will ascribe her evident discomposure to her husband's sudden appearance. *God, you made me jump!* (If he asks who she was speaking to, she might deploy the 'honesty principle' – *Oh, it was my lover* – in the hope she will not be believed.) There's a stage illusion which incorporates both misdirection and the honesty principle. I display two large boxes, to demonstrate that they are empty, then 'nest' the bigger of the two over the other. The Lovely Kim bursts theatrically through the top as if from nowhere. Cue applause. The audience is now invited to imagine they are backstage, viewing from the rear as I repeat the same illusion to a fictitious audience portrayed on a painted backdrop which has been lowered. The premise is that the real audience is to be allowed the rare privilege of witnessing how a 'trick' is done. I follow the same procedure as before, displaying the first box to the make-believe spectators, then setting it back down. As I go over to the second box alongside it, Kim, by means of secret panels, sneaks out of this box and enters the first, in full view of the real audience but concealed from the pretend one. Once again, I nest the boxes. There is an air of amused enlightenment mingled with dissatisfaction as the spectators discover how disappointingly unmagical the methodology is. This, however, is transformed into astonishment as the top bursts open to reveal . . . not Kim, but a male stage assistant. Kim has vanished.

The Backstage Illusion featured in my (so far) unique television appearance, as one of the finalists in a national contest for up-and-coming conjurors on the club and cabaret circuit. 'Up-and-coming' meaning under thirty; I snuck in with a few months to spare. I came third. My supporters in the studio audience were Rosa, Paul Fievre, Taaffe and his wife, Dympna and John. Paul obtained a recording of the broadcast for me, which contains the only action footage I have of Rosa.

For a week or so after she died I couldn't tolerate the thought of going through the scores of photographs of her, and of us, that filled two albums. Those prints pinned to the corkboard in the kitchen or displayed in clip-frames, I took down. But, coming across her passport photo among the items in her bag jolted my obsession into reverse, from total avoidance to compulsive gorging. I couldn't get enough of her. Within hours I'd festooned every room with all the pictures I could find, so that wherever I went I was accompanied by Rosa. Rosa laughing, Rosa pulling a face, Rosa riding her bike – Look, no hands – on the tow-path, Rosa and me kissing, Rosa's hair blowing in the wind, Rosa tossing a pancake, Rosa and Dympna drinking cocktails, Rosa hugging Merlin, Rosa dancing, Rosa in her dressing-gown, Rosa in bed with flu, Rosa naked through a translucent shower curtain, Rosa cooking, Rosa gardening, Rosa and me on a fairground ride, Rosa applying burgundy eyeshadow, Rosa cross-legged on the floor ripping open Christmas presents, Rosa smoking a cigarette. The one of her gardening, caught by surprise while pruning roses, was the last I took before she died. I didn't know it then, but I was already losing her.

It was during this phase of photo addiction that I looked out the video cassette. I slotted it into the machine, fast-forwarded to the appropriate sequence and watched it over and over. Rosa was in shot for only a few seconds, as the camera panned slowly across a section of the audience. My supporters, clapping enthusiastically. Rosa has her left thumb and middle finger in her mouth and you can make out a high-pitched wolf-whistle above the general applause. Still in shot, she lowers her hand and leans to say something into the ear of the woman sitting beside her, Dympna. Rosa can be seen from the chest up. She is wearing a bright lemon-coloured cotton shirt made silky by the studio lights, her hair is up and unnaturally black, her eyes and lips are daubed with streaks of yellow. Her ear-rings and bangles emit chips of reflection. Her lips are slightly parted. It is Rosa, and it is not Rosa, just some strange woman captured fleetingly on the telly – anyone's lover, daughter, sister, friend. Happy, clappy. She could've been an actress planted in the audience to make out she was having the time of her life; only if you know her can you tell this extremity of emotion isn't faked. After replaying the scene several times, I freeze-framed it with Rosa in centre-shot. She is captured fractionally out of focus. Fuzzy at the edges, the colours of her are bleeding. She's open-mouthed. She might be talking or about to sneeze, a moist tip of tongue discernible between parted teeth. Staring at her in that frozen moment, I was reminded of a head-and-shoulders picture, flashed up behind a newscaster, of the victim of some awful crime or accident. Always, in these snapshots or home-video stills, the person appears by their expression – their *eyes* – to be in prescient anticipation of death, as though the portrait captures an essence of impending tragedy in its subject. I wondered if it was *me*, with hindsight, reading something that wasn't there. Or Rosa, like all of us, containing at all times the blueprint of mortality. Every photograph of a person is the photograph of a person who will one day die. I released the freeze-frame, allowing Rosa to become animated again. She laughed, gave another wolf-whistle, then the camera cut to Peter Prestige and The Lovely Kim, on stage, bowing.

Kim phoned to ask how I was coping. Her word: *coping*. She also asked, less directly, when I was likely to resume work. I said I didn't have any idea. I offered an assurance, unsolicited, that she'd continue to be paid her retainer. *Red, it's not me I'm thinking of, it's you. Maybe you need to . . .* I thanked her. If there was anything she could do – absolutely anything at all – I was to let her know. I thanked her again and hung up.'

Kim possesses a flair for misdirection far exceeding the customary requirements of a magician's assistant. With her participation, I have been able to introduce more effects – and more elaborate ones, at that – into my act; it is, to quote Paul, as though there are two illusionists on stage. As I stared at the telephone, its cradled receiver still resinous with unevaporated condensation from my touch, I suppressed an urge to call her back. Instead, I phoned Dympna. It was the day after my visit to her bedsit; I'd come away burdened by so many unanswered questions that my resolve to respect her reticence gave way. I had to know what *she* knew. She hadn't told lies, but she had lied by concealment, by evasion. *Don't tell any one any thing about me.* How many of us had been similarly primed? I was sure Dympna had also lied by misdirection, though with no great finesse. Her hostility towards me after so many months of, albeit shared, friendship had been in the guise of loyalty to her *true* friend, Rosa. Antagonism bolstered by suspicion. Even if she didn't know the reason why Rosa was leaving me, she had the fact of this desertion as a basis for her distrust. But I'd spied something else in her manner – not just anger or wariness or disdain, but fear. Reflecting on our meeting, I came to the interpretation that Dympna was literally afraid to talk to me. I rang her. Not to confront her, nor to rake over the previous day's conversation, but to pose a question I'd neglected to ask.

'Dymp, was Rosa seeing someone else?'

'No!'

'Be honest with me.'

'Red, she wasn't.'

'Was she ever? While she was with me, I mean?'

'No.'

I paused. 'OK.'

'She'd have told me if she was.'

'Yeah.'

'*Red.*'

'Yeah, I'm sorry, Dymp. I just . . . I needed to know.'

I told her the police had taken away the things she'd been asked by Rosa to collect. I'd been given a copy of an itemized receipt which they got me to sign; everything would be returned in due course along with those contents of her shoulder-bag which were no longer required for investigative purposes. They didn't take any of the photographs, though DI Strudwick had been visibly startled by the sight of so many of them about the house. Dympna sounded surprised too, when I informed her of what I'd done. She also softened towards me, I could tell. A little, but not enough.

I believed her when she said she didn't think Rosa was being unfaithful to me. Which isn't the same as saying I believed in Rosa's fidelity. There were so many puzzles surrounding her death, but one thing I did understand was that Rosa had been leading a double life of which I knew nothing. I've heard it said that when two lovers meet for the first time they have a subliminal premonition of what it is between them that will, ultimately, cause their division. With Rosa, I sensed from the outset it would be sex. She was so sexual, I couldn't believe I'd be enough for her. She had been so ready to fuck me, I couldn't believe myself to be the last man in her life to be so readily fucked. Even before she died, even before I began to decipher the mystery with which she'd enclosed half her life, I'd grown convinced that she was concealing something from me. And that something was the fact that I was in the throes of losing her to someone else. I tried to explain some of this on the phone to Dympna. The softness left her voice. *Jesus, Red, Rosa's been killed and all you can think about is whether she was sleeping around.* She didn't say 'Rosa's dead,' she said 'Rosa's been killed.' Her exact words: Rosa's been killed.

'Why, Dymp?'

'Why what?'

'Why was she killed?'

'I didn't say . . . I didn't *mean* killed. Look, don't twist . . .'

I began to interrupt, but there was a click and the line went dead.

Pancake Day

Rosa was making pancakes. It wasn't Shrove Tuesday, wasn't any Tuesday. I arrived home from rehearsals to find the kitchen worktops spattered with milk, flour, fractured eggshells and semen strands of raw albumen; Rosa was on the point of tipping batter into a frying-pan from a glass bowl. Smoke rose from the pan.

'*Pannekoeken.*' She waved a spatula as she spoke. 'I could eat these things till they're coming out my ears.'

'Panna-what?'

Rosa looked at me, then back at the pan. 'Just a word some guy in London taught me. Dutch guy. He was a chef.'

It was the first time she'd cooked since moving in. Mostly, we'd snacked or dined out or eaten take-aways; now and then I'd rustle something up. I watched Rosa cover the surface of the pan with a liquid film of yellowy-white. On another ring, the contents of a saucepan simmered. Ham and mushroom in cream and white-wine sauce, she replied, when I raised the lid by way of inquiry. *Woite woine.* A half-empty glass stood within reach on the counter. I went over to the fridge and looked inside.

'Where's the rest of the plonk?' I asked.

'In here.' Rosa indicated her stomach. Tapping the side of her head, she added, 'I'd say there's a fair bit in here as well.'

I lost count of the *pannekoeken* we ate that evening. They were delicious. She confessed without modesty that they were her speciality; no one cooked them better, and anyone who said they did was talking crêpe. I remember finding this quite funny at the time, but we'd drained two more bottles of wine by then. We lay stretched out on the sofa, listening to CDs. It must've been after midnight. We were interlocked, somehow – all arms and legs – yet, after much positional experimentation, comfortable. I was stroking Rosa's hair, her left hand rested on my pancake-distended stomach. It was the longest we'd spent in physical proximity, albeit fully clothed, without one or other of us initiating sex. Even when she eased a hand inside my shirt the contact was affectionate rather than suggestive. I wondered aloud if she was glad she'd moved in with me; she said it was the worst decision she'd made in her entire life. This remark terminated in an indiscreet belch for which she made no apology.

'You ever lived with a bloke before?'

She moved her head, though pressed as it was into the crook of my shoulder, I couldn't tell whether or not this was an affirmation.

'Eh?'

'Yeah, sure.'

'One? More than one?'

'Never more than one at a time.'

I laughed. 'How do I compare?'

'Oh, now.'

Cramp. I withdrew a leg from beneath hers and flexed it, bringing my foot to rest on the arm of the sofa.

'What happened, with the others?' I asked.

Rosa's breath was warm against my neck. 'Don't let on, like, but I'm not living with them any more.'

'No, I . . .'

Let it go. I fancied a cigarette, but that would've meant untangling myself to retrieve the pack. I continued playing with her hair. We'd rarely discussed our previous lovers – or rather, I had made occasional, tentative attempts to raise the subject and she'd swatted each one dead like a fly. Once, when I persisted, Rosa reminded me of a scene in *Four Weddings and a Funeral . . . you know, where your man wants to know how many fellers she's shagged and your woman reels off a list this long.* Point made. Sometimes, an involuntary image of Rosa with another man would make me nauseous with anxiety; other times, fantasizing, I could arouse myself with these hard-core pictures playing on the screen of my imagination. That night, on the sofa, she surprised me by resuming the conversation where I'd left off.

'It fucks up.'

'Always?'

'Always, so far.'

'Why d'you think that is?'

Her turn to laugh. 'Ever thought about becoming a counsellor?'

'Sorry, I'm just . . .'

'Jesus, Red, I'm drunk as a skunk. Don't let me have any more wine.'

'There's none left.'

'Well, go out and buy some and then don't let me have any.'

'OK.'

The room was warm, making me sleepy and relaxed. I laid a hand over hers on my stomach. Her fingers were cool, mine were warm. She said, 'It's like I fill a hole they didn't even know they had.'

'Oh, yeah?'

'Fuck off, I'm being serious.'

'What d'you mean, "a hole"?'

'Like, their life is empty, only they don't realize it. Then I come along.' She exhaled. 'I don't know what I'm saying.'

'I don't get how this causes things to fuck up.'

'I'm talking about the ones where it's more than just shagging, yeah?'

'Sure.'

'It's . . . I don't know; OK – *I'm* their life now.' She laughed. 'Dymps reckons I'm an invasion. *A physical and emotional invasion.*'

'What, and they can't handle it?'

'Usually it's me, actually – I can't handle them not being able to handle me.'

After a moment's reflection, I asked, 'So what sort of bloke is your type? Your *ideal man.*'

Rosa kissed my ear, made it ticklish with the damp brush of her lips. She whispered, 'My ideal man is always the one *after* the one I'm seeing at the time.'

Since Rosa died I've discovered the truth about where she learned to make pancakes. *Dutch guy*, that much wasn't a lie, but he was no chef, and they didn't meet in London. His name was

Nikolaas. *Is* Nikolaas. A name and number on a sheet of paper torn from a notepad in her shoulder-bag. A clue to Rosa's fatal journey, and to Charity Jackson; though I had no idea then, as we gorged on *pannekoeken*, that Nikolaas even existed, let alone any notion of just how significant he would become to me, nor how elusive.

I rang him from Paul's place, and from telephone kiosks. I rang him so often I no longer needed to refer to the notepaper for his number. But, no matter what hour of the day or day of the week, I was invariably greeted by that brief recorded message in a language I didn't understand. Finally, in exasperation, I left my name and number and declared myself to be a friend of Rosa's. As soon as I replaced the receiver I sensed that I'd made a mistake. To be honest, the feeling wasn't as well defined as that; if it seems so now, it is by virtue of hindsight. At the time, all I had was an unaccountable desire to retract my message, to erase the identifying words I'd imprinted on that tape which now belonged irretrievably to someone else. 'Flashing', we magicians call it. A momentary lapse in technique or concentration, or inadequate checking of audience sight-lines, which allows the onlooker a glimpse of something he shouldn't see.

I leaned against the glass wall of the booth. It was dark. Rain was overlaying the pavement with a sheen of reflected street-lamps. I dialled Lena's number. With her, I had endured even less success – no reply, no answering machine, nothing. The calls had become habitual; I listened to the repetitive and seemingly infinite ringing tone as though that, in itself, were the purpose. Each time I would slip into a trance-like state between boredom and meditative contemplation. So it was, on that wet evening, that I was startled by the click of a connection. A woman answered, so clearly she might've been standing beside me. Dutch. I was so taken unawares that I didn't reply right away and, after a pause, she said something else. I gabbled. Hello, did she speak English?

'Yes. Who is this?'

'I'm . . . my name is Red. I'm a friend . . . I'm ringing about Rosa.'

'Red?'

'R–E–D, as in the colour. I'm a friend of Rosa's.' Another pause. 'Is this Lena?'

'I don't know any Red.'

'Am I speaking to Lena?'

'Where are you calling from?'

'England. Oxford. I lived with Rosa here in Oxford . . . I got your number . . . What it was, your name and number were on a piece of paper among her things.'

'I don't know you, Mr Red.'

Her English was virtually flawless – almost unmarked by accent, though there was an indefinable lilt that characterized her as a non-native speaker. She sounded young, a young woman with a clear, confident manner that came through despite her caution at this unexpected call. I couldn't make out any background noise.

'Rosa died. Did you know that? She died a couple of weeks ago.'

'OK, I think you have a wrong number.'

'Please, I think Rosa was killed. Someone killed her.' Silence. 'Lena? Are you still there? I think she was coming to see you in Amsterdam when she was killed.'

'I'm sorry, OK, you have a wrong number.'

'Don't hang up. Please. I need to know what happened to Rosa.' No reply. But she didn't disconnect me – I could hear her breathing at the other end of the line.

'I cannot talk with you, Mr Red, until you identify yourself. OK.'

'I told you, my name is Red. I lived with Rosa – I mean, she lived with me for a year up to the time she died. Red's . . . it's not my real name. My name is Fletcher Brandon. I'm a professional magician.' Silence. 'I don't know what else you want me to say.'

'I cannot talk with you.'

'Lena, please . . .'

'I am hanging up. OK, you must not call me again.'

'Who is Charity Jackson?' Silence. I thought she'd gone. 'Who's Nikolaas? Is he a friend of yours?'

'You have spoken with Nikolaas?'

'No, I . . . his answering machine. I left my name and number on his answerphone. What . . . ?'

'What is his number you called?' The alarm in her voice was palpable. I told her the number. There was a long silence. I was about to say something else when the woman resumed speaking. 'Mr Red, I am going to tell you this and then I am hanging up. OK. That number is not safe.'

'I don't understand.'

'That number is not safe for you. Bye-bye.'

Click. When I redialled, there was no answer.

Twice in consecutive days, a woman had hung up when I'd tried to make her discuss Rosa. First, Dympna; now, Lena – if it was Lena I'd been speaking to. I stood in the booth for a while, thinking, listening to the insistent ringing tone of an Amsterdam telephone. Then I cradled the receiver and walked home in the rain.

It's all girls here. Some of them are OK, some of them aren't. I still have to go to school. I thought they'd teach you here but they don't. Which is a bollix but it's OK really cos I get to stay friends with Nicola. Some days we bunk off down the shopping centre or somewhere, but the staff here always find out and someone – Dave or Jilly, usually – comes to your room and gets you to talk about it. That's what they want you to do: talk. All the time. Talktalktalk. Last week, Dave goes, 'Rosa, how d'you feel about missing school yesterday?'

And I go, 'Dave, I feel fucking great.'

Auntie Niamh doesn't visit. She didn't even send me a card on my birthday. I was fourteen last month and the only cards I got were from Nicola and Amy. Amy has been to see me a couple of times since she got me in here. She says they're hoping to 'place' me with a foster family and I think, oh yeah. I got a letter from Auntie. She said I was a slut. She said Uncle Michael had fallen from grace cos of me and I would burn in eternal hell-fire just like my daddy would. He isn't going to prison, Uncle Michael. There isn't even going to be a court case.

A lot of the girls are into stuff. There's a guy called Luke comes round the back gate every couple of days. Luke's Sandwich Run, he calls it. He's about twenty, I reckon. He says he lived in a home like this one from when he was eight. Most of the girls fancy him something rotten. The first time I met him, he was outside when I came back from school. He said hello and I was new wasn't I? I said yeah and he asked what my name was and I told him. He said his name was Luke. We shook hands, which made me laugh cos who the fuck shakes hands with anyone? We talked a bit. He's from Manchester or Liverpool or somewhere, only he's been down here for years.

I sit in his car with him sometimes. We don't go anywhere, just park in the road outside the home, smoking. Marlboro. I like Marlboro best of all. I say I hate it here. I say I don't hate it as much as living with my auntie and uncle but I still hate it. I tell him things, all sorts. I tell *him about Uncle Michael. Luke doesn't ever say much, he just sits there listening — really listening, like — and nodding and smoking and staring out the windscreen. I tell him loads.*

Necromancy

Here's a fact about Houdini: when his mother died, he employed mediums to contact her. Sure enough, during one séance, the dead woman's spirit communicated with her son. The snag was, she used English, a language she could barely speak when she was alive. Houdini, thereafter, devoted himself to exposing the charlatanism of clairvoyants. Another fact: despite his scepticism, Houdini told his wife Bess that, if he died before she did, he would try to reach her from beyond the grave. To safeguard against fakery, they devised a code known only to them. Houdini died on Hallowe'en, 1926. For ten years, Bess staged a séance on the anniversary of his demise. Several of the mediums claimed to convey messages from the great escapologist's spirit, but she was having none of it. The séances ceased. Houdini's widow came to believe what I believe: necromancy – that is, communication with the dead by a process of divination – is complete bollocks. Don't fall for it. And if I can't spot a lie, then who can? After all, conjuror and clairvoyant alike thrive on the propensity of people to be deceived.

Rosa and I devised no private code for posthumous intercourse. Death, hers or mine, was never discussed. None of this *I hope I die first cos I couldn't live without you bollix*, as Rosa might've said. I was twenty-eight when we met, she was pushing twenty-five; you don't contemplate your own death when you're that age. Frankly, I wasn't even certain we'd still be together by the time I was *thirty*, let alone imagining the pair of us jockeying geriatrically for position at death's door. I was right. I'm nearly thirty now, and Rosa is no longer with me. Her absence is more immense than her presence ever was. Her absence, on that night when I returned home drenched from the phone-box . . . What I did, I went upstairs, stripped off my wet clothes and sat naked on the unmade bed where we'd fucked and slept so often. There, alone, in silence and in the dark, I tried to make contact. But this was no tacit acceptance of the bogus, no self-delusion; it was that purest, most magical of deceits – illusion, the misinterpretation of a true sensory stimulus. Sitting cross-legged on that bed, I shut my eyes and revived the smells, tastes, sounds, sights and touches of her. I made a dream of her that was so real to me, in that moment, I felt I had only to open my eyes and she would be there before me, to hold and to talk to and to kiss. If she spoke to me, it was through my own thoughts; like all spirits of lost loved ones, she told me what I already knew, or what I wanted to hear, or what was within me in the guise of being without.

Two coincidental occurrences broke the spell. The first was Merlin, creeping on to the bed and investigating, in his whiskery, damp-nosed manner, the intriguing odours of my exposed genitals. The second was a voice, calling my name. Someone was in the house. I spilled the cat from the bed and went out on to the landing, looking over the banister to see my brother standing at the foot of the stairs.

'The door was unlocked,' said Taaffe. 'I've been phoning you for days.'

I began to descend. 'I left the machine on,' I replied. 'I didn't feel like talking to anyone.'

'You know, Red, your prick's smaller now than it was when we were lads.'

I stopped half-way down the stairs. 'I'll go and put some clothes on.'

We drank bottled beer in the living room. Taaffe told me he'd been worried about me. I said I was fine. He said that was crap.

'You look awful. The house is a fucking tip. When did you last eat?'

'It's just, I've let things go a bit without Rosa here to keep me in line.'

He laughed. 'What was it? "Rosa would rather stab herself in the eye than do any housework." I'm quoting you. Red, you used to *iron* your tea towels.'

I shrugged.

'Paul called me,' he said. 'He thought it might help if I popped round.'

'Why, what's wrong with him?'

'Yeah, good one.'

'Taaffe, I tell you what it is, right, it's called *grief*. You know? Someone dies and you get fucked up by it. Try it one day. I can recommend it.'

'This isn't grief, it's a failure to function. It's self-pity, actually.'

'Well, you've not been here five minutes and I'm feeling better already.'

He held his bottle up to the light to inspect its contents. 'This beer's good.'

'Belgian. Rosa's favourite.'

Staring straight at me, he said, 'The woman had good taste.'

Taaffe and I share a distinct brotherly resemblance, though he's slightly darker and rounder faced. We're about the same build, the difference being, I keep fit – out of consideration for my stage appearance – while he has a sedentary job (building society, assistant manager) and a compulsive aversion to any form of physical exercise. He has an unnerving ability to read my thoughts. Taaffe was named after the winning jockey on Gay Trip in the 1970 Grand National, the race taking place the week before he was born. Another of Dad's lucrative winners. Taaffe is a year and a half younger than me, but he has a wife and three children, lending him a maturity that persistently casts me in the role of kid brother. He says I should invest in a Personal Equity Plan. Once, drunk, he'd confided *I wish I was the sort of bloke a girl like Rosa would fall in love with*. Rosa liked him. She said he was a *gas ticket*.

I lit a cigarette and checked my watch: just before midnight. I thanked Taaffe for coming round and he told me not to be so soft.

'Heard from Dad lately?' I asked.

'Day before yesterday. Three in the morning.'

'Pissed?'

He nodded. 'He call you as well?'

'Not for a few weeks.' I took a swig of lager. 'You tell him about Rosa?'

'No.'

The curtains were open. I went over and closed them. There was a full ashtray, two empty beer bottles and a half-eaten slice of garlic bread, days old, on the window-sill. I switched on a lamp and flicked off the main light, softening the tones of the room and somehow making it seem less unkempt. Taaffe was using a stack of newspapers as a footrest. I sat back down on the sofa and resumed smoking and drinking.

'D'you think Mum has ever forgiven him for what he did?' I said.

He looked at me. 'Would you, if you were her?'

'We're talking ten years ago.'

'I wouldn't expect to be forgiven.'

'You wouldn't do it.'

Taaffe smiled.

'What?' I said.

'I used to fancy her like fuck.'

'Who, *Monica*?'

'The number of wanks I had, fantasizing about her.'

'Jesus.'

'Don't tell me you didn't.'

'Fuck off. No, I fucking didn't.' I shook my head. 'I hated her. I think I hated her more than I hated him.'

The truth is, I did fancy her. If she'd given me even the slightest come-on, I'd have . . . what would I have done? I'd have had a wank on the strength of it, probably. When I was a teenager I used to masturbate while imagining Monica with my *Dad*, for fuck's sake. Which is pretty sick when you think about it.

'D'you remember those mags we found in his study?' I asked, smiling.

'*Found*. You mean, when you forced the lock on his desk?'

'Yeah, well, all right.' I pointed at him with the neck of my beer bottle. 'I don't recall you refusing to look at them.'

'I must've been – what? – eleven. I'd never seen anything like that before.'

'Taaffe, I don't think age is the issue – a lot of people go their entire lives without witnessing a woman giving an Alsatian a blow-job.'

My brother laughed. We were quiet for a moment, giving way to sporadic fits of mirth. More beer. I finished one cigarette and lit another. I asked Taaffe if he was hungry and he said yes. There was bread, I said, just about fit for toasting, nothing to put on it, the last of the Kerrygold having gone in Merlin's dish that morning. I went out to the kitchen, cut four slices off the rump of a loaf and laid them under the grill. I stood for a moment, not doing anything. The door to the cupboard under the sink was wide open. I took two strides across the room and kicked the door so hard it slammed shut with a tremendous crack that reverberated off the walls like the report of a rifle shot. Taaffe appeared in the kitchen doorway. Neither of us spoke. My foot hurt. I saw to the toast, conscious of being watched the whole time as I turned the bread and slid the grill pan back beneath the flames. My brother came right into the room and had a nosey around, peering into the fridge and one or two of the cupboards.

'Tomorrow, after work,' he said, 'I'll come round and we'll go to Tesco's.'

I looked at him. 'Am I more like Dad or Mum, would you say?'

'Dad, definitely. Mum only used to grill the toast on one side.'

He took me shopping the next day, as promised. My sister-in-law came as well, along with my two nieces and my nephew. They all stayed for tea and afterwards I was persuaded to perform a show for the two older children. It was the first conjuring I'd done since Rosa died. I showed Gemma how to stick a pin in a balloon without bursting it. She liked that a lot. She asked if Auntie Rosa had gone to heaven. I told her I didn't know. What else could I have said? You can't tell a child of seven you don't believe in all that shite.

The Intruder

I'd been boozing with Conal Riordan, Rosa's boss at *Erin*. We'd
started at the Head of the River, then, when a college rowing
crew turned up in fancy dress and started playing drinking games,
we downed our pints and escaped to the Folly Bridge Inn. *This
fucking city is university challenged*, said Conal. I had hoped to pump
him for clues, but it became apparent that he was, genuinely,
oblivious of Rosa's double life. Didn't know what she got up to
on those days when she was supposed, as far as I was aware, to
have been at work; no idea why she was off to Amsterdam; never
heard her mention a Vicky. Conal knew less than Dympna;
either that, or he was better at lying. Fuck all to do with the
I R A, of that much he was certain.

'Your woman was the least political person I ever met,' he
said.

'Do the police still think someone on the paper had something
to do with it?'

'Those fuckers. They're convinced any cunt with nationalist
sympathies must have Provo connections.'

So what *was* she up to? With each fresh intake of beer, the
theories became increasingly implausible. Soon, we'd given up
altogether on speculation, degenerating into an alcoholic melancholia of shared mourning. *Great girl. Best girl in the fucking world.
Fucking tragedy. Fucking . . . fucking tragic.* I cycled home drunk.

I stood Rosa's bike in the front garden without chaining it,
because they could nick the fucking thing for all I . . . The
security light, dazzling me, and I saw her whitewashed face that
first night, that first kiss. Steps. One, two, three. Door. I rescued
my keys from an entirely different pocket to the one I thought
they were in and the lock, the lock, fumbled one into the lock.
Jesus. The door shuddered open. I stepped into the hallway and
switched on the light. Too bright. The coat-stand. What the

fuck was, the coat-stand was lying on its side. Coats everywhere. Had I just done that? No. I never touched the . . . Merlin. Must've been Merlin. I put the stand upright. The coats. How had they been so flung about? But if I didn't have a piss in the next thirty seconds. Upstairs. Up. The. Stairs. I might've been whistling, I can't remember, I whistle when I've had a few. Perhaps it was the whistling he heard, or maybe it was the noise I'd made coming in. I don't know.

The stairs, as I reached the top of the stairs, he came at me across the landing. Fast. No words. He was in the bedroom doorway, then he was right there in my face. Gloves, a balaclava with pink lips through the slit in the wool. Did I say anything? Did I shout? He hit me. I *saw* him hit me, his arm raised, and there was something in his hand – black – and I was off balance, and the ceiling light swam. I must've grabbed – his jumper, his jacket – because . . . woah! backwards down the stairs, and him on top. And then, and then – what? – in a heap in the hallway, and I was on top of him now, on his lap. No pain. Not any pain. Just, I was going to be sick. We sat there for a long time, hours and hours, or maybe only for a moment . . . I was hurting now, watching something – a heavy black torch – roll from stair to stair to my feet. He was up, beneath me, pushing me off. I picked up the torch and turned to swing at him with it, only the stand I hit the coat-stand instead, and it was between us with its wooden arms and I saw a referee trying to separate two boxers. The torch hit the floor. All this grunting and breathing, he was . . . with the coat-stand he knocked me back and I was on my arse watching him make for the door. After him. After him. Through the doorway. We were in the bright white light and I swung him round, tearing grabbing pulling at his balaclava. His face, I saw him: black hair, messed up and sweaty; sallow skin damp, gleaming, the eyes. Then his arm went up again.

Lying on my back on the steps. I wanted to sleep. Just sleep. Sleep.

Merlin revived me, sniffing, lapping at the side of my face. I touched where he was licking and my fingers came away moist with blood. I couldn't sit up. I was cold, stiff, each breath stabbed me. The cat was on the steps beside me, as though pondering the oddity of my predicament. For a moment, I thought he was going to use my prone body as a means of strutting from top step to bottom, just for novelty's sake.

Rosa and I used to fight. I'm not referring to the time she punched me. We fought in bed for fair shares of the duvet; we had Sunday morning pillow-fights; we wrestled on the living-room floor for custody of the TV remote-control. We fought for real, too, and not necessarily when we'd been boozing. She tipped a bowl of washing-up water over me in response to some remark I'd made. She bit my ear and drew blood. She hurled a potted plant at me as I left the house one day, and I can't for the life of me remember what we'd been quarrelling about. She pronounced 'violence' *voilence*.

The coppery-haired sergeant dropped by, unaccompanied. Paul let him in. The officer had to remind me of his name: DS Crookes. *How could I have forgotten that?* I said. A mistake. It hurt to laugh. I was flat on my back in bed, head propped up by two pillows, neck supported by a surgical collar and naked upper torso swathed in tightly bound bandages. The detective looked as exhausted as ever.

'Two broken ribs, a loose tooth and ten stitches,' I explained, in response to his inquiry. 'Concussion, at the time. And I dislocated my thumb punching the coat-stand.'

DS Crookes nodded.

'Where's Inspector Strudwick?' I asked.

'Dentist. Impacted wisdom tooth. *Excruciating*, by all accounts.'

We shared a smile. The sergeant drew up a chair and sat at my bedside. I could hear Paul downstairs, hoovering.

'The worst of it is I can't smoke,' I said. 'Too painful.'

I was conscious of my speech being made staccato by an inability to utter more than a couple of words without a shallow, jabbing breath. A coughing fit reduced me to a chill sweat.

'You're better off than the other bloke,' he said. 'Ruptured spleen.'

'Terminal, with any luck.'

'We're optimistic of having the opportunity to question him.'

I'd learned from a uniformed officer who attended the scene of what was, at that stage, an 'aggravated burglary' that the intruder had been apprehended after collapsing in the street not far from my house. The internal injury had been caused, presumably, by his cushioning my fall when we crash-landed at the foot of the stairs. There was nothing by which police could identify him, and he'd yet to be declared fit for interrogation following an emergency operation.

'You didn't know him?' asked DS Crookes.

'Never seen him before.'

'And he didn't say anything to you?'

'No. Not a word.'

He made a note. 'So, basically, what is it makes you think this is more than just the disturbing of a straightforward burglary?'

I reiterated what I'd told the constable the previous day. The intruder had made an untidy search of the house, but no easily pocketed items of value had been taken – credit cards, cash, an expensive camera; and, having apparently come on foot, he was hardly able to make off with the television, video, CD player or personal computer. To judge by the evidence littering the place, he'd been more interested in paperwork – personal letters, documents, diaries, address books, official correspondence, note-books. He'd turned out the pockets of those of Rosa's clothes that remained in the house, as well as most of mine. My PC had been switched on and disks were strewn about the desk but, without the password, he'd failed to log on.

'He was after information,' I said.

'What sort of information?' asked DS Crookes.

'Why don't you ask him that?'

'We will. In the meantime, I'm asking you. '

A shrug was out of the question, in my condition. I formed my face into an expression intended to signify *Search me*.

'If you don't know what he was after,' the sergeant continued, 'how can you be so sure this had something to do with Miss Kelly's death?'

I debated whether or not to inform him of the message I'd left on Nikolaas's answering machine, and Lena's subsequent warning that the number wasn't 'safe' for me. But that would've meant telling him about the piece of paper in Rosa's bag and confessing – *explaining* – my concealment of it.

'I'm not *sure* of any connection,' I said. 'I'm just suspicious.'

'And nothing's missing, as far as you know?'

'No.' I pushed with my heels to ease myself into a less uncomfortable position. I asked, 'Did he have anything of mine or Rosa's on him?'

'No.'

I indicated the water on my bedside table and asked if the sergeant would mind helping me. Holding the glass beneath my chin, he directed the tip of the straw between my lips. Water dribbled. He apologized, adjusting the angle of the glass. When I'd finished, he set the drink back down on its coaster. I thanked him. Then, I said, 'Have you come here to go over everything I told your colleague?'

He shook his head. 'I was hoping we might talk about Miss Kelly.'

'What about her?'

'Certain matters have come to light since we last spoke. Concerning her past.'

'Let me guess – when she was sixteen she went out with a boy whose father's next-door neighbour's best mate knew someone who had a cousin in the IRA.'

He smiled. After a moment's deliberation he said, 'I have to say we're drawing nothing but blanks on that particular line of inquiry, Mr Brandon.'

'So what *have* you come up with?'

He told me the police had traced Rosa's adoptive parents, her aunt and uncle. At least, her uncle had died of cancer a couple of years ago. But Aunt Niamh was still alive, a patient in a long-stay psychiatric unit in north London. *Chronic alcoholic, basically, with associated mental illness.* She was fifty-eight years old, said the DS. Officers had also tracked down one of the social workers who'd been instrumental, all those years ago, in taking

Rosa into local authority care. Amy Judd. She now worked for a children's charity but was currently on leave, visiting relations in St Lucia.

'Rosa really *was* taken into care?' I asked.

DS Crookes nodded. 'When she was thirteen. Nearly fourteen.' He paused. 'Not for the reason she told you, though.'

'Why, then?'

He hesitated again, gaze fixed on the point where my unshaven chin rested on the rim of the surgical collar. I thought he wasn't going to respond, when finally he said, 'She was on the at-risk register. The CPU – Child Protection Unit – made a successful application for her to be removed from the adoptive home.'

'At risk of what?'

'Abuse.' At last he made eye contact. I wish he hadn't. '*Sexual* abuse. Her uncle, apparently – Michael Kelly. There's a file on him, but he was never prosecuted.'

Neither of us spoke. Downstairs, the phone rang and I heard Paul's muffled voice in one-sided conversation, not so much a distraction as a surreal counterpoint to the impact of the detective's words. When he resumed speaking, I had to force myself to concentrate on what he was saying. The children's home where Rosa lived had since closed, he explained, and officers were still trying to trace the senior staff who worked there at the time. Amy Judd had remained involved in Rosa's case for some years, but in her absence it was proving difficult to establish what had happened to Rosa after she left council care.

'From the age of sixteen, to the commencement of her friendship in London with Dympna O'Neill and then her job in Oxford at *Erin*, we have nothing on her at all,' said DS Crookes. 'Five years, more or less. No employment or benefit data for that period, no criminal convictions, no local authority records of residency or electoral registration, no bank or building society accounts . . . zip. Basically, there's a bloody great hole in her life. It's as though, for five years, your Miss Kelly ceased to exist.'

We're at his brother's — me and Red — and we're having a great craíc. Sunday dinner. Leg of lamb looks like it came off a cow. Home-made mint sauce. Red's been doing magic for the kids and they love it; they think he's the bee's knees, especially Gemma. She's six and she's wild for her Uncle Red and he's wild for her, and I watch them play together and I think — this is fucking evil, if you ask me, but I can't help thinking it anyway — give it a couple of years and he might want to shag her. His little niece. I mean, for fuck sake. Look at her, so fucking innocent, and I want to tell her, I want to do her growing up for her. But you can't. And I look at Red and he's about as far away from wanting to shag her as it's possible to be. He's great with her, actually. Even with the little one, who doesn't do much except sleep and cry and shit herself, he's still interested, like. He holds her and talks to her, he even changed her. 'When I say the magic words . . .' The Illusion of the Disappearing Pooh, he called it. Fucking hoot. He'd make a brilliant dad, though I wouldn't ever say that to his face. As for him and Gemma . . . I hate myself for the way my mind works.

Like I say we're eating Sunday roast and Red's on good form and Taaffe's great. I can tell Lisa, the wife, doesn't like me much — the way I look, or the way I talk or something, or the way the kids are with me, I don't know — but she's polite and she smiles a lot and she doesn't cut me out of the conversation or anything and basically I couldn't give a fucking shite what she thinks of me. It doesn't spoil things. What nearly spoils things is Taaffe. I think I'm the only one who notices, because he's not at all obvious about it. I give him no encouragement, not a bit of it, and I don't give him a warning-off look either cos that gives the game away just the same. I can survive this. Nothing's going to happen, ever, and he knows that and I know that, and as long as Lisa and Red never catch on, everyone's happy. I won't tell Red. He thinks the world of his brother. So everything's fine, it's cool.

Then, I'm in the bathroom. Taaffe's washing up. Red's in the garden with Gemma and Daniel, and Lisa's settling Katy in her cot. Only, when I unbolt the door and step out on to the landing, Lisa's standing there. No smile, now.

'Don't even think about it,' she says.

I could play dumb, but I don't. 'He's the only one thinking about it.'

'And why d'you suppose that is?'

In her head she's looking me up and down, I can tell. Up till now I'm siding with her on this, but now I think, Screw you. 'I should dress up like one of those Muslim women, is that what you're saying? Fucking veil and that, so he doesn't get a stiffy every time he claps eyes on me?'

She could slap me. She's close to it, but she doesn't. She might cry instead. I go soft on her. 'Lisa, he won't do anything about it, he's not the type. I know.'

I can see by her eyes the real problem is the idea of him even imagining it. Him thinking of me while he's shagging her, or something. 'Sins of the mind,' Father Horan used to call it. And I think, jesus, if you can't handle that you might as well never have anything to do with any of them ever again.

Like I say, I won't tell Red any of this. When I'm not in his life any more, Taaffe will still be his brother.

The Living Doll

This is the Illusion of the Living Doll:

A tall tripod is isolated centre-stage, standing on a platform. On top of the tripod rests a life-size head (female) made of plaster. The head is unadorned, it is bald, its eyes and lips are closed. Music, spotlight. Enter Peter Prestige, the Prodigious Prestidigitator, wearing formal evening attire. I am wheeling on to the stage a trolley in the design of a dressing-table and laid out with cosmetics paraphernalia. With stylish flourishes, and appropriate, entertaining patter, I begin to make up the plaster head. I apply eyeliner, I pencil in the eyebrows and eyelashes, I powder it to give skin tone, I use blusher to add definition; I daub cobalt-blue eyeshadow on the upper lids; I paint her lips ruby red. I fasten a pair of pendulous gold ear-rings that glister in the spotlight. Each gesture, each touch, oozes the sensuousness of an erotic caress. Once the face is complete, I place a wig of lustrous, shoulder-length blonde hair upon her head and style it lovingly with the tips of my fingers. Finally, I fasten a long red cape at her throat and drape it around the tripod upon which the head rests. I kiss her. And, when I withdraw from the kiss and step aside, the eyes flicker open and the lips form into a smile. It is The Lovely Kim. She pushes apart the folds of the cape to reveal a lithe body clad in spangled bikini. Stepping down from the platform (now empty: no tripod, no plinth) she approaches me and reciprocates my kiss. We turn hand-in-hand to the audience, bow in unison and exit together, stage left, to rapturous applause.

The key to the success of this rather simple illusion is, as ever, presentation. Our ability, mine and Kim's, to play our respective parts – to *act* – transforms this from a story to a plot. It isn't the 'trick' in itself which is magical but the manner of its performance. Kim is a natural. On stage, and off, she possesses an unerring awareness of the effect she has on those watching her and –

significantly – a facility to manipulate that effect to suit her own purposes. The subtlety with which she does this makes her prowess as an actress all the more awesome. After meeting her for the first time, following her recruitment as my stage assistant, Paul Fievre warned me. *Red, that woman will fuck you up.* I asked if he meant professionally or personally.

'As a magician, she could be the best thing that ever happened to you,' he said. 'As a man, as an *engaged* man . . . all I'm saying is, if you don't want to get wet, don't stand out in the rain.'

'Too cryptic for me, Paul.'

'You know what I'm getting at.'

'If you're saying what I think you're saying, it won't be Kim who fucks me up, it'll be me fucking myself up over her.'

Which is what happened, of course. One long-running affair, innumerable lies and evasions, infinite distrust, one incontestable moment of exposure, one ex-fiancée. Kim's fault or mine? She knew I was engaged, so did I; she chose to seduce me, I chose to be seduced; she enabled my infidelity, I was the unfaithful one. I stood out in the rain and got wet, to borrow the euphemism of my friend, manager and agent.

It was during a presentation of the Living Doll illusion that Kim initiated the seduction. Venue: Fairfield Halls, Croydon (so don't tell me we were inebriated with the heady romance of our surroundings). I kissed the 'plaster' figure, as the illusion requires, and, brought to life, The Lovely Kim stepped down from the platform and reciprocated. The apparent passion of this second kiss was to be feigned, as usual, for the audience's benefit. What happened, on this occasion, was that Kim insinuated her tongue into my mouth for the duration of our embrace. She'd been my assistant for only a few weeks, but the sexual *frisson* Paul would later refer to was already developing. Off stage, too, the rapport between us had become taut with possibility. That evening, in Croydon, we milked our applause and retired. In the dressing-room, with the door locked, we fucked on the floor on a makeshift bed of Restoration-comedy costumes filched from a wardrobe.

Kim visited me the day after DS Crookes had. She'd heard, via Paul, of my mishap and arrived bearing fruit and flowers and a novel by an author I'd never heard of. I was still confined to my bed. Paul made us tea then retreated downstairs to continue Operation Clean-up. Kim sat on the chair beside the bed, as the detective had done. She looked well; she *always* looked well. Often, I'd seen her first thing in the morning after a few hours' sleep, hung-over and without make-up, and she invariably looked as fresh and sexy as ever. Today she wore a sleeveless yellow summer dress that stopped just below the crotch; her blonde hair, bleached by the sun, was unfettered. She inquired after my health and I said I felt better than I had done the previous day.

'Better for seeing me?'

Indicating the newly replenished bowl on my bedside table, I replied, 'I'm certainly better off with regard to fruit.'

She smiled. 'You know, I've really *missed* your charm.'

'It's not being able to smoke is what it is. Makes me contrary.'

Kim removed the flowers from their wrapping and arranged them in a vase on the window-sill. Peach and scarlet carnations, most of the blooms not yet fully open. I watched her, silhouetted against the daylight, her bare burnished limbs, her forearms pricked with blonde hairs picked out by the sunshine of a gorgeous spring morning. She returned to my bedside. She was wearing a necklace I'd bought her ages ago.

Her face became serious, concerned. 'How are you, generally?'

'Not so good.'

She nodded, her features exuding sympathetic reassurance as she manufactured a silence that invited me to elaborate.

'You never took to her, did you?' I said.

'I won't lie to you, Red. There was just . . . something about her.'

'Sure. It doesn't matter.' I tried to sip my tea. 'I don't think you were exactly her favourite person either.'

Kim averted her gaze, concentrating on smoothing her dress with the palms of her hands. She looked up, towards the window. 'I suppose we were both jealous of one another, deep down.'

'Rosa wasn't the jealous type.'

She looked at me, now. '*Everyone* is the jealous type, in my experience. It's a question of how you deal with it.'

The thing with Kim, once you know her, every word, every gesture, every facial expression, every *pose*, has to be analysed and decoded for signs of calculation. *She's all subtext*, according to Paul (Eng. Lit. graduate). In this respect, she's far from unique: putting on an act according to circumstance – that is, exhibiting some aspects of ourselves while concealing others – is a common enough trait. Kim, however, has a tendency to be taken in by her own display; her 'true' identity is as obscure to her as it is to those for whom she performs. Now, at my sickbed, she was casting herself in another role, the solicitous and intimate well-wisher, a friend, a colleague, a former lover. Subtext? Rosa had been dead long enough for Kim to offer me a demonstration of her own vibrancy. Whatever, I didn't have the energy for emotional games. Not on her terms, anyway.

'How's Tony?' I asked.

'Oh, he's fine.' The hesitation was almost indetectable. Less well disguised was the implied disparagement in the tone of her additional remark: 'Same as usual.'

I winked. 'He's a lucky guy.'

She laughed. 'You're only saying that because it's true.'

Mission accomplished: I'd diverted the conversation away from the subject of Rosa and my bereavement, and by making a parody of flirtatiousness, I'd defused the sexual tension she'd generated. We were more at ease, our exchanges became less stilted, less choreographed. We chatted. For nearly an hour, Kim raised my spirits and made me smile in a way that I hadn't done – sober – in some time. We even discussed, albeit vaguely, the prospect of resuming work. But the very mention of it panicked me. A return to normality, in whatever guise, was a progression towards consigning Rosa to the past. *Moving on*. As for being paid to entertain and amuse . . .

'I'm not there yet,' I said. 'Fuck's sake, I just can't.'

'Hey, come on. Red, it's *all right*.'

I weighed what she'd said and the way she'd said it. *Support. Understanding. Unconditional friendship.* I shouldn't have been talking to her like this. Not yet. For the first time I recognized that I'd harboured an illogical resentment of Kim for being with me in Bradford when, one hundred and sixty miles away, Rosa was killed beneath the wheels of a train. I ought to have been with Rosa, not Kim. As though sensitive to my altered mood, she steered us into safe territory, relating an anecdote about a mutual friend that I'd have enjoyed immensely if it hadn't been for the pain in my ribs when I laughed.

'Sorry to interrupt the party,' said Paul, appearing in the bedroom doorway. He said he had to pop out for an hour and was there anything I wanted before he went?

It was Paul's departure which caused another marked change in the atmosphere between me and Kim. The mutual awareness, as the front door banged shut, that we were alone in the house, in my bedroom, turned relaxed jollity into awkwardness. We became conversationally clumsy. We became polite. It wasn't long before we lapsed into silence. I simulated an interest in the dust-jacket of the book she'd fetched, then replaced it on the bedside table. Kim studied my face until my eyes snagged on hers. Smiling uncertainly, never letting loose my gaze, she eased a hand beneath the duvet. I was already semi-erect before she found me. Within her enfolding fingers, I thickened still further. I reached under the covers and, taking her by the wrist, wrenched her hand away. Her eyes flared. I let go. She continued to sit there quietly for a moment before getting up and walking out of the house.

I didn't appreciate, at the time, how alike Kim and Rosa were in one essential respect: a predisposition for deceit. Which is not to say their lying was manifestly or tactically similar. Kim's greatest skill lay in falsification, making you believe things about her which weren't true; Rosa's lay in concealment, screening off parts of herself and her life. Often, Kim would become convinced by her own fabrications; Rosa was never under any illusions about herself. As actresses, Rosa *played* a part whereas Kim *was* the part. Yet Rosa it was who duped me the more comprehensively, without once arousing my suspicion. Frankly, I didn't have the fucking foggiest about the woman.

Rosa's most elaborate deceit – the lie she lived, the lie of what she was – began to be revealed to me by chance when I visited her Aunt Niamh. DS Crookes, after conferring with the head of the residential psychiatric unit, supplied me with its address in north London. *Take care how you raise the subject of Rosa*, the sergeant had advised, *and whatever you do, make it clear to her you aren't Old Bill.* He explained that a uniformed colleague's questioning had made her so agitated the nursing staff had been compelled to terminate the interview. Mrs Kelly – screaming, tearful – accused the constable of trying to trick her into letting them take her Michael away.

'I thought he'd died years ago,' I said.

DS Crookes remained deadpan. 'We're talking about a woman who spends all day knitting baby clothes for her grown-up children.'

He wondered why I wanted to see her. She was Rosa's aunt, I said. She had, in effect, been a mother to her for five years, from the age of nine to fourteen. I wished to share whatever memories she had of the girl who grew up into the woman I fell for. I needed to talk about Rosa. *You have your gaps to fill in, sergeant, I have mine.*

We were sitting in a garden at the rear of the building, on a bench at the extremity of a pink stone path that lolled from cavernous French windows like a tongue from a mouth. The windows gave on to a communal lounge where Mrs Kelly had been knitting when I arrived. A care assistant had conducted me to her, raising her voice above the drone of a television perched high on the wall. *Niamh, there's someone to see you.* At fifty-eight, Mrs Kelly did a passable impression of a woman in her seventies. Then she looked up and gave a smile that peeled years from her face. She called me Liam.

'Who's Liam?' I muttered to my escort.

'Her son. One of them, anyway.' She grinned. 'Couple of weeks ago, one of the maintenance lads was "Liam". She had him sit with her drinking tea for an hour.'

Mrs Kelly, oblivious to these whispered exchanges, demanded to know if I'd been in a scrap. She was peering through her spectacles at the wound inflicted by the intruder, which still bore the livid zip marks of recently removed stitches.

'You ought to know better at your age,' she said.

It was a close day and the lounge reeked of urine and stewed tea. Most of the other occupants were asleep or watching TV. I suggested we go outside. *Good idea.* Mrs Kelly had wedged her knitting down the side of the seat-cushion and risen to her feet, heading off with disconcerting haste and making straight for the bench. *My bench.* We sat side by side, gazing out over the pink path with its flower borders. She clasped my left hand between both of hers. A smashing day, she declared. For the sake of a reply, I remarked that the tulips were out early this year.

'Global warming,' she said. 'London will be a desert in ten years.' I gave her a sidelong look. She added, defensively, 'They said, on the telly.'

For someone who'd lived most of her adult life in England, her accent remained unmistakably south-western Ireland – a gentle sing-song, less brazen than the Dublin of Conal Riordan and Dympna O'Neill. It was, I imagined, pretty much how her sister, Rosa's mother, would've spoken; a hint of Rosa, too, though *her* accent had been mangled by London school-days and working alongside 'the Dubs' at *Erin*. Mrs Kelly's permed dark hair was overrun with grey, her complexion rouged by years of drinking. Now and then the lenses of her glasses became bright discs of sun. She inquired after the well-being of people I'd never heard of – Liam's wife and children, I guessed – and I told her they were all fine. They were always in her prayers, I was to tell them.

'Julia was here the other day, with her latest, and I'd a letter from our 'Raidy. *Airmail.*' She smiled. 'Mrs Ferucci, she calls herself now. He's Italian, from Boston.' Lowering her voice, she added, 'One of ours, I'd say.'

Having gained Mrs Kelly's confidence by default, it was easy to continue in the role which I'd been assigned by her confusion. If she wanted me to be Liam, I was Liam. Then she threw me by talking *about* Liam, and after a moment's bewilderment it dawned on me that, for a sentence or two, I'd been recast as her other son, Declan.

'So, how've you been keeping?' I asked, steering the conversation into less complicated territory.

But she was gone. Mumbling to herself and gazing anxiously about the garden as though trying to pick out a familiar face in a crowded room. Her eyes alighted on a woman walking with a frame across the distant patio. Mrs Kelly smiled.

'The priest comes on Mondays,' she said. 'Father Nicol. English.'

A bee landed on the path just in front of us, stumbling drunkenly before taking off again in the direction of a rockery banked with pansies and sweet-william and an unkempt clump of lavender. Much of the garden was in sunlight, but we were shaded by a canopy of rhododendron. One or two other residents were out and about, and a gardener passed by wheeling a barrow of pungent compost.

'Do you . . . ?'

'The years my Michael put into this garden, and they trample all over it.' She made a vigorous shooing motion with her hand, shouting, 'Get off! Go on, get off!'

We continued like this for a while, meandering incoherence interspersed with long silences and odd instants of lucidity – a five-minute discussion of a TV programme we'd both watched – that passed for normal conversation. Holding hands the whole time. I picked my moment, and feigning idle curiosity, I asked, 'Did you ever hear what became of Rosa?'

Her grip tightened. 'That one,' she said, staring straight ahead in the direction of the French windows.

Be jovial. Be chatty. 'She'd be – what? – twenty-five by now.'

'If your father catches you saying her name . . .'

'Don't you ever wonder about her, after all these years?'

Mrs Kelly released my hand, uniting hers in her lap. I'd lost her. She appeared to be studying with disinterest a plume of midges zigzagging above us.

'I want to go in now, Liam.'

I accompanied her in silence to the lounge, where she retrieved her wool and needles. I thought she was going to sit down and resume knitting, indifferent to whether I stayed or left. She headed instead for a doorway leading into a short ill-lit corridor, glancing over her shoulder as though in expectation that I would follow. The corridor smelled of floor polish. As I fell in step beside her, she whispered, 'There's something I want you to do for me. A little job.'

Her room was a shrine to the Madonna, pictures cluttering the walls. Over the head of the bed hung a crucified Christ in ornately carved wood. The only secular ornamentation was a set of framed photographs arranged on a lace doily on the bedside table, portraits of people I assumed to be Rosa's Uncle Michael and the four cousins who became her adopted siblings. Mrs Kelly's sons were dark-haired, one bearded, the other clean-shaven; the younger of the daughters was exceptionally pretty. I looked at Michael Kelly. Close-set eyes, and his eyebrows met above the bridge of his nose, but handsome and strong-featured with an engaging smile. Mid-fifties. He could've had only a few years of life left when he posed for that photo, though he showed no sign of impending decline. I pictured him with Rosa, an ordinary bloke fucking his little niece.

'I'm glad you shaved that fuzz off,' said Mrs Kelly, gesturing towards one of the portraits. 'Never suited you.'

She was standing beside me. Taking my elbow, she steered me towards one of two armchairs. The chair was winged, its armrests and back draped with protective squares of embroidered cotton. I sat down. She went to the wardrobe and opened it with a key threaded on a loop of cord she wore like a necklace. From inside the wardrobe, she produced a shoebox jammed with letters and postcards, mostly frayed or discoloured with age. The box had been repaired with clear adhesive tape.

'Here's the letter from 'Raidy,' she said, handing it to me. 'Go on, read it.'

I made a pretence of reading the congested blue scrawl. The date caught my eye – the day of Rosa's funeral. Mrs Kelly, maintaining an unintelligible private monologue, searched the contents of the box as though it were a file index, offering me a succession of items of family correspondence spanning several years. A card from Declan, from a Greek island; another from Mairead, bearing a photograph of Niagara Falls; a six-page letter from Julia; greetings cards – birthday, Christmas, Mother's Day – even one from me (Liam, that is). My handwriting was atrocious. Whatever she gave me, I showed interest. The last was another airmail letter.

'From that slut,' she said.

'From *Rosa*?' I inspected the handwriting on the envelope – hers, for sure. Mrs Kelly was watching me, my hands, as I held the letter. I tried to keep the tension out of my voice. 'When did this come?'

'This turns up, and next thing you know the police are here, asking after her. They must take me for an eejit.'

'You got this *recently*, in the last few weeks?' I examined the envelope again; it was too dog-eared, surely. The postmark read Amsterdam, but I couldn't make out the date. I looked up at Rosa's aunt, who was standing expectantly before me.

'She *said* they would come looking for her.' She indicated the letter. 'Well, not with my help they won't.'

'D'you mind if . . . ?'

'D'you know they did it in your old bed?' Her hands were shaking so violently I thought she would spill the contents of the shoebox or drop it altogether. 'She made him do it to her while she had her monthlies, so it would be like going with a virgin. That's what she told him. Her *own uncle.*'

I relieved Mrs Kelly of the box, setting it down on the bed with the letters she'd handed me, and helped her into the other armchair. She rummaged in the sleeve of her cardigan for a handkerchief, but held it crumpled in her fist rather than using it. Tear tracks stained her face like streams of damp on an off-white wall.

'I want you to burn it,' she said matter-of-factly, when at last her discomposure was spent. She was more focused than at any time since my arrival. 'They're sure to find it next time they come snooping round.' She drew my attention to an enamel wash-basin. 'Do you have matches? I'm not allowed any.'

I gestured at the ceiling. 'What about the sprinkler?'

'*That?* Those things are for show. If there was a fire in here, we'd have no chance.'

I searched among the letters I'd laid down, then frisked my jacket pockets for a lighter. I went over to the basin. 'You sure about this?'

'I want it burned.'

Holding the blue airmail envelope by one corner, I snapped the lighter beneath it. The flame was slow to catch, but once it did the letter soon became engulfed. I let it drop into the basin. It continued, briefly, to burn, exhaling wafery fragments of charred paper into the air. We watched, Rosa's Aunt Niamh and I. When the flames had exhausted themselves, I turned on the tap to flush the blackened debris down the plug-hole. I wiped the bowl clean then rinsed my hands. Apart from an unpleasant smoky odour, no trace of the letter remained. She thanked me.

★

When I left, Mrs Kelly kissed me and pressed a pound into my hand and told me not to spend it on sweets. I put the coin in my pocket. The same pocket into which I'd ditched Rosa's letter before setting fire to the one from Mrs Mairead Ferucci.

There's this . . . it's a sort of I dunno sort of like you're buzzing. Awake. I mean so awake it's unreal. You're bursting to do things — dance, run, whatever. And you think, yeah, fucking yeah, this is the biz. Me, I go round talking to everyone, and if we're dancing I'm dragging them up on the floor with me and it's like it's me they're all watching cos I'm the best dancer there ever was and I feel so cool so fucking ace cool. I talk to them. Guys and that. People I don't even know who the fuck they are or nothing but I'm jabbering away. Brilliant. It's just so fucking brilliant you can't believe it, like hyper. Luke goes, we're talking energy, only he says it N-R-G, with a capital 'N'. He calls me Jilly Whizz. He says I'm a whizz kid. But the next day, fuck. I mean, fuck sake you never got a hangover like this. Jesus. I go, 'My head, my head.'

'What goes up must come down,' he goes. And then he says, 'This is the Appliance of Science. You want O-level physics, I'm your man.'

I sell them for him, at school. I've stitched a pouch inside the lining of my jacket, to keep my stash. A secret pocket. You wouldn't know it's there or nothing.

The envelope contained a single sheet of thin blue paper and a colour snapshot. In the photograph a man and a woman, their faces pressed together, cheek to cheek, were toasting the camera with glasses of lager. Their heads filled most of the frame. They were beaming. The man had short blond hair spiked with gel, a neat goatee beard, a solitary ear-ring and a complexion made caramel by suntan; the woman was Rosa. No doubting it, despite the poor quality of the print and the surprise of her youthfulness. It was her. She looked about sixteen. Her glossy black hair was tied in a pony-tail, she was made-up in shades of lavender and cerise and wearing hooped silver ear-rings the size of beer coasters. The hand in which she held her glass sported a ring on each finger. The illumination, along with the juxtaposition of her tanned companion, made Rosa's skin unnaturally pale, her face reflecting light while his absorbed it. Their pupils, his and hers, were reddened by flash. Their smiles appeared forced. Rosa, in particular, wasn't smiling in the spontaneous and uninhibited way she did in so many of the photographs I have of her. She looked tired and drunk and unsure of herself. There was nothing written on the back of the print to indicate where or when the picture was taken, or to identify the blond, goatee-bearded young man with his face pressed against Rosa's. I set the photograph aside and picked up the letter. Green ink. Each word inscribed so firmly that the blank reverse of the sheet was brailled with indentations. The handwriting was hers, those characteristic looping flourishes and the inverted capital 'N', an untidy note filling half the page. The letter was four years old, written when Rosa was nearly twenty-one.

Dear Auntie Niamh,

I know you hate me but I'm writing to you because your my Mammys sister and because I dont have no body else I can write to in England. Please dont show this to Uncle Michael or throw it away.

Ive been living here in Holland for nearly three years. Im very unhappy but some people are trying to help me. The thing is I dont know wether I can believe them only I have to because there isnt no one else. Im frightened.

If any thing happens to me the Police will tell you because your my family. Please give them this letter and the photo inside. They will go to the flat in Pijlsteeg and they will find the man in the picture and then they will make him tell them about me.

Don't show this to the Police untill they say any thing has happened to me or no body can help me at all.

Rosa   xxx

Rosa had been living with me for three months when she came down with flu. Conal sent her home one Monday; by Tuesday she was bedridden, buried beneath blankets and duvets. *Oym doying. I swear, Red, oym fickin doying.* I asked for the name of her GP, but Rosa said she couldn't remember. Besides, every doctor she'd ever known was an *utter bollix*. I fetched provisions instead: orange juice, paracetamol, cough linctus, Beecham's powders, throat pastilles, a large box of Kleenex mansize. Every couple of hours I'd prepare a fresh dose of Miss Kelly's Miracle Cure, a fragrant concoction of whisky, honey, cloves and hot water made to her own recipe and which, she asserted, depended for its efficacy on the proportionate composition of its ingredients (four parts whisky to one part everything else).

'That won't make you well,' I said, 'it'll just make you drunk.'

'Sure and I won't give a shite how sick I am.'

After forty-eight hours her condition was deteriorating. I offered to contact my GP but Rosa made it plain I was to do no such thing. We quarrelled. I told her she was being stubborn, stupid and irrational. She told me to fuck off. I didn't fuck off. I brought her whatever she needed; I let her sleep when she was tired; I kept her company when she wanted company; I nursed her. Gradually, she improved.

'I stink like a hole,' she said, on the fourth night of her illness, as I cuddled up to her in bed.

'I know.' I kissed her.

'Whatever I've got, you'll be after catching it yourself.'

'I expect so.'

'Now who's being *irrational*?'

'It's because I love you.'

You could have fallen into the silence, you could've lost yourself in it. So much time gaped before she replied I began to doubt whether I'd said the words, or whether she'd heard them. I hadn't planned them, they just came. In the awful pause of their aftermath I lay beside her and inhaled the warm odour of stale sickliness, wondering about the truth of what I'd told her, and about its timing. Then, at last, she spoke.

'Red, you haven't a fucking clue what you're talking about.'

Once he had recuperated sufficiently from his operation, the man who broke into my house participated in an identity parade. I picked him out. The other men assembled in that room at St Aldate's police station shared few physical or facial similarities with the suspect, but I would have recognized him whoever had been selected to complete the line-up. Those features were incised on my memory. Seeing him again through the mirrored glass, it was as though he was captured once more in the glare of a security light as I ripped away his balaclava. In fact, ten days had elapsed since his arrest and hospitalization. It had taken the police that long to establish who he was. Initially, the doctors said he was too weak to be interviewed; then, after being declared fit, the man refused to give his name or answer officers' questions. He wouldn't utter a word. His fingerprints and photograph didn't show up on police records. At a preliminary hearing, magistrates remanded him in custody as 'A. N. Other, address unknown'. For declining to divulge his name in court, and even to say 'yes' and 'no' when required, he had a charge of contempt added to those of aggravated burglary and assault. The day before the line-up, he was still protecting his anonymity. As D I Strudwick put it *We're staging an identity parade for a man without a fucking identity*.

Then, on the morning of the parade, a breakthrough. The owner of a lodging house off Botley Road, just a few minutes' walk from my place, reported a missing person. One of his guests hadn't been seen for more than a week though his belongings were still in his room and he'd paid for two weeks up front. The police hadn't been notified sooner, the landlord said, because it wasn't uncommon for lodgers – *his* sort of lodgers – to disappear for days on end. Officers searched the missing man's room. Among his abandoned possessions was a passport, its photo bearing an exact likeness of A. N. Other. By the time I arrived at the station, a potted biography had been assembled from various items recovered from the lodging house. The police knew his name, his date of birth, his home address, his shoe size, his occupation (printer), his preferred brand of toothpaste . . . *So, who is he?* I asked D I Strudwick. The man's name was Freddie Roos, and he was Dutch.

Three interesting facts about Freddie Roos:

1) 'Freddie Roos' was a pseudonym; he had gained entry to Britain four weeks earlier with false documents. His real name was Max van Dis. Born in Luxemburg of Dutch parents, resident in Amsterdam since childhood.
2) He had a criminal record in the Netherlands, mainly car crime, theft and burglary in his younger days, but recent offences included the possession and supply of drugs.
3) Among his belongings were more than twenty photographs of Rosa at various ages and with various alterations in hairstyle; several of the pictures had been taken recently, in Oxford, with the aid of a telephoto lens. There were also pictures of me.

As an illusionist, you become accustomed to the thrill of surprise on the faces of your audience as you bring a magical effect to its climax. I witnessed a variation of this expression in detectives Strudwick and Crookes in the wake of the Max factor. The discovery of the photographs – combined with Max's country of abode, his criminality, the odd circumstances of his break-in at my house, and the fact that Rosa was bound for Amsterdam when she died – transformed the detectives' disposition towards the case. They were electrified. However, this heightened urgency and seriousness did not take the investigation much further forward. At least, not immediately. Max was no more forthcoming, nor was I much help with my insistence, under tediously repetitive interrogation, that I had never known Rosa to have anything to do with drugs. *Did she ever use or keep drugs in the house?* No. *Did you ever see her use drugs?* No. *Did she ever display symptoms of drug use?* No. *Did she ever associate with people who used or supplied drugs?* No. *Are you yourself, or have you ever been, a drug user?* No. (Actually, I smoked a few joints while I was a student, but it didn't seem necessary for the police to know that.) *Did she ever offer drugs to you?* No. *Did she ever have visits or phone calls which gave you grounds for suspicion?* No. *Was she ever in possession of large sums of money which she was unable satisfactorily to account for?* No. *Can you explain why a known drug dealer has a dossier of photographs of Miss Kelly, and yourself, in his possession?* No. *Are you telling the truth?* Yes. Yes I am.

A few days later, DC Crookes paid a visit. After preliminary conversational courtesies, he got to the point. In the light of recent developments, he said, CCTV recordings from security cameras at Reading railway station on the day of Rosa's death had been requisitioned by CID. Film footage of passengers disembarking from the Oxford–Reading train on which she'd been travelling had been analysed.

'Our man, Max, can be clearly identified alighting on to the platform,' said the detective. 'He was on that train.'

I let him continue.

'As the passengers make their way towards the exit another man is seen to fall in alongside him, as if meeting him. You can see them talking to one another. We've got them together on film again in the station concourse, still talking. Outside, they join the queue at the taxi rank and get into separate cabs.'

'Any idea who this other bloke is?' I asked.

Crookes nodded. 'You remember one of the witnesses who gave evidence at the inquest, a Mr Terence Farr?'

'The old boy who was having trouble getting his case off the luggage rack?'

'That's him. We got him to sit through the film with us to see if he could pick out the man who pushed past him just after Miss Kelly. You know, the witness who followed her into the end section of the carriage and never came forward to testify.'

'Yeah, I remember.'

'Gave us a good ID, did Mr Farr. Basically, the missing witness is none other than the bloke talking to Max on their way out of the station.'

I digested this information. 'You're . . . what are you saying – that they're accomplices or something?'

The sergeant paused. 'I'm here to inform you, Mr Brandon, that as of now, we are formally treating Miss Kelly's death as a murder inquiry.'

The ideal audience? A theatre full of mathematicians, philosophers and scientists. Ask any conjuror. The more intelligent – the more rational – a spectator, the more readily he will be deceived. Because what you are doing in magic is creating the *semblance* of a chain of cause and effect. I do this, then this happens; I do that, then that happens. Basic logic. And a logical mind, receptive to a connection between each apparent cause and its apparent effect, is more prone to surprise when an illusion reaches its 'illogical' climax. If it is a paradox to describe intelligence as a bar to comprehension, there's irony too in the common misapprehension that the closer you are to the magician the easier it is to 'spot the trick'. My other category of ideal spectator, therefore, is the one right under my nose. Believing himself to be in prime position to discern the methodology, he'll be all the more impressed when he cannot.

And there I was, a magician – but also a maths graduate, a lover, a member of the audience – being taken in by her. By Rosa. I accepted the logical account of what she purported to be; I was too intimate, too close. Don't let anyone tell you it's easier to deceive a stranger than a loved one. It isn't. It fucking well isn't. You can lie to someone you know well because you understand the deception they're most vulnerable to. You know what it is they want to hear. And they make allowances for you, blinded by their own preconceptions, complacent; sometimes, even if they're suspicious, they choose credulity in preference to the awful alternative of confronting the lie and all that it signifies. They trust. That's what I did, I trusted Rosa. You know the worst thing? Not her deceitfulness, but the realization that she never trusted me enough in return to disclose even the smallest, most innocuous, part of the truth about herself. And I can imagine her riposte: *Like it's any of your fickin business.*

I moved in with Paul Fievre after the launch of the murder investigation. Police advice. My *domestic security* and *personal safety* had been compromised by my association with Rosa. Max van Dis may have been the first to track me down, they said, but he wouldn't necessarily be the last. For starters, his as yet anonymous accomplice on the train was still at large. So, my agent became my landlord. Merlin accompanied me, briefly exploring (seemingly, unenamoured) his new home, before beating an enforced retreat to the summit of a tall bookcase so that the Fievres' toddling twins could no longer yank his tail (ears, whiskers) whenever they pleased. He would venture down only when they weren't around. We slept, Merlin and I, on a camp-bed on the floor of the study. *Stay as long as you want*, Paul told me; I sensed Penny's welcome was less sincere.

I was watching television at Paul's, babysitting while my hosts celebrated their wedding anniversary. I'd already been out to the back garden twice in the gathering dusk – to smoke, strict house rule – and was contemplating a third trip when the doorbell chimed. My first reaction was self-interested concern that the twins would wake and require attention. I went to the door, and leaving the hall in darkness, peered through the spyhole. There, in fish-eyed distortion, was a woman bearing an uncanny resemblance to Whoopi Goldberg. I didn't recognize her. She was alone, standing in half-profile, with the unaffected demeanour of someone unconscious of being observed. I flicked on the light and drew the door ajar on the chain. The woman came to attention, making eye contact through the narrow opening; she smiled, all teeth and lips and purple gums. She asked if I was Mr Fievre. London accent, no trace of Caribbean. I told her Mr and Mrs Fievre were out. Another broad smile.

'Then, you must be Mr Brandon. Yeah?' Seeing my expression, she added, 'The police gave me this address. Sergeant Crookes. It was *you* I came to see.'

Her attention shifted from my face to my feet. Merlin was

gazing inquisitively at her from the doorstep. She greeted him (*Hey, brother!*) and bent to stroke him. I began to warn her about his tendency to scratch, but the woman hoisted him off the ground and nuzzled her nose against his.

'Cats love me,' she said. Merlin, as if by way of affirmation, gave her face an unmistakably affectionate lick. 'Dogs, now that's a different story. Either they growl or try to hump me.'

We both laughed. The informality made my continued use of the security chain an embarrassment. I released the door. The woman was almost the same height as me, dressed in jeans and a cardigan unfastened to expose a T-shirt with an image of twin volcanoes above the legend 'Get Twice as High in St Lucia'. She had big hair.

I said, 'I'd invite you in, only . . .'

A frown. 'Only what?'

'Only I've no idea who you are.'

'What am I *like*?' Her momentary anxiety was superseded by another flush of infectious laughter. She set Merlin down, spending a moment unhooking one of his claws from the chunky knit of her cuff. Offering her hand to me, she apologized for calling unannounced. 'My name's Amy Judd. I used to be Rosa's social worker.'

We sat in the lounge, drinking beer from cans, conspicuously not smoking, though Amy didn't ask, so I assumed her to be a non. I emptied a pack of peanuts into a bowl and invited her to help herself; she declined, saying she'd not long had dinner. Almost immediately, however, she scooped up a handful and began slotting them into her mouth. I accepted effusive compliments on what a nice house I had, then reminded her it wasn't mine, and that set us off laughing again. Merlin slept on her lap.

'He was Rosa's,' I said. 'Got him from a sanctuary when he was a kitten.'

She stroked between his ears and along the length of his spine. His tail twitched but he remained still, eyes tightly closed. 'I can feel him purring,' she said, without looking up. 'You ever touch his throat and feel him purr?'

'I can't afford to lose a finger.'

She smiled. 'What's his name?'

'Merlin. Rosa called him Kerrygold. Insisted he was a she, as well.'

'Uh-huh.' Amy's expression became serious. Still stroking Merlin, but her gaze firmly fixed on mine now, she said, 'I was so sorry to hear Rosa died, Mr Brandon.'

Died. Most people, if they referred to her death at all, phrased it *Sorry to hear about Rosa* or *Sorry about what happened.* I asked her to call me Red. She inquired after me and Rosa, and I told her – how we'd met, how long we'd lived together . . . Amy listened. When I'd finished she conducted her own explanations. DS Crookes's idea, her visit. Short notice, but they'd brought her to Oxford anyway, to assist with police inquiries, so she'd taken a chance on finding me at home. At someone *else's* home, anyway. The sergeant was concerned about me, about how I was *coping.* I said, 'D'you think he went for Bereavement Counsellor and some kind of cock-up with the psychometric test papers landed him in the police?'

Amy enjoyed that one. 'He likes you,' she said. 'Don't knock it.'

I swallowed some beer, still sharp with cold from the fridge. I asked how she'd found out about Rosa. The police, she replied, had made contact after her return from a holiday at her grandparents' place. She indicated the T-shirt. *They used to grow bananas, now they grow old.* She'd been involved with Rosa for just over three years, from the time she was put on the at-risk register. She hesitated.

'It's OK,' I said. 'I know about what went on with her uncle.'

Amy nodded, visibly reassured. It was she who'd been instrumental in taking Rosa into care and securing her a place in a children's home, she told me, maintaining irregular contact with her even after she was old enough to discharge herself from local-authority supervision. This was the period about which detectives Strudwick and Crookes had questioned Amy most closely.

'Not much I could tell them,' she said, chasing another peanut with a swig of beer. 'I only kept tabs on her for a year after she left care. Less than that. Not even part of my case load, officially, but . . . you get to caring for someone. You shouldn't, but you do. Yeah?'

'So she'd have been – what? – seventeen when you lost touch?'

'Uh-huh.'

'Where was she living? London, still?'

'Yeah. She moved in with this guy – guy called Luke. Older than her. I used to see her at his flat, when he wasn't around, or we'd meet up for a coffee or something.' She corrected herself. 'I say "his flat", but they must've lived in three or four different places during that time. Always north London, though.'

'What happened? I mean, how come you lost touch with Rosa?'

A shrug. 'I'd arranged to call round, but she wasn't there. They'd moved out a few days before. Done a runner. No forwarding address, nothing. Usually, when they moved, Rosa would let me know, but this time . . .' Amy gave another shrug.

'She never contacted you?'

She shook her head.

'He wasn't Dutch, was he, this Luke?'

'Dutch?' She frowned. 'No. He was from Liverpool, I think. Yeah, scouser.'

'What was he . . . you know, was he OK? A nice guy?'

Amy paused, her beer can half-raised to her lips. She lowered it. 'You don't know any of this? About why she was with Luke?'

'No.'

She sat back abruptly, causing Merlin to jolt awake. He stood up, stretched, made himself comfortable again and closed his eyes. Amy looked at me across the room, her black skin varnished by the glow from an overhead wall-lamp. 'Luke was a *pusher*. Speed, dope, coke, LSD, heroin . . . you name it.'

I said nothing. I thought I would be the first to break eye contact, but it was Amy – studying her beer can as she set it down on an occasional table beside her chair. No coaster. Another drumbeat message of this house: *drink = coaster; all surfaces, at all times*. I visualized a ring of condensation and dribbled alcohol forming on the veneer. Rosa, after her first visit to the Fievres', described it as *the kind of place where you want to stub your ciggie out on the sofa.* Jesus, how I craved a cigarette. I stood up, dealt a coaster from a desk on the sideboard and slipped it under Amy's can.

'Was he *her* pusher?' I asked.

I was conscious of her watching me as I returned to my seat. 'That's why – *one* of the reasons why – I went on seeing her,' she said. 'To persuade her to go into detox. And kick Luke into touch while she was at it.'

I cleared my throat. 'What was Rosa on?'

'Speed, to start with.' She paused. 'I think she might've been into smack as well by the end. By the time I lost touch with her, I mean.'

'*Heroin?*'

Amy nodded. 'Luke was a known user. Rosa . . . it would've been a probable progression for her, being with him for so long.' Another hesitation. 'I'll be straight with you, Red, when the police told me Rosa was dead my first thought was drugs.'

I told her I needed a cigarette, and did she mind if we went outside? That was fine by her. I led the way, binning the empties and collecting two more cans from the fridge *en route* to the rear garden. We stood on the patio, its neat pattern of hexagonal flagstones etched in light from the kitchen window. It was chilly, but not unpleasantly so; the freshness reinvigorated me. We drank, and I smoked, in silence for a moment.

'She wasn't into anything the whole time I knew her,' I said, at last, the quality of my voice in the night air startling me after the absorbent cosiness of the lounge.

'That's what they told me. The police. I mean, they said you'd told them that.'

'Amy, she was *clean*. I don't give a fuck what Strudwick thinks. Christ, he had Rosa down as an IRA terrorist to begin with.' Amy laughed and I couldn't help joining in. 'If you're telling me she was into drugs . . . all I'm saying is, that was eight years ago. You knew her then, and I didn't. But I do know she wasn't into anything while we were together.' I raised my cigarette and my beer can. 'Apart from these.'

'The stage she was at the last time I saw her . . .' said Amy, 'well, she needed proper help – and sooner, rather than later. Maybe she got that. Somewhere, somehow. By the time you came along, maybe she was well into recovery. Who knows?'

I stared out into the darkness of the Fievres' garden, looming indistinctly with trees and shrubs huddled black-on-grey against the sky like a clandestine gathering of cloaked men. There were no stars to be seen, only clouds.

'What I don't understand,' I said, 'is, if everyone knew what this guy Luke was up to, how come he wasn't banged away?'

'Everyone *didn't* know, that was the problem. We suspected, sure. God knows how many times he got searched or raided – the police were spying on him for *months*. But he was too shrewd to give them any actual proof.'

'Apart from Rosa.'

'OK, so how do you prove who supplied her?' Amy cut across my next remark, adding, 'And if you're about to ask whether we could've got her to testify . . . she was as hooked on *him* as she was on the gear he got for her.'

'You're telling me she was in love with this bloke?'

'Red, she was seventeen. *Fourteen* when she met him. He was older, he had a car, plenty of money, somewhere to live, he showed an interest in her.' Amy looked at me, her teeth and the whites of her eyes picked out in the illumination from the kitchen window. 'The life she'd had up till then, she took her comfort where she could find it.'

I made no reply, drawing on my cigarette and spinning the spent butt into the gloom beyond the perimeter of the patio. In the morning I would have to retrieve it.

'When she confided in Luke about her uncle,' Amy continued, 'she wasn't talking to some do-good social worker, she was talking to a guy who'd been where she was – a guy who'd lived in care for most of his childhood, who was eight years old the first time he was buggered by his stepfather.'

Neither of us spoke for a long while in the aftermath of that remark. The only sounds were of dogs barking, distant traffic noise and, nearby, occasional voices in the street, footsteps, and the clunk-clunk of car doors being opened and closed. I tried to see Rosa, as she would've been then; I tried to imagine her with Luke. I tried to conjure up a picture of her popping pills or shooting heroin into a distended vein. But that was a Rosa almost as unfathomable to me as my own teenage self had become with the distance of a decade. Instead, I began to unpick my memories of the Rosa I *did* know for clues to the one I didn't. But they were clues planted retrospectively, rather than ones I'd detected – or been allowed to detect – at the time. I looked at my watch. Paul and Penny would be home soon, and I ought to check on the twins.

Carole-Ann goes, 'Who was the first guy who told you he loved you?'

'My uncle.'

'No, I mean . . .'

Then she sees my face and she says sorry and she shuts the fuck up. Then I say sorry as well, cos if I don't she'll be off and I'm not supposed to be here to make her cry. I tell her it doesn't matter. I get her talking again and she's OK and we end up having a right laugh practising ways of saying 'I love you' to each other.

'You know I love you Rosy, you do know that don't you?'

That was Uncle Michael's name for me. His little Rosy. Usually he told me he loved me while he was sticking it in me hole. All hot breath and sweat and his string vest making red rings on my skin.

'I love you, I love you, I love you . . .'

Away and fuck yerself ya great cunting gobshite fucker.

With Luke, the first time, it was 'What would you say if I told you I loved you?'

I must've told him I loved him about a hundred times by then and all he could come up with was this What would you say . . . bollix. About fucking time, I should've said. But I didn't. You don't, do you? You should do, but you don't. You hug him or kiss him or something and you feel like crying because it's all you've wanted to hear him say for so long it seems like your whole fucking life.

I never told Nik I loved him. Not once, in three years. And he never told me.

And now Red's saying it. He's holding me and saying, 'Because I love you.' I'm lying in bed feeling like shite with the flu and I'm telling him I just want to curl up and die with it and he goes, 'Don't die.' Quiet, whispery. 'Don't die.'

And I go, 'Why not?'

'Because I love you and I don't think I could live without you.'

I can feel his breath on my neck while he's talking. I think about it for a bit and then I tell him he's talking out his arse. He is, too. They always are. What they're doing is they're either lying to you or they're lying to themselves or they're so fucking stupid they don't know what the fuck they're saying but they feel like it's the thing to say so they say it as though saying it makes it true. It's all shite, I love you, when you think about it. At the end, with Luke, I was screaming at him, 'You said you loved me . . . you said you loved me!' Know what he said, the bastard? He said, 'I meant it at the time.' Well what fucking use is that? Fuck all, that's what. That means . . . what that means, any time anyone tells you he loves you he might've stopped meaning it the moment he's finished saying it, for all you know. Christ sake.

So Red tells me he loves me. That's his problem, not mine. As for that don't-die-because-I-couldn't-live-without-you bollix . . . What I should say to him is, 'OK, kill yourself. If I die, kill yourself. Or don't fucking say it.' Because otherwise it's shite. It doesn't mean shite.

A week after I told Rosa for the first and, as it turned out, the only time that I loved her, she assisted in preparations for a rare *al fresco* performance by Peter Prestige, Prodigious Prestidigitator, and The Lovely Kim. A carnival in South Park. I'd been booked to stage a ten-minute magic show every hour, on the hour, from noon until six. Rosa and Kim helped load the van for the short drive from the Port Mahon to the swathe of parkland, where the city rises steeply towards Headington Hill to yield a picture-postcard panorama of Oxford's spires, bell-towers and domes. My pitch was flanked by a fortune-teller's tent and a portrait artist drawing caricatures at five quid each. I put Rosa to work on curtains and scenery while Kim and I assembled the props and apparatus. It amused Rosa that I never let her in on the magical mechanics of my act. *If it's not about secrets, why are you so secretive?* I corrected her: magic wasn't *just* about secrets, was what I'd said.

'Illusion is the art, methodology is the brush with which I paint.'

'C'mere, Red, you know what you're full of?'

'Wouldn't be *shoite*, would it?'

'Fucking right it would.'

I called out to Kim, 'You should hear us when we're *quarrelling*.'

Kim was upstage from us, wheeling one of the frames into position for the Girl through a Glass Plate illusion. Her smile in response to my remark excluded Rosa. The pair hadn't spoken to one another all morning, beyond what was strictly necessary. Rosa and I, in contrast, were full of talk, our words flooding the void that had followed my ill-received declaration to her in her flu-stricken state. I hadn't thought her the type to sulk, but for days she'd conveyed the impression of a woman in a strop with me, with us, with herself, or with life at large. And once she was well enough, she avoided me altogether by working all day and boozing every night with her colleagues from *Erin*. When she departed at short notice to London, to stay with friends whose names I'd never heard her mention before, I convinced myself she'd be returning only to clear her things from my house. I rang my brother. *I told Rosa I loved her and, the way she's reacting, you'd think I'd told her the exact opposite.* Taaffe said little Katy had an ear infection. He said I wasn't entitled to talk about love until I'd discovered what it was to continue loving a baby daughter who'd kept me up all night screaming with earache. Then he hung up. Rosa came back the day she said she would; she didn't leave me. The sulking stopped. She made no reference or allusion to what I'd said, and neither did I. It was as though those three small words had vanished. Except, and I'm an authority, nothing truly vanishes – it is only made to seem so.

Carnival day, Rosa and I were chattering away again. Kim and Rosa weren't. Together, we got the act ready in good time for the first performance. The summery weather drew hordes to the park. The noon show went well, apart from one awkward moment when, by magically exchanging a stick of candyfloss for a toffee apple, I reduced a boy to tears. In a break between performances, Rosa, Kim and I joined Paul, Penny and the twins for a picnic on a grassy slope overlooking not just the carnival site but the whole of Oxford. Paul insisted on a photograph – *great for posters* – of me and The Lovely Kim in costume against this backdrop. We posed, he took the picture. At the time we couldn't comprehend why Penny was so amused. Not until the film was developed did we realize Rosa had sneaked into shot, undetected. The print, never used for publicity purposes, is among those adorning my house. Kim and I are in the foreground, the dreaming spires behind us; also behind us Rosa – bending over, skirt raised and knickers lowered, to expose the dark cleft and twin white domes of her arse.

Vicky was less obvious in the photographs the police showed me – stills produced from the CCTV footage of passengers disembarking at Reading station. 'Vicky', a name at the head of a gin-rummy scoresheet, whose handwriting matched that on a parcel containing Rosa's shoulder-bag. The last person, apart from the killers, who'd seen Rosa alive. Tracing her had, unsurprisingly, become of vital concern to detectives Strudwick and Crookes. Every female passenger captured on film sporting a bag resembling Rosa's had been freeze-framed and enlarged in the hope of obtaining a positive identification. DS Crookes called at Paul's house one morning with a dozen pictures for me to inspect on the off chance I might recognize one of the women. The sergeant also returned most of the contents of Rosa's bag as well as other items the police had removed from my house. Black sacks, bulging with her belongings; he thought I'd prefer to keep them at the Fievres' for the present. I thanked him. I thanked him, too, for having encouraged Amy Judd to drop by.

He made a dismissive gesture.

'Seriously,' I said, 'it helped me a lot, talking to her.'

'How about Niamh Kelly, any joy there?'

I fashioned an account of my visit to Rosa's aunt that was similar to what had actually occurred in all but the essential respects. I told him she'd mistaken me for her son and, as a consequence, we'd managed to talk about Rosa without her becoming suspicious or unduly upset. Since my return from London I'd debated handing Rosa's letter over to the police but – for motives as obscure to me as those which prompted the concealment of Charity Jackson's passport and the phone numbers for Lena and Nikolaas – I'd decided to keep it to myself. It was more than just an indefinable sense of unease at making the police privy to what I knew; rather, the more I unearthed about Rosa's past the more possessive, the more proprietorial, I became. She was mine, not theirs. By releasing her secrets into their custody, I would be relinquishing what little I still had of her that remained private. Seeing DS Crookes, I wondered again whether I was doing the right thing. That letter and its enclosed snapshot were stowed only a few feet from where the detective and I were sitting; it would've been so simple to betray them to him. Only now there would be the added complication of having to explain why I'd not done so sooner. So I said, and did, nothing.

Rosa's letter stayed where it was and Crookes, oblivious to its existence, removed the set of stills from their folder and went through them with me.

I'd told him before that I knew of no one called Vicky in Rosa's life, so it was with little anticipation of success that we trawled those grainy, ill-focused prints. In some instances the quality of the image was so poor I'd have been unable to put a name to the women even if they were intimate friends. As for those whose features were captured more clearly, and face-on rather than in profile, there wasn't a spark of recognition. They were just women with black shoulder-bags, strangers unwittingly filmed going about whatever business had brought them to Reading that day; I'd never seen them before. With one exception. A young woman, early twenties, maybe, with dark hair styled in a bob; she was looking towards the camera, though not directly at it, her head tilted back slightly and her right hand apparently caught in the process of hooking a stray strand of hair behind her ear. Her expression was serious, unsmiling, though not dissimilar to those of the other women with their vaguely hassled air of travel endurance. DS Crookes's voice startled me.

'Know her?'

I was peripherally aware of him seated beside me, studying my expression as I studied hers. He must've sensed something in my manner because I had spent no more time on this photograph than on the others I'd looked at so far. I laughed.

'No, no. It's just . . .' I glanced at him, feigning embarrassment. I gave another laugh. 'Actually, I was just thinking I wouldn't kick her out of bed.'

The detective laughed too. I saw him switch his attention from me to the photo and back again. He searched among the other stills, producing one of a curly-headed blonde. Smirking, he said, 'I'd sooner have this one, given the choice.'

After he'd gone, I re-created the image of that dark-haired woman in my mind and tried to recall where I'd seen her before. The thought of her nagged at me for the rest of the day, frustratingly elusive. If only I'd still had the photograph, but Crookes had taken them away and it would've been impossible to ask to keep that one without rekindling the suspicion I'd managed to allay. It wasn't until that night, on a camp-bed in the study, that I was jolted awake with the realization of how I came to recognize her. I sat up, cracking my head on the underside of Paul's desk.

Her name wasn't Vicky, it was Carole or Caroline, or something like that. I got out of bed and switched on the light, rummaging urgently among Rosa's newly returned possessions. Bollocks. Her address book wasn't among the items the police had handed back. I'd *met* this woman. Only once, more than a year ago, but I was sure I'd met her. Her hair had been styled differently, but there was no doubting it was her. I could picture her now, with Rosa, in a noisy, smoky pub in Oxford; they were at opposite ends of a table, moving it so two groups of people could drink together. They didn't sit side by side, as I recollected – this Carole or Caroline sat at the head of the table, while Rosa positioned herself opposite a man she didn't know, a man who was about to beguile her by causing ash to appear, as if by magic, in the palm of her hand.

In the morning I phoned Dympna – who had also been there that time in the Eagle and Child, with John. She played dumb; I got angry with her; she got even angrier with me and slammed the phone down. When I redialled, her number was engaged. I rang each of my friends in turn among those who'd witnessed the stigmata illusion to see if they could identify any of the other party. One name stood out, the friend of a friend and one of the reasons why the two groups had united in the first place. I called her, but she had only a sketchy memory of a boozy session many months ago; anyway, she was a workmate of John's and didn't really know Dympna, never mind Dympna's friends. She vaguely remembered Rosa, *because of the trick with the ash*, but had no recollection of any Carole or Caroline. I tried Dympna again: engaged. I went round to her house, but the curtains were drawn and no one came to the door. I visited the *Erin* offices; Conal Riordan told me Dympna had phoned in sick that morning.

At a loss to know what to do next, I went home – to *my*

home, not Paul's – to collect the post. Usually, Paul did this for me every two or three days, but it wasn't far from Hythe Bridge Street to Osney, so I remounted Rosa's bike and headed off. The house was cold and musty from having been unoccupied. I'd entered by the back way, to avoid being seen from the street. Going through to the hall, I saw the doormat was patchworked with envelopes and junk mail. I binned some and opened the rest: a newsletter from the Magic Circle, the latest issue of *Abracadabra*, a letter from my accountant and an electricity bill. I pocketed the post and checked the answering machine: no messages. It was this last action, combined with the electricity bill, which gave me the idea. I ran upstairs to the spare bedroom, where a wardrobe serves as a filing cabinet for all manner of domestic and professional paperwork. In a buff-coloured folder crammed with documents, I found what I was looking for – a telephone bill for the most recent quarter. Stapled together were three sheets of itemized calls. Scanning the dates, I noted down the numbers dialled around the time of Rosa's death. Some, I recognized: Paul, Taaffe, the *Erin* office, Dympna, the Port Mahon, a Bradford number relating to a call I'd made to the hotel where Kim and I would be staying after the show. Other numbers, I checked against my address book: bank, home-insurance agent, credit-card booking line for rail tickets. Two numbers remained which I couldn't identify. I rang the first: home-delivery pizza. The second, also with an Oxford code, had been dialled twice – two days before Rosa died, and again on the day itself. This call, fifty-two seconds in duration, was timed at 10:01 – after I'd left for Bradford, but before Rosa had made the series of cash withdrawals prior to boarding the train. I picked up the phone once more and tapped in the digits. A female voice answered: *Hi! You're through to Sheena and Carole-Ann . . . sorry, we can't come to the phone right now, but please leave a message after the long beep and we'll call you back soon as poss. Thanks a lot!*

I waited for the tone. I gave my name and Paul's telephone number and said I wanted to speak to Carole-Ann; I said it was urgent, I said I was hoping she might be able to put me in touch with *Vicky*. Then I hung up, left the house, again by the back way, and cycled to Jericho to feed Merlin and to wait for her to ring.

Detective Inspector Strudwick and Detective Sergeant Crookes were already there, in the lounge, talking to Penny while the twins used a uniformed constable as a climbing frame. The talking ceased when I entered the room. Penny looked at me, Crookes didn't. It was Strudwick who spoke. Something had cropped up and would I mind *popping along* to St Aldate's with them. When I asked why, he glanced at Penny and said he would explain the situation on the way to the station. He did. What he said, as we negotiated the Oxford one-way system in an unmarked police car, was: 'Late last night, the Metropolitan Police apprehended a man believed to have been on the train with Max van Dis when Miss Kelly died.'

He paused. I waited in silence for him to continue.

'He was brought to Oxford for questioning,' the inspector added. 'During the course of these interrogations last night and this morning, the man indicated to us that he and van Dis had been promised a sum of money to . . . kill Miss Kelly.'

'Who by?' I asked.

There was another, even longer pause before DI Strudwick answered. 'He says by you, Mr Brandon.'

Can you tell us what happened the night of the alleged burglary?

You know what happened. I came home drunk and disturbed a man who'd broken into my home. We fought and he got away.

You didn't know this man?'

. . .

Suspect shakes his head.

What's this 'suspect' crap?

You'd never met him before?

No.

Can you tell us anything about why this man broke into your home?

I don't know. He was after something, information or something. I've no idea.

Information about what?

About Rosa. Something to do with whatever Rosa was up to.

What was Rosa up to?

I've told you, I don't know. I wish I did, but I don't.

I'm showing the suspect photograph 1b. Do you recognize this man?

No.

You don't know him?

No.

You didn't meet him in a public house in Oxford on Wednesday the eighteenth of March?

No.

You didn't meet him and Max van Dis to discuss the contract killing of your girlfriend, Miss Rosa Kelly?

No I fucking didn't.

Did you meet them again on the Friday of the following week to hand over the first instalment of the sum agreed?

Is it all right to smoke in here?

Suspect doesn't respond.

I've never met either of them. The first I knew of van Dis was when he broke into . . .

Can you account for your whereabouts on either of those evenings?

Not without checking my diary, no. I might've been performing, I don't know.

Was . . . ?

Hang on, the eighteenth was the day after St Patrick's Day. Yeah. Yes. We were wrecked from being out on the piss the night before, so we had an early night.

Who's 'we'?

Me and Rosa.

Just the two of you?

Yes.

You didn't go out at all that evening, the eighteenth?

No.

And no one came to the house?

No.

Did you receive any phone calls?

I can't remember. How am I supposed to remember that?

What about the following Friday, the twenty-seventh? Where were you that night?

Like I say, I'd need to look in my diary. It's at the house – Paul's house – if you want to send someone to fetch it.

Dave, can you see to that? Detective Sergeant Crookes is leaving the room. Now, Mr Brandon, if we can talk again about the alleged burglary. Is it the case that van Dis came to your house to demand the remainder of the money?

Jesus, how many times?

You hadn't paid up. He came round to find out why, and you came to blows. That what happened?

Is that what he says?

I'm asking you, is that what happened?

The place was a tip – you were there, you could see he'd been going through my and Rosa's things.

You could've done that yourself.

Fucking hell, I was unconscious.

Not when our officers arrived, you weren't.

This is ridiculous. This is absolutely fucking ridiculous. Why would I want to have Rosa killed, for Christ's sake? I loved her. I loved her.

. . .

. . .

OK, let's wrap it up for now. Interview terminated, 11:17.

They fetched my diary. Friday 27 March was blank. Strudwick interviewed me again that afternoon, for three hours. We discussed drug smuggling and the internecine feuds which beset criminal gangs. He noted down my bank and building-society details in order to obtain statements for the period when a downpayment was supposedly made to van Dis and his accomplice. In the meantime, I was released – without charge – on police bail, pending further inquiries. Among the conditions was a stipulation that I had to continue to reside with the Fievres; also, I had to surrender my passport. On the way out of the station, I asked my escort, DS Crookes, why the allegation of my involvement was being taken so seriously.

'They both named you, basically,' he said.

'So what? They're obviously in collusion on this.'

He shook his head. 'They haven't seen or spoken to each other since van Dis was arrested. When was this collusion supposed to have taken place?'

For much of my repertoire, I, as conjuror, am cast in the controlling role. I am the performer. Kim is there, as her job title suggests, to assist; even in Assistant's Revenge where, if you recall, she secures me by the wrists and ankles to a board, the climax is my turning the tables on her. There *is* a magical feat, however, in which the roles seem truly to be reversed: the Dizzy Limit. I employ it occasionally as an opener, it being a spectacular illusion with which to launch a show. It is also hard to conceive of a more dramatic means of introducing myself to an audience.

What happens is the curtains open to reveal an empty stage. The Lovely Kim enters left – smiling, stunning, bathed in spotlight. Applause. She gestures towards a point high above the stage, immediately picked out by a second spotlight. Into this circle of white is lowered a large net containing in its fold none other than Peter Prestige, magician. Applause. I am suspended in the net some thirty feet or more above the stage. At a signal from Kim, the net suddenly falls open, amid gasps from the audience as they anticipate my plunge on to the wooden boards below. But their exclamations are transformed instantly from alarm to amazement . . . for I have vanished. There is the net, open; there is the stage, empty but for The Lovely Kim; there is no magician. More applause. Enter Peter Prestige, stage right – smiling, unruffled and unharmed.

Don't ask how it's done, because I won't tell you.

Suffice to say, Kim – despite the semblance of being the one orchestrating the feat – plays no part in the 'magic' of it; hers is a presentational role. As soon as I walk on stage, the audience has forgotten all about her and is thinking only of me and my miraculous escape. The Dizzy Limit was a favourite of Rosa's. *One day, you'll land on your fickin head with any luck.*

We stayed up late, drinking. Paul listened, he said all the right things. *It's their word against yours, this van Dis and the other bloke . . . No evidence . . . All sorted in a day or two . . . The police can't prove you did something when you didn't, can they?* I smiled. I expressed gratitude for his faith and support, prompting him to remind me indignantly that he was my friend as well as my agent.

'If I go down for conspiracy to murder,' I said, 'do you get to serve 10 per cent of my sentence?'

After we'd retired to our beds, I used the phone in his study to dial the number of the woman who hadn't returned my call and who went by the names of Vicky and Carole-Ann. Answering machine. I left another message, modifying my previous one to impart the information that I'd been helping the police with their inquires all day and would appreciate it if she could shed light on whatever the fuck was going on. I was still speaking when someone picked up. Female – youthful, but without an especially feminine lilt; her accent was broad north-east. I tried to match the voice to the face in the CCTV photograph and to the woman with Rosa that night in the Eagle and Child. She spoke rapidly, almost in a whisper.

'Red, listen, tell them nothing about me, not a thing, right – not my number, nothing. I don't know how the hell you got hold of me, but *they* mustn't.'

I managed to interrupt. 'What about Rosa's things? Why did you . . . ?'

'The bag was a mistake. I fucked up with the bag. If the police haven't already got it, get shot of it. If they ask you about what's in it, you don't know shit.'

'OK, OK.' I was trying to calm her down. 'Two men have been arrested. The police think they killed Rosa somehow, I don't know . . . pushed her off the train.'

'I didn't see nothing.'

'But you were with . . .'

'I never saw what happened.'

'Why did they kill her? That's all I want to know, why she died. Why was she going to Amsterdam?' I listened to the silence. 'Who's Charity Jackson?'

'Do the police have Charity's passport?'

'No.'

I sensed her relief. 'If they find out about her – if they ask the blokes they've nicked about her – then word'll get back and she'll end up the same as Rosa.'

'And you?'

There was a pause. 'Aye, me an' all.'

With that, Vicky – Carole-Ann, or whoever she was – disconnected me before I had a chance to say another word.

This one's special, Luke says. Two hundred quid. I go, What's the story? And Luke goes, It's a two-hander. One fucks, one watches. I tell him I don't want to know and he says it's OK cos he'll be in the next room if they start anything. He's seen my picture, Luke says – the one who wants to watch, this is. Mr Peters. Fifty-something and loaded. The guy's gone for me in a big way. Smitten, like.

'How come he don't want to do it himself, then?'

Luke shrugs. 'Gets his kicks watching pretty girls go with pretty boys.'

'Boy?'

'Seventeen, same as you.'

'How old is he, Luke?'

'Mr Peters, you do what he says. OK?' Luke looks at my face, like, and he can see I'm not up for it. He goes, 'Two hundred. Think about it.'

I tell him to tell Mr Peters and his toy boy to shove it. Luke just shrugs like he couldn't give a fuck. Like, so what? Then he says he'll hold out on me. Not shouting or nothing, just dead normal like he's telling me what's on telly or something. He won't sort me for fuck all until I'm begging for it.

'I'll sort myself. I don't need you.'

'You found a place where they dish it out for free?' he says. 'Where's that? Where's it dished out for free, Rosa? Will you show me? I'd like to see that place. They dish it out for free, I'll be first in line.'

'I don't need you.'

'You got a car? A phone? Maybe you got your own flat I don't know about? You got someone to look out for you? Or maybe you'd be happier on your own down some alleyway – just you and the trick. Hang around on the streets and turn some trick who takes you down an alleyway and fucks you up the arse with a broken bottle. Sound good to you, Rosa, does it? You think the guy'll pay two Cs for that?'

★

We're in Luke's bedroom, me and the boy and Mr Peters. Luke's in the kitchen. I can hear him moving about, I can hear the radio. Mr Peters keeps his clothes on the whole time and he doesn't wank or nothing. He just watches and tells us what to do. He's OK, actually, Mr Peters. Friendly and that, calls me by my name. Suit and tie, flash watch. He's got this silk hanky poking out his pocket. He says I'm to call him Jan. Yaan. The way he talks, I ask if he's German and he just laughs. The boy's about fourteen. I never get to find out his name. He looks like some guy off the cover of a teenie mag. Scared shitless, I have to show him what to do and all the while we're doing it, I'm thinking twohundredquid, twohundredquid, twohundredquid.

Mr Peters — Jan — goes off to see Luke. Me and the boy take turns to shower and get dressed. We sit in the bedroom, waiting; we don't have shit to say to each other. Then Luke and Jan come back in and Jan's smiling and looking at me. The way he looks, I turn to Luke and ask what's going on. Luke won't look me in the eye, he just stares at the floor, the walls, the ceiling . . . any place except me. I ask him what the fuck's going on but he doesn't say nothing and he doesn't look at me. And all the time this Jan feller's got a smile on his face a mile wide.

He goes, 'Rosa, dear, have you ever been to the Netherlands?'

I sat staring at the phone for a long time. Eventually, I picked up the receiver and rang a different number. We talked, hung up. I got dressed again, slung a few things into a travel-bag, said a hushed goodbye to Merlin (who ignored me) and made sure to leave the house without disturbance. I had everything I required, for now – clothes and toiletries, of course, a small amount of cash. Also, documents: my address book, Rosa's airmail letter, the photograph of her with a goatee-bearded young man, the piece of paper bearing phone numbers for Lena and Nikolaas. And the passport. Not mine, which remained in the safe keeping of the police, but Charity Jackson's. Other essentials could be bought, or acquired, along the way. I let the front door click gently shut behind me and set off on foot. One thirty. Nobody was about, and only a few windows were showing a light. I avoided main roads, wherever possible, plotting a circu-itous route through the side streets of Jericho and then Osney, bypassing my own house and continuing along a footpath that skirted between a school and an industrial estate. The path led on to playing fields running parallel to a main road but separated from it by a tract of houses. Something moved a short distance ahead. A cat. Startled by my approach, it leapt on to a tall fence and perched there, watching me go by. It was a mild night, moonless, the sky textured with low cloud, and I was warmed by the exertion of walking, the bag chafing my leg at each stride. In the dark the expanse of grass beside me became a grey, calm sea. I could see my breath. I could hear the sound of my own footsteps. I followed the perimeter path to a point where it bisected a stand of trees to give on to a street lined with red-brick terraced houses. The car was already there, parked at the kerb, its headlights doused and the engine switched off. I let myself in the passenger door. I looked at him. Before I could speak, Taaffe said, 'Red, don't tell me . . . I don't want to know.'

My brother and his family live in Abingdon, a small town close to Oxford. They live, like me, by the Thames. We tried an experiment last summer: I tossed a red plastic ball into the river near my house and we spent the day at the foot of Taaffe's back garden waiting for it to drift past. It didn't. His eldest, Gemma, made us keep watching until it was too dark even to see the water. She was out there again first thing, perched on a chair to peer over the hedge. When my sister-in-law yanked her indoors for breakfast, Gemma threw a tantrum, blaming me for failing to *magic* the ball's reappearance. I said it must've floated by while she was asleep, which didn't mollify her in the least.

We're friends again now. (We were friends again by the end of breakfast, if I remember rightly.) When I came downstairs the morning after my late-night flit from Paul's house, Gemma gave a stiff-legged jig in celebration of Uncle Red's surprise visit and dangled herself from my neck until it was time for school. Her departure was conditional upon the promise of a conjuring show when she returned home. I watched the car drive away, Lisa at the wheel and the kids strapped in, one asleep, two waving out of the window. Taaffe was in the kitchen, reading a newspaper and trying to eat toast without spoiling his clothes. He worked a few minutes' walk away, at a building society in the town centre; I knew he'd have to leave soon. I tried to appear relaxed about that. But I can't conceal much from my brother.

'You won't be here when Gemma comes home, will you?' he said.

I shook my head.

'D'you want to talk about it?'

'No.'

'Fair enough.'

'Taaffe, it's best you know as little as possible.'

He glanced at the paper, then laid it down again on the kitchen table. Tea, toast. He swept crumbs off his lap. He looked at me. 'Do you need money?'

'No, I'm OK.'

'Thank fuck for that.'

I couldn't help smiling. 'If anyone asks, I wasn't here. OK?'

He nodded. Draining his tea, Taaffe stood up, brushed himself down again, took his suit jacket from the back of his chair and put it on. He stacked his breakfast things in the sink. 'Don't worry if you don't have time to wash up before you go.'

'When have I ever done the washing up?'

'Bob-a-job week, 1978.'

'Seventy-seven,' I said. 'Seventy-eight, I washed Dad's car.'

Taaffe shook my hand, which embarrassed us both. Then he hugged me. I was to take care of myself, he said. Then he left the house.

I didn't have much time before Lisa would return with Katy, having dropped the other two off at school and playgroup. I already had one of the items I required – Taaffe's credit card, lifted from his wallet amid the confusion of three children being hurried from kitchen to bathroom to car. In its place was a note informing him of the theft, so he wouldn't assume the card to have been mislaid, or stolen by someone other than me. All I could hope for, then, was that he wouldn't have the card cancelled. Imitating his signature would be straightforward enough – Taaffe's writing was barely more sophisticated than the storybook letters Gemma used to form her own name. Finding the second item was more problematic, and more time-consuming. But, after a painstaking search, I found what I was looking for in an alphabetically indexed file-box, under 'P'. His passport was one of the older, pre-European Community types; its bearer's photo-graph had been taken eight years before. I studied the picture closely. Not a bad likeness. Not *too* bad, anyway, for brothers who'd come to share a decreasing resemblance with the passage of time. It was just about conceivable that – to a bored, overworked official – the real Fletcher Brandon, aged twenty-nine, and a two-dimensional Taaffe Clarke, aged nineteen, might pass for two versions of the same person. So that was me, in my new role as Mr Taaffe Clarke. What you do is play the part. Neither confident nor apprehensive, nor behaving in any way that might attract undue attention. If you are who you purport to be, there is nothing exceptional for you in travelling under *your* name, with *your* documentation. So you act normal. From the moment I left his house, I was me playing an actor playing my brother. For someone accustomed to being me playing an actor playing a magician, this was a breeze.

The credit card bought me a train ticket at Abingdon station, also, an air ticket from the KLM desk at Heathrow. And the passport secured my admittance into the departure lounge and beyond boarding control. By midday, I was disappearing into cloud cover hundreds of feet above southern England.

PART TWO

Amsterdam

'Mulder, the truth is out there . . . but so are lies.'

— *Agent Scully*, The X-Files

'Your cheatin' heart will tell on you.'

— *Hank Williams*

Busking

As the aircraft banked steeply for its approach to Schiphol, my window seat presented a vertiginous panorama – treacly sea yielding to unremitting cultivated flatness, a partially completed children's puzzle of interlocking pieces, its neat green and brown rectangles patterned by a lattice of waterways. *Dykes, polders, land reclamation . . .* the nomenclature of long-dormant geography lessons, returning to annotate the living map unfolding beneath me. Once upon a time all this was water. The plane veered again, adjusting its course with what felt like unnecessary compensation; my first sight of Dutch soil was replaced with a sweep of featureless white that could've been any sky, anywhere. Our descent was choppy. My neighbour had his eyes closed and was gripping both armrests. Flying doesn't bother me, to be honest – the mathematician in me takes comfort in the statistical improbability of death by air crash. Smoking is what *should* scare me, but it doesn't. Rosa told me she'd never been up in a plane. (Me: *Afraid?* Her: *Never had any fickin place to fly to.*) Another of her lies. Any moment we would touch down in a land where she'd lived during her missing years and where she'd been destined on that final journey. The exhilaration of my escape from England began to subside. My world had closed in on me there, as I exhausted each source of information on Rosa's double life; *events* had closed in on me: van Dis, the police. I'd had to break free. But there was no sense of liberation. What I felt, as we landed, was a nebulous, anticipatory dread. This was no business trip, no tourist excursion; this wasn't even about my status as fugitive. It was about Rosa. My pursuit of the truth of her would succeed or fail in the days that followed, here, in her hidden city, and I was petrified. Daunted by what I'd let myself in for, afraid of the magnitude of the mess I'd left behind. Frankly, I didn't know what I was doing.

The pilot announced the time and temperature in Amsterdam. He apologized for the turbulence (*Bit blowy out there, I'm afraid*) and told us to hang on to our hats upon disembarking. I hung on to my bag of duty-free: two hundred B & H and a bottle of Johnny Walker, courtesy of Taaffe Clarke's plastic money. Now all I had to do was convince Dutch customs and immigration officials I was my brother.

Three queues. I positioned myself in the one filtering past a young uniformed officer who looked like he couldn't give a fuck about anything, ever. When it came to my turn, I handed him Taaffe's passport; he gave it back without a word and with only a cursory inspection of the photograph, or of me. I thanked him in Dutch – acquired from a phrase book purchased at Heathrow – and he replied in English, wishing me a good trip. A doddle. I suppressed a smile, unable to believe how easy it was. Maybe it was this, the latest in a sequence of successful deceits, that made me complacent about the invulnerability of my assumed identity. Within minutes, I was in trouble. I'd made my way through baggage reclaim to the airport terminal's main concourse and was attempting to obtain a large cash advance, in guilders, on Taaffe's card. The teller in the foreign-exchange bureau asked me, in almost flawless English, to wait while she phoned for authorization. Standard procedure. I watched through the security window as she made the call. Short blonde hair, high cheekbones and pale blue eyes; her face was tanned and free from make-up. She jotted a note on a pad and hung up. Taaffe's passport and credit card and the incomplete money-exchange form lay on the counter in front of her. She compared the signatures. Unsmiling, she spoke into the mike.

'I have to ask you a couple of questions, please, to confirm your ID.'

'Sure.'

Fuck. Fuckfuckfuck. Act natural. It was important to behave normally and to maintain eye contact. And my mind, all the while, was frantically seeking an escape route. An 'out', as we conjurors call it, for when something goes wrong in the middle of an illusion. She had the passport, the plastic; I had only a few pounds in sterling. I had my own credit card, but no matching ID and, besides, no way of using it without the risk of my presence in Amsterdam being traced. Either I answered the questions or I was fucked. *What* questions? If she asked for a codeword . . . Jesus, what hope of guessing Taaffe's codeword, even if I had all day to think about it, never mind a few seconds? I hoisted my travel-bag off my shoulder and set it down on the floor.

'Your date of birth?' she asked.

I told her my brother's birthday.

'And your mother's . . . um, *maiden* name? Maiden, is that correct?'

I gave my first truthful reply: 'Cooper. My mother's maiden name was Cooper.'

'Thank you, Mr Clarke. That's fine.'

My first purchase with the stack of newly acquired guilders was a glass of beer in the airport bar. *Een pils.* More froth than lager; when I asked the barman to top it up, he declined with a dismissive wave, as if to say *You want beer pulled the English way, piss off back to England.* So you have a second glass to make up for the short measure, and a third – by which time the post-traumatic stress of ordeal-by-foreign-exchange has turned into amused relief. I drank a private toast to my good fortune.

My second purchase was a rail ticket. I'd never seen a double-decker train until I stepped on to that platform at Schiphol. With its smart blue-and-yellow livery and gleaming, streamlined modernity, it resembled not so much a train as an aeroplane on wheels. The short journey into the city centre was noiseless and smooth, apart from a momentary embarrassment when a ticket inspector drew my attention to the fact that I was sitting in first-class. My ejection to the adjacent carriage precipitated a mass exodus – with concomitant banter – of similarly mistaken Britons. I've performed magic in fifteen countries – in Europe, east and west, in North America, in Australia and New Zealand, in *Japan*, for fuck's sake – and there I was, on a short hop across the North Sea, reduced by a combination of drink and nerves to the role of novice day-tripper. I found a corner seat where I was permitted to smoke – according to the signs – and stare out of the window. Our passage through the south-western suburbs was characterized by high-rise housing estates and broad avenues flanked by precision-straight columns of trees made lush with spring leaf. Every available piece of exposed concrete was tattooed, it seemed, with graffiti.

At Centraal Station, I bought a city plan from a newsstand and emerged into a stiff breeze, its chill mitigated by tentative mid-afternoon sunshine. Stationsplein, a wide, irregularly shaped plaza overlooked by the gothic edifice of the railway terminus, was congested, interwoven with cyclists, pedestrians and clanking yellow trams. I evaded the surreptitious attentions of several youths – pushers or touts or chancers of some sort, milling edgily among the throng with deleted expressions. On a bench, a woman slept beneath a grubby red blanket. A short distance beyond her, a large barrel-organ was playing to a semicircle of spectators. The smaller children watched in fascination as its gaily painted parts kept rhythm with the music in a mime of perpetual motion. The organ-grinder was collecting coins in a felt cap. I'd done my share of busking in my early days, as well as street performances at the Edinburgh Fringe and other festivals, but this looked like money for old rope – assuming you could afford the initial outlay for the organ. It wasn't even hand-powered, as far as I could tell. I gave him some change, if only for the reason, the curious coincidence, that he reminded me, by his rotund jollity, of a Dutch magician I'd once met and who was the one potential ally I had in the whole of Amsterdam. Synchronicity, I suppose you'd call it, if you believe in that sort of thing. Which I don't.

I found the taxi rank and asked a driver to take me to a reasonably priced hotel in or close to the city centre. He shrugged. He said Amsterdam was full. *Everybody comes to Holland now, for the bloemen.* Also, there was a music festival (Beethoven, Brahms – he wasn't sure) and an international conference. *No beds nowhere*, he added, activating the meter and setting off into the traffic.

Forty minutes and ten hotels later, he came out of the lobby of a place called the Terdam and gave me the thumbs up. A leafy crescent, lined with cars parked diagonally to the pavement. I spied a nameplate: Tesselschadestraat. The hotel appeared neither too shabby nor too exclusive. I had no idea where we were. Spreading the map open on the roof of his cab, I asked the driver to show our location. He pointed vaguely beyond a huge and magnificently blossoming horse chestnut: *Leidseplein here*, he said. Then, in the opposite direction: *Vondelpark*. Finally, somewhere between the two: *Rijksmuseum*. His tone implied, What more could I ask? I paid him, recovered my bag from the boot and went into the hotel.

All I had was his name and address, a two-year-old entry in my address book — legacy of a fleeting friendship formed at a symposium in Madrid organized by the International Brotherhood of Magicians. We hadn't written to one another since then, and I had no phone number for him. For all I knew, he could've moved home. I decided against asking the hotel switchboard to find the number for me; instead, I took the lift down to the lobby and borrowed a telephone directory from reception. Thumbing through the pages, I came to the surname I was looking for and checked the initial and address. It was the current year's edition, and the details matched those in my address book. I wrote down the number. Back in my room, I made the call.

'Huting, dag.'

'Hello? Is that Denis Huting?'

'Yes, Denis Huting. Hello?'

'Hi! Hi, I don't know if you remember me — my name's Fletcher Brandon. *Red*. You know, Peter Prestige. We shared a room at Madrid, the year before last.'

'Red! Shit, yeah, I remember you. You never wrote me.'

'Yeah, I know . . . I'm sorry, you know how . . .'

'So what, I never wrote you.' He gave a wheezy laugh. 'How you doing?'

'Fine. I'm fine, Denis.'

'Still working?'

'Yeah . . . I mean, not for a few weeks, but yeah. You?'

'I just got back from a show, funny enough. It was good, actually.'

'Look . . .'

'So why are you phoning me?'

'I . . . I'm in Amsterdam.'

'Shit, so am I!'

We laughed. 'I got here today, just now. I was thinking, maybe we could meet up for a beer or something. If you fancy.'

'Sure. Let's do that.'

'How . . . I know it's a bit short notice, but what are you doing this evening?'

'I don't have time for you tonight.'

'Oh, right.'

'Tomorrow is better. Why don't we have lunch?'

I agreed. He asked me where I was staying and named a café close by, giving me directions and stating a time for us to meet. We said goodbye and hung up. Nearly twenty hours before I would be able to see him. I undressed, intending to have a nap before showering and going out to eat. But impatience got the better of me; I picked up the phone again and dialled the number I had for Lena. I hadn't tried to contact her since the one time I'd been connected, only to be cut off in mid-conversation in a rain-soaked Oxford payphone. This time, a ringing tone. I let it ring for ten minutes without an answer before giving up. On the same scrap of paper which bore her number was Nikolaas's. I hesitated. The fearfully insistent tone of Lena's warning against calling him – *this number isn't safe for you* – had left its impression, as had the consequences of my last call to that number. Even in the anonymous sanctuary of an Amsterdam hotel room, these were more potent forces than my desire to speak to this man. I replaced the handset without dialling.

'Fancy a long weekend at the seaside?' That's how he got me here. Only, it's not just the two of us – it's Kim and her feller as well – and it's not a proper holiday, cos Red's playing three nights at Brighton. A working holiday, he calls it. I've only met your man Tony once and we've done fuck all socializing as a foursome, and here we are on a weekend away together like we're the best of friends. They're in the next room to us at the hotel and the beds creak and the walls are cardboard. So, Friday night, we're banging away and we can hear them banging away as well, and Red says it's putting him off his stroke and let's do it on the floor so they won't hear us. So we do. Me on all fours, him doing the biz. Anyway, when he comes, his arse loses it and he lets rip with a real cheek-slapper. Well, the two of us are in a heap on the floor laughing fit to piss. Saturday morning, at breakfast, we're sharing a table – me and Red, Kim and Tony. No one's looking anyone in the eye and no one's saying much except 'Could you pass the butter, please' and 'Looks like it's going to be fine today' and all that shite. Then Red tries to break the ice with, 'The beds are a bit noisy here, aren't they?'

And Kim gives one of her smirks and says, 'At least ours doesn't fart.'

It's Saturday night now – Red and Kim are on stage, me and Tony are in the audience. They're doing the Basket trick. I must've seen this half a dozen times and I still haven't a fucking clue like. This is what happens: Kim stands in this wicker basket – it's about two foot high and four foot long – and Red covers her with a cloth. She sinks down into the basket and Red whips the cloth away and puts a lid on the basket. Then he goes round sticking one sword after another into the wicker till there's no way she's not going to be skewered. Red pulls the swords out, puts the cloth back over the basket and takes the lid off, gets into the basket himself and sits down in it. When he gets out again, the cloth rises up out of the basket like a ghost . . . Red whips it away, and there's Kim flashing her teeth. Tony whispers in my ear, 'Trapdoor.'

And I think, is it bollix, cos I've watched them rehearse this one and there's no trapdoor upstairs at the Port Mahon or Kim'd drop arse-first into the public bar. So I tell him this, and Tony goes, 'So how's he do it, then?'

I can feel his lips against my ear. And now it's me, whispering, 'She's a blow-up doll — all he has to do is let the air out and then blow her up again.'

Tony thinks this is a hoot.

In the interval, the two of us hit the bar. Tony's a gym instructor. Personal Fitness Consultant, he calls it. He looks at me and grins and says, 'D'you reckon if we left now we could get to the hotel and back here again in time for the end of the show?'

I don't say anything.

He goes, 'They wouldn't ever have to know.'

I give him my best smile. 'Tony, don't take this personal, like, but why would I want to shag a cunt like you?'

Morning. The Dam was cacophonous with traffic and the pulsating music of a funfair, its Ferris wheel dwarfing the whalebone-white phallus-structure of the national monument. Tour buses offloaded parties of Germans, Japanese and Swedes into the pubic fuzz of people at the monument's base. Across the way lay Pijlsteeg, a narrow lane separating a hotel from a café-bar displaying the red, black and white Heineken tricolour. Not so much a thoroughfare as a gap, unremarkable and, seemingly, unnoticed by the eddy of passers-by. Entering Pijlsteeg from Dam Square was like emerging from an all-night party into the dead silence of solitude. What little light there was seeped from a misshapen strip of sky framed by the rooftops which gave the alleyway its definition. The walls, lined with bicycles clamped to every pipe and ventilation grille, reiterated the clop-clop of my footsteps on grey brick cobbles. One bike, still secured to a street sign, had been grotesquely crippled; another was missing a wheel. Litter and gobbets of unidentifiable detritus had collected in doorways and in the drain grates. Glancing further along the lane, I saw an incongruous chrome and tinted-glass atrium: an arcade of shops selling cheese and chocolate, restaurants, a wine bar with mullioned windows. No. 37 stood on the right, some thirty metres before Pijlsteeg turned posh, a narrow building tapering to a high gabled point with a pulley-beam beneath the eaves. Its windows were rendered opaque by grime or frosted glass; those at ground-floor level were heavily barred. The white wooden door was psychedelic with graffiti. Set into the wall beside it was an intercom panel, its four buzzers labelled hs, 1e, 2e, 3e; the corresponding name slots were blank. I craned my neck to gaze at the uppermost storey, the 'III', I assumed, in the sender's address on Rosa's letter to her aunt. A solitary sash window, firmly closed. I tried to picture a teenage Rosa at that window, smoking, raising the sash to flick a cigarette stub into the passage below. Or clattering down three steep flights of stairs and letting herself out through this very door, with its spray-paint expletives and slogans and the esoteric insignia of youth gangs. A bike, chained to a drainpipe. Her long black hair, getting in the way as she stooped to free the lock; Rosa, swinging into the saddle and propelling herself towards Dam Square to be engulfed in the throng of tourists. She'd *lived* there. Years ago, she'd lived there, in that building, and written a letter full of fear and pleading to a woman who would always detest her. No sign of life at the third-floor window, nor at any of the others. The intercom panel. I could have pressed each buzzer in turn and waited for someone to come. I couldn've asked after Rosa. But if she'd been desperate to leave, maybe I shouldn't be so impatient to venture inside without some idea of what to expect. I'd been in Amsterdam less than twenty-four hours; No. 37 Pijlsteeg was there before I arrived and would still be there the next day and the next. I'd *seen* it – that was enough, for now. So I left the buzzers well alone. I walked away. As I retraced my steps to the Dam, I was startled by steam escaping from a vent just above my head. On the adjacent brickwork was another piece of graffiti – a telephone number, beneath the message *Black girl, 14, wants big cocks to suck and fuck.*

A child's mind – I'm talking about a small child, not a teenage fucker and cocksucker – is broad and deep and untainted by the cynicism of accumulated experience. A child encounters novelty and gives it a hug. As an illusionist, you might assume this to imply that an audience of kids will be more naïve, more gullible, more susceptible to simple deceit than will an audience of adults. You'd be wrong. I've said it before: the easiest people to dupe are those most convinced of the subtlety and sophistication of their perceptive powers; children – the younger the better – are free from such pretension. Don't assume, either, that you can get away with lower standards of magicianship as a children's entertainer. You can't. No one is quicker than a kid to cry 'Cheat!' if slipshod conjuring gives him a glimpse of the trick.

Any parent or grandparent, any aunt or uncle, any teacher, will tell you: children see what they see and they don't take any crap from anyone.

I learned this for myself, performing (as Peter Prestige, and as Uncle Red) for kids of all ages; I learned it, too, from Denis Huting. Denis is a professional children's magician, the best I've seen. Stage name: Oranjekip, or 'orange chicken'. He wears a chicken costume, coloured bright orange and specially tailored to accommodate his girth. Denis calculates that, if he were a real chicken, his cooking time – at so many hours per pound – would be just under a month. Egg productions and disappearances are a feature of his act, and he is – as far as I'm aware – the only magician ever to perform the Sawing a Fox in Half illusion. At the symposium in Madrid someone asked why he chose to entertain children rather than adults, and he replied *Because children are wonderful. By that, I am saying they are full of wonder.*

The café where we'd arranged to meet – constructed of wood, decorated like a fairground ride – was an architectural hybrid of scout hut and end-of-pier cafeteria at a 1950s English seaside resort. It sold pancakes and *poffertjes*, whatever they were. Denis Huting was already there when I arrived, the sole customer seated at one of the interior tables; others were savouring the sunshine on the boarded verandah. We shook hands warmly and he informed me I was six minutes late. I apologized.

'We Dutch are a punctual people,' he said.

'I'll try to remember that.'

'You know that game you play in England, "What's the time, Mr Wolf?" Our children don't see the point of this game because they already know the time.'

'Is that true?'

'No. I made it up.'

We laughed. Denis sat down, gesturing at the vacant seat opposite his. He looked even heavier and rounder than I remembered. I said it was good to see him again, prompting a brief reminiscence of three days' cohabitation in a Spanish hotel for Hocus Pocus '96. *Remember ringing room service at 2 a.m. and ordering scrambled eggs? . . . Did I? . . . And when the guy came, you* opened the door dressed as a chicken and screamed . . . Yes, I recall: 'You've murdered my babies!' Denis was in his mid-forties and more or less bald. When he laughed his eyes disappeared among folds of skin and his fleshy jowls flushed deep pink. He took two menus from a rack and handed one to me. His fingers were so plump the knuckle joints had lost definition, yet I'd witnessed sleights with those hands that bewildered even me, a fellow pro. He spoke English with a phlegmy emphasis, turning 'g' and 'ch' into throat clearance.

'When you did not write me,' he said, becoming serious, 'I thought maybe I have disgusted you.'

I hesitated. 'Denis, you're not the first guy who's made a pass at me.'

'I was drunk.'

'Thanks. I'm flattered.'

'No, I mean I was drunk to make a pass. When you are a children's magician it's not so good for people to know you are gay.'

'D'you think so?'

'Sure I think so. You like fucking men, you like to fuck little boys.' He gave a shrug. 'I tell you, it's what people think.'

'I like fucking women, but it doesn't mean I want to fuck little girls.'

'You're not people.' I didn't say anything. Denis caught the attention of a waitress. As she made her way towards our table, he smiled at me and said, 'It was the chicken costume put you off? Or it was me being so fat and ugly?'

'Fat and ugly, definitely.'

Denis loved that. The waitress had to wait for him to finish laughing before she could take our order: *poffertjes* for him, a cheese pancake for me, two coffees.

'What are *poffertjes*?' I asked.

'You can have one of mine,' he said. 'And you will never want to eat any other food as long as you live. I promise this.'

We were sharing a booth enclosed by ornate wooden panels painted claret and sky blue and trimmed with gold, in keeping with the café's general décor. Those diners seated on the verandah were obscured by a smoky veil of heat-shimmer rising off the griddles and deep-fat fryers. The air reeked of fresh coffee and hot oil and sweetness.

'So, tell me, Red, why are you come to Amsterdam?'

'Just a holiday, really.' I shrugged. 'I heard it was an interesting place.'

'Tulips, cheese, Anne Frankhuis, the Van Gogh museum? Sure.' He winked at me. 'Or maybe have a good time with one of the window girls and smoke some hash?'

I reciprocated his smile. 'And look up my old friend, Oranjekip.'

The waitress fetched our coffees, a solitary biscuit perched in each saucer. The cups were small, dainty. Denis stirred two heaped spoonfuls of sugar into his.

'So, tell me, Red, why are you come to Amsterdam?'

'You know, I feel like I just entered this time warp where people keep asking me the same . . .'

'You can tell me why, or you can tell me to mind my business . . .' He ate his biscuit whole, dabbing crumbs from his lips before adding, 'But don't lie to me. OK?'

As we talked, his eyes left mine only to attend to his coffee or to the transfer of biscuit from saucer to mouth. Denis locked his gaze on yours in a way that compelled you to not look away. I nodded, in response to the challenge of his remark. I disclosed the context of my visit, enough to have him believe me, at least. I told him how Rosa died and about her letter, headed with an address in Pijlsteeg; I showed him the picture of her drinking with the tanned, goatee-bearded young man; I cited the involvement of Max van Dis, and of Lena and Nikolaas and 'Vicky', and of a passport in the name of Charity Jackson; I said Rosa had been *en route* to Amsterdam when she was killed; I told him about Rosa, and about the two of us. What I didn't tell Denis Huting was of my interrogation by the police, nor of my fraudulent escape from England.

'Drugs?' he asked, when I'd finished.

'Don't know. Like I say, she was a user when she was a teenager and there's the van Dis connection, but I just . . . it doesn't fit in with the Rosa I knew.'

His tone was matter-of-fact, almost dismissive. 'I don't get why you do this, coming here like you are a policeman. What can you do?'

Before I could answer, the waitress returned. She set my food in front of me, then Denis's. Occupying his plate was a mound of what looked like small dumplings, festooned with powdered sugar, sliced fresh strawberries and whipped cream.

'There. *Poffertjes,*' he mouthed the word as though it were the name of his lover. 'Balls of pancake . . . how do you call it?'

'Batter.'

'Yes, balls of batter, deep fried.' He forked one on to my plate. 'Go on, try.'

Another wink, then I lost him to his food for several minutes. As for mine, the pancake was almost half a metre in diameter and layered with thin slices of molten Emmental, its characteristic holes elongated into ellipses by the melting process.

'Rosa's speciality,' I said, using my knife as a pointer. '*Pannekoeken,* the only word of Dutch she taught me.'

'You loved her?'

I looked at him across the table. 'Yes, I did.'

'She's not here. You know that?'

'I know.'

I was distracted by the persistent clanging of a bell somewhere nearby, a warning to pedestrians of an approaching tram, Denis explained. He'd demolished his meal in the time it had taken me to fold my pancake into a more manageable form and make two or three inroads. He pushed his plate aside and reclined in his seat.

'Tell me, whatever became of The Lovely Kim?'

'She's still my assistant.'

'You still fucking her?'

I laughed. 'I thought we were discreet in Madrid.'

'That illusion, where you make her on fire . . . I was very impressed by that.'

(This is the Fire and Water illusion: at one end of the stage is a platform, at the other is a huge glass tank filled with water;

168

Kim, in a bright yellow bikini, stands on the platform while Peter Prestige wraps her in swathes of paper; taking a cigarette lighter from his pocket, he touches the flame to the paper; his assistant is immediately engulfed by fire; the magician pauses for the audience's gasps of horror to subside before drawing their attention to the glass tank; The Lovely Kim – intact, unblemished, and still wearing the yellow bikini – is swimming in the water, smiling. Applause. Don't ask . . .)

I smiled. 'It worked very well that night.'

'When you helped her from the water,' he said, 'the way you held hands, the way you looked at each other before you take your bow . . . that is how I know.'

'You're the detective here, not me.' I conceded defeat with the pancake. Denis raised his eyebrows by way of inquiry; I gave the nod, and he helped himself to my leftovers. When he'd finished, I took out a pack of B & H. 'D'you mind if I smoke?'

'Yes, I do.'

I put the cigarettes back in my pocket without a word.

He shrugged. 'You ask me, I tell you.'

I couldn't help laughing. He joined in, eyes disappearing among the creases of his face. We broke off talking while the waitress cleared our table and made a note of Denis's request for two more coffees. When she'd gone, he said, 'The phone numbers for Lena and Nikolaas, can you write them down for me?'

'Sure, why?'

'Cees, he has a sister who is working with PTT – the post and telecom, here in Amsterdam. Maybe she can find the address for these numbers.'

'Cees is your, um . . .'

'Yes. He is my "um". This is your word for it now, in England?'

'Absolutely.'

We shared another smile. I produced the piece of paper bearing Nikolaas's and Lena's numbers, copying them on to a paper napkin. As I did so, he said,

'Also, the address in Pijlsteeg. Maybe, we can find who lives there.'

I added the necessary details. Denis took the napkin from me, studied it for a moment, then folded it into a square and slotted it into a compartment of his wallet. The coffees arrived. He ate his biscuit whole, as before, then raised the cup to his lips, the tiny handle pincered between fat thumb and middle finger, his little finger cocked. He set the cup down, only it wasn't a cup that sat in his saucer now but an egg. The cup had vanished. Tapping the egg with his spoon, the shell split jaggedly in two to release a plastic miniature chick, coloured bright orange.

'A souvenir,' he said, handing it to me. He winked. 'Keep it by your bed and every time you go to sleep you will think of me.'

Sunday Mornings

Sunday mornings, we'd stay in bed – sleeping, smoking, reading the papers, drinking coffee, listening to the radio, fucking. Lunch-time, we'd shower, sling on some clothes and go to a pub where they had food and live music. Sometimes, however, especially on the cold, damp winter days of penetrating and relentless grey, we wouldn't surface until the evening session; bedridden, the passage of time was marked by an alteration in the quality of light through the curtains. Rosa once told me I was the only guy she'd ever spent an entire day with without quarrelling. *What day was that, I must've missed it? Go on, ya bollix.* It would be me despatched to collect the papers from the doormat, to make coffee, to fetch platefuls of buttered toast, to put food, milk and a dab of butter out for Merlin. Me, always. Rosa would rise only to use the bathroom and even then she'd take the duvet with her, wearing it like an oversize cape and leaving me in naked protestation on the stripped bed. One afternoon she had me carry the television upstairs because there was a black-and-white film she wanted to watch. *A fillum.* I parked the set at the foot of the bed. No picture, no aerial socket. So we hauled the whole lot – mattress, sheet, duvet, pillows, telly – downstairs and remade the bed on the living-room floor. Ten minutes into the film, Rosa declared it a *poil of shoite* and switched off. We fucked, instead. And when we'd finished, Rosa said, 'Now, tea, would be *lovely*.'

So it was me, nude, who went out to the kitchen. My semi-tumescent prick flapped at the insides of my thighs, spilling silvery strands of stickiness that patterned the floor like slug trails. Merlin, sniffing in my wake in feline impersonation of a tracker dog, seemed unimpressed. He sat by the back door, as though expectant that I would save him the trouble of letting himself out through the cat-flap. *She's teaching you bad habits, Merl.* I opened the door. He lost all interest in going outside, slinking off to nuzzle indifferently at the mound of food in his dish. I shut the door. Merlin nosed two biscuits and a lump of rabbit on to the lino, ate nothing, and left the house via the flap.

'That cat is sick in the head,' I said, placing Rosa's mug within reach.

'Ah, leave her alone.'

I set my own drink down and eased back beneath the covers of our makeshift bed. Rosa's skin was hot to the touch. She was sitting up, practising a trick I'd taught her using a five-pound note and two paper clips: you shape the fiver into an 'S', fix each clip to it, tug sharply at the ends of the note and the clips fly into the air . . . no longer separate but linked together. As if by magic. This was one of several basic feats – simple to perform but visually effective – which she'd acquired in order to entertain her colleagues during idle moments at the *Erin* offices. It wasn't working. I showed her the correct way to attach the clips to the note and she tried again. Bingo.

'It's putting the things on – you know, *casual* – so's it looks like they could go on any old how . . . that's the bit I can't manage.'

'Practise,' I said. 'Do it again and again until you don't have to think about it.'

'I'm all thumbs, like.' She performed the trick a second time and a third. 'See?'

'You have to get the audience watching *you* rather than what you're doing.'

A fourth attempt. The paper clips spiralled into her tea. *Ah, for fick's* . . . Rosa fished them out. I remarked, to no amusement on her part, that she'd written herself into the conjuring textbooks by inventing a new climax to a traditional trick.

'I thought women were supposed to be more patient than men?' I said.

'Not this woman. Not with this shite, anyway.'

'You don't like doing magic, don't ask me to show you how.'

'C'mere though, Red, d'you never get bored *rigid* with all this practising?'

'No.'

172

Rosa shook her head.

'What?' I asked.

'Nothing.'

'No, go on, what?'

She lay back abruptly in bed, her long hair strewn about the pillow and one or two stray wisps levitated by static. Her eyes, usually so blue, were made deep grey by the half-light from the closed curtains. A redness lingered around her slightly parted lips, the soft skin so recently stubble-chafed where we'd fed on one another's mouths while we fucked. Staring up at the ceiling, Rosa eventually said, 'D'you ever wonder what it is you see in me?'

'Christ, what brought this on?'

'No, go 'way and listen, if I wasn't such a great shag you'd be off.' She turned her head to look at me. 'Wouldn't you? You would. Out of here like a shot.'

'I *live* here.'

'Don't be a smart arse.'

'Rosa, for fuck's sake.'

She rolled away on to her side, her back towards me. 'Ignore me.'

'Where did all this come from? One minute you're . . .'

'Like, ig-*nore* me. OK?'

It wasn't unprecedented for Rosa to unburden herself of a crisis of confidence, although her confessionals were rare and – so far – invariably drunken. *How long d'you give us?* was one theme, demanding a prognosis from me as though I were a doctor and our relationship a terminally ill patient. *We'd both be better off on our own* was another. The happier we were, the more prone she was to insecurity; happiness, it seemed, served only to foreshadow its opposite. The subtext was that I would be the first to give up on us, on *her*. Which I found bizarre, because all along I'd suppressed a nagging conviction that she would be the one to effect the self-fulfilling prophecy of our demise. Her, not me. Yet there she was – *Rosa* – sober, on a wet Sunday afternoon, seeking reassurance. I watched the duvet rose and fall with her breathing.

'Who says you're a great shag, anyway?'

She didn't respond. When I nudged her in the ribs, she withdrew to her side of the mattress.

'How long since you moved in?' I answered my own question. 'Six months. Do you think we'd have lasted this long if sex was the only thing I liked about you?'

Rosa's voice sounded disembodied, as though the figure in the bed had nothing to do with the words projected. 'What's the longest you've been with someone?'

I thought for a moment. 'I don't know. Couple of years.'

'Kim?'

'Yeah. Only half that time doesn't really count. And we never lived together. There was a girl years ago, at the poly . . . about fifteen months, I was with her.'

'How come Kim didn't move in?'

'Don't know.' I paused. 'We started out as an affair and somehow – even when we were legit – the idea of being a "proper couple" never really seemed right.'

Rosa rolled on to her back again. She looked at me, her lips betraying a half-smile. 'And we're a proper couple?'

'Fuck off, you know what I mean.'

'Fuck off yourself,' she said, giving me a dig in the arm.

'I know your favourite colour. I know what size shoes you wear. I know how many sugars you take. I know you don't believe in God, Father Christmas, life after death or a divided Ireland.'

'I'd say you've got me taped, so.'

I reached for my cigarettes, lit two and handed one to Rosa. We leaned into one another, lying in silence for a moment and exhaling smoke ceilingwards at irregular intervals. Her entire body was warm, except for her feet.

'What's *your* longest relationship?' I asked.

'Oh, now . . . *relationship*.'

'You know what I mean.'

'I was shagging one feller for about three years. Two-and-a-half, maybe.'

'*Three years*. When was this?'

'I was seventeen when it started.'

'In London, yeah?'

Rosa took a deep draw on her cigarette, holding the smoke in and releasing it with her response. 'Yeah, London.'

'Was he the one who taught you how to make pancakes?'

'That's your man.'

'What was his name?'

She twisted her head to get a better look at me. That half-smile again. 'You wouldn't be jealous, would you?'

'You're on a train or something, and you want to impress someone – you going to make them a pancake? Or show them a card trick?' I returned her smile. 'I deal in the art of the possible.'

'Shite is what you deal in, Fletcher Brandon.' We kissed. 'Grade-A shite.'

'Anyway, you still haven't told me his name.'

'Nik,' she said. 'All right? His name was Nik. So now you know.'

'Were you in love with him?'

Rosa lowered her head. I wasn't sure she was going to reply at all and, when she did, her speech was muffled by the pillow. 'I thought I was, at the time.'

The phone rang. The answering machine cut in and I listened to my voice, then to my brother's as he left a convoluted message about meeting up for a beer. Rosa reached across me to drop her fag end in the dregs of my tea. She appeared to have relapsed into the melancholia of a few minutes ago. I finished my cigarette and added it to the remnants of hers. Making my voice soft, I said, 'Is Nick the reason you're not sure about us? I'm not saying do you still love him, I mean did something happen between you that . . . ?'

Another kiss, to silence me. Her breath, on my face, was warm and smelt of tobacco. As suddenly as her mood had deteriorated, it improved again – she smiled, she effervesced; looking me directly in the eye, she swatted my question with her own.

'Go on then, clever shite, what's my favourite colour?'

'Green.'

'Hah, well that's where you're wrong.'

'You told me so yourself!'

'So I'm a liar.'

I bought a phone card and went to one of the booths on Leidseplein to ring Taaffe. I dialled his work number, hoping that, even if the route of my escape had been plotted as far as my brother's place, the police would be unlikely to monitor calls to his office. Switchboard asked my name before putting me through. *Eric White*, I said. (An Anglicized corruption of Ehrich Weiss, the real name of the man known as Houdini.) Taaffe, who understands better than most the way my mind works, deciphered the pseudonym right away.

'Hello, Mr White,' he said, as soon as the telephonist connected me. 'Has the new credit arrangement been to your satisfaction?'

'Yes, thank you, Mr Clarke. It's been very useful.'

In the background, I heard a door close. Taaffe, his voice lowered now but the alteration in tone unmistakable, said, 'You must take me for some kind of a cunt.'

'Taaffe . . ,'

'Where the fuck are you?'

I didn't answer.

'I had Messrs Plod round last night, waving an arrest warrant under my nose and asking if I'd seen you or heard from you.'

'What did you tell them?'

'Gemma was still up when they came, and they asked *her* – right there in front of me and Lisa – if she'd seen her Uncle Red lately. D'you know what she did? She lied. *Seven years old*, and she covered up for you . . . I didn't even have to tell her.'

'Taaffe, all I can say is I'm sorry.'

This exchange of recriminations and apologies continued for a moment before my brother calmed down sufficiently to tell me what I needed to know. The police had no idea where I'd gone after I left the Fievres' house, although according to Taaffe, they refused to believe Paul was similarly ignorant. *He was down the nick for hours . . . I'd start looking for a new agent if I were you*. My brother was questioned as a matter of course, as were other family, friends and associates; my storage room at the Port Mahon had been searched in case I was hiding there. Even my father was asked if I'd made contact. His reply, apparently, *Yes, Christmas 1982*. The police – oblivious to the theft of Taaffe's passport and with my own in their possession – were working on the assumption that I remained in Britain. I had time, though how much was anyone's guess. And, given the Dutch factors in the investigation, Amsterdam was the first place the police would come looking once they began to suspect I'd left the country.

'You realize how stupid you've been, doing a runner like this?'

Taaffe elaborated. He'd heard, from Paul, that the inspection of my bank and building-society accounts revealed no unexplained transactions around the time when I was supposed to have paid for Rosa to be killed. And with only the unsubstantiated claims of Max van Dis and his fellow hitman to go on, the police had come to regard my alleged involvement as increasingly dubious. Until I chose to jump bail. Now, my face was in the papers: Murder Link To Magician's Vanishing Act.

'We have to hide them,' he said, 'in case Gemma starts a scrapbook.'

We go out, it's got to be with one of the guys — usually Nikolaas or Max or Wim. Or Rennie. Rennie is Mr Peters' nephew so you have to watch what you say with him, like. I don't hardly see Mr Peters at all, unless he turns up for a private show with a bunch of his 'special clients'. Rennie doesn't get to be in the shows or the films cos he's got something wrong with his skin which means he hasn't got no face hair. He's from Zimbabwe — Rhodesia, he calls it. Max is as bad. Worse, actually. He laid into Renata over something the other day and . . . fucking hell, the state of her. He got a right bollixing, though, cos she won't be working for a while. Wim's OK. Thick as shite, but OK. And Nikolaas is a good craíc and a great one for the booze, only there's something . . . I don't know. Like, he's an odd one out. I go, 'Nik, we're two of a kind, you and me.'

He shakes his head. 'One and one don't make two, it makes one and one.'

Weird. I can't suss if he's clever, or just talks clever. Nik's the one who sorts us. Good gear too. Some of the girls are into it and some aren't, though I don't know how you can do half the stuff they tell you to if you're not dosed up. I mean, fuck sake. The girls are OK, mostly. Not that I see much of them, except when we're working. Jan — Mr Peters — doesn't like us being too friendly, worried we're going to form our own branch of De Rode Draad or something. Fat fucking chance.

I'm in my room and like I've just cooked up a shot . . . and it's mmmm mmm I'm swimming fucking like . . . fucking mmmm and there's . . . I didn't see him only there's Max in the doorway and I didn't hear him or . . . or shit and he's saying I'm wanted downstairs . . .

'Two o'clock,' I go. 'Two o'clock.'

'It's five after.'

Like his mouth's moving and the words are somewhere . . . they're not . . . they're somewhere else and I'm fucking mmmm and where's

my watch? Max is looking at the stuff on the floor and he's . . . he says
I'm wanted downstairs like fucking now. Like now. I'm laughing . . .
I'm . . . it's giggling it's giggles . . .

'How's goan van Dick?'

Van Dick . . . he fucking hates that van Dick cos it's not . . . it's
what is it? It's Dis D-I-S van Dis not Dick . . . and he's looking at
me and . . . more words swimming . . . I can't hear now and I can't
see and I can't hear what he's . . . he's what he's saying . . . he's taking
his belt off and I'm where am I? I'm sitting on the floor and he lifts his
arm and it's . . . I don't feel anything I don't feel any fucking thing at
all . . . my hair he's it's in his hand and he's pulling me and I'm . . .
he's pushing me out the . . . the ground he's holding me out the window
and there's the ground and bicycles and it's like they're right there and
they're so far away . . . down . . . and he's . . . words . . . he's going
to drop me he's going to . . . and I don't I can't.

Nik . . . it's Nik now and Max is I don't know where he is but he
isn't because it's Nik here now and I'm sitting on the on the bed. The
bed. I don't hurt.

'He dropped me.'

'It's OK, he didn't drop you.'

'He dropped me.'

I'm on the bed and I don't hurt.

The Apartment

My room at the Hotel Terdam was on the top floor, its walls
and ceiling meeting at an oblique angle to accommodate the
slant of the roof. There was a rail across the window above the
bed, preventing the curtains from dangling on to the pillow.
Décor and furnishings were minimalist – blacks and whites and
clean, straight lines; the spacious *en suite* bathroom, a dazzle of
chrome, white tiles and mirrored glass. I was in the shower on
my third morning in Amsterdam, my skin pinking beneath the
torrent, when a telephone's shrill tones penetrated the noise of
the water. Wrapping a towel round my waist, I went into the
bedroom and picked up the receiver.

'Hello.'

'So you are Fletcher Brandon, you are Red, you are Peter
Prestige, and now you are Taffy Clarke.'

It was Denis Huting. I corrected his mispronunciation of my
brother's name. He said I wasn't to blame him, but the hotel
receptionist who'd put the call through. Denis's voice gladdened
me; I had reined in my impatience at hearing nothing from him
since our meeting nearly forty-eight hours earlier.

'So how come you are Mr Clarke?'

'Denis, you don't want to know.'

'I do want to know. That is why I ask.'

'OK, I don't want to tell you.'

Was I happy for him to divulge information by phone or
would I prefer a secret assignation, some place where we could
be secure in the knowledge our conversation wasn't being mon-
itored? *If you like, I can wear dark glasses and carry a copy of De
Telegraaf . . .* I said it would be fine to talk over the phone. *OK,
information.* We have a surname to go with Lena: *Gies, G-I-E-S*;
also, an address corresponding to the telephone number I had
for her. Kerkstraat. Church Street, in English.

I made a note. 'Anyone else at that address?'

'No, it is just Lena Gies.'

'How about Nikolaas?'

'This is interesting, now,' said Denis. 'Because the telephone number you have is for an address where there is no Nikolaas. Your information is old.'

'OK, give me the address anyway.'

'This is the other interesting thing. The address for that number is the same as you write down for me the other day: Pijlsteeg, 37 III.'

'You mean Nikolaas lives – or used to live – there, in Pijlsteeg?' I asked. 'Is there any way of checking that?'

He laughed wheezily. 'I already done that. Cees's sister checked for me who has lived at that address, historically. There was a Nikolaas van Zandt for seven years, from June 1990 until last November.' He spelled the surname for me.

'Any forwarding address?'

'Sorry, no. There is nothing.'

'Who's resident there now, since November?'

'The apartment is empty, this is what PTT records say.'

'Who's the owner?' I asked.

'I don't have this information.'

A thought occurred to me. 'Denis, you know the telephone number – I called from England a few weeks ago and got an answering machine. Surely, if the apartment was unoccupied, the line would've been disconnected?'

'No, there is a telephone still. The people who manage the building pay for this – a property company, you know? This is what Cees's sister tells me.'

'Did she give you the names of people living at the other apartments?'

'I did not ask her this.'

'How about no. III? Was anyone else registered at that address besides Nikolaas van Zandt? I mean, during the time he was living there?'

'Miss Rosa Kelly, for example?'

'Yes.'

'No. I have some names here – four names – but no Kelly.'

All female. He read them out in chronological order. Three of the names meant nothing to me. The second of the four – resident at Pijlsteeg, 37 III from June '91 to April '94 – was Bernadette Houlihan. A conflation of Rosa's confirmation name and the surname she was born with.

As soon as we'd hung up, I retrieved my bag from on top of the wardrobe and took out Rosa's airmail letter. It was dated 10 March 1994. I felt sure, now, that the 'Nick' she told me she'd lived with for three years in London, and who'd taught her the art of making *pannekoeken*, was Nikolaas van Zandt; and it wasn't London where they'd been lovers, but Amsterdam. Nikolaas, whose phone number wasn't safe for me. Nikolaas, photographed enjoying a beer with a teenage Rosa. Nikolaas, the man she said the police should seek if anything happened to her. I re-read her letter.

. . . They will go to the flat in Pijlsteeg and they will find the man in the picture and then they will make him tell them about me . . .

. . . Im very unhappy but some people are trying to help me. The thing is I dont know wether I can believe them only I have to . . .

. . . I'm frightened . . .

Written in the month before 'Bernadette Houlihan' ceased to reside at No. 37, third floor. What I didn't know was why she'd been so desperate to flee and whether she was escaping *from* Nikolaas or with his help. Nor did I comprehend the 'how?' and 'why?' of Rosa surviving her clandestine departure from Amsterdam only to die four years later while trying to go back there.

The building, its façade painted black and cream, stood four storeys high on the corner of Kerkstraat and Utrechtsestraat. The ground floor was given over to a clothing shop, with a black door to one side of this affording access to the flats above. This section of Kerskstraat was pedestrianized. On a stand, some dozen cycles were lodged into racks designed to take half that number. Each time a tram trundled by along Utrechtsestraat, the vibrations excited the bikes into metallic chatter. On the second floor, window-boxes displayed a profusion of red pansies. The windows were shut, despite the warm weather. A name card in the intercom panel confirmed the information supplied by Denis's contact at PTT: this is where Lena Gies lived.

I pressed the buzzer. No answer. I pressed it again, without response. A window was open on the first floor, so I tried that buzzer, and after a short pause a woman's voice crackled in Dutch through the speaker. I hurriedly produced my phrase book from a jacket pocket.

'Hallo . . . hallo, spreekt u Engels?'

'Nee.'

'Um . . . alstublieft, waar is Lena? Twee . . . second floor. Twee.'

'Ja, ja, Lena. She come Donderdag.'

'Thursday?'

In the background, I heard a baby crying; the woman sounded preoccupied, anxious to extricate herself from this conversation. 'Ja, Donderdag. Thurs-day.'

'Thank you. Bedankt.'

The crackling ceased. Lena wouldn't be home for two days. By Thursday, I would've been in Amsterdam almost a week, each day bringing nearer the time when the police in Oxford would pick up my trail. I considered inconveniencing the woman in the first-floor apartment again, to see if she knew where Lena was – but this would be beyond the scope of my Dutch and her English. A note in Lena's letter-box, asking her to contact me at the hotel? No. Too dangerous – I didn't want to give away where I was staying. What I did, instead, was something that proved to be even more reckless.

An intercom panel, a sequence of buttons. Not a black door in Kerkstraat, however, but a white one diseased with graffiti in a shabby alleyway off Dam Square. Pijlsteeg, 37. I buzzed the third floor, keeping my thumb on the button, as though the duration of this action increased the likelihood of someone answering. Yet the response, when it came, made me start. A voice, not over the intercom, but from someone standing close behind me.

I wheeled round to see a man and a woman, side by side. The man was holding a bunch of keys in one hand, a lighted cigarette in the other. When he spoke again, he used English, though I'd said nothing to give away my nationality.

'Can I help you?'

'Do you live here?'

'Yes.'

The man was a few years older than me, and shorter – no more than five-eight – with wispy brown hair and no eyebrows whatsoever, giving his face the appearance of a new-born infant. A blue sweatshirt was draped over his shoulders, its arms knotted at the chest. The woman, much younger than her companion, wore a white sleeveless cotton shirt and denim miniskirt; her limbs were so bleached by the glare of the sun that they seemed almost translucent. A natural redhead, her mass of curls was piled up on her head in a style that reminded me of Rosa's friend Dympna.

'Are you on the third floor?' I asked.

The man studied my face for a moment, drawing on his cigarette. He shook his head. 'Second. The apartment above us is empty.'

His English was correct but heavily accented, possibly South African. Beside him, with his relaxed confidence, the woman looked ill at ease. She looked *ill*, to tell the truth. Although I addressed both of them, clearly he was the one to do any talking. I asked if they'd been living there long, and he said no. Did he know Nikolaas van Zandt, who used to live on the third floor? Another pause, another shake of the head.

'Been empty the whole time we've been here. Don't know no Nikolaas.'

'I was told he only moved out a few months ago, in November.'

'Nah.' For the first time, he smiled. His next remark was a question, intoned as a statement of fact. 'Maybe you got the wrong place.'

For a moment we were looking directly into one another's eyes, his appearing small and oddly positioned beneath the incline of skin where his brows should've been. He raised the cigarette to his mouth for a final time, inhaled, and discarded the stub in the direction of the gutter. All the while, the woman shifted her weight from one leg to the other, as though in need of the toilet. I became conscious of standing between them and the door to the apartments. The man swung the keys loose on their ring and enclosed them once more within his fist.

'Yeah,' I said, 'maybe I made a mistake.'

I stepped aside. The man moved past me to open the door. Placing a hand in the centre of his companion's back, he ushered her inside – seemingly propelling her, yet without applying any pressure. She glanced at me for a fraction of a second before disappearing from view. The man smiled again. Then he was gone, the door shut. I stood outside. A woman came by on a bicycle, with a young girl riding pillion, sitting side-saddle and swinging her feet back and forth. She was singing. Having given the man and woman ample time to climb the stairs to their second-floor apartment, I tried the buzzer. I waited. I tried again. No answer.

I turned away from No. 37 and walked towards the Dam. It was one thirty; I hadn't eaten since breakfast at the hotel. At the end of Pijlsteeg, a café-bar fronted on to the square. I went in and ordered a beer and a sandwich, the barman gesturing at a vacant table by the window and intimating, by a combination of sign language and broken English, that he would fetch my order. I sat down. I was in the process of lighting a cigarette when the redheaded young woman in the miniskirt appeared, as if from nowhere, in the seat across the table from me. She looked petrified.

I can help ye find Nikolaas. Her first words to me in that café-bar at the end of Pijlsteeg, populated by tourists and Amsterdammers and pungent with cigarette fumes, coffee and cooked meat. Not her first words, strictly speaking. What she said, as she sat down in the haze of my newly ignited B&H, was, 'Ah've no got long, he thinks ah'm oot fae fags.'

'He' being the man with no eyebrows. She glanced with the repetitiveness of a nervous tic in the direction of the door, as if he might appear at any moment. She was breathless – from running, she said, to catch up with me. Her thin arms were peppered with freckles, her pale face drenched in light from the window which looked out on to the Dam. I was conscious of the covert attention she attracted from men in suits seated on high stools at the bar. I pointed with my cigarette towards Pijlsteeg.

'What's the story there?'

'Listen . . .'

That's when she said she could help me find Nikolaas. I asked if she knew him.

'Aye, ah know him.'

There is an illusion I seldom perform – requiring, as it does, the expense of hiring a second stage-assistant. The Bangkok Bungalow illusion, or Now You See Him, Now You Don't. It opens with Peter Prestige directing his audience's gaze towards a doll's house on a curtained platform. I close the curtains. I state that a person hiding inside the doll's house will be made to appear. When I open the curtains, a man – tall, well built – is standing on the platform. Announcing a reversal of the process, I close the curtains momentarily before opening them again to show the man has gone, supposedly back inside the doll's house.

At this point I pick up the doll's house and hand it to The Lovely Kim, who carries it off-stage. The spectators aren't having any of this, drawing vociferous attention to a suspicious bulge in the folds of the curtains. Amid much clamouring for me to expose the man hiding there, I whip the curtains away and cast them to the floor. The platform is bare, the man has truly vanished. Applause, etc. I shan't tell you, so don't ask. All I am prepared to say is that the man is at no time inside the doll's house.

The barman arrived, giving the table a brisk wipe and setting my beer down on a paper coaster. The young woman spoke to him in Dutch and he gave a curt nod. When he'd gone, she resumed our conversation, hunching forward over the table. Her upper half was duplicated in a reflective gloss left behind by the barman's damp cloth.

'He used tae live there, at thirty-seven,' she said. 'Ah'm no certain where he's at now, but ah know someone who might know.'

I looked at her. 'What's your name?'

'Tha' disnae matter. Wha' the fuck dis tha' matter?'

'It matters to me.'

As though selecting a name at random, she said, 'A'right, so ah'm Kirsty.'

'Where you from, Glasgow?'

'Fuckin' hell, ah've got about *two minutes*.'

Despite a vague physical resemblance to Dympna – the hair, the complexion – Kirsty reminded me more of Rosa, with her verbal spikiness and a cavalier disregard for the impression she made on those around her. *This is me, take it or leave it*. The contrast between her demeanour in the shadow of her companion outside No. 37, and there in the café-bar, could hardly have been more pronounced.

'He scares you, doesn't he?'

'Look, d'ye wannae find Nikolaas, or no?'

'They didn't have the right brand of cigarettes at the bar, so you had to hunt around. He believed your excuse for going out, you can make him believe that as well.'

She shook her head. 'It disnae work like tha', no wi' him.'

The barman returned with my sandwich and a pack of Camels. He slipped a till receipt under my coaster than spoke to Kirsty. She produced a small purse from a money belt around her waist, rooting in it for coins. I said I'd pay for her cigarettes. From the barman's expression, you would have thought I'd just farted. He retrieved the receipt, noted down the extra amount in biro and went away without a word.

'Barman a good friend of yours?' Kirsty didn't answer. She was preoccupied, glancing over her shoulder towards the door. 'How long you been over here?'

'Ah need cash,' she said, turning to face me again. She was fretting at the pack of Camels as though it were a rosary. 'Ye ken whit ah'm sayin'?'

'If I want to find Nikolaas, I've got to pay. Yeah?'

'Five hundred guilders. Half up front, half when ye get tae see him.'

I did a quick mental calculation: £160, give or take. I smiled. 'How much gear will that buy?'

As a reflex, she placed her right hand over her left bicep. She took her hand away again just as quickly. 'It's eczema,' she said. 'It's no whit ye think.'

'Go on,' I said, picking up my sandwich and taking a bite out of it.

'What?'

'Piss off out of here.'

Her fleeting look of alarm – almost panic – transformed into one of indifference. Feigned indifference, it seemed to me. She watched me eating for a moment. Her eyes – hazel, underscored by shadows – followed the motion of my fingers, my mouth. At length, tapping the unopened cigarette pack against the edge of the table, she said, 'If that's me oot ay here, then that's you: no Nikolaas.'

I replaced the half-eaten sandwich on its plate. Wiping my lips, I asked, 'How old are you, Kirsty? Eighteen? Nineteen?' Her veneer of nonchalance remained intact. 'Bilingual, working overseas, nice boyfriend . . . you've done well for yourself.'

'Dinnae patronize me, ye wanker.'

'How about Nikolaas, was he your boyfriend?'

Kirsty lowered her head. She didn't say anything. When she lifted her head again, she turned to look out of the window and I saw by the play of light that her eyes were moist. Outside, in Dam Square, a couple were explaining the workings of their camera to a passer-by so he could take their picture in front of the national monument.

'I need to find him,' I said, almost whispering.

She looked at me now, composed, back in control. 'Like ah say, five hundred.'

'You'll get your money after I've seen him. If I pay you up front, I might as well flush the money down the bog.'

'That's me, then.' She stood up, her chair scraping on the floor. 'Ah couldnae gi' a fuck if ye find him or no. S'your problem, pal.'

I held her wrist. The joint was so thin my thumb and middle finger completely enclosed it. I made her sit down. The barman and several customers were watching us. One of the men in suits muttered a remark to his drinking companions which provoked laughter. Kirsty's expression was moulded into a leer of contempt that encompassed me as well as them. I told her she'd have her payment, cash on delivery.

She extricated her wrist. I pushed my plate across the table, one sandwich untouched, the other half-consumed.

'Here, you look as if you haven't eaten for a fortnight.'

She looked at me and then at the food, peeling back one of the slices of bread to inspect the contents. She slid the plate back to me. 'Ah'm vegetarian.'

'You want me to order you something?'

'Ah'm oot ay here.'

She stood up again and this time I made no attempt to stop her. As she turned to go, I said, 'Five hundred, COD. Do we have a deal?'

She hesitated. I imagined her calculating the number of fixes she could score with that sum, weighing this against the risk of me failing to pay up – or, much worse, being found out by the man in the apartment at No. 37, who was, by now, wondering what was taking her so long. I needed her to be desperate enough.

'Aye, OK, deal.'

I leaned back in my seat. 'How soon can you find him for me?'

'Not today. Ah've tae make a couple ay calls.'

'Tomorrow, then. I'll be in here, same time.'

'No here.' She thought for a moment. 'D'ye ken the Bloemenmarkt, where they sell all the flowers and shit. It's on Singel.'

'I'll find it.'

'Two o'clock tomorrow.'

She left, pursued by the eyes of half the customers. When she'd gone some of them turned their attention momentarily to me. I finished my beer and sandwiches and revived the cigarette that had lain neglected on the lip of an ashtray. Smoking, gazing out of the window at the goings-on in the Dam. I didn't know what to make of Kirsty. I knew that I didn't trust her. However, I wasn't sure exactly what it was I didn't trust about her. What I felt confident about: one, she needed funds to feed her junk habit; two, she was palpably afraid of what awaited her at No. 37 if our deal was discovered. I stubbed out my cigarette. A gang in overalls was working the square, moving among the throngs of tourists, emptying rubbish bins into a yellow crusher-lorry and sucking up litter with an industrial vacuum cleaner. The café window vibrated with the noise as the men and their machinery went by. I settled my bill with the barman. It was only as I stood up to leave that I noticed something which, at that moment, seemed innocuous enough; it would be more alarming for Kirsty, when she realized, than for me. An oversight, that was all. An ironic one, even so, given the pretext for her subterfuge in coming to find me in the first place. The implications of what she'd done, albeit inadvertently, did not become apparent to me until later. Until it was too late. And, when they did, I cursed myself for failing to appreciate them sooner. Had I done so, the awful consequences of our meeting in the flower market the following afternoon would have been averted. At the time, however, I couldn't resist a smile as I saw that Kirsty, in her hurry to get back, had left the packet of cigarettes behind.

The first night, after the trick with the ash, Red asks how come I wear a ring on every finger and both thumbs. 'Tooms,' he says I call them.

I go, 'So it'll hurt you when I give you a hand-job.'

Anyway, he got me to go through them finger at a time and tell me all about where I got each one and how long I'd had it and what it's made of and what it 'signifies' – like, they're just rings and whoever gives a fucking shite? They're rings, and I wear them. The claddagh, he wants to know all about that one cos it's Irish and I'm Irish, so it's like he's finding out about me. And I think jesus christ will you spare me. And then I think fuck it Rosa your man's just interested. So I'm showing him.

'It's two hands holding a heart – see, there's the hands and there's the heart. If you wear it so the heart's pointing out, it means your heart's not given to anyone . . . the other way round means it is.'

Course, mine was pointing out.

He goes, 'Have you ever worn it with the heart the other way?'

'No. And don't hold your breath waiting for me to turn it round cos of you.'

Like I say, that was the first night. It's . . . what is it now? Fucked if I know, eight months? Just over. And I'm wearing it the other way. Didn't say nothing to Red, just turned it round one morning – had to use soap so's I could get the ring off my finger – and waited to see if he'd notice. Took him nearly a week. Then, today, I'm practising a card trick and he's watching and he stops me and takes hold of my hand and looks at the ring. Then he looks me in the face and smiles – not a proper smile, but like he's not sure if he should be smiling or not. But I can see he's well chuffed. He doesn't say nothing, he just keeps on holding my hand – rubbing his thumb over the ring – and then he gives me a kiss on the cheek. I look at the ring myself then, cos knowing him the bastard, he's probably done some trick and the fucking thing's pointing the other way again. But it isn't. I laugh at myself. And when he asks why I'm laughing I tell him and then he's after laughing as well.

Two lies, about the claddagh. I lied when I told him I'd bought it for myself – it was a present from Nik, for my eighteenth. And I lied when I told Red I'd never worn it pointing in.

A Big Hand for the Girls

It was the first time my fidelity was tested, I suppose, since I'd met Rosa. Brighton. I was booked to play a couple of nights. It was a weekend, and I suggested Rosa and Tony join us to make a holiday of it. I thought it would work out, but Rosa didn't take to Tony, and seeing as how she and Kim weren't exactly kissy-huggy at the best of times, conversation became strained. We quarrelled about it, Rosa and me. The second afternoon in our hotel, as I was getting ready to go to the theatre, I said, 'You don't make much of an effort with people you don't like, do you?'

'Who, those two?' She jerked her thumb at the wall dividing our room from theirs. 'Who says I don't like them?'

'It creates an atmosphere when you act like this.'

'Oh, *atmosphere*, is it?'

And so it went on, degenerating into an argument made ludicrous by the need to keep our voices down to avoid being overheard by Tony and Kim. It was this, the element of farce, which ultimately defused the row. *Who the fuck are you whispering at . . . ? You're the one who's whispering . . . Don't you lower your voice at me . . .*

'C'mere, Red, you can be OK when you stop taking yourself so serious.'

I left it at that. With Rosa, I'd learned to be patient. Sure enough, towards the latter part of the holiday she was more her usual self, talkative, ready with a smile. This improvement in her spirits, however, coincided with a decline in Tony's; now, he was the one creating the atmosphere. And I think I know why. Something occurred that Saturday night at the theatre and – somehow, I don't know how – he'd intuited it.

We were backstage, Kim and I, getting changed and cleaned up after the show in time to meet the others for a drink and something to eat. A shared dressing room, though this wasn't uncommon given the limited facilities at some provincial venues. During our affair, of course, it hadn't been a problem. But once that had ended and we'd begun new relationships, we tried to respect one another's privacy no matter how cramped and potentially intimate the arrangements. That night in Brighton Kim came up behind my chair as I was removing my make-up. Our eyes engaged in the dressing-table mirror. I was stripped to the waist; she was wearing a white towelling bathrobe. Her hair was wet. Smiling at my reflection, she referred to the enthusiastic copulation we'd overheard through the walls of our adjoining rooms the previous night.

'I have to admit, I got quite turned on listening to you and Rosa.'

I smiled back. 'Did you?'

She nodded. 'I couldn't help picturing the two of you . . . you know.'

I didn't tell her I'd become similarly aroused, thoughts of Kim and Tony firing my imagination as Rosa and I fucked. Kim's hand came to rest on my shoulder, where the skin had been dampened by droplets of water from her hair. We continued to watch one another's faces in the mirror, hers oddly lopsided when viewed in reverse.

'Shall I tell you what else makes me horny?' she asked. I didn't reply. 'The idea of you and me fucking, in here, while they're in the bar waiting for us.'

We didn't fuck. There was a knock, followed by the appearance of one of the theatre staff with a batch of programmes for us to autograph. By the time he'd gone, the moment – the mood – had passed. I wondered then, and again now: would I have succumbed if it hadn't been for the interruption? Truth is, I don't know. But I believe the possibility of what *might* have happened left a subliminal trace that eluded Rosa but which Tony detected. There was a transformation in him that evening. Sullen, uncommunicative. From then on, it was a matter of surviving the weekend.

I never told Rosa what nearly took place between me and Kim

in that dressing room. There wasn't an appropriate opportunity – at least, not one that coincided with a moment when I had the courage to say something.

Someone dies, and you fill your life with things that aren't grief. You busy yourself; only, you can't do that for ever and you can't do it every minute of every day. It finds you, grief does. I phoned Denis Huting from my hotel room. *I miss Rosa*, I said, when the sobbing ceased and I was able to speak. My eyes alighted on the miniature plastic chicken – bright orange – he'd presented to me, which now stood on the bedside table. *I miss her.* He told me to eat. It was unhealthy to cry on an empty stomach. *Eat sugar. Then, at nine, I will come for you and we will go to the walletjes.*

At one minute to nine, reception called. I took the lift down to the lobby, where Denis was flirting with the young clerk on the front desk. One of his favourite pastimes, making straight guys blush. We walked to the Leidseplein. Denis hailed a taxi, gave instructions to the driver, and we set off into the night-time traffic, chiefly comprised of cyclists riding without lights. Which made me think of Rosa again.

'What's this place you're taking me to?' I asked.

'The *walletjes* is not a place, it is an area. It means "little walls", because this is the area of the city walls, historically speaking. Now it is the red-light district.'

'If you're taking me to get laid, forget it.'

Denis, who filled most of the rear seat of the taxi, gave my knee a slap. 'Don't worry, Red, no getting laid. I'm taking you to a show.'

We came to a halt in a sidestreet just along from a large, unattractive church – the *Oude Kerk* – a medieval building, incongruously denoting the geographical heart of Amsterdam's sex zone. Denis paid the driver and we got out. The theatre was flanked by a bar and a neon-lit shop selling porn videos, magazines and erotic accessories; the centre-piece of its window display was a pink dildo at least a foot long. As for the theatre, its frontage was more discreet – black walls adorned with 'Acht en Twintig' in neat white lettering, the name evidently derived from the street number of the premises. A billboard advertised that evening's entertainment:

Tonite – Magic Show

Denis bought tickets from a kiosk inside the entrance and we went up a steep staircase; at the top, a professionally cheerful hostess led us through heavy curtains into the auditorium. Pillars clad in mirrored mosaic gave glimmering reiteration to the sole source of light – candles, in red-tinted glass bowls, at each of some fifty tables formed in a horseshoe around a stage. Most were occupied, mostly by men; there was a hubbub of combined conversations. A nebulous pink plume of cigarette smoke hung beneath the ceiling. In one corner was a bar, the waitresses – all young, all dressed in skimpy cheerleader-style outfits – swarming to and fro with trays of drinks and snacks.

'Not your sort of hang-out, I wouldn't have thought?' I remarked to Denis, as we sat down. He didn't hear me, preoccupied as he was with tipping the hostess. She left, smiling, to be succeeded almost immediately by a waitress.

'Beer?' Denis asked, still breathless from the stairs. I nodded. He ordered *twee pils*, and something else I didn't catch, then turned to me and said, 'Great place, yeah?'

'Are you serious?'

Evidently uncomfortable, he claimed a second chair and repositioned himself, one buttock on each. Mopping his forehead with an orange handkerchief, he stilled my next question (*What are we doing h . . . ?*) by gesturing towards the stage. A musical introduction – taped, warbly – was being played, the noise in the auditorium was fading, a solitary spotlight picked out the point where the stage curtains met. The voice of an unseen compère welcomed the audience in four languages. At the moment when our waitress arrived with two frothing glasses of beer and two apple pastries, the curtains parted and, to a roar of approval, a magician and his assistant stepped into the spotlight. You could tell he was a magician because he wore a top hat and carried a wand. These items apart, he – and his pretty assistant – were stark naked.

Goedenavond, guten abend, bon soir, good evening . . . I am the great, the one and only . . . Nudini! [he smiles] Tonight I give you . . . Fucking Magic!

. . . the assistant (slim and tanned, her pubic hairs trimmed into the shape of a heart) turns her back to the audience and bends over, legs apart. Cheers, wolf-whistles. We see that something protrudes from her labia. The magician removes it, raising the object aloft: a ping-pong ball. He produces another and another, more than twenty in all – the illusion culminating in the assistant expelling the final ball from her vagina with such force that it arcs through the air and lands in the lap of a startled, but delighted, member of the audience. Huge cheers, laughter. Applause . . .

. . . the assistant lies on her back and, with a wave of Nudini's magic wand, she begins to levitate – rising two or three feet, then returning to the floor; he tries again, but cannot sustain the levitation. As though struck by an idea, the illusionist causes her to rise once more and while she hovers horizontally positions himself between her legs and enters her, so that it seems his penis is all that keeps her aloft. Cheers . . .

. . . the Great Nudini displays a length of cotton thread and half a dozen razor blades. The magician winds the cotton into a ball and places it in her vagina. Next, he inserts one blade after another. Gasps, groans. In four languages, he asks if a member of the audience will step on to the stage and fuck her. More laughter. Nudini makes a play of trying to drag one spectator from his seat. The man declines. Returning to the stage, the conjuror taps the assistant with the magic wand and, searching between her labia, slowly pulls out the length of cotton – now threaded, as if by magic, with the razor blades. Applause, whistles . . .

. . . an upright cabinet is wheeled on-stage and the assistant is shut inside. The Great Nudini dismantles the cabinet into four box-like sections which he reassembles in a different order, stacking them one on top of the other. When the doors to each box are opened, the hips, thighs and heart-shaped pubes are revealed at the top, the breasts and stomach are visible in the second box, the head and shoulders in the third, and the legs and feet in the fourth. The magician begins at the top, fingering and licking the exposed vagina; after a moment, he turns his attention to the second box, caressing the breasts and sucking at the nipples; next, box three – he kneels so that his erect penis can be placed into the mouth of the assistant's apparently severed head. She gives him a blow-job, which concludes with semen dribbling down her chin. Rapturous applause. He closes the doors to the four sections and puts them back together in the correct order. The assistant steps out, smiling, her lips still shiny with the magician's discharge. To a standing ovation, the Great Nudini and his pretty assistant take a bow . . .

. . . *Dank u, en tot ziens; danke, und auf wiedersehen; merci, et au revoir; thank you, and bye-bye* . . .

Ice-Cream

I have performed each of those illusions with The Lovely Kim; at least, variations of them. I've produced ping-pong balls from her mouth . . . I've caused her to levitate, supported by my little finger beneath the base of her left heel . . . I've made her swallow razor blades then reeled them from her mouth on a length of thread . . . I have enacted the Illusion of the Mismade Girl, tickling her belly button and stealing a kiss from her severed head before putting her back together again. I admit this. I admitted as much to Denis Huting when he challenged my criticism of the Great Nudini.

'He is a magician, like you,' said Denis. 'He makes new ways of performing old tricks. That is all.'

I shook my head. 'He's a pornographer.'

'First, he's a magician. Second, he's a pornographer.'

Midnight in an ice-cream parlour on Leidseplein. We were both ravenous after beer and hash cookies at the bar next door to the Acht en Twintig theatre.

'What do you do to The Lovely Kim?' He swallowed a mouthful of honey-and-praline. 'You tie her up, you cut her into pieces, you put sticks and swords into her, you lock her up inside a box, she appears and disappears when you say so, you make her on fire . . .' he smacked one palm against the other '. . . you crush her.'

'Magician as violator, is that what you're saying?'

He gave a shrug. 'She is a body, and you abuse her.'

I'd heard Rosa's friend Dympna propose a similar theory one drunken night in Oxford. *Why are magicians so obsessed with bondage and penetration?* I wanted to tell Denis what I'd told her – the premise of a performance was irrelevant because magic, above all, was about illusion, conjuror and assistant alike being subservient to that end. The significant relationship wasn't that of male conjuror to female assistant, but that of conjuror/assistant to illusion. But how did that fit the logic of my objection to Nudini's act on the grounds of its sexually explicit content? So, I merely said, 'I once asked Kim if she felt exploited.'

'What did she say?'

'She said, "If we're talking about how much you pay me, then yes I do."'

Denis smiled. He ate more ice-cream. 'But it isn't exploitation. It is – what's the English? – you make an object of her.'

'Objectification.'

'Yes. If you make someone just an object, you can abuse her and feel nothing yourself because you are the superior one. She is nothing to you.'

'What we saw *tonight* was an objectification of women. And about as crude an example as you could get.'

'Crude? Or honest? You think it is more honest for you and Kim to keep your clothes on and pretend what you do is nothing about sex?'

'I'm talking about subtlety of presentation.'

'So long as you are subtle, it is OK? It is *art*.' He shook his head. 'Red, my friend, you are dishonest if you believe this.'

'All right, all right, what about striptease? Should the woman, the artiste, begin fully clothed and . . . and slowly *unveil* herself, or would it give you a bigger turn-on to see her stark naked from the moment she steps on stage?'

Denis arched an eyebrow, *faux camp*, and we both burst out laughing. And, with that, discussion gave way to companionable silence. When we'd finished our ice-cream, I reclined in my seat and tried to gauge whether the effects of the hash-and-beer binge were wearing off. No, the unequivocal answer.

'You still woozy?' I asked, tapping the side of my head.

'So-so.' Denis dabbed his mouth with a serviette. His face was flushed. He surveyed his dessert carton, perplexed by its emptiness. 'When you're so big as me, some of the drugs get lost trying to find their way to your brain.'

I removed a pack of B&H and a lighter from my jacket

pocket, looking around for no-smoking signs. 'Is it OK in here, d'you think?'

'In Amsterdam, it is OK anywhere.' Another smile. 'Unless you are with me.'

'For fuck's sake.' I put the cigarettes away. ''Been Rosa, she'd have lit a fag and shoved it up your nose.'

When we left the ice-cream parlour I accompanied Denis to a taxi rank on the opposite side of the deserted square at Leidse-plein. A fine drizzle was falling. The tramlines glinted beneath an anaemic white light cast by the streetlamps, undispersed water globules accumulating like perspiration on their greasy surface. There were no taxis. I said I'd wait to see him off before making the short walk back to my hotel.

'You will get wet.'

'I don't mind. It's quite refreshing, actually.'

Denis had raised the hood on his coat and drawn it tight so that only his eyes, nose and mouth remained visible. 'How are you feeling now?'

His question caught me unawares. I had to think for a moment. 'About Rosa?' I asked. He nodded. 'OK. OK, really. I think it helped, having a night out on the town with you.' Another pause. 'I feel like shite, if you want the truth.'

He didn't say anything.

'Fact is, I want her not to be dead.'

A drip had formed on the end of Denis's nose. He blew it off. Staring vaguely in the direction from which a taxi might appear, then turning back to me again, he said, 'I lost a good friend. My "um", before Cees. AIDS, you know? Pneumonia, but AIDS. I could not live for two years without him.'

'I'm sorry, I didn't know that.'

A car shooshed past on the wet road, then another. 'Then, after two years, someone says to me, "He is gone, but your love for him is not. Believe only in that – your love for him – because it is better to hold on to something which is alive than something which is dead."' Denis looked at me. 'So that is what I did.'

'Did it work?'

'No.' He laughed, and so did I. We laughed for a long time,

each time we stopped we'd set one another off again. At last, serious again, he managed to add, 'They are only words.'

'But they help?'

'Yes. A little.'

A taxi had arrived, parked with its engine idling. The driver waited with what appeared to be a mixture of patience and complete indifference for us to terminate our conversation. He was smoking, gazing out of the windscreen at the wet night. Denis raised a hand, pressing his thumb firmly to the corner of my mouth.

'Ice-cream,' he explained. He licked his thumb clean. 'Blueberry cheesecake.'

We said good-night. Then he let himself into the taxi, the vehicle visibly sinking on its suspension as he sat down. The driver eased the car away from the kerb without indicating and drove off. I thought I saw Denis waving to me out of the rear window, but it was dark and the glass was grimy and rain-spattered; for all I know, he may just have been lowering his hood.

The bar at the end of Pijlsteeg. We're guzzling. It's been . . . I don't know. Hours. I don't know how many hours since the last shot and Nik's holding out on me. For my own good, he says. Like, fucking yeah. He says he'll make me a 'pannekoek met marihuana' to keep me going. Fuck sake. He just shrugs and says if I want to kill myself that's my problem, but he's not going to help me do it. Wim. What's Wim saying? He's going on about something . . . a photo. He wants to take a photo of me and Nik. Fine. Fine. I mean, do what you fucking like.

'Get my best side,' I go.

Wim looks at me, like there's this fucking puzzle in his head and it's so fucking com-pli-ca-ted. Nik's got his arm round my shoulders and he's leaning his head close and we're holding our beers. A toast. Wim's fiddling with the camera. And I'm thinking few hours ago, jesus christ that hand – Wim's hand – was shoved up to the wrist inside my arsehole.

He takes the photo. I say I'm going to the loo. Renata's supposed to come with me, but Nik's taking a picture of her and Wim now and anyway everyone's too slaughtered to give a fuck.

I'm sitting here trying to piss and I feel . . . I'm feeling so fucking shite. Just shite. I look at my watch. Another half-hour and we're due back at 37. Bunch of American businessmen – floor show, then solos – so no shot till after and that could be, like, hours away. Fucking three or four in the morning. I've been in here too long. I go out to the basins. I'm bending over, splashing water on my face, and there's this woman washing her hands. I stand up and I can see her in the mirror, gawping at me. Too long. Like it's a pick-up or something, only she doesn't look the type as far as you can tell. Tall, dark-haired, pretty; older than me by a few years. I don't remember seeing her in the bar, but she must've been there somewhere. She gives me this smile. Fuck sake, it is a pick-up. Only, she goes, 'You OK?'

I don't say nothing. I go over to the dryers. Your woman comes over as well. She's looking at the door now. She looks scared. I'm drying my hands and face. Then she shoves something in my back pocket.

I go, 'I don't do dyke for free.'

She nods at the door. 'OK. You're happy with these people, don't call me.'

Close up, it's a wig. Your woman's wearing a fucking wig. I go, 'Yeah, sure, I'll call you.'

She touches my shoulder. But she doesn't say nothing, just gives me a squeeze and walks out, back into the bar. I take the paper out of my pocket and unfold it. Maybe there's a twist of H or rock inside, but there isn't. Just writing. 'Lena'. And a phone number. I look at it for a minute, then screw it up and drop it in the bin. I'm almost out of there when I stop and go back and stand gawping at the bin like the bin's going to make my mind up for me. Any second now, Renata's through that door wondering where the fuck I've got to. I can't find the piece of paper right away, but I rummage around for it and there it is. I fold it up into a tiny square and slide it under my biggest, chunkiest ring so the ring's tight on my finger now and you can't see the wedge of paper, but I can feel it, digging into the skin.

You were purchasing some bulbs, perhaps? Or sightseeing, taking photographs?

Yes, sightseeing.

So. You are looking around the bloemenmarkt. What time was this?

I don't know. Two o'clock, something like that.

Two o'clock. And you were alone?

Yes.

There is no one with you in Amsterdam?

No, I'm here by myself. Just a holiday.

What is your job, in England, Mr Clarke?

I work for a building society. Mortgages, savings, that sort of thing.

You are not married?

Oh, yes. Lisa.

Children?

Three. Two girls and a boy.

A married man with three children, on holiday by himself. In a city like Amsterdam, this is not altogether unusual, if you understand me.

That's not why . . .

Please. You are a man and so am I.

. . .

Anyway, perhaps this is for the evenings. Hey? But this afternoon, something different.

. . .

How much time did you spend there, looking at the flowers?

Not long. Half an hour, maybe.

So. You look around for thirty minutes. Then where did you go?

I went into a kind of alleyway off the Singel.

Why did you go there?

I . . . was looking for somewhere to eat. I was hungry.

You did not have your lunch until this time? Two thirty?

I just wanted a coffee or something. A cake, you know.

You wanted coffee and a cake?

Yes.

And you went into the steeg to get this?

There was another street, at the end of the alleyway – parallel to Singel. It looked . . . I thought there might be a coffee shop or something.

Reguliersdwarsstraat?

I don't know its name.

You are in the steeg. So. You are by yourself?

Yes.

You see, because there is a witness who saw you walking with a young woman.

No.

A woman with red hair and very white skin. Not so tall. Very pretty. You were talking to her?

No.

That is what our witness tells us.

Then your witness must be mistaken.

There were a lot of people? Perhaps this woman is walking nearby and the witness thinks you are together – is this possible?

Maybe, I don't know. I can't think of any other explanation.

No. I cannot, either.

. . .

The steeg was busy?

I don't remember.

And you are just walking by yourself?

I told you, yes. Jesus.

. . .

Sorry.

. . .

. . .

What happened then, Mr Clarke?

★

Tulips, in every variety and colour. I have never seen so many in one place. Row upon row of them arranged in trays that stretched all the way along the street, on the ground and on trestle tables, beneath great canvas awnings and makeshift shelters of plastic sheeting puddled with the remnants of morning rain. Mostly tulips, but many other flowers besides – pansies, chrysanthemums, marigolds – and a host more I couldn't name; an expanse of colour, the cool air impregnated with an almost overwhelming perfume. Plants, too, and countless trays and sacks of bulbs and display boards arrayed with packets of seeds. The stalls formed a narrow ribbon running the length of the Singel, some fronting on to the street while others occupied floating pontoons and flat-bottomed boats moored along the canal itself. People, everywhere – browsing, taking pictures, bargaining with the stall-holders; impossible to move through the market at anything more than a shuffle. I checked my watch. Five to two. Somewhere amidst all this confusion, I was expected to find Kirsty. Or she would find me.

I strolled aimlessly, distracted, scanning the kaleidoscope of bodies and faces for a glimpse of someone who might be her. At one point I jolted into a stand of bulbs, almost dislodging a tray from its shelf and reaping a torrent of Dutch invective from the stall-holder. Five past . . . ten past. My meandering became more methodical. I'd start at Muntplein and work my way along the street as far as Koningsplein, then return through those stalls afloat upon the canal, their wooden floorboards rolling and pitching gently, almost imperceptibly, beneath my feet. Twenty past . . . twenty-five past. I'd completed several painstaking circuits of the bloemenmarkt, resigning myself to the probability that there was to be no meeting. She'd stood me up. Whether she had chosen not to come or been prevented from doing so, I'd no idea. Perhaps Kirsty had never intended to meet me . . . . whatever, she wasn't there. It was only once my attention drifted, and I began taking in the sights and smells, the vibrant bustle of the market, instead of scrutinizing every passing face for hers, that she appeared. The sound of bells diverted me, drawing my gaze skywards to an ornate stone clocktower whose carillon was chiming a melodic tune. When I lowered my gaze again Kirsty was standing in profile before me, our bodies too close in the press of people. She was feigning interest in a display of verbena. Rubbing one of the leaves between thumb and middle finger, she raised her hand to her face and inhaled.

'Ye widnae think a plant could smell so strong ay lemon,' she said, as though speaking to herself. She didn't look at me.

'What am I supposed to say: "I hear the tulips are blooming in Berlin"?'

I swear she almost let slip a smile. She was wearing her hair down, making her face smaller and rounder. Heavy make-up; more soberly dressed than before, however – a navy-blue woollen jumper, jeans and sneakers. She looked at her watch.

'I'd more or less given up on you.'

'Aye, well, it wisnae easy tae get away.'

Seemingly without orchestration, we'd moved away from the display and fallen in step, walking casually along a congested aisle between racks of souvenirs: decorated clogs, picture postcards, pieces of blue-and-white delft ceramic. Kirsty made a cursory inspection of the postcards. We stood in such forced proximity I could smell her: a powerful scent of coconut. She pretended to kiss the side of my face.

'Ye got the dosh?'

'You give me Nikolaas's phone number,' I said, returning her fake kiss. 'And when I've spoken to him, you'll have your money.'

'I can dae better'n tha', I can take ye tae him.'

'What, *now*?'

'Aye. Coupl'ay minutes frae here.' She returned my gaze unwaveringly, pushing a strand of hair away where it had snagged at the corner of her mouth. 'So?'

'Let's go, then.'

'Five hundred.'

'Five hundred, COD.'

She checked her watch again, then turned in the direction from which we'd just come and led us out into Singel; we were walking more quickly than before, but still with the natural, easy gait of sightseers.

'Another five hundred, we can go tae your hotel afterwards,' she said, matter-of-factly, without so much as a sideways glance. 'If ye like.'

'I don't think so.'

'Suit yesel.'

'Besides, I heard the window girls charge fifty.'

'Aye, an' that's whit ye get – a fifty-guilder fuck.'

We continued in silence for a moment, then turned off into one of a series of pedestrianized alleys, similar to Pijlsteeg only shorter and less dilapidated. There were few people about: a man, pausing by a flight of stone steps to refasten a shoelace, an elderly couple – tourists, by the look of them – aiming for a point where the steeg was truncated by a much busier street. Kirsty gestured up ahead, explaining that Nikolaas was waiting for us in a coffee shop. A pigeon, startled as it investigated a mess of compressed burger, fled almost from under our feet and flapped away to a high ledge. Kirsty flinched, emitting a yelp of alarm, her reaction quite out of proportion to the incident. I was about to say something to her when the man by the steps stood up from tying his laces and, waving an unlit cigarette at us, asked in broken English if we had a light. Curly blond hair and threadbare moustache. I stopped beside him, reaching into my jacket pocket. Kirsty kept on walking. As I produced my lighter, I saw that, far from slowing down, she'd quickened her pace, not waiting for me or even glancing over her shoulder to see what I was doing. I called her name. In that instant, the man gripped my arm and drew me roughly towards him, spilling the lighter to the ground with a clatter. In the hand with which he'd been holding the cigarette there was now a knife. The flat of the blade pressed cold and hard against my mouth. His breath smelled of mushrooms. I tried to pull away, but another pair of hands was holding me – my neck, my left elbow – a second man having waylaid me from the rear with such stealth I hadn't even registered his footsteps. Kirsty was running now, sprinting towards the end of the alley without once looking back. The second man – black, unshaven, his face pressed cheek-to-cheek against mine – said, 'OK, this is no problem.'

They positioned themselves either side of me, walking me along the uneven brick cobbles in simulation of two friends helping a drunken mate home from the pub. No sign of Kirsty now. At the head of the steeg, a car had pulled up in the main road, engine running, the front and rear nearside doors open. The two men were marching me towards it. I said nothing; my mouth filled with unuttered words like the internal scream of a nightmare. Suffocation. It was all I could do to breathe, to open my mouth and gulp cool air. I wasn't even conscious of walking, of putting one foot down and then the next; my legs had become inert appendages, scuffing uselessly along the ground. I was dependent upon these two men; without their support, I would fall and I wouldn't be able to get up again. The car. Grey. Its doors wide open, waiting for us. Only a little way now and I would be able to sit down. Then, a door banged open directly in front of us and a man in workmen's blue overalls emerged backwards, carrying a small table. There was a collision, the table hitting the ground with a sound of splintering wood. In the confusion, both men relaxed their grip on my arms – only for a moment, but long enough for me to wrench myself free. I wheeled away, turning to run. But one of them regained a hold of my wrist, tugging me off balance and swinging me headlong towards the wall of the alley. My left shoulder took the impact. They were both on me now, pinioning me against the wall so that my face was pressed into the brickwork. One of them punched me; one of them kicked me in the back of the leg. Someone was shouting in Dutch: the workman in blue overalls. I couldn't see him, though I heard his shouts, and the scuffling of feet; I didn't see what he did to them. But suddenly I wasn't up against the wall any more. A car horn blared twice. I turned to see the blond one sitting on the ground several feet away, holding a hand to his face, trying and failing to stand up. His accomplice and the workman were heaving and grunting like two wrestlers. That car horn again. The first man was up now, unsteady. His nose was a mess, slopping clots of blood on to the ground as he stooped to reach for something. Going over to the other two, he punched the man in the overalls – once, twice, three times in the ribs – while he was still trapped in a sumo embrace. A flurry of uppercuts, each blow forcing a gasp of ejaculated air. Car horn, a long persistent blast. I ran. I ran away from the car, from the three men fighting; I retreated full tilt along the alleyways towards the market. A blur of people, of voices. Flowers. Someone lurching, arms outstretched as if to hug me. But all I could see, in my mind, was a man's fist: punching, punching, punching. Enclosed in his fist was a knife, its steel blade stained red up to the hilt.

The Calling Card

An illusionist's essential concern is to enable his audience to appreciate the 'trick' without exposing the trickery. His challenge, therefore, is to make them simultaneously attentive and inattentive, alert and dull-witted, perceptive and unobservant – to cause them (individually and collectively) to notice some things while failing to notice others. His talent is guile. His medium is the fallibility of the senses. To those who deride the *science* of magic, I say: we live in an age when science has been sapped of some of its power to make us marvel. A rocket blasts off into space and we sit in our own living room and watch it as it happens, *taking this for granted*. Yet I, a mere magician, can hold an audience spellbound; I can make people marvel; I can make them ask, How the fuck does he do that? What it is, the accomplishments of modern science are so complex, so far outside the scope of our comprehension, that we give up even trying to understand them. We simply accept. It isn't necessary to know how a space shuttle – a video recorder, a mobile phone, a CD player, a computer – *works* in order to use one. With magic, however, the 'workings' of an illusion seem knowable, albeit frustratingly poised just beyond our grasp. And so, we engage with the pretence of the magical in a way in which we seldom can with the fact of technological miracle. I put this idea to Paul, a while back and, imitating Rosa, he replied that I was talking out of my arse.

I was simultaneously attentive and inattentive, alert and dull-witted, perceptive and unobservant. Me, a magician. In a steeg between Singel and Reguliersdwarsstraat, I believed Kirsty was escorting me to a meeting with Nikolaas van Zandt. I believed the blond man who'd been tying his shoelaces was genuinely seeking a light for his cigarette. Also, I believed I saw him land three punches to the ribs of the workman in blue overalls who had come to my aid. Punches, not stabs – I didn't see the knife until after the ultimate blow. Which is why, under interrogation by an Amsterdam police inspector, I puzzled him by one of my replies. Q: *Did you witness the stabbing?* A: *I must've done, because he had a knife in his hand.* He asked me to be more explicit; I described what I saw and how I saw it. At first, the police thought I was a party to the stabbing, the officer who apprehended me at the end of the steeg, assuming that my absconding from the scene was evidence of culpability. While he held me his colleague gave chase to my supposed accomplices. But the two men reached the car awaiting them and were driven away at speed. Their pursuer was left to attend to the workman, slumped in approximation of the Muslim prayer position. Beside him, an upturned table with one fractured leg; the blood had pooled in such a way that, from a distance, it appeared to be issuing from the table rather than the man. It was an eyewitness – an office worker overlooking events from a first-floor window – who informed the police that I had, in fact, been trying to resist an assault by the two escapees when the other man intervened. An attempted mugging, was her assessment, or a random, unprovoked attack. She couldn't be sure. I confirmed this interpretation during questioning at the police station. I persisted, however, in refuting the evidence of another eyewitness – a stall-holder in the flower market who said he'd seen me and an attractive young redhead walking together along Singel shortly before the stabbing. My interrogator – Inspector Oosterling – didn't believe me. At least, he made it plain that he was dubious about the non-existence of my female companion and this, in turn, appeared to cast doubt in his mind over my status as victim of an indiscriminate crime. The redhead bothered him. But, for the time being, and in the absence of conclusive evidence to the contrary, he let it go at that. I signed a statement; I gave the name of my hotel. My identity was verified – passport details and home address obtained by telephone from the Terdam and entered into a computer. I noted the irony that Insp. Oosterling was so preoccupied with distrusting what I *said* that he neglected to distrust who I *was*. If I presented myself as Mr Taaffe Clarke and possessed the documentation to substantiate this, then, as far as he was concerned, I was Mr Taaffe Clarke. Each time he addressed me by name, I had to suppress the surge of exhilaration and guilt that accompanies successful deceit. Interrogation over, I was free to leave. However, it would be necessary, the inspector said, for me to remain in Amsterdam for a few days to assist with further inquiries. Was that a problem? No. A police doctor examined me. *Bomps and bruces. Maybe some shock. Take a painkiller and go to bed.* Oosterling conducted me out of the building. As we paused beside a patrol car waiting to take me back to the hotel, I asked if the man who'd been stabbed was going to be all right. The inspector looked at me, then looked away.

'I'm sorry,' he said. 'But he already died.'

A Thursday afternoon. I know it was a Thursday because it was Rosa's birthday, and her birthday fell on a Thursday last year. She'd been living with me for nine months and in all that time I'd only phoned her once at the *Erin* offices – that one call earning a fierce rebuke and an insistence that under no circumstances was I to do so again. *Your man can't abide us having personal calls while we're working.*

'What if it's an emergency?' I asked.

'Like what?'

'I dunno . . .'

For months, I made sure not to phone her at work. Then, on her birthday, I came home from morning rehearsals to find a message on the answering machine. It was from a local florist, informing me that she'd been unable to deliver the bouquet I ordered because the recipient wasn't at the address I'd given. I rang the florist. *Our girl went to the newspaper, but they told her Miss Kelly was off today.* I arranged for the flowers to be brought to the house instead and hung up. Rosa had left as usual after breakfast, perfectly well and saying nothing abut having a day off. I checked the *Erin* number, picked up the handset and dialled. I gave my name and asked to speak to Rosa, but it was Dympna who came on the line. She sounded artificially breezy.

'Hi, Red.'

'Is Rosa there?'

There was the slightest hesitation. 'No.'

'Only, I sent some flowers – you know, for her birthday – and the florist said Rosa wasn't there when they tried to deliver them.'

'Oh, right.'

'So, what . . . was she on her break or something?'

'Yeah, I expect so.'

I paused. 'Is she on another break now?'

'No. No, she's . . . the thing is, she's in with Conal at the moment. Going through some filing he wants her to do. I can't really disturb them, because . . .'

'Because Conal *can't aboide* his staff receiving personal calls.'

Dympna gave a cheery laugh. ''Fraid so.'

'OK.'

'Look, I'd better go.'

A scene imprinted itself on my imagination of Conal and Rosa locked inside his office, the pair of them fucking across the desk. Which was ludicrous because, as far as I knew, she wasn't even *at* work, let alone shagging her boss. But she was shagging someone, somewhere – I convinced myself of that, in the three hours between making that call and Rosa's return home. Why else go through the pretence, the subterfuge, of leaving for work? Why else deceive me and get her best friend to cover for her?

She came in at the usual time. The bouquet was on the kitchen table, still in its ribbons and wrapping. She read the card, then hugged me. The lack of response caused her to withdraw. *What's up?* I explained. When I'd finished with facts, I set about the speculation. The argument, the accusations and protestations of innocence, raged, counter-accusations too – Rosa was infuriated that I'd checked up on her. I was jealous, possessive, insecure. I was pathetic. I was spying on her, and I was pathetic. I said if she wanted to fuck someone else, she could at least have the decency to fuck off first.

'You know where I was?' she said. 'I was at *work*.'

'So how d'you explain these?' I gestured at the flowers.

'You explain them, 'cos I'm bollixed if I have to.'

She went out, returning after midnight and sleeping in the spare room. In the morning, she'd already left the house by the time I got up. That evening, Rosa told me nobody at *Erin* knew anything about any flowers. So she'd made some inquiries and it transpired that the delivery girl had knocked at the door of the company occupying the ground-floor offices, instead of going up to the first floor. The receptionist there had blanked at the name Rosa Kelly, and the girl – *thick as shite, I shouldn't wonder* – must've gone away without trying the other premises. I pointed out that the florist said the girl had been told it was Miss Kelly's day off. Rosa shrugged.

'She fucked up the delivery, and now she's lying to get herself out of trouble.'

I didn't say anything.

Rosa pointed down the hallway. 'Go on, then, if you don't believe me. Ring your woman in the office downstairs and see what she says. Go on.'

'There won't be anyone . . .'

'They don't finish till half six. *Go on.*'

I didn't make the call. What I did, later that evening, was ask Rosa how the dictation had gone with Conal the previous afternoon. Her perplexed frown appeared genuine. *I wasn't taking dictation*, she said. *I was filing.*

In my room at the Terdam, I locked the door, shut all the windows and sat on the bed. After some time, I undressed and showered. My shoulder was sore, and I had to soap myself with one hand. I left the shower, dried myself, then had another shower. I had three showers, one after the other. Then I sat naked and wet on the bed for a while before having another. Then I puked copiously into the toilet. It was six in the evening. I took two of the painkillers the police doctor had given me, drew the curtains and went to bed. I lay with my eyes shut. When I opened them again it was dark outside, but I hadn't slept. The pain in my shoulder had been reduced to a dull ache.

I got the cigarettes out of my jacket pocket, but I couldn't smoke because my lighter was still lying in a steeg off the flower market. I fetched a glass tumbler from the bathroom and poured whisky into it from the duty-free I'd bought on the flight from London. I drank. I dialled room service and ordered a box of matches. I sat on the bed, waiting. When the matches came, I smoked for a while and drank more whisky. And the whole time – whatever I did, whatever I tried to make myself think about, regardless of whether my eyes were open or closed – all I had in my head, filling it, was the stabbing, in ceaseless replay. The sound of fist against ribs, driving the blade in: thwock, thwock, thwock. Air, expelled in gasps from the man's lungs. Bright blood, on bright metal.

It was later that evening, after another failure to sleep, that I decided to go out. A walk. Fresh air. A few beers in a bar somewhere. I retrieved my jacket from the floor. The wallet wasn't in its usual pocket. It wasn't in any of the pockets. It wasn't in my trouser pockets. It wasn't to be found anywhere in the room. I thought carefully about this. The wallet must've fallen out during the scuffle, I decided; it would be lying somewhere in the steeg, already recovered by the police during their inspection of the murder scene, or stumbled upon by a passer-by. Six hundred guilders. Thankfully, the remainder of my cash – as well as Taaffe's passport and credit card, Charity Jackson's passport, the addresses and phone numbers for Lena Gies and Nikolaas van Zandt – were stowed in my room's safety deposit box. Six hundred guilders. Shit. If the police found the wallet, I'd have the money back soon enough; if not . . . well, it was gone. Alternatively – and this thought occurred to me with a nauseous dread – the wallet had been pickpocketed. Lifted amid the congested aisles of the bloemenmarkt; two bodies compelled into close confines – beside a display of lemon verbena, perhaps, or during a pretend kiss in front of a stand of postcards. Kirsty. Jesus fuck. What else was in the wallet? I tried to think. A photo-booth picture of Rosa that made her hair purple . . . a few British stamps . . . a fluorescent yellow calling card for an Oxford taxi firm . . . another, white, on the reverse of which

I'd made a note of my brother's office phone number. And on the face of this card were the corporate crest, name, phone and fax numbers, and full postal address of the Hotel Terdam.

'This is you, this is you, this is you . . .' he goes, and he puts on this daft eejit walk like it's supposed to be me. And I go, 'This is you, this is you . . .', and I'm pulling a face, like he does when he's talking. We do it again, over and over '. . . this is you, this is you . . .' until we've run out of ways to rip the piss and we end up just laughing our heads off so much we can't even speak. Kids. You behave like kids, for fuck sake, like you were twelve or something. I nearly tell him I've never felt like this about anyone before, but I don't. I don't. You can't, can you, because it always comes out sounding like shite and anyway, once you say it, you're stuffed. So I don't. But he can tell. And if he can't then he's the biggest stupid blind bollix I've ever known.

Dymps knows.

'It's written all over your face,' she says.

'Oh, great.'

'Both your faces.'

'An' there's me thinking I only had the one.'

Carole-Ann knows. I told her. She's always getting me to talk about him: Red this, Red that. The Ash Man, she calls him. Anyway, I told her. She says I deserve him and I ask is that good or bad, and she laughs and gives me a hug.

Kim, she knows as well. The Lovely Kim. Me and him and her are in the bar after a show the other night – London, some club or other; no Tony, he's ancient history. Her words. 'Ancient' meaning, like, two weeks ago. Like I say, we're in the bar and Red's off for a leak so it's just me and her staring into our booze and swilling the stuff around in our glasses like it's the most fascinating fucking sight you ever saw. Only one of us has got to say something eventually and it's her. She gives this smirk of hers and says, 'It's really good to see him so happy.'

'Red? You reckon?'

She nods, long and slow. Her smile is saying: when it comes to understanding the way Red is we've got two brains between us and she's pretty sure she's got one and three quarters of them all to herself.

'You've transformed him.'

'Transformed, is it?'

'Absolutely.'

'From what to what?'

This is a bit complicated for her. She just gives a shrug and another of those smirks. Her hand's on my arm now, cool and dry against my skin. She goes, 'Rosa, believe me, you're the best thing that ever happened to him.'

I think, I'm going to have to make a joke out of all this or she'll have me hoicking down her cleavage. 'The best shag, you mean?'

She lets out a little laugh. Her head hangs forward a minute and she tips it back again, flipping her hair out of her face. Smiley. She goes to say something but I see her stop herself and I look where her eyes are looking and there's Red, moving towards us. She swaps one kind of smile for another, sips her drink. She's watching him and I'm watching her. There's an olive in her drink, kebabbed on a cocktail stick. Green with a piece of red shoved inside. I mean, fuck sake, an olive. What I want to do is pull the cocktail stick out and poke it in her fucking eyes.

I rang Denis Huting. No answer, no answering machine. I called him at intervals during the evening, from my hotel room and subsequently from a payphone in a bar off Leidseplein, where I stowed myself until it closed at 2 a.m. Turned out on to the streets – tired, drunk – I phoned Denis again, in urgent need by then of somewhere safe to sleep; again, there was no reply. If Kirsty *had* pickpocketed my wallet, I dared not return to my hotel for fear that her friends would seek to redress the failure of their previous ambush. So, where to go? With the illusion of being warmed by so much beer and whisky, I contemplated walking the streets or dossing down on a bench. But it was raining, and I had in my pockets all the cash and other valuables from my safety deposit box. I could've walked to Denis's place – on my map, it looked to be no more than three miles – but if he and Cees were away, I'd be stranded outside in the drizzle at three in the morning in some anonymous suburb of Amsterdam. And then what? I stood in the phone booth, sheltering, dialling his number again for want of something to do. How tempting it was just to slump on the floor of that booth and sleep. An idea: go to Lena's place. No. Pointless. According to her neighbour, Lena wasn't due back until that day, so I could hardly expect to find her at home in the early hours. Besides, I didn't know whether she'd talk to me at all, let alone offer me a spare bed. As for checking into another hotel, assuming I could find one with a vacancy, what prospect was there of a drenched, luggageless drunkard being admitted at this time of night?

For an hour, I cruised the area around the Leidseplein in the hope of finding an all-night bar or café – even a club, though I was hardy dressed for it – but everywhere was closed and shuttered. The streets were deserted. I pissed in the doorway of an Indonesian restaurant. I was exhausted. Still inebriated, but increasingly wet and cold. My jeans were saturated, sucking at my legs as I walked; my feet ached and I was out of cigarettes. I craved comfort. I longed to be warm and dry, to lie down and allow myself the luxury of sleep. At last, I reached a point where fear was overhauled by desperation and an irresistible desire for rest. I headed back to the Terdam.

Concealed in the recessed entrance of an office building some way along from the hotel, I spent a few minutes observing the rows of parked cars, the doorways, the ill-lit pavements and the columns of black trees that flanked them. Silence. No sign of life among the shadows. I hurried across the road. The double glass doors, as usual, were unlocked; the night-duty receptionist, as usual, barely troubled to glance up from a portable television as I came in. I had my room key at the ready but, as on previous nights, wasn't required to produce it as proof of residence. To gain illicit admission to the hotel it was necessary, I suspected, merely to traverse the foyer with the confident stride of one who belonged.

At the top floor, I got out of the lift and trod carefully along the corridor to my room. I paused outside, listening. In a neighbouring room, someone was snoring, the bagpipe descant preventing me from concentrating on the less easily detected breaths of the awake, of men who might be beyond the locked door to my own room. Key in hand, I hesitated, afraid to move lest a rheumatic floorboard gave me away. No. Dazed with fatigue though I was, my soft bed beckoning, I couldn't bring myself to go in. Even if no one lay in wait. I couldn't be sure that the few remaining hours of the night would elapse without someone breaking in to catch me slurred and defenceless with sleep. I moved away. Returning to the lifts, I pressed the call button, although I had no idea where to go. The *walletjes*? Slumped asleep in an all-night sex cinema, flanked by men jerking off to hard-core. The police? Revealing the truth about the attack in the steeg, about *me*, and ensuring myself of at least a cell for the night prior to deportation. Maybe walking the wet streets wasn't such a bad option, or hunkering down in some dark doorway. I pressed the call button again. While I waited, I noticed a narrow door along from the lift well. A walk-in store cupboard; on my way down to breakfast the previous morning I'd seen a maid loading a trolley with clean bedding and towels from this room. I tried the handle. The door opened, releasing an aroma of freshly laundered linen. I stepped inside, switching on the light and closing the door behind me with a discreet click. The storeroom was small and cramped, but spacious enough for my purposes. And it was warm, almost suffocatingly so, serving as it did as an oversized airing cupboard. I removed my damp clothes and shoes and made space to spread them on the wooden slatted shelves. I towelled myself dry, fashioned a bed out of blankets and sheets piled deep on the floor, turned off the light and went to sleep.

Magic incantations – abracadabra, hey presto, open sesame – are infrequently uttered by today's illusionists. The wand, too, isn't the fashionable conjuring accessory it once was, now employed chiefly as a decorative pointer rather than as a focusing agent for magical powers. Myself, I use these totemic tools of the trade only at children's events or where a more traditional approach is expected. At the seaside, for example, where performers of all kinds tend to modify their acts in deference to the nostalgic ambience of time-stood-still. Indeed, there are illusions in my repertoire that I wouldn't consider performing except at coastal resorts and holiday camps. One such is Bathing Beauty. What happens is this: The Lovely Kim appears on stage wearing a bikini, sunglasses, a pair of sandals, and with a beach towel draped around her shoulders. You can be sure that one or more of the men in the audience will greet her entrance with wolf-whistles. She poses, and I pretend to take her picture – handing her the camera, which she takes off-stage on the premise of having the film developed. Kim returns a moment later with a large colour print, almost lifesize, showing her in the same attire and pose – the difference being that, in the photograph, she is standing at the sea's edge as it laps at a sandy beach. Kim exits. I display the picture, then fold it in half. I tap the picture with a magic wand and say *Abracadabra!*, emphasizing each syllable in the time-honoured manner. From within the fold I begin to fish out one item after another on the end of the wand: sunglasses, a sandal, another sandal, a towel, then, to more wolf-whistles, a bikini top followed by a bikini bottom. Once these have been tossed aside, I ask if the audience wish to see the photograph again. Naturally, this prompts a chorus of (male) affirmation. I string them along for a while, before giving the picture a final tap of the wand. With a cry of *Hey, presto!* I unfold the print to reveal The Lovely Kim, in water so deep that only her head and bare shoulders are exposed above the surface. *What a pity,* I declare, *the tide has come in!* Groans, laughter, good-natured jeers, applause. Thank you and good-night, Morecambe, Great Yarmouth, Bognor Regis . . .

I mean, for fuck's sake.

The root of the word 'Abracadabra' is reputed to be Hebrew: *Ab* (Father), *Ben* (Son) and *Ruach Acadsch* (Holy Spirit). Prior to its adoption by magicians, the phrase was invoked by physicians to counter ague, flux and toothache. Beats me why the Holy Trinity should concern themselves with curing flux (whatever that is) or assisting in the Bathing Beauty illusion, but there you have it. And if quasireligious mumbo-jumbo enhances the presentation of an illusion, then that's fine by me, because – as I've said before – the art of stage magic lies in its *performance*. And what more appropriate way to simulate magic than by the simulation of a magic password?

Lena Gies required a password from me. A word agreed between her and Rosa, and so jealously guarded that its use by an outsider guaranteed that person's trustworthiness. Anyone unable to specify the password was to be treated with suspicion, regardless of circumstance or their credentials. That was why, when I phoned Lena from Oxford and declared myself a friend of Rosa's, she said she could not speak to me. That was why, when I called her again – this time from an Amsterdam payphone the morning after my night in a hotel store cupboard – she hung up immediately upon hearing my name. Not that I guessed at the existence of a password until I rang her once more, seconds after being disconnected. I was in Amsterdam, I . . . She interrupted me, her voice edged with exasperation.

'If you are truly a friend of Rosa you must say something to prove this.'

'What? Say *what*? I don't understand.'

'OK, you are not able. Goodbye, Mr Red.'

I went to the junction of Kerkstraat and Utrechtsestraat, to Lena's apartment. That black-and-cream-fronted four-storey building, with flats above a clothing shop on the corner and flower boxes on the window-ledges. The sash window on the second floor was open this time, only by a few inches – but enough for the tails of a pale blue curtain to be agitated by an erratic breeze. As I stood on the pavement, looking up, I thought I heard music playing in Lena's flat, but the sound could have been emanating from any of the windows, most of which were ajar. The rain of the previous days had abated, the cloud cover was higher and less menacing; occasionally, it fragmented to admit spring sunshine into the streets like spillages of weak yellow dye. My clothes had dried and I felt refreshed, if somewhat stiff, after a few hours' sleep among the bed linen. My injured shoulder ached. I decided against announcing my presence over the inter-com, certain that Lena would refuse to see me. Instead, I waited for a break in the traffic, crossed the main road and went into a bar diagonally opposite her building. I needed time to plan my approach – my seduction, if you like. The password could've been anything – a solitary word, a phrase, the name of a place or person . . . something of private significance to Rosa and Lena, Rosa, probably – and I didn't expect to be allowed to hazard several guesses. So, if I was unable to crack the code required to gain Lena's confidence, I'd have to find another way of convincing her to trust me.

I chose a window seat looking out across Utrechtsestraat, hung my jacket over the back of the chair and set my day-pack down under the table. A barman approached, addressing me in Dutch then switching comfortably to English as I placed my order. He was barely out of his teens, dressed in a crisp white shirt and black jeans. Shortly, he returned with a coffee and twenty B&H,

my own supplies, stupidly forgotten, remaining out of bounds in my room at the Terdam. He removed the clear wrapping from the cigarette packet, flipped open the lid and peeled off the protective foil. I was beginning to speculate that the service might extend to inserting a cigarette in my mouth and lighting it for me, when he simply laid the carton on the table beside my drink and presented me with a till receipt. I paid him. Lighting up, I took a moment to survey my surroundings. This was one of Amsterdam's traditional bars – a *bruine kroeg*, or brown café; its panelled walls, subdued lighting, heavy maroon curtains and smoky atmosphere lent it the public-bar ambience of an English local. The place was quiet. Most of the other customers were drinking beer, one or two reading newspapers from a rack on the wall. A TV and juke-box stood idle, the only noise coming from sporadic conversations or the hiss of Grolsch being drawn off from a stainless steel contraption the size of a canteen tea urn. I smoked, sipped coffee and gazed out of the window.

I was on my second cigarette, debating whether to order another coffee or a sandwich, when my attention was diverted with a jolt by the sight of a hand appearing from the open window of Lena's apartment. I sat forward abruptly in my seat. The hand – recognizably female – reached out, the forearm to which it was attached (and which was all I could see of its owner) being loosely clad in a sleeve of blue-and-white horizontal stripes. I watched the hand untangle the end of the curtain from the window-box, where it had snagged. The hand withdrew inside, taking the curtain with it; the window closed. I was still monitoring the building for further signs of activity when the front door opened and a tall blonde woman stepped out. She was carrying a large plastic bag, slung over her shoulder like Santa's sack. She wore grey leggings and a baggy top, in the style of a rugby shirt, patterned with blue-and-white hoops.

I grabbed my jacket and day-pack and left the bar, following Lena – for surely that's who she was – at a discreet distance. She was heading along Kerkstraat. At a point where the street broadened into a small square of scrubby urban parkland, she halted by a doorway and swung the burden from her shoulder.

I saw her push the door open, dragging the bag inside after her. I continued on the opposite pavement until I drew level with the building – a coin-op launderette, numerous figures within blurred by a film of condensation on the plate-glass frontage. Lena's stripy top was visible as she bent to load a machine with the contents of her plastic sack. I sat on a bench in the square, watching the launderette. Behind me, boys – kitted out in the red-and-white of Ajax or the tangerine of the Dutch national team – were scuffing a football around a dirt pitch with metal goalposts. If Lena stayed inside, I decided, I would retreat to my observation post in the bar and intercept her on her return. But she didn't. She re-emerged with the empty bag scrunched up in her fist and set off in the direction of home, checking her watch. I followed, keeping pace at first, then drawing closer. Her bobbed blonde hair swung slightly with the rhythm of her stride. At the main road she had to wait for a tram to pass, enabling me to close the gap and, as she crossed, I fell into step alongside her. I said hello. I smiled and said, *Hello, Lena.* I didn't introduce myself, nor did I need to. She skipped sideways away from me and put out an arm in the manner of a rugby player fending off a tackle. Shaking her head, not looking at me but straight ahead at the black door to the apartment building towards which her long legs were propelling her with urgency.

'You must go away. OK?'

'Please, Lena, I need to talk to you.'

I went to take hold of her, but the sudden movement made me wince with the pain in my shoulder. Even so, she flinched, yanking her hand away as a reflex. For a moment, I thought she was going to slap me. But hers, too, was a phantom gesture, another inchoate pose in a mime of two people fighting. We were a few feet from the door, Lena scrabbling in the pocket of her leggings for a bunch of keys. I stood in her way, desperate to delay her disappearance long enough for one final appeal.

'Lena . . .'

'Fuck *off.*'

Her exclamation attracted stares from two workmen replacing a broken window in a neighbouring building. They exchanged smiles with one another. I was made to feel like what they surely assumed me to be – a jilted lover making a fool of himself. Lena, self-conscious now, lowered her voice – reducing its pitch but not its tone of indignant irritation.

'I cannot talk with you. I cannot be seen with you.'

With that, she barged past me and made for the door. As she inserted her key in the lock, I clutched at the one word I'd been able to think of that might save me from being excluded from her trust. One word of countless thousands I'd heard Rosa speak that stood out from the rest for its oddness and for its special significance to her here in Amsterdam. The door juddered open in Lena's hurry to escape inside.

'*Pannekoeken*,' I said. 'Rosa's password is *pannekoeken*.'

She halted on the threshold, turning to look at me. Her blue eyes, her lips, were smileless. She shook her head. 'You don't know that.'

I didn't reply.

'It is a guess,' she said, 'or you would say it before.'

I could have lied, in the hope of being believed; or I could have told the truth, inviting rejection. Her eyes held mine, scrutinizing me, waiting for my response.

I gave a shrug. 'She cooked me pancakes one time, in Oxford. Taught me the Dutch name for them.' Inhaling deeply, I didn't so much speak the next words as let them free on the outward breath. 'So, yeah, I was guessing.'

Lena continued to regard me for a moment. Then she held the door open wide and, with an almost imperceptible motion of the head, signalled me to go in.

Talking to Lena (1)

The window was open again, the breeze dishevelling the curtains, only, now, I was on the inside, gazing down at the bar where, a short while ago, I'd been drinking coffee, smoking. Lena was making sandwiches. *I have to eat*, she had said, almost as soon as we'd climbed the stairs to her apartment. *You want some?* I'd said yes, if it wasn't any trouble. She'd shrugged. She returned from the kitchen, plates in her hands, bumping the living-room door shut with her bum. She fetched the food to an occasional table and sat down on a sofa, inviting me with an impatient wave to occupy one of two armchairs. The suite was upholstered in an abstract African design of deep reds, browns, oranges and greens that dominated the otherwise austere décor: white walls, beige carpet, blond-pine bookshelves and those flapping, pale blue curtains. Sitting by the window, Lena was honeyed in natural light, hair made fairer still by a corona of sunshine, the downy nape of her neck speckled with gold and silver. A CD was playing unobtrusively, the same music I'd heard earlier, looking up at the apartment. Everything but the Girl. Lena kicked her shoes off, folding her bare feet beneath her as she sat cross-legged.

'I forgot the drinks,' she said, gesturing towards the kitchen. 'There's some beers, if you want.'

Her English was heavily accented, each 's' aspirated through pursed lips like a kiss. *Shome beersh*. In Denis Huting this sounded comical, but Lena's speech had a sexy quality that compelled you to watch her mouth rather than her eyes when she was talking. I made my way to the door.

'Can I get you one?'

'No. Coke.'

I fetched two Cokes, the cans ice-cold to the touch. I handed one to her and set the other down on the table beside the plate of sandwiches she'd made for me.

'You know, you didn't even make a good guess.' She popped her can and took a swig. 'OK. The password isn't *pannekoeken*, it is something different.'

'So how come you let me in?'

She shrugged. 'I didn't want you outside making a noise in the street.'

'Sure.'

'You want another reason, Mr Red, you make one for yourself because I don't have one. Maybe when you eat your sandwich I ask you to go.'

'It's just Red. No need for the mister.'

'Mr Red is good. I like it better.'

I smiled, so did she. 'You make me sound like a character in *Reservoir Dogs*.'

'I don't see this movie.'

On the wall, directly above her head, was a monochrome photograph of a canal in winter, flanked by trees whose bare branches were duplicated in the metallic surface of the water. Noting the direction of my gaze, Lena turned to look at the picture.

'Leliegracht,' she said, facing me again. 'I took it myself.'

'You're a photographer?'

'OK. I take photographs.'

She ate. No explanation of the differentiation. Her tone implied a philosophical nuance rather than a straightforward distinction between professional and amateur status. The picture was superb. I was about to say so, when she swallowed and asked, 'So, tell me about Rosa.'

'She died.'

'I know this.'

'I'm trying to find out why.'

'I know this also.'

I looked at her. Fine. I'd tell her things she didn't know. So, I told her about me and Rosa, about how we met and the year we spent together. I talked about Rosa, the way I remembered her. Lena listened without interruption. By the time I'd finished, the food was gone and the cans stood empty on the able. I was smoking, she wasn't.

231

'You're a magician?'

'Yeah.'

'You know, there is a Dutch magician – Jasper Grootveld. Very famous.' She thought about this, frowned. 'Very famous in Holland, anyway. Many years ago he is in Amsterdam, making graffiti on cigarette advertising. Everywhere, he writes "k", for "kanker".' She drew a 'k' in the air with a finger. 'OK. Cancer, in English.'

'Is this a subtle way of telling me you'd rather I didn't smoke in here?'

Lena uncrossed her legs and stretched them out so her heels rested on the table. Leaning back on the sofa, she clasped her hands behind her head, the loose sleeves of her stripy shirt slipping down to her elbows. She looked at me. When she spoke next, her voice betrayed no inflection to correspond with the shocking change of subject.

'You think maybe it would be nice to fuck me?' She might've been asking if I'd had enough to eat. As though anticipating my denial, she continued dismissively, 'I can see, in your eyes. Maybe you'd like to lick me in the pussy?'

'Lena, I *don't* want . . .'

She shook her head. 'I tell you about cigarettes. There is a guy I know, before, he was angry with me. He ties me to the bed. I don't have clothes on and this man, he takes his cigarette – it is burning, OK – and touches it to my pussy.' Lena mimicked the action with her right hand, pressing the tips of her thumb and middle finger against the crotch of her leggings . . . six, seven, eight times. 'Like this.'

I looked away.

'You want to see how my pussy looks now, Mr Red? You want to lick it? You want to put your cock in my pussy?'

'Fucking hell, Lena . . .' My eyes were stinging. 'Why are you telling me this?'

'The man who did this to me, you know him. He is called Max van Dis.'

★

232

We were drinking beer. Lena had put on another CD. She'd been telling me about her time at Pijlsteeg: fifteen years old – a runaway, a junkie in the making, living in a squat and touting for business every night at the Dam – when she was picked up by a man posing as a punter. They went to a graffitied alley off the square, where she expected to perform the usual two-minute, twenty-guilder blow-job in a doorway. Instead, he invited her into No. 37 with a promise of regular food, drugs, money and somewhere to sleep. Her previous pimp saw her in a bar a week later and gave her a beating. The following day, she said with a shrug, his body was recovered from the Amstel. Lena worked at Pijlsteeg for two years before incurring the wrath of van Dis, her minder, for brokering private deals with clients for extra services. That was when he mutilated her.

'I couldn't work, so they made me go.'

Back to the squats. And to the streets. Unable to fuck for a while, unable even to urinate without pain, she figured oral and manual would provide enough guilders to feed her, and to feed her habit. But her wounds became infected and, as her condition deteriorated, a fellow squatter dialled 112. It was in hospital that her addiction was diagnosed, she said. As soon as she was well enough, Lena was admitted, voluntarily, to a detox and rehab project. After more lapses and relapses than she cared to recall, she was weaned off heroin and on to methadone, then off methadone. She'd lost thirty pounds in weight, and hadn't menstruated for eighteen months.

'I'm clean now,' she said. 'For six years, no drugs.'

The sun had gone in, the room had become cooler. Lena closed the window. I took a long slug of beer and stood the bottle back on its coaster.

'Rosa used to pick off the labels with her nails,' I said, smiling at Lena. 'Like a nervous habit.' She nodded but didn't say anything. I mumbled something about how Rosa would only drink Belgian lager, the sentence trailing off into nothing. I exhaled. 'Did . . . Rosa, did she do the same work as you when she was at Pijlsteeg?'

'Of course.'

'She was a prostitute.'

'You don't like this word?'

'No.'

'You think it's better to be a prostitute's trick?'

'I'm not saying . . .'

'OK.' Lena frisked her hair away from her forehead. 'You don't like the idea to be in love with a woman who was a prostitute . . .'

'I didn't mean it like that.'

'. . . who made blue movies and live-fucking shows. To live with her one year and not know this.'

'*No.*'

The resentment in my voice stilled the conversation. Lena stood up and went to the CD-player, switching it off and effecting a rude silence in the room. She adjusted another of her framed photos, which had tilted out of alignment, a black-and-white picture I recognized, from my city guide, as the 'dancing houses' – a higgledy-piggledy row of buildings whose foundations of log-piles had become warped and rotten over the centuries, exposed to oxygen by the vicissitudes of Amsterdam's water levels.

'Did she go through what you did?' I asked. 'Rehab, I mean.'

Lena nodded.

'Here?'

'No. England.' She paused. 'It was hard for her, actually. The methadone. She was taking this for a long time.'

'To get her off heroin?'

'Sure, but methadone, you know, is very nice. Nicer than heroin I think.' Lena was leaning against the long glass-fronted cabinet which housed her music centre, arms folded. Watching me. 'Rosa had a bad time,' she said at last.

We might have been discussing a stranger. Her Rosa wasn't mine, the life she described wasn't a part of the life of the woman I'd known. I tried to envisage another Rosa: fucking for money, shooting up, wracked by withdrawal; petrified, as Kirsty had been. But this Rosa was still too new to me to be absorbed into a greater whole.

'How long did you know her?' I asked.

'I met Rosa the first time in a bar at Dam Square, by Pijlsteeg,' said Lena, with a slight smile. 'I followed her into the toilet. This is maybe five, six years ago.'

'I know that bar.'

She looked up sharply. 'You've been to Pijlsteeg?'

'I . . . walked past. You know, just to see the building.' I told her about Rosa's pleading letter to her aunt, with its Amsterdam address and the clue to her imminent escape. 'Were you the one helping her out of No. 37?'

'Not only me.'

'What are you, the Red Thread?'

'You heard of them?'

'I read something about it.'

Lena shook her head. 'We are nothing to do with them. OK. De Rode Draad is a labour union for prostitutes. We are not this. We are only people who have worked in Pijlsteeg and other places the same. If a girl wants to run away, we help her. We help her run away and we help her stop drugs. That's all.'

'You started this group yourself?'

'Not me. A woman from England. I heard about her through one of the nurses at detox, you know?' Lena checked her watch. '*Shit*. My clothes.'

'I'll walk along with you to the launderette.'

'No. It is not safe for us to be together outside.'

It is not safe. The phrase rekindled memories of an earlier conversation, when she'd warned me against dialling a certain Amsterdam telephone number.

'Is Nikolaas van Zandt your contact at Pijlsteeg?'

Lena had begun clearing away the debris of our lunch. 'Nik is gone.'

'They killed him?'

A shake of the head. 'He is hiding someplace.'

I followed her to the kitchen. She rinsed the plates and stacked them in a plastic draining tray. The window above the sink afforded a view of a cramped patchwork of back gardens towered over by buildings seemingly constructed with the sole purpose of blighting one another's space. A cat, entirely black, was asleep on the ledge, though I couldn't see how it had attained this second-storey vantage point. I asked if it was Lena's and she said it wasn't.

'I've got a cat like that,' I said. 'Merlin. You know, after the sorcerer? Rosa insisted on calling him Kerrygold. It was her present to me when she moved in.'

Lena laughed. She was drying her hands on a tea towel and raised it to her face to conceal her mouth.

'What's so funny?'

She turned to look at me, still smiling. Her blue eyes caught chips of light from the window. 'When we helped Rosa run away, she lived in a house in Amsterdam for one or two days before someone can go with her back to England. OK. You know the first thing she wants when she is in the safe house?'

'Kerrygold butter?'

'Yes, of course. Toast, with Kerrygold butter. At Pijlsteeg, the girls can have anything – drugs, drink, anything – but they only have margarine. No Kerrygold. Don't ask me why this is.' She gave another laugh, this time, I sensed, at my expense.

'Go on.'

'OK. *Kerrygold*. So now you know Rosa's secret word.'

Under the wig, she's a blondie. Lena. I don't know if that's her real name but it's the one she told me so that's what I call her. I have another name of my own now: Pauline Wright. Pauline. Fuck sake. I go, 'How come you get to be Lena and I get to be Pauline?' She thinks this is a hoot. They're getting me a passport – British, like – made out for this Pauline Wright character, only it's going to have my picture in it. The photo's a copy of the one Wim took of me the night Lena did her pick-up routine in the loos – with Nik's pretty mug and the beer glasses cut off so it'll just be me, head and shoulders, looking spaced.

Lena. Christ, I hardly know the woman. Twice, we've met: two minutes in the ladies and half an hour in a hotel bedroom where I'm supposed to be shagging a client for three hundred Gs, only it's not a client it's her, and we don't shag we talk about how it's going to happen. The ins and outs. The timing. I've gone over and over everything in my head – where I've got to be, what I've got to do, what I have to say, what to do if this or that happens or if things go wrong, passwords . . . it's, like, my head's splitting with so much to remember I can hardly sleep for dreaming it's happening. And in my dreams it always fucks up. Always. I get caught. I get killed. I dream it's a set-up. Lena cheats on me. And Nik. They set me up.

Two and a half years, and I still haven't a fucking clue about Nik. Three years, nearly. I'm not supposed to talk to him about this. None of it, not a word, in case we get overheard. It's got to happen without any of them sussing he was in on it. And sometimes I get to thinking if he stays I might as well stay too cos what's the point . . . I mean what's the fucking point of going back to England if he's still here? What is there for me in England anyway? Fuck all.

The other day, me and Nik are in the kitchen making pancakes and there's no one else around so I ask him if he'll come with me. He just shakes his head. I don't know if he means 'no' or if he's telling me it isn't safe to talk. He looks jumpy.

I go, 'So that's it then, is it? That's us.'

'Yes.'

Yes. One word. Nice while it lasted, now fuck off. I stand there looking at him, watching him cook. And I'm fucked if I'm going to touch him or say anything else and I'm fucked if he's going to see me cry. So bollix to him. Only, the thing is I don't know if he means it or if he's just saying it so it'll be easier for me to go, to escape. To leave him behind and never see him again.

Talking to Lena (2)

I asked Lena if she'd ever taken a photograph of Rosa. A portrait. Or did she confine herself to atmospheric scenes of Amsterdam? She replied, more or less in these terms, that when she took a picture of a person in Amsterdam, it *was* an Amsterdam scene. Unless I believed that cities consisted only of buildings and streets and canals?

I smiled. 'I'm not being rude, but did Rosa ever tell you you were full of shite?'

'Sure. Every day she tells me this.' Her own smile broadened, as she gave a passable impersonation: ' "C'mere, Lena, will ye stop troin to ficken con-*fuse* me?" '

We laughed at this giving of a voice to the unarticulated bond between us. Then, sadness as the fleeting re-creation of Rosa lent perverse emphasis to her absence. Lena left the kitchen. A moment later she called me and I traced her to the bedroom. The bed was made, a suitcase lying there open and partially unpacked. A KLM tag was strung to the handle. Lena produced a heavy rectangle sheathed in bubble-wrap from the wardrobe and set it down on the foot of the bed. She unwrapped it.

The photograph, in black and white and mounted in a wooden frame, showed Rosa in half-profile. Only the upper half of her body was in shot, one breast partly exposed by the opening in a dark-coloured dressing gown that made her skin especially pale by contrast. Her face was free from make-up, her black hair bedraggled and, apparently, wet. She held a mug in her left hand, frozen in the process of raising it to, or lowering it from, her mouth; each finger and the thumb were adorned with rings. The picture's most striking feature was the relaxed naturalness of the subject, anyone viewing it sharing the photographer's experience of catching Rosa entirely unawares. Her gaze was aimed off camera at something or someone unseen, her face wearing a smile of absolute and irresistibly attractive inhibition. She looked so alive.

Lena eased my face into her shoulder with no concern, it seemed, that I was trailing dampness down the front of her shirt. The more I tried not to cry, the more noisily and profusely the tears came. Her hand was warm against my neck, her body scented with something sweetly floral. Neither of us spoke. I tried to, but the words stalled and, in any case, Lena hushed me with the merest increase in the pressure of her embrace. When, at last, I managed to stop, she produced a tissue. My withdrawal coincided with hers; in that instant of separation, ours was no longer a gentle intimacy but an awkwardness of mutual embarrassment. We became clumsy. I wiped my face and we stood apart at the foot of her bed, solemnly resuming our study of the picture.

'I took this after she has ran away from Pijlsteeg,' she said.

'At the safe house? Or in England?'

'Yes, England. Maybe one year later.'

I indicated the suitcase, with its airline label. 'Is that where you've just come back from?'

Lena shot me a smile. 'OK. It is funny – you are here in Amsterdam, looking for me, and I am in your country visiting my friends.'

'Where?'

'At a refuge. Don't ask me the place, because I don't tell you.'

My face felt flushed, my eyelashes still dewy with tears. Lena's photograph revealed little of the location, the background comprising a rectangle of white wall and the unruly foliage of a houseplant that appeared, with the deceit of perspective, to be sprouting from Rosa's back. It could've been any room, anywhere.

'I went with Rosa,' Lena continued. 'I helped her to go from Amsterdam.'

'Is there a woman called Vicky who works there, at the refuge? Or lives there? I think her real name might be Carole-Ann.'

She didn't reply. I mentioned the parcel of Rosa's belongings; 'Vicky' on a gin-rummy scoresheet; the passenger with dark hair in a bob, filmed on CCTV walking along the platform at Reading; the friend of Rosa's in the pub the night I performed the stigmata illusion; the woman whose number I traced from an old phone bill and who picked up mid message while I spoke to her answering machine. Geordie accent: . . . *Tell them nothing about me, not a thing* . . . And, when I tried to ask why she'd sent me Rosa's things: *The bag was a mistake. I fucked up with the bag* . . . All the while, I had the impression I wasn't telling Lena anything she didn't already know.

She said matter-of-factly: 'Carole-Ann doesn't live any more at the refuge.'

'She was a prostitute as well? Here in Amsterdam?'

'Of course.'

I took another look at the portrait, conscious that before long Lena would stow it away again, like treasure returned to its place of concealment. The mood between us was tilting subtly towards the proprietorial: her picture, my Rosa.

'I have loads of shots of her,' I said. 'But nothing as good as this.'

Lena wrapped the frame carefully and eased it back on the shelf among a stack of similar packages. *Too many pictures, not so many walls.* She closed the wardrobe. With the photograph gone, so was our purpose for being in the bedroom; we became gauche again. Lena *had* to reclaim her clothes from the launderette, she said. I felt a surge of anxiety – she was all I had of Rosa, there in Amsterdam; my only connection.

'D'you want me to go?' I said.

'No, no. Please, you must stay.'

She'd be back soon. *Help yourshelf to beersh.* A hostess's laid-back charm. However, I detected in her eyes, in her manner and voice, the same panic. She was as afraid of letting go of me as I was of losing her. What I couldn't fathom was why?

Once Lena had gone, I got a beer, lit a cigarette and, with a guilty excitement reminiscent of being home alone as a boy, I nosed about the apartment. Drawers and cupboards, the letter rack, the pockets of jackets and coats – seeking nothing in particular, finding nothing exceptional. The contents of the suitcase were no more revealing: clothes, a paperback novel (in Dutch), toiletries, two canisters of used film, a Hothouse Flowers CD in a W. H. Smith bag with a receipt dated the previous day and issued at a London branch. There was a phone on her bedside table. I rang Denis. He answered and we spoke briefly: yes, he'd been away (booked at short notice for a festival in Germany); no, he hadn't heard about the stabbing near the bloemenmarkt; yes, of course I could crash at his place. As I hung up, there was the sound of a key in the front door. I slipped back to the living room in time to see Lena appear in the doorway, hugging a bulging black bag, cheeks slightly flushed, breathless from hauling her load along the street and up two flights of stairs. She grinned, pleased to see me.

'If she'd been so anxious to escape, why was she going back?'

'To Amsterdam? Rosa was coming here many times.'

'No, on the train, the day she . . .' It was difficult to read Lena's expression. 'You're saying that wasn't her first trip?'

'OK. You want to talk about Rosa. But this is about the group – it isn't safe for you to know so much. Also, it isn't safe for us.'

'Rosa was killed?'

'Sure.'

'Sure. That's all you can say?'

Lena stood up, crossed the room and switched on the light. The afternoon had turned prematurely gloomy, a bank of charcoal-grey cloud dulling the sky. I stubbed out my cigarette, waiting for her to say something and half expectant that this time she really would tell me to go. But she didn't. Lowering herself on to the sofa, she said, 'That trip was the first for a long time. Fifteen, maybe eighteen months. Before, she was coming here two times a year or something.'

'Why?'

'To take people away from Pijlsteeg. The British ones – Carole-Ann, others.' Lena elaborated: 'She would bring money, also a passport – because, at that place, the women aren't allowed these things. Also they are afraid, or sick with so much drugs, or not so clever. OK. They need someone to be with them who knows what to do.'

'How come Rosa stopped making the trips?'

'They were looking for her.'

'The men from No. 37?'

'She saw Max van Dis following her one time in the street in London, close to where she lived. So she had to go live someplace else and then another place. Oxford, not London.' She shrugged. 'No more trips to Amsterdam.'

'Until that last one.'

'Sure.'

I thought about this for a moment. 'How come they were after Rosa? I mean, Rosa in particular.'

'No. It was all of us. Me, Rosa, Nikolaas. Others. They would like to find all of us. But Rosa, she is in England and they think maybe if they find her they can find the refuge.' Lena smiled. 'Also, Rosa is good. You know, she takes a lot of women from Pijlsteeg and this is a problem for them because women is how they make the money.'

'They wanted to put a stop to your group?'

She nodded. There was something about Lena that made me suspect I was only hearing the partial truth. Something in her expression, but also in what she'd told me – and it took me a moment to identify what it was.

'If they were hoping Rosa would lead them to the refuge,' I said, 'surely she'd have been more use to them alive than dead?'

Lena didn't answer for a long time. Eventually, she said, 'They found out she was having sex with Nikolaas . . . OK, the big boss of No. 37 – he's called Jan Peters – anyway, he found out about Rosa and Nikolaas and he was so . . . *jealous* he wanted them killed. This is why it was dangerous for her to come back here.'

'What are you saying, Rosa was his . . . ?'

Lena halted me with a vigorous shake of the head. 'No, not Rosa – Nikolaas. Jan was fucking Nikolaas.'

From the apartment below came the sound of a baby crying. I mentioned my conversation over the intercom and asked whether the woman downstairs was a friend. She nodded. Lena looked after the baby sometimes. *He has four lungs – two for breathing, two for screaming.* I thought of my youngest niece, Katy, who hardly ever cried and would produce a smile at the slightest encouragement. Rosa used to have her chortling away, reaching out with bunched fingers at this funny grown-up's face as though trying to grab a piece of the happiness for herself.

'Mr Red, you must tell me something. OK. You have a passport for Charity Jackson . . . do you have this? In Amsterdam?'

'You spoke to Carole-Ann?'

Lena hesitated. 'Actually, yes.'

I nodded.

'Where is it, the passport?'

I pointed towards my day-pack, slumped in a corner of the room. Lena looked at the pack. I went over to it and opened one of the zippered compartments, taking out the passport and placing it between us on the coffee table. She didn't pick it up.

'Is this why you didn't want me to leave while you were at the launderette?'

She smiled. Then her features were masked by a swathe of fine blonde hair as she leaned forward in her seat. When she raised her head again the smile was gone. She asked whether the police back home knew I was in Amsterdam. I said they didn't. *And the police here?* I hesitated. *Why would I have anything to do with the Dutch police?* Lena shrugged and suggested that, if I was trying to find out about Rosa, perhaps I believed they could help. I shook my head, told her I was working solo – apart from a guy called Denis Huting. I explained about Denis. Lena listened. One more question: she wanted to know if anyone had seen me or spoken to me when I visited Pijlsteeg.

'I told you, I just took a look at the building where she used to live. I wanted to see it for myself.'

She nodded. After a long pause during which neither of us spoke Lena finally said, 'You know why she was coming here, that last time?'

'Yeah.' I exhaled. 'Yes, I do.'

We discussed my willingness, then the practicalities. The risks. I would hold on to the passport, they would supply the money, the air tickets; they would devise the tactics. *Maybe you are the trick, she comes to your hotel, we lose the minder somehow . . . something like this*. I was to go to my friend's place and wait for a message. At the door, as I left her apartment, Lena kissed me on both cheeks and told me to be careful. I wasn't to visit her again, I wasn't to phone her. I wasn't to make further attempts to contact Nikolaas. And under no circumstances was I to go anywhere near Pijlsteeg. *They don't know you. This is good for us*. We said goodbye. In the few hours I'd spent with Lena, I had discovered the purpose of Rosa's final journey to Amsterdam, and a purpose of my own: to complete the task she'd been prevented from accomplishing.

I knew so little of Rosa. Only one year of her life – the last year – had been spent with me; I had my observations, the facts of our existence together, the facets of herself she chose to present to me or which became manifest despite her. The preceding twenty-four years were a sheaf of blank pages interspersed with partial and indistinct sketches: drawn by her, drawn by others who'd known her before I had. Some truthful, some not. From Lena, another portrayal: Rosa the prostitute.

Rosa.
Her tendency to obliterate
 . . . to conceal
 . . . to rage
Her capacity to endure.
Were these the symptoms I saw of the past revealed to me by Lena? A self-protective defiance – a denial – of her vulnerability.
When someone dies, you regret the words left unspoken

between you. Your words, the things you never got round to saying. Me, I wanted Rosa back to hear *her* words, her replies to the unanswered questions that had stacked up in my head until I was afraid of being mad with them. Nosy, she reckoned I was. Always scavenging for scraps of her past and of her past selves. *I'm here now, aren't I? This is me. Isn't that enough?* These weren't her actual phrases, but they were implicit in her reticence, her evasiveness, if I probed too deep or too often. Those glimpses she had occasionally given, already precious to me, have become priceless in the weeks and months since she died. Since she was killed.

Rosa the child, for example.

A pizza restaurant in Oxford – a small boy at another table, throwing a tantrum, prompting us to discuss childhood. Gradually, I manoeuvred our conversation from the general to the specific: what had Rosa been like as a girl? For once, she was willing – or, at least, not unwilling – to satisfy my curiosity about a period in her life which had hitherto been draped in vagueness.

'You mean, like, personalitywise?'

'Yeah.'

She bit into a slice of garlic bread. Lips, greasy and freckled with crumbs. She said she'd been a very shy child . . . wouldn't say boo to a goose, afraid of her own shadow, a proper shrinking violet and all that. I laughed and said I didn't believe her. As it happened, she didn't give a good shite whether I believed her or not.

'How come you're so different now?' I asked.

'People change.'

'Not that much.'

'Red, you'd be surprised.'

I asked what was her earliest memory? Falling down some steps when she was two and a half, she said. She raised her chin, inviting me to inspect the scar; I couldn't see any scar and she said in that case I must be fucking blind. She tapped the skin with her fingernail. *There. It's right there.* I still couldn't see it.

'Two stitches, I had.'

I told her my earliest memory: riding on a donkey at the

seaside and screaming to be let off. It wasn't being so high off the ground that scared me, but the hot musty stink of the animal. I'd have been three or four years old. Even now, I said, I could still re-create the sensation of that odour just by thinking about it.

'So what kind of child were *you*?' asked Rosa, smiling.

'Always had to be the centre of attention.'

'A show-off, is it?'

'Yeah. If Mum and Dad were watching the telly, I'd go and stand right in front of the screen. I don't remember doing that, but that's what they've told me.'

I wondered aloud whether we'd have liked one another if we'd met as children; Rosa said she didn't think so. Besides, her mammy and daddy hadn't approved of her playing with older boys. Too rough, too much foul-mouthing. I'd seldom known her to volunteer information about her parents.

'Who d'you take after most, would you say, your mum or your dad?'

She looked at me for a moment then, loud enough to be heard by diners at the neighbouring tables, replied, 'I don't have a prick, so I s'pose it must be my mother.'

The walk from Lena's place to Denis's took an hour. He lived in the suburbs to the south of the city, on the outer fringes of a district known as De Pijp. The Old South, a network of narrow terraced streets hemmed in by brick tenements, each five or six storeys high. There were plenty of people about, despite the darkening skies and the prospect of rain, and the area had an appealing bustle. I found Denis's block with the aid of the directions he'd dictated over the phone. The ground floor was occupied by a Surinamese restaurant decked out in green, white, red and yellow, and spilling tables on to the pavement. Its proprietor, preparing for the evening session, paused to return my greeting with a flash of his teeth. Glass doors alongside the restaurant gave entry to a dingy lift-well. I went up to the fourth floor, following an enclosed walkway to a bright orange door decorated with a cartoon chicken waving a magic wand.

It was Denis who answered. He wore a multi-coloured poncho with tasselled hems, a plain white sarong, football boots and a beret.

I smiled. 'You never told me it was fancy dress.'

He called out over his shoulder, 'Cees, there is a man at the door with a sense of humour.'

I heard the distant reply, 'Tell him we already got one.'

Denis beckoned me into the flat. We found Cees sitting cross-legged on the floor in the living room. For some reason I'd expected him to be young and pretty, but he was older than Denis and had the drooping features of a bloodhound, made less canine only by the presence of glasses and the absence of long floppy ears. He wore a trilby, a purple T-shirt, the waistcoat to a pin-striped suit, luminous lemon cycling shorts and cherry-red Doc Marten boots. Denis, indicating a mound of clothes, hats and shoes dominating the centre of the room, explained that they'd been to a jumble stall at the market in Albert Cuypstraat and bought up almost the entire stock.

'Floyd died,' he said. 'We try to make ourselves happy.'

From the direction of his gaze, I understood Floyd to have been one of the tropical fish in a glass tank perched on a stand in the corner. I set my bag down and sat on a wicker chair that creaked beneath me. Cees spoke to Denis in Dutch, then asked if I wanted coffee. I said yes, and he went off to make it.

'You look hot,' said Denis, hoisting himself off the floor and on to a futon sofa.

'I've been walking.'

'You *walked*. From where?'

'Kerkstraat.'

'Why do you do this?'

'Exercise.'

He shook his head. 'No. We don't have this word in Dutch.'

Lolling on the sofa, the poncho and sarong billowing about him in voluminous folds, Denis resembled a collapsed marquee. His bald pate was flushed, the eyes made small as he enjoyed his own joke. That familiar wheezy laugh. Then, serious again, he fixed me a look and said, 'You in shit, Red?'

'I think so.'

I gave him the details I'd withheld when I rang from Lena's. I told him about Kirsty and the stabbing, and about my interrogation by the police. I told him why it wasn't safe for me to return to the hotel. I told him about Lena, and of my recruitment into the operation to spring Charity Jackson. *This isn't shit, Red, this is diarrhoea.* As we talked, Cees brought coffee – three dainty cups, each with a thin biscuit like a comma in its saucer. I wondered what Rosa had made of this Dutch custom, given her practice of serving coffee in a large mug, accompanied by at least half a packet of chocolate digestives. Denis ate his biscuit whole. He said I was welcome to stay as long as I wished, provided I was content to sleep on the futon. I watched Cees's face. If he minded this intrusion, his expression gave nothing away.

'Do I have to dress up?' I said, nodding at the pile of jumble.

Denis laughed, Cees didn't. But he smiled. He smiled at me, then at Denis, and I saw that everything was all right; I also saw, by the contrast between the two smiles, that a dozen unexpected visitors couldn't diminish their privacy, their intimacy. And, if I'm honest, it made me sad, so fucking sad, to realize I'd never loved or been loved as exclusively as this.

We ate pasta. We talked, we drank wine, we watched a film (in English, Dutch subtitles); every so often I would slip out on to a narrow balcony to smoke and gaze down on an unattractive suburban stretch of the Amstel river. My hosts remained in jumble costume all evening, although Denis eventually removed the beret because it made his scalp itch. Their attire was as eclectic and as eccentric as the décor of their living room, with its flock wallpaper, chintz floral curtains, a kilim rug thrown down on stripped pine floorboards, huge pop-art prints alongside horse brasses and framed photographs of Italian footballers, a mismatched suite (futon, wicker chair, beanbag), the fish-tank, its water and occupants tinged with pink by a concealed neon striplight, several dozen varieties of small potted cacti, an antique grandfather clock, and wall-mounted spotlights that indiscriminately cast bright pools of illumination while leaving other parts of the room in darkness. I loved it. I loved being with them.

After only a few hours in their home, I'd become so relaxed, woozy with wine and easy company, that Denis's advice, when it came, was all the more shocking in its abruptness. And in its perceptiveness, giving voice to the thought that had been nagging me since I'd fled the Terdam. When the film ended, he doofed off the TV and, with no preamble, said, 'Red, you must tell the police where you are.'

'I know.'

'If they find you are not in the hotel, this looks bad for you.'

I rang Inspector Oosterling that evening. It was late, he wasn't there. I left a message, giving my name – that is, Taaffe Clarke's name – and Denis's number. I also rang the hotel, explaining my temporary absence and asking if they could hold the room for me for a few days. They took some money in advance, noting down Taaffe's credit-card details. In the morning, I was shaving when Cees rapped on the bathroom door and said there was a call for me. My face half-covered with foam, I went out to the hallway and picked up the handset from the upturned packing case that served as a telephone table. The inspector didn't seem fazed by my disappearing act, in fact he wasn't even aware of it, having had no cause to contact me since our interview. He thanked me for the courtesy of informing him of my whereabouts. My explanation that I'd decided to spend a few days with a friend seemed of little interest. What did interest him, this being the purpose of his call, was something uncovered only that morning by one of the officers working on the murder inquiry. The eyewitness who claimed to have seen me in the bloemenmarkt with a young redhead had been shown a file of photographs of known and suspected prostitutes working in the city, whether legally or illegally. From among these, she'd identified a woman whose name, according to police records, was Mary Ruth McAllister. British citizen, nineteen years old, no criminal convictions. Miss McAllister's picture, said the inspector, had been circulated at the morning briefing. One of the investigation team recognized her as someone he'd seen the day before the stabbing. The officer, off duty at the time, had been drinking with friends in a bar at the Dam Square end of Pijlsteeg when he saw Miss McAllister in the company of a Caucasian male, aged about thirty, medium build, approximately six feet tall, with short, dark brown hair and a suntanned complexion. The man and the woman had been conversing in English. In the light of this latest development, Oosterling wondered if I would care to call in at the station at my earliest convenience.

Today, I made another personal mandala, like Dympna taught me:

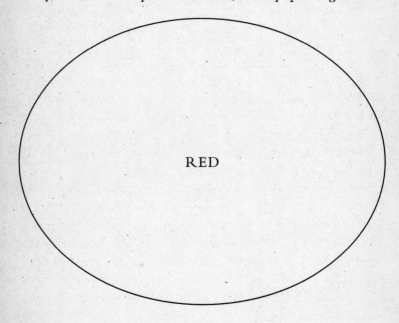

RED

When I'd done it, I screwed it up and threw it away so he wouldn't ever see it.

A spectator is at his most gullible when he believes he has discovered something which the illusionist hadn't intended him to discover. Take the illusion of the Magic Light Box. A tall cabinet stands centre-stage, its walls made of thin translucent panels illuminated from within like a paper lantern. I show the cabinet to be empty, then close the door. A silhouette slowly forms on the front panel, as though a woman's shadow is being cast on to the paper screen by the interior light. The silhouette, in turn, gradually transforms into a recognizable figure, a pretty young woman in sequinned costume, smiling, apparently having been made to materialize inside the cabinet. Then, the image flickers like a faulty television screen and, even though the picture returns to normal, there is a realization in the audience that this isn't a real woman but merely the projection of a film. This sense of a fraud being discovered is heightened by the performer feigning appalled embarrassment at having his methodology exposed by a technological glitch. The spectators' amusement edges towards gloating superiority; the 'living' image of the woman is rendered ridiculous, a testimony to my incompetent charlatanism. It is at this moment that the paper panel bursts open and the figure – the very real, very lovely, Kim – steps out with a flourish from the cabinet. Cue astonished delight, rapturous applause. Peter Prestige savours the moment. Not only have I fooled the audience, I have fooled them into mistaking me for a fool.

I intended to effect a similar sleight on Insp. Oosterling, deflecting his attention from the real 'trick' by allowing him the delusion of uncovering a lesser one.

The interview room was the one where I'd made my initial statement on the day of the stabbing: that missing ceiling panel exposing dusty pipes and cable ducts, that elliptical necklace of cigarette welts on the table's white Formica surface. Pale green walls, dark green floor. No window, other than the small rectangle of meshed glass in the door. The same two men in suits – Oosterling, and a colleague with a Polish-sounding name which I'd forgotten since our previous meeting and wasn't reminded of. As before, he said nothing during the interview, preoccupied with note-taking or operating the tape; occasionally a question, or my reply, would cause him to glance up with melodramatic significance – a habit that appeared to disconcert the inspector more than it did me.

Oosterling was tall and skinny with a pudding-basin cut of dark-blond hair ill-suited to his angular face and a robust moustache that overhung his upper lip and upon which he would suck moistly from time to time as an aid, it seemed, to concentration. Instead of the conventional smart shirt and tie, he wore a mustard-coloured polo shirt beneath his suit jacket, unbuttoned at the throat. His attire complemented a casual manner that lent the proceedings an incongruous atmosphere of informality. Only in the words he used did his seriousness and professional diligence manifest itself. Words selected with ponderous deliberation, though it was hard to say whether this was due to acute interrogative strategy or the encumbrance of having to conduct an interview in an alien language. I liked him. I had the impression this feeling wasn't reciprocated.

'So. You know this woman, Mary Ruth McAllister,' he said. A statement, not a question, uttered with no difference in emphasis to our inconsequential preamble: the weather, my journey (by tram) that morning to the police station. 'She is a friend?'

'I don't know her.'

'You were witnessed drinking with her.'

'I didn't *know* her – I'd only met her a few minutes before we went to the bar. She told me her name was Kirsty.'

'Kirsty.' He paused to refer to a notebook. Looking up at me again, he asked, 'You went to the bar together with her?'

'I went by myself, then she followed. We'd . . . arranged to meet there.'

'Where did you see her before?'

'In Pijlsteeg.'

A flicker of reaction. 'How was this?'

I hesitated. 'She was soliciting.'

'She was a prostitute? You know this?'

'Yes, I knew it.'

'There are no windows in Pijlsteeg.'

'She's not a window girl.'

'So. Tippelen.' After a muttered exchange in Dutch with the other detective, he added: 'A street girl. You know, it is forbidden in this part of Amsterdam.'

I shrugged. He aped my gesture. *Sure, it happens.*

'This is why she wants to go to the bar with you?'

'Maybe. I don't know.'

Inspector Oosterling watched me light a cigarette, nudging a foil ashtray across the table towards me. I thanked him. He asked how much she was charging, and I told him: five hundred guilders. He smiled. His colleague shot me one of his looks.

I addressed the inspector. 'You think I was being ripped off?'

'Ripped off?'

'Too much money for a fuck, d'you think?' No reply, the obvious response left unsaid: *Depends who you fuck and what sort of a fuck it is.* 'Anyway,' I added, 'I never got my fuck and she never got her five hundred guilders.'

He fretted at his moustache, delaying his next question. 'Why did you not have sex with her that day, when you have been talking in the bar?'

'She was worried her pimp would find out. This was a . . . private arrangement, I suppose you'd call it, between me and her. I think she was a junkie.'

'You think so?'

'Yeah, she needed cash to pay for drugs. Heroin.' I tapped my arm. 'There were needle-marks, you know?'

He waited for me to continue.

'Also, I didn't have that much money on me.' As I said it, I wondered whether this was one elaboration too many; I decided to simplify things, get to the point. 'We arranged to meet again the following day, at the flower market.'

'You were to go where with her, Mr Clarke? Your hotel?'

I shook my head. 'I didn't want to risk smuggling her past reception.'

'So. Where?'

'She said she'd take me somewhere. An apartment. She didn't tell me where.'

Oosterling's eyes tracked my hand to the ashtray then back again. I inhaled and let out a cloud of smoke that briefly obscured him before dispersing into the thin soup of accumulated fug beneath the ceiling. I nodded, in anticipation of his next remark.

'Sure, it was a risk.' Another drag on the cigarette. 'I was very stupid.'

'You have five hundred guilders cash and you go with a street girl some place you didn't know.'

'Like I say, stupid.' I tried to read him. 'I . . . she was English. *Scottish*. I suppose I trusted her more than I should've done.' He wasn't buying that, I could tell. 'OK. To be honest, I wanted her so much I didn't know what I was doing. I mean, I didn't think. My prick ruled my brain. D'you have this saying in Dutch?'

He sniffed. 'You have been with other prostitutes in Amsterdam?'

'No.' I hesitated. 'Yes. Yes, I have.'

'And you pay five hundred guilders every time?'

'No. Fifty, with the window girls – maybe more, it depends on the girl.'

'Five hundred, you get to fuck a junkie.'

Again, there was nothing about him to suggest he was becoming more probing, more confrontational – apart from the words he used. To leave his inquiry unanswered was tantamount to conceding the point.

'For five hundred, I was buying a couple of hours with her, not just twenty minutes. Also, I was getting whatever I wanted. *Anything goes*. That's what she said.'

'This is the purpose of your holiday, to have sex?'

'Yes.'

He nodded, studying his notepad once more. 'So. You told

lies to me before. About your visit to the bloemenmarkt, and about this girl. You said there was no girl.'

I looked down at the table. 'I was afraid my wife would find out. If there was no girl involved, it would be just another random attack on a tourist. A mugging gone wrong.' I paused. 'I thought I could get away without having to mention her.'

'Your wife thinks you are here on business?'

'Yeah.'

'Building-society business.'

I looked at him. He leaned back in his chair, clasping his hands behind his head. As his jacket lifted, I glimpsed twin ovals of sweat staining the armpits of his shirt. His face was inscribed with what I took to be intense dissatisfaction. Before he could formulate this into a question, I said, 'If this . . . look, if my wife found out, that would be it. Finished.' I swallowed. 'The thought of losing my family, my *children* . . .'

In his eyes, I saw disdain. *What kind of father – what kind of a husband – goes to Amsterdam for sex?* If Oosterling had a daughter, I imagined she'd have been about Kirsty's age. To him, I was pathetic. Which suited me just fine, because I'd rather he regarded me as pathetic than conniving, deceitful, suspect. I didn't care whether he liked or loathed me, as long as I was believed.

'You think she plans this robbery?' the inspector said at last, ending an uncomfortable silence. 'This Kirsty – Mary Ruth McAllister – she –' he conferred, with his colleague, 'she sets you up?'

'Yes. Yeah, it was a set-up. An ambush. I'm sure of that now.'

I explained how she'd behaved oddly in the moment before the man tying his shoelaces made his move, how she'd walked away, more or less ran off, without looking back or summoning help as the two assailants, her accomplices, set about me. If it hadn't been for the intervention of the man in the overalls, I said, the robbery would've been irresistible. At best, I'd have been roughed up and five hundred guilders poorer; at worst, it could've been me lying stabbed and dying in that alleyway. I didn't put this conclusion into words; I didn't need to – it hung between us like an admission.

Oosterling produced a photograph from a folder, said something in Dutch then, switching to English, asked, 'Is this the girl?'

I took the picture. Flame-red hair and alabaster skin; slightly younger, healthier, but unmistakably Kirsty. The coconut smell of her flooded my nostrils. I nodded.

'Please, for the tape.'

'Yes, that's her.'

He searched again among his papers, impatiently, apparently having difficulty locating something specific. I extinguished my cigarette, waiting for him to continue. His colleague stared at me, unembarrassed even when I returned his gaze. I removed another B&H from the packet, then changed my mind and put it back. As I did so, the inspector pulled a photographic contacts sheet from the file.

'The two men who attacked you, are they here?'

I took the sheet from him. A dozen faces in all, some black, some white. I studied them closely. None of them resembled either of my assailants, though four of the white men were immediately familiar. My stomach lurched. If I admitted that I knew them, I would have to reveal everything I'd succeeded in concealing from him – my true purpose in coming to Amsterdam, my illegal entry into the Netherlands, my fugitive status from the British police, my connection via Rosa with the racketeers at No. 37 Pijlsteeg, my *name*. I would be arrested, taken into custody, sent home – denied the chance to fulfil Rosa's mission. Among the men in the photographs were Kirsty's minder, the man with no eyebrows; Max van Dis; van Dis's accomplice on the train, whom I'd seen captured with him on CCTV footage. The fourth man whose picture I recognized was Nikolaas van Zandt. I examined the contact sheet a little longer, then handed it back to the inspector.

'No,' I said, truthfully. 'None of these men attacked me.'

Here's a tale, told to me by Inspector Oosterling one morning in a smoky interview room with pale green walls and a missing ceiling panel. A tale of prostitution and the vice squad and No. 37 Pijlsteeg, outside of which I had unwittingly been ensnared by a young Scottish hooker known by police to be resident there.

'For years, we watch this place. We know what happens there. Sometimes, we go in – we make a *raid*. So. We make many raids. We arrest one or two peoples, we take away films and magazines, some drugs.'

'But you don't close them down?' I asked.

'What is there to close? Prostitution is not illegal here. Pornography is not illegal here. There are no children . . . the place is clean and is not so noisy and they have papers – you know, a safety certificate – for fire. The drugs? The drugs are for "personal use". We find small amounts only. No dealing.'

'What about violence, exploitation, intimidation?' Conscious of the inspector's curiosity at my sudden agitation, I toned it down. 'Kirsty, this Mary McAllister – she was scared stiff, you could see it. Afraid of what would happen to her.'

I wasn't thinking of Kirsty, I was thinking of Lena being stabbed repeatedly between the legs with an imaginary cigarette. I was thinking of Rosa.

Oosterling spread his hands. 'Someone is afraid. Where is the crime?'

'You don't think the women are coerced . . . I don't know, almost like slaves?'

He smiled. He was warming to me – at least, less hostile – now that my earlier deceit had been admitted. I suspect he was also amused to be marking my card – me, Mr Taaffe Clarke, an English building-society deputy manager on a sex holiday –

about how I'd tangled with one of Amsterdam's more intractable criminal gangs.

The inspector shook his head. 'We have no witnesses, no proof of nothing. We talk to the girls, they tell us – always, they tell us – they are happy. They like it there. They have money, food, some place to sleep. Nobody hurts them. Nobody makes them do this. This is what they tell us.'

'And you believe them?'

'No, of course, we do not believe them.'

Another tale, told by Denis Huting, about prostitution and the history of Amsterdam. In 1345, in a house in Kalverstraat, a dying man received the last sacrament, only to bring it back up into a bowl. The piece of holy bread was tipped on to an open fire; the following day it was found intact, undamaged by the flames. A miracle was declared. The chapel that was later erected on the site became a place of Christian pilgrimage, attracting thousands of visitors and helping to establish Amsterdam as a focus for trade. Ships came. With the ships came sailors, and the sailors, at sea for weeks with their fellow men, wanted women. And so another kind of trade, the oldest kind, began to flourish. Denis smiled. To this day, the procession in Kalverstraat remained an annual event in the religious calendar. To this day, he hardly needed to add, there were those who came to the city not to worship, but to fuck.

I was back at Denis's having been released with a formal caution for wasting police time; I wasn't to return to Britain without notifying the Dutch authorities. *For the moment it is better you stay with your friends in De Pijp.* Officers had gone into No. 37 Pijlsteeg with a warrant, but Mary McAllister wasn't to be found, nor any men fitting the description of the pair who'd attacked me. I recounted these latest developments to my hosts over a game of cards. (A game punctuated by Cees's allegations that Denis and I were using manipulative skills to cheat.) I told them all about Pijlsteeg, prompting Denis's historical anecdote.

'You see, Amsterdam is built on the illusion of a miracle!'

I needed a miracle, too, if I was to win a hand of poker with

260

ten high. I folded. Denis won with a pair of kings, raking the
pot – five chocolate biscuits – towards him. He ate two and
stacked the rest with what remained of his previous winnings.

We'd been playing for half an hour when the phone rang.
Denis went out to the hall, returning a moment later and raising
his eyebrows at me.

'Oosterling?' I asked.

He shook his head. I hurried to the phone, but when I picked
up the handset there was no one on the line. I spoke uselessly
into the mouthpiece, then hung up in annoyance. Almost immediately, it rang again. This time, my anxious 'hello' received
a response – brusque, businesslike, but unmistakably sibilant.

'Hello, Mr Red.'

'Lena.'

'Do you have something to write?'

'Yes.' There was a pad and pen beside the phone. 'What . . . ?'

She dictated a few words then rang off. This was her message:
Tomorrow. The Kabin Klub, St Annenstraat. Girl no. 6.

Over post-coital nicotine, Rosa once asked if I'd ever been with
a prostitute. I said I hadn't, which was true. She asked if I ever
would. I said I didn't know, which was also true. Would it have
bothered her if I'd replied in the affirmative to either question?
She didn't answer, except to remark upon my use of the phrase
'replied in the affirmative'. This, the extent of our first and last
conversation on the topic of prostitution.

Denis's reaction, when I revealed her former profession, was
curiosity. Could I tell, from the way she was with me, and with
the benefit of hindsight, that there'd been a time when she'd
done it for cash?

'D'you mean, was she good?'

'Was she?'

'Yeah, she was. She was unbelievable.'

He nodded.

'But always on her terms,' I said. 'What we did, how we did
it, how *often*.'

'You think maybe prostitutes do it on the client's terms?'

'I'd say so. I mean, sure, she sets the price, but . . . Look, he wants a blow-job, she gives him a blow-job. He wants her on top, she goes on top. He wants kinky, she gives him kinky. Once he's handed over the money, the client's the one in control.'

'Control.' Denis considered this for a moment. 'OK . . . OK, say he wants to fuck someone who wants to fuck him. Who really *wants* to. Who really wants to fuck *him*. For sex and, also, because she loves him. How much does he pay for this?'

I walked the maze of alleyways. Some of the rooms were in use, heavy purple curtains drawn across a glass-panelled door; a few were empty and unlit, a handwritten or printed notice fixed in the window – '*kamera te huur*' – followed by a telephone number; the remaining rooms boasted their business. Each occupant, in a condition of elaborate undress, posed on her threshold like an animated lingerie mannequin – a pout, a smile, a wink, a beckoning finger; a muzak of enticements in Dutch, German, English, issued into the jostle of gawpers and cruisers that thronged the narrow lanes. Each door stood ajar to disclose the interior of each small, square room: an enamel washbasin, mirrored walls, tiled floor, plain white ceiling, a single bed neatly made up with white sheets – the whole, blushing with suffused red light. A tall black girl in a basque grinned at me, showing white teeth and gums the colour of bruised cherries. *Hey, vous êtes français? Italia? Hey, where you from?* I went by, avoiding eye contact. In a neighbouring doorway, a peroxide blonde teenager tugged the 'V' of her panties to one side. *Boys, you like shave pussy?* I pushed through a knot of men – youths, mostly – who'd been halted by the flash of smooth cleft flesh. Their faces described what they'd witnessed. With a window girl, you know – you're *absolutely certain* – she'll let you fuck her. The moment you set eyes on her, a fuck – any variety of fuck you want – is yours for the asking. Guaranteed fuck, right now. How many women do you encounter in your daily life who you can say that about? None. That's how many: none. I saw it in the eyes of those men, I sensed it in myself. *I can do this. I can step inside that room, hand over the cash, and fuck her.* And that would be about as complicated, as involved, as it got. I edged round a corner into the next steeg. There, a few paces ahead – where the alleyway spewed into St Annenstraat – gaped the gaudy entrance to the Kabin Klub.

Not a club, though it did have cabins. Dozens of them. Each partitioned cubicle housed a seat, a video screen, a complimentary box of tissues, a door that bolted, and walls reinforced with stainless-steel panels to prevent holes being gouged by customers interested in watching one another wank. A coin-slot activated a private film show, a control button enabling the viewer to surf forty channels of continuous hard-core porn. Every taste catered for. I'd seen such cabins before (1991 European Festival of Magic, Hamburg – eight of us on a stag-night outing to the Reeperbahn. For the remainder of our stay in Hamburg, whenever one of us went off to the toilet he would be pursued by a chorus of *Channel Twenty-one!* Don't ask, you don't want to know).

That day in Amsterdam, I wasn't interested in videos, I was there for the live action. A revolving stage surrounded by cubicles from which voyeurs watched a naked performer writhe erotically to music, each punter feeding coins into a slot to prevent a screen from descending over his viewing window. A board by the cash kiosk displayed photographs of the performers – seven women and a transvestite. The pictures were numbered. I studied the shot of Girl no. 6. Slightly older than the others – mid twenties, at a guess – she had shoulder-length brown hair streaked with ash-blonde highlights, hazel eyes and an expression intended to be alluring but which lent her a moody, sullen air. She was cupping a breast in each hand; the breasts seemed incongruously large in relation to her slender frame. Her pubic hair was mani-cured into a thin vertical line like an exclamation mark. According to the caption, the girl's name was Kola. There were booths where you could pay for a one-to-one with the artiste of your choice, provided she wasn't otherwise engaged. When I arrived, a digital panel showed Girl no. 2 was on stage, no. 3 – the TV – was on standby, and no. 1 was on her break. Several men were loitering, waiting for a changeover of performers on the revolving platform. I stepped into one of the one-to-one cabins, bolted the door, made myself comfortable and pressed '6' in a set of call buttons.

I tell her about the things we do together, the places we go . . . the stuff we talk about. Lovey-dovey shite is mostly what she wants to hear. Bedtime stories, she calls them.

Carole-Ann goes, 'When you're not here, I have to make up stories in my head about you two.'

She's only met him the once. In the Eagle and Child, just before her latest relapse. The Relapse Queen they call her in here. Like none of them had any fucking problems coming off. Like, they just snapped their fingers and that was it. Carole-Ann reckons that trick with the ash is the most romantic thing she saw in her whole life.

She's doing OK. Down off the meth bit by bit. She's eating again. She's sleeping better. But she still needs the stories and the card tricks. She still needs me to tell her: You can. I did, so can you. She still needs me. I got clean, I got out of here, I got a job, I got a place to live, I got Red. Red is, I dunno . . . to her, me and Red are the next hook. It's like she's weaning herself off on to us. On to me.

'You don't need this place any more,' she says.

'My arse.'

'You don't.'

'You think I only come back to see you?'

'I look at you, Rosa, and I see myself in a year's time.'

'Well, fuck your luck.'

When she laughs, it's like there's something still going on inside her that isn't bollixed.

I fetch flowers and magazines. Thursdays and Fridays. She's my 'project'. My mission. She says doesn't Red mind me spending so much time with her? And I say no he doesn't, cos if I tell her he doesn't know anything about it it means I'm deceiving him, and – the way her mind works – if you deceive each other you can't be Mills & fucking Boon any more. So I deceive her instead.

Nice days, me and Carole-Ann sit outside or go for a walk with some

265

of the others. Picnics and that. Wet days, we play scrabble, cards, charades. We drink tea. We eat chocolate. We smoke. The only men here are the ones we talk about, and the ones in our heads we don't talk about. There's a sign on the wall says:

YOU DON'T NEED HIS DRUGS
YOU DON'T NEED HIS MONEY
YOU DON'T NEED HIS DICK

Only, someone's crossed out the last one. Which is a hoot, if you ask me.

I lit a cigarette. As I did so, someone entered the cubicle to my right, the sound of the bolt sliding home and of my neighbour settling on to plastic upholstery clearly audible through the plasterboard division. I stared straight ahead, studying my reflection in the large glass panel separating me from a pink armchair that dominated the other half of the booth. A figure – white, naked – emerged from behind the chair, where a curtain hung across a dark recess; she sat down, my mirrored features now superimposed over hers. Girl no. 6: Kola. She resembled her photograph so exactly it was uncanny. Gone, though, was the moody pout, in its place a portrait of tedium that a practised smile failed to disguise. She wore her nakedness unselfconsciously, like comfortable clothes. Assessing me: *another wanker*. Muffled voices penetrated from the adjoining booth, a man and a woman talking in Dutch. I gave Kola a smile.

'Hi,' I said.

'English? American?'

'English.'

'Thirty guilders,' she said, indicating a small table beside her chair, bearing half a dozen dildos in a variety of colours, shapes and sizes, and a tube of KY Jelly. 'You can play with yourself too, if you want.'

Her accent sounded French. I eased a folded slip of paper through a slot in the glass. The voices ceased next door, to be replaced by the waspish drone of a vibrator. Kola seemed oblivious. Opening the note, her bored expression, her imitation smile, vanished as she read the message; her eyes, when they met mine, were attentive in their reappraisal. She was alert, almost apprehensive. The note, its solitary word, *Kerrygold*, was set aside on the table. I took care not to let my gaze wander from her face to her breasts, her neatly manicured vertical slash of pubic hair (the latter disappearing from view, in any case, as she crossed her legs). She was wearing a delicate gold ankle-chain.

'My name is Red.'

'I am Kola,' she said, glancing at the partition between us and the neighbouring cubicle. She lowered her voice. 'Did you see him go in?'

'No.'

We listened, her caution infecting me. The vibrator was accompanied now by feminine whimpers of, presumably, feigned arousal and the creak-creak-creak of plastic upholstery as the punter, I imagined, responded appreciatively to the performance. *The sound of one hand clapping*, I said. Kola didn't get the joke.

'Is there somewhere we can go?' I asked.

A shake of the head. 'It's better here.' She relaxed, apparently satisfied that we weren't being spied upon. Even so, I had to lean forward to catch her words, my own steaming the window that divided us.

'Have you talked to Lena?'

She gave a shrug. 'Naturally.'

'I want to help.'

'She told me this.'

Kola picked up a dildo – large, black and remarkably similar in design to the ubiquitous *Amsterdammertjes*, phallic roadside posts sporting the city's triple-X crest, which keep motorists from veering on to pavements or into canals. She switched it on and laid it back down on the table, its hum adding to the aural backdrop.

'Do you have a pen?' she asked.

The biro just fitted through the slot in the glass. Kola took it, and scribbled on the reverse of the note I'd given her.

'Here.'

Neat, undecorative handwriting. *263 Prinsengracht*. I looked up.

'You must go to this address tomorrow. Eleven a.m.'

'Is this where Nikolaas lives?'

'He will meet you there.'

And do what? Supply me with money and tickets to convey

the woman posing as Charity Jackson from Dutch soil to British? Or brief me: how and where to meet her, how to effect her escape from No. 37 Pijlsteeg . . . times, places? Perhaps the plan would be put into effect there and then, and I would need to go prepared for a hasty departure. Kola shrugged off my queries, faintly irritated, I sensed, by my anxiety. *I can't tell you*. Nikolaas would explain, she said. I looked at her, picturing her with the young man in the snapshot of Rosa. His latest lover? I wondered if she knew about Rosa, about Rosa and Nikolaas. And about Nikolaas and Jan Peters.

'How come he lets you work in a place like this?'

She gave a snort. 'He *lets* me?'

'OK, how come you work here?'

None of your business, said Kola's expression. But her disdain turned at once into a display of ostentatious indifference. A working girl – streetwise, resourceful – she was too adept at handling hassle, at handling *men*, to be fazed by my crude curiosity.

'Money. Why does anybody work?' She gestured at her surroundings. 'Also, I am on the inside. I see things, I hear things. You understand?'

I tried a different tack. 'How long have you been with him?'

'I don't work for him,' she said, after another pause; choosing to misconstrue my inquiry. 'I don't work for anyone.'

'You just pass on messages from him to people he doesn't trust.'

Her eyes held mine. 'You follow Lena, you speak to her – she doesn't know you. Nobody knows you for sure. The men at Pijlsteeg, if they find Nikolaas they will kill him. So, naturally, we don't trust you.'

I didn't respond. Kola pushed her hair back from her forehead, the highlights catching reflected shimmer from a concealed wall lamp. Her breasts rose and fell with the movement of her hands. She caught me looking.

'Lena says you are doing this because of Rosa.'

'Did you know Rosa?'

She shook her head. 'I heard she died.'

'Yeah.' *She died*. That was all there was to say about her, the

269

reduction of her life to the fact of her death. Rosa was a dead person. 'I'm not . . . I'm not doing it for her, I'm doing it for myself.' I hesitated. 'I'm not *just* doing it for her.'

Kola's annoyance visibly receded. At least, she appeared to be making an effort to keep it in check, to repair the atmosphere between us. She apologized. The circuitousness, the subterfuge, the elaborate procedure by which I was allowed to meet Nikolaas, she explained, were an insurance against my exposing him, deliberately or unwittingly, to danger. As for my motivation, it was immaterial to her – *you do this for yourself, but this isn't about you*; the only people who mattered, she said, were Nikolaas van Zandt and the woman who was Charity Jackson. Next door, the sounds of mutual masturbation stopped. Voices, a rustle of clothes, a bolt being drawn back, a door opening, footsteps. Kola told me to wait five minutes before leaving. With that, she stood abruptly and let herself out through the curtain. Her knee jolted the table. A small dildo was dislodged, rolling with slow-motion inevitability across the top and falling to the floor. The large black one, which she'd neglected to switch off, continued to vibrate, its whine amplified in reverberation against the table's wooden surface. The curtain twitched. From the shadows, a cat appeared. Siamese. It sprang gracefully up on to the armchair and, pausing only to register my presence beyond the glass screen, insinuated itself among cushions still impregnated with Kola's residual warmth.

I don't use live animals in my act, never have done. (Nor dead ones.) I've never produced a rabbit from a hat, only toy bunnies at the kids' shows; I've never caused white doves to appear in, or vanish from, a cage. As an experiment, I once spent a wet Sunday afternoon trying to train Merlin to place a paw on a particular playing card among a line of twelve arranged face down on the living-room carpet. He sat watching with apparent fascination as I repeated the procedure – dealing and re-dealing, issuing the spoken command which, with constant reiteration, I hoped would prompt him to select the correct card. Then he stalked off. Rosa, spectating, thought it was a hoot.

More trouble than they're worth. Besides, when Kim applied for the position of stage assistant she stipulated that she couldn't work with animals because she was allergic to *anything with fur, feathers, four legs or an unsatisfactory IQ*.

'What about dolphins?' I asked.

'You pull a live dolphin out of a hat, you don't need me working for you.'

That remark clinched the interview, I don't care what anyone says about my employing Kim because of her appearance. In fact, an early routine I devised after she joined the show required her to wear a cat costume – head, tail, the lot – rendering her looks irrelevant. The Nine Lives illusion. Nine separate illusions, in effect, constructed on the premise that I was a callous cat owner intent on killing off an unwanted pet. I blew her up, shot her with a crossbow, tied her up in a sack and dumped her in a tank of water, sawed her in half, decapitated her in a guillotine, impaled her on a sword, set her alight, crushed her between two beds of spikes . . . and each time, as I proclaimed her demise, The Lovely Kim, in the guise of the black cat, would emerge unscathed, aloof, prowling the stage on all fours in a remarkable facsimile of feline disdain. The climax, the ninth life, was a disappearance – I laid a large mat down, to preclude the use of a trapdoor, and enticed her on to it with a saucer of fresh cream. The cat sat on the mat. As she lapped at the cream, I draped a thin silk cloth over her. When I whisked the cloth away: no cat, just the mat and the saucer. I addressed the audience. *At long last, I've got rid of that* . . . Laughter. Applause. People pointing. I turned to look behind me and there, in the dark recesses at the rear of the stage, Kim's grinning mouth, complete with whiskers, was floating, disembodied, against the backdrop of a pitch black curtain.

Kim was always naked inside her cat costume. *Too bloody hot in there*. When she peeled off in the dressing room, her skin would be pinkly luminous, her blonde hair damp and tousled and flattened against her forehead, the swathe of dark curls between her legs jewelled with perspiration.

★

We dined at the small Surinamese restaurant downstairs from their flat, Denis and Cees tutoring me through an unfamiliar menu. The wine came compliments of the owner. *Without us, no profits*, Denis explained in a whisper. He even claimed credit for the addition of the un-Surinamese dish of *poffertjes* to the list of desserts. It was over this last course that talk turned to my visit to the Kabin Klub. I described Kola to them, recounting our conversation as best I could between Denis's persistent questions and Cees's hiccups – legacy of too much spicy food.

'You think they trust you, now?' Denis asked.

'I don't know.'

'Maybe this Nikolaas van Zandt will not come.'

I shook my head. 'They need my help.'

He forked another *poffertje* into his mouth, washing it down with white wine. 'What is this place where you have to meet him?'

'A house, I think. In Prinsengracht.'

'Where in Prinsengracht?'

'Number 263.'

Denis and Cees exchanged glances.

'You know this address?' I asked.

They laughed. It was Cees who answered. 'Everybody in the world knows this address. Well, OK, they know the girl who was living there.' He hiccuped. excused himself then hiccuped again. 'Prinsengracht 263,' he said, 'is the Anne Frankhuis.'

The bells of Westerkerk struck ten as I crossed the bridge over Prinsengracht. Beneath me, a sightseeing boat disturbed the water, vents in its curved glass roof open to admit the breeze. Passengers were taking snapshots. I followed the canalside road, its cobbles resonant with each passing car. Columns of mature elms made an avenue of the canal, their laden branches overhanging houseboats that sighed on their moorings in the wake of the tourist craft. And there, a short distance from the church, some two hundred people stood in line, a long spindly finger pointing the way to the Anne Frank House. I'd arrived early, on the advice of Denis Huting: *Always, there are queues.* Even so, it was hard to see how I would gain admission in time for my meeting with Nikolaas. I was wearing sunglasses, a baseball cap and ill-fitting clothes loaned by Cees, and I'd taken a roundabout route to the museum to ensure I wasn't followed.

Beside No. 263 was a construction site, screened by gaily coloured hoardings. The wooden panels formed a temporary exhibition, displaying a sequence of children's paintings under the heading: *de rechten van het kind.* The rights of the child. Eleven in all, each with an accompanying illustration: Right to Protection; Right to an Education; Right to Life; Right to a Homeland; Right to Play; Right to Friendship; Right to Equality; Right to Freedom; Right to Grow Up; Right to Self-Expression. One title was missing, above a picture – by *Heleen, 12 jaar* – of children standing on yellow ground against a blue sky, five facing one way while a sixth child addressed them. Right to be Heard? Or maybe it was a sermon: Right to Faith. I wondered how Rosa might've interpreted it; but, truth was, I didn't have a clue what she'd think. A young woman directly ahead of me in the queue leaned against her companion and remarked, in English, that there was no Right to Love.

'You'd think that'd be a basic right,' she said. '*Love*, yeah?'

The friend nodded. Their heads were touching, her dark hair fanned on his shoulder. They kissed; their faces, in profile, were so close I could've reached out and touched them. How d'you enshrine 'love' in a Bill of Rights? How d'you *make* people love? I didn't say anything. I just stood in line, edging almost imperceptibly towards the museum entrance. The young woman's partner gave her a nudge.

'With all these people hanging around outside every day,' he said, 'makes you wonder why the Nazis took two years to find her.'

When was the beginning of the end with Rosa? The day we met is the cynical answer. And, in a way, that's true; but that's always true, about everything. The *potential* was there from the word go, but that's always true as well. On the morning after the night of the stigma, when Rosa invited herself to move in, we talked of future fuck-up. Of an ending. So you have to search somewhere else for a cause, for the origins of an actual – *the* actual – cause. As I stood outside the building where Anne Frank had hidden, I wondered whether her discovery came with the impact of an inevitability – fulfilment of an ending she'd feared and foreseen for herself from the day her family took refuge. *This is how it ends*. The unconscious dread made conscious, made fact. Betrayal. Capture. Death. And, between beginning and end, two years of living in hope that it might turn out otherwise. A different ending. For me and Rosa there was also a moment when the possibility of a different ending disappeared. And our demise, too, owed itself – as I'd always suspected it would – to betrayal.

1) An act of sexual infidelity.
2) Rosa's claddagh ring, reversed so that the heart no longer pointed inwards.

We were gardening, preparing for the imminent onset of spring: pruning roses, gathering the mulch of fallen leaves neg-lected since the previous autumn, giving the back lawn its first trim of the year. We'd been working for an hour, going about our separate tasks, our breath made visible in the chill air of a Sunday morning. It was five days before Rosa died. I took a photograph, catching her by surprise as she tackled a bloomless bush with a pair of secateurs.

'An Irish rose,' I said.

She didn't say anything.

'You're blushing.'

'It's the cold,' she said, resuming her work with a methodical intensity.

I returned to my own job, mowing the lawn. Rosa had been quiet for a couple of days, quiet for *her*; she hadn't smiled as often as usual and when I had managed to make her laugh, her responses seemed forced. Just tired, she said, when I asked if she was OK. So I let it go. Gardening – gardening *together* – had been my idea to bring her out of herself, and to close the distance between us. But, that morning, ours wasn't a companionable silence. We worked independently, self-contained. The picture – the last I ever took of her – prompted our first significant exchange of words. The second came when I caught sight of Rosa hurrying indoors. I went after her. She was standing at the kitchen sink, douching her hand. The water was pink, splashing over the unwashed breakfast things.

'It's only a nick.'

'Let me see.'

'I'm *all right*.'

I took her by the wrist, drawing her hand towards me. Blood dripped on to the floor tiles, making a cluster of scarlet stars between our feet. There was a razor-thin incision near the tip of her middle finger, oozing copiously; messy rather than serious.

'Thought I'd prune my fingers while I was at it.'

'I *told* you to wear gloves.'

She withdrew her hand, placing the injured finger back under the tap. I fetched antiseptic, cotton wool and sticking plaster and between us we cleaned and patched the cut. It was then that I noticed her ring – the claddagh, reversed. She saw me register the change. She also saw, as our eyes met, that I suspected the

275

reason for it. We stood close in the kitchen for a moment without speaking, then I went back outside.

The primary cause was us, Rosa and me – our predisposition to behave, and to react, in the ways that we did. Even before she died, I was losing her. Even before the *betrayal*, I was losing her. The fact is I never trusted her; and once there's distrust, you start to seek the signs that substantiate it. And that really is the beginning of the end.

Quarter past eleven. Late. It was only as I paid the entrance fee that I realized I wasn't sure if the meeting was supposed to occur inside or outside. I had the impression I was to go in, though I couldn't recall Kola being specific. *He will meet you there.* If I was meant to wait outside, surely Nikolaas would've approached me in the queue? But if we were to meet in the museum, he too would have had to stand in line for more than an hour, exposing himself to recognition. Perhaps he had arrived much earlier and was already waiting inside – my role, to mingle with the throngs touring the exhibition until he appeared, as if from nowhere, at my side. This thought, triggering a memory of my clandestine liaison with 'Kirsty' in the flower market, almost sent me fleeing into the street. But I took my entry ticket – distracted, queasy with anticipation – and went in.

I removed the cap and sunglasses in what felt oddly like an act of reverence. The English couple were above me on a steep staircase, her thick-soled shoes clonking on the floorboards, a hand fretting self-consciously at the back of her brief denim skirt. At the top, a bottleneck of people filed into the first room for a video show. I stood at the side through three screenings, surreptitiously scanning the audience for him. It was eleven thirty when I moved on, passing beyond an imposing hinged bookcase that had once served to conceal the door to the hideaway in the back annexe.

A variation of a Houdini anecdote occurred to me: *A building stands empty. Eight Jews enter the building. The building is still empty. Where did the Jews go?*

The route directed us into a room where one wall was calibrated with pencil lines recording the heights of Anne Frank and her sister during their time in hiding. A middle-aged woman was looking at the marks. She held one hand to her mouth; a man put his arm around her, squeezing. Others waited respectfully for the pair to move away before taking their turn to look. None of them was Nikolaas. A group encircled a display case – a doll's house re-creation of the interior of half a century ago, complete with furniture; in the real room, visitors gazed out of the window, once screened off but now a whitewash of light. No Nikolaas. I browsed, dallying, scrutinizing a jaded map of Normandy, allowing crowds to pass by. Each fragment of blond hair, of beard, of tanned skin, each half-seen figure in the procession, brought a fleeting promise of Nikolaas, and then was not him. I moved on. In my pocket was a picture, his features frozen beside Rosa's in a beery toast – features I'd studied so often I no longer had to look at the photograph to remind myself of him. I expected a face, a glimpse of a face.

But, in Anne's room, it was voice and a brush of physical contact that made me start. As I inspected a board pasted with pictures of pre-war film stars, someone standing right beside me spoke two words: *Shirley Temple*. I hadn't noticed him, yet he'd drawn so close our shoulders were touching. Turning sharply from the picture of the child star to the man who'd uttered her name, my excitement was transformed instantly into disappointment. Thinning grey hair, aged flesh; his remark hadn't even been aimed at me, but at the woman to his left. He exuded an overwhelming odour of stale tobacco. Reacting to *my* reaction, the man who was not Nikolaas withdrew half a pace, casting me a look of puzzled irritability before ushering the woman away. I was left alone with Shirley Temple, fossilized in childhood, cupping her cherubic face in her hands in a goldilocked pose of happiness. I don't know how old she was when that picture was taken – seven? eight? – but already she'd learned to give good face.

No Nikolaas, not in Anne's room nor in any of the others. Nor was he among those standing three deep at a series of display boards in the exhibition area. It was midday, an hour after we were due to meet. I was drifting, absorbed into the hordes of visitors but, unlike them, not preoccupied with what there was to be viewed. My mind wasn't filled with Anne Frank or the holocaust, nor even with Rosa, but with Nikolaas; I was conducting a one-way conversation with him in my head, two questions in endless repetition: *Where are you? Why aren't you here?* So, when I saw her, I was taken unawares. Long brown hair, glasses, dressed entirely in yellow – she was ahead of me, turning from one of the information panels at the far end of the room. Her eyes caught mine – no, she was already looking at me when my gaze met hers and caused her to flush, briefly, then look away. *Lena.* The hair must've been a wig, but I saw enough – mouth, eyes, the shape of her neck – to recognize her. She made for the exit. I went after her but, in the crowds, it was hard to hurry. She was reduced to a flash of bright yellow fabric among figures funnelling out of the room. I jostled my way to the door, peripherally aware of the muted annoyance I left in my wake; down some stairs two at a time, and into the museum shop. Busy, people jockeying for position among the souvenirs. No Lena. Women, women with dark hair, women with glasses, women in yellow; but the woman with dark hair and glasses and a yellow dress had gone. I went outside. In Prinsengracht, the line for the Anne Frankhuis now stretched as far as the Westerkerk; half a dozen folk drank coffee at tables lining the pavement; others, who had preceded me through the exit, were streaming away in all directions. No yellow, apart from a man with a lemon-and-white-check sweater over his shoulders. I'd lost her. I'd lost her, and I didn't understand how she could've gone so far or so quickly; but if she was still in the museum – if, somehow, I'd missed her or she'd contrived to be missed – there was no way I could go back inside without rejoining the queue.

I didn't have to. As I turned to look back at the exit door, it opened and the woman in yellow emerged on to the steps descending to street level. It was her, the woman I'd glimpsed across a congested exhibition room: same dark hair, same glasses, same dress. When she reached the bottom step, I was there, obstructing her path. For the second time, our eyes met, only now, her face was so close we could've kissed. So close I could inhale her perfume and detect the textured surface of foundation applied to her skin. Her bespectacled pupils dilated in a flare of surprise, but with no recognition of me beyond the faint acknowledgement that this was the man who'd caught her staring at him a few moments ago. I also saw that, whoever the woman was, she wasn't Lena.

What you should do . . . What you should do is say, 'I don't love you any more.' Just say it. 'I don't love you any more.' Over. Finished. Then, the fuck is fine because it isn't that kind of fuck now. It isn't a lie. It doesn't make lies of everything else you ever said or did.

If the fuck is how you say it then what kind of a way is that to tell someone? I mean jesus christ isn't it enough to make you ashamed of yourself?

Or, I don't know, I don't know, maybe the fuck is the way you both find out. The fuck is the words, the fuck is what makes the words true even though you haven't said them yet. Even though you haven't even thought them.

Excuses. Bollix. Shite.

A fuck.

So I take the ring off. I have to use soap cos it won't shift and then it does and I put it back on again so it's pointing the other way. And I'm crying. I'm crying my fucking eyes right out of my head.

Next thing I do is call the refuge. I tell them I'm doing the Amsterdam run.

'You sure about this, Rosa?'

'Yeah, I'm sure.'

'A week. We need a week to set it up.'

'Fine.'

I can wait a week. A week is OK. In a week I'll be gone.

The Lost Princess

Imagine a Cleopatran tomb. The Lovely Kim enters, stage right, in the guise of an Egyptian princess. I swathe her from head to foot in bandages then stand her in an upright, open sarcophagus. I give it plenty of patter. Soon, the princess's diaphanous image, translucent and unswathed, is seen to appear before the sarcophagus, in the manner of a ghost emerging from her own mummified form. This beautiful apparition drifts towards the audience, slowly fading until she vanishes like a mirage before their eyes. I go to inspect the mummy, but the moment I touch the bandages they collapse in a small pile at my feet. The sarcophagus is empty. Cue applause.

The illusion of the Lost Princess – don't ask how it's done, because I won't tell you. All I will divulge is that at no point does The Lovely Kim die and go to heaven. Also, she wears a black wig, because who ever saw a blond Egyptian princess? (Not that the wig has anything to do with the methodology.)

'Magic is a form of seduction,' I said. 'It leads you astray, up here.' I tapped my head. 'People fall for me. When they watch me as Peter Prestige, I get to screw every one of them.' We both laughed. 'You know the prostitute's slang for sex with her clients?'

Denis Huting shook his head.

'Turning tricks.'

She wasn't Lena, she wasn't anyone. I left her there, with her embarrassment. I walked from Prinsengracht into the city centre and out again to Rembrandtplein and followed Utrechtsestraat as far as the junction with Kerkstraat, with its apartment building with the black door and the window boxes and the nameplate saying *Lena Gies*. With Lena. I would sit with her and we would drink beer and eat sandwiches while she explained the reason for no Nikolaas. *No Nikolaas?* Maybe she'd be surprised to hear he hadn't turned up. Or she wouldn't, she'd know: *OK, this is what happened*.

'You are fucking me around.'

'No. Sure, we don't do this, Mr Red.'

It wouldn't happen like that because we would sit drinking beer and eating ham sandwiches that she'd made, laughing about no Nikolaas and the woman I mistook for Lena. *Now you see us, now you don't!* She would arrange another time for me and Nikolaas, so no need to say to her, *You are fucking me around, Lena.*

Lena Gies, it said.

I pressed the buzzer, waiting for her voice from the pattern of holes. Out of breath, I was, from walking so far so fast from the Anne Frankhuis with no food and no beer and no cigarettes because all I wanted was to be talking to Lena. I lit a B&H. I was sweating, my hands making damp stains on the filter. I pressed the buzzer again. Again. Fuck, Lena. You are fucking with me. Again. The other buzzers then, one after another; I didn't get the Dutch woman with the crying baby, I got a man.

'Excuse me, I want to see Lena Gies. She lives on the second floor.'

'No, she is come.'

'Come? What d'you mean she is come?'

'*Come.* Two days, she is come.'

'I don't understand.' Then I did. The man wasn't saying 'come', he was saying 'gone'. 'When will she be back?'

'No. Another persons is living there now.'

Think. Think. 'Do you know where she's gone? Her address?'

'I don't know this. Sorry.'

The crackle of the intercom died. Her windows closed, curtains half-drawn and a different colour to the ones I'd seen before. I tried to imagine her photographs of Amsterdam, rehung on other walls. Gone. But the scarlet flowers remained in the window boxes, her name was still there in the panel. A teenage girl on a bicycle rang her bell and I had to step out of the way. A tram went past on the main road.

In the 'brown' bar on the opposite corner, I ordered a Grolsch. It wasn't the barman from the previous time – white shirt, black trousers – it was an older man in a cardigan. The beer was so cold it hurt my throat. I drank some more, smoking. I ate olives from a small glass dish. Acting normal, trying to calm myself, to moderate my behaviour – my mood – in front of him. Patient. Did he know the woman who used to live in the second-floor apartment? I pointed out of the window. He shook his head.

'Lena Gies,' I said. 'Blonde hair. Young. Very pretty.'

'No.' He was making coffee for a man in a smart suit, waiting for the screech of the machine to cease before adding, 'I don't know her.'

'She must've come in here sometimes, drinking.'

'Young? Very pretty?'

I nodded. 'Yeah.'

He gave me a wink. 'I think I seen this girl in my dreams, you know?'

He was still laughing to himself when he set the coffee down, placing a biscuit in the saucer. He wasn't looking at me, he was looking at the man in the suit. They spoke to each other in Dutch. The man in the suit looked at me then looked away.

'Did she come in here? Lena Gies.' I made stripes with my hands on my chest. 'Sometimes she wore a blue-and-white shirt, like a rugby shirt.'

The barman moved away to serve someone else. I watched him, then finished my beer, put too much money on the counter and left. I talked to the assistant in the shop beneath the apartments, I talked to neighbours. And to the woman who worked in the coin-op launderette where Lena had gone when I followed her that time.

'She used to do her laundry here. Lena. Blonde hair.'

'*Ik begrijp het niet.*'

'Lena Gies.' I pointed along Kerkstraat. 'She lived in the apartments.'

'*Ik begrijp het niet.*'

'You don't know her?'

A young man with long hair said, 'She says she doesn't understand.'

I took a tram back into the city. In the Kabin Klub, the picture of Girl no. 6 showed a woman weighed down with great folds of flesh, her bosom veined like blue cheese. *Jucey Mama*. None of the photos was of Kola. I asked the guy in the change kiosk about her, but he said he didn't know no Kola. *I only bin here one weeks.*

'I saw her yesterday, in one of the booths.'

He shrugged.

When I kept on at him, when I started swearing and banging the Perspex screen and causing small stacks of coins to topple, two bouncers appeared from nowhere and dumped me in the steeg like a sack of rubbish.

Did you know the truth about us, Lena? About me and Rosa. Is that why?

A while ago – at the beginning of all this, when I began to lay out my memories – I said there were three things, three occurrences, that had reduced my life to what it is now. One was Rosa's death, another was the arrival of the parcel containing Rosa's bag – a mystery, followed by a clue to the mystery. I didn't want to talk about the third thing, the third occurrence; frankly, I didn't even want to think about it. I still don't. But I must, because if it hadn't happened the other two events might never have taken place.

We were in the rehearsal room at the Port Mahon, perfecting the illusion of the Lost Princess. In costume: me in the usual DJ, Kim wearing a flowing, sleeveless white gown – more Roman toga than Egyptian. Our dilemma was the 'blocking', the sequence of movement required for Kim's ghostly image to appear to emerge from the mummy. She made the slow walk, with me as her audience, noting any misalignment then repositioning the sticky-tape markers that plotted her path across the bare boards.

'Fancy a break?' I said.

'I thought I was the impatient one?'

'Do I sound impatient?'

Kim came over. 'Impatient, bored, irritable, fed up . . .'

'Hungry and in desperate need of a fag,' I said, finishing her sentence.

'*Hungry?* It's not even eleven yet.'

I opened the curtains. 'My breakfast . . . met with a mishap.'

Kim took a cigarette from me, I held the flame close and she leaned into it. She withdrew. I lit mine, then replaced the lighter and pack on the window-sill. The glass vibrated with the passage of a lorry outside. It was raining, the street below busy with umbrellas and cars leaving trails in the wet.

'Rosa?' she asked, exhaling smoke against the window pane.

'The bowl hit the sink from ten feet away,' I said. 'Most of the cereal didn't make it that far.'

'What was the quarrel?'

'You know, I'd love a quarrel. A quarrel would be so relaxing.'

She laughed, raising the hand that didn't have the cigarette to her mouth. As I shared Kim's reaction to my words, I felt the tug of guilt, of complicity in amusement at Rosa's expense. Of intimacy, in her absence, with a woman who wasn't her. Also, the shame of my own embarrassment at Rosa's temperamental excesses when I was far less bothered by her spontaneous, soon forgotten, rages than I would've been by hours and days of moods and sulks and dreadful silences.

'I like her,' said Kim.

'No you don't.'

'I do.' She took a drag, breathed out. 'She's good for you, actually.'

'Sure.'

'So, what was the argument about?'

We'd stopped looking out and were standing facing into the room, absorbing warmth from the radiator beneath the window. Someone was hoovering downstairs in the pub, preparing for opening time. I tapped ash into my cupped hand.

'I think she's fucking around,' I said. 'Not *around*, I mean fucking someone. Some guy. Her boss, possibly.'

'And you told her this?'

I shook my head. 'The argument was about the washing up, whose turn it was.'

'Yeah, right. No subtext.'

'I'm not allowed to use big words any more.'

Kim gave me a look. 'You've really got it in for her, haven't you?'

I told her about the unsolved Interflora mystery on Rosa's birthday, the trips to London – always by herself – to see friends I'd never met. I could see from Kim's expression she wasn't impressed by the evidence I'd accumulated in support of my suspicions.

'The other night she had a phone call – she told the caller she'd ring them back and when I asked who it was . . . well, she said it wasn't anyone I knew.' I exhaled. 'But she seemed put out. Uncomfortable.'

Kim drew on her cigarette. She knocked her excess ash into my palm, and, by nothing more than her silent attentiveness, extracted a tumble of words from me that encapsulated my doubt, my fear, my gnawing jealousy. By the time we were ready to resume rehearsals, I was all talked out. I went to the gents and sluiced my face at one of the basins. When I returned to the rehearsal room the curtains had been closed and Kim was in position, spot-lit. She paced out the steps – close to being bang on this time. I joined her, kneeling on the floor beside the line of black crosses.

'It's just these last few,' I said. 'You were drifting out to the left.'

She knelt down too and we began realigning the markers. As Kim picked at the tape, I glanced up from what I was doing and saw one bare breast fully exposed in profile through the slash in the side of her toga. When she realized, she stopped.

I'd like to say I was drunk, but I wasn't.

I'd like to say Kim reached out to touch my cheek, but she didn't.

I'd like to say she made it easy, so all I had to do was slip my hand inside the gaping material, but she didn't, she sat bolt upright and started to get to her feet.

I'd like to say I let it go at that, but I didn't.

What I did was grab her by the arm and kiss her and go on kissing her, even when she twisted her face from mine; what I did was yank her robe loose with my free hand despite her resistance. Then, as suddenly as I'd started, I stopped. I let go of her. We knelt in enforced proximity on the floor, heaving hot breath in and out, dishevelled; Kim's face was flushed. She shoved hair out of her eyes, drawing back the drooping tresses of black wig. I tasted blood on the inside of my upper lip. There was a silence, perforated by its own shocking resonance, and by muffled noises from the bar, and by our breathing, and by an insistent clatter of rain against the skylight directly above us. The room had become darkened by the downpour.

Eventually, Kim said, 'Is that how *she* likes it?'

I shook my head.

Kim looked at me, intently, apparently seeing my face – *really* seeing it – for the first time and finding countless points of fascination there. As though she believed the secret to what might happen wasn't contained in my next words or deeds, nor even in my eyes, but in the very pores of my skin. I went to speak, but stopped myself. There was nothing to say. She knew as well as I did that I wanted her but I also wanted not to cheat, and that these two desires were incompatible in the absolute. I had to choose. I had to fuck her or walk away. I stood up. I undressed; when I'd finished undressing myself I undressed her. She went to remove the wig, but I held her hand.

'No,' she said, freeing herself from my grip and taking off the hairpiece so that her blondeness spilled from its confines. 'It's me, not her.'

And there, hidden behind a screen on the wooden floor of the rehearsal room, I fucked Kim.

On my final morning at Denis's place, I received an unexpected visit from a policeman – not Oosterling, someone in uniform. He gave me a package. My wallet. Handed in by a refuse worker, who'd found it near the flower market. The cash was missing, but the rest of the contents – including the card for the hotel – were intact, if somewhat damp. So I hadn't been pickpocketed after all. I couldn't help smiling. Walking wet streets into the small hours for fear of returning to my room, the uncomfortable night in a laundry cupboard, all this time in hiding at Denis's apartment . . . and there never had been any risk of my assailants in the steeg tracing me. Amusement, then panic, at the thought of the police having stumbled upon my true identity; but the only name among the items in the wallet was that inscribed on my brother's business card. Taaffe Clarke. *My* name, to all intents. I signed for the wallet, the officer left.

I turned my smile on Denis. 'I didn't need to live here, with you.'

'If you don't live here,' he said, indicating the newly closed front door, 'I don't get to flirt with the pretty policeman.'

We rejoined Cees in the kitchen. He was cooking for three, the officer having declined – with embarrassment – Denis's entreaties for him to have lunch with us. The room was steamy. Cees, stirring the contents of a pan, had his Walkman on – seemingly oblivious to the utensils and ingredients that decorated every surface like abstract art. I was reminded of Rosa, trashing my own kitchen with pancake debris.

'You okay?' Denis put a hand on my shoulder.

'Yeah, fine. Just . . . you know.'

He fetched three beers from the fridge, opened them, put one within reach for Cees and stood the others on the table. He sat opposite me. Bigger than ever, a male version of the new Girl no. 6, *Jucey Mama*. I thought of Kola, her slenderness, the delicate ankle-chain. Where was she, now? Where was Lena? And Nikolaas? Charity Jackson? I swigged from the bottle, went to light a cigarette, then remembered the house rules and slotted it back in the pack. Charity Jackson. The arrogant young face in the fake passport I'd found among Rosa's belongings, still working at Pijlsteeg. Or worse. An aroma of tomatoes, accompanied by the tinny beat of the Walkman. Denis raised his beer, drank, lowered it again. Glistening lips. Rosa − *look, no hands!* − using her lubricated mouth to roll a condom over a punter's cock.

'What you going to do now, Red?'

I shrugged.

'You think they will contact you again?'

'I don't know.'

He was watching my hands. My hands, repetitively tapping the base of the beer bottle against the table; I wasn't even aware I was doing this until I saw him watching. I stopped, then started again and had to stop myself a second time.

'What about the hotel?' he said. 'Or maybe you want to live there again now it is safe?' He gave one of his wheezy laughs. 'Too many nights on the futon, listening to two men having sex.'

'What music's that?' I twisted in my chair. Cees had his back to me, head going in rhythm with whatever tune was filling his ears. 'Hey, Cees?'

'He can't hear you.'

Facing Denis again. 'I thought I recognized it, the music.'

Denis drank some more beer, his eyes on mine over the tilted bottle. Serious.

'That plastic chicken you gave me,' I said, 'it's still on my bedside table at the Terdam. Unless they stole it, the cleaners or someone.'

He didn't answer. I stood up, went over to the French windows. I wanted to go out on the balcony and smoke and look down into the streets, the river, but I couldn't get the handle to work. I stared out instead, through the glass. The sky was absolutely white. In an apartment across the way, a young woman was ironing.

Denis's voice. 'Now maybe you have to say OK, I quit. I go home.'

In a porn movie she wouldn't be ironing, she'd be on the sofa: naked, bored, playing with herself. Someone enters the room – the guy from next door, a workman, she's left the door unlocked – or it's her husband, home early with one of his mates . . . smiles, a few words of dialogue, then the sucking and fucking. She's up for it. Porno women are always up for it, for anything with anyone anywhere anytime.

'Red?'

'What?'

I turned, went back over to the table and sat down. Cees was distributing place mats, plates, cutlery, condiments. I was conscious of Denis watching me the whole time. Cees moved away and I heard the shoosh of water.

'Denis,' I said, 'have you ever been unfaithful to Cees?'

Without even glancing in his partner's direction, Denis replied, 'No.'

One word: no. Simple as that. I frowned, swilling beer around in the bottle and watching froth collect in the thin green neck. I went to speak, then had to clear my throat. I said, 'I was unfaithful to Rosa. With Kim.'

Denis didn't respond.

'A week before she died.' I looked at him, holding his gaze. 'You're the only person who knows. No, you're the first person I've *told*.'

After lunch, I told Denis I was going home. I would catch the tram to Centraal Station, go to Schiphol and board the first available flight to London. No more Taaffe Clarke. *You're right, Denis, I've done all I can.* Forty-eight hours since Nikolaas had failed to show, and not a word. Something had gone wrong, the plan had been aborted, and they couldn't – or wouldn't – tell me why. What could I do? Nothing. Without them, I was useless. I reeled off the itinerary again: pack, leave the flat, go to the station, go to the airport, go home. I could be in Oxford by nightfall.

'OK,' he said.

'Yeah.' I nodded, interested in the sensation of my head going up and down, up and down. Hard enough, and you could dislodge your brain. 'Yeah.'

'Go straight home, Red.'

'I'll phone you, soon as I get there.'

In the doorway, we shook hands. We hugged. Cees hugged me as well, and then I shook Denis's hand a second time. He looked me in the eye, the way he does.

He said, 'You don't know for sure she's still there.'

'Who?'

'Even if you find her, you can't help her by yourself.'

I let go of his hand and picked up my bag. I thanked him for everything.

'They *know* you,' he said.

'Who knows me?'

'Or you think you can hurt them? Is this it, to hurt one of them?'

I laughed. 'Denis, it's OK, I'm going *home*.'

'Maybe you want most of all to hurt yourself?' He lent this remark the weight of a realization that, having eluded him, was suddenly obvious. 'Hey? Let them do the same to you they did to Rosa?'

'I'm going home.'

He came down with me, to the street, and watched me go. I turned to wave a couple of times and he waved back. My hands were clammy on the plastic handles of the bag. I walked away from Denis's place, heading for the tram stop. When the tram came, I got on. I looked out of the windows. At Leidseplein, the tram stopped by the café where Denis had eaten *poffertjes* on my first morning in Amsterdam. Off again towards the Spui, and the heart of the city. Before long, the tram would draw to a halt outside Centraal Station. But I wouldn't be on board. I would be elsewhere. I would be crossing Dam Square – with its monument, its traffic, its pimps, touts and pushers, its tourists, and its bar with the Heineken sign. Heading into Pijlsteeg.

★

Here's what I think: the liar and the magician set out to deceive, but only the liar depends on being believed. The magician merely conceals the *method* of his deception; for the liar, this is never enough – he must hide the very fact of it. Another essential difference: once the methodology – the trick, if you like – is exposed, magic ceases to be magical, while a lie remains a lie even after the liar is caught out.

I lied to Denis.

I lied to Rosa.

In the days between the rehearsal of the illusion of the Lost Princess and that morning in the garden, when Rosa cut her finger, I lived a lie of omission by neglecting to tell her I'd fucked Kim. This lie, the common refuge of a man who, faced with a choice between fidelity or infidelity, decides to cheat, then tries to get away with it.

I lied, and I was caught out.

I have to give away the trick, I have to tell you how it's done.

First thing, Kim is not inside the bandages – the mummified form in the upright sarcophagus is actually a 'jimmy', a collapsible wire frame. Kim has let herself out of the false back of the sarcophagus, and through the screen which stands directly behind. Concealed from the audience by this screen, she slowly traverses the rear of the stage, her path plotted precisely by sticky-tape markers. A backstage spotlight illuminates her, a mirror in the wings is angled to reflect her image on to the front of the stage. There, at the apron, a plate-glass sheet is suspended – the lighting in the auditorium designed to conceal its presence. The mirror projects Kim's image on to the glass so that, to the audience, she is see-through – emerging from her own mummified form and approaching them like a ghost. The spot is gradually dimmed and then extinguished, causing Kim to fade with each step before disappearing. The bandages collapse, empty. As if by magic, The Lovely Kim has completely vanished.

The illusion of the Lost Princess, effected with traditional techniques from the magician's repertoire – the use of mirrors and the principle of Pepper's Ghost – as well as basic geometry and a reliance on people to believe their own eyes.

While we fucked, Kim thought she heard the rehearsal room door open. We paused, listened, heard nothing but rain on the skylight, and resumed fucking. Then the sound of the door again, banging shut. *It's the Invisible Man*, she whispered in my ear. In fact, the system of accidental airlocks in the Port Mahon was such that the use of a door in another part of the pub sometimes caused ours to open and close, apparently of its own accord. No matter how often this happened, it never lost the capacity to startle.

When Rosa failed to meet me for lunch that day, as arranged, the truth – the appalling possibility of what had occurred – didn't sink in. I assumed she was still angry over our fight at breakfast. Even her uncharacteristic quietness, her distance from me, in the days that followed didn't impress their significance upon me. She was tired. Not until I saw her inverted claddagh ring was I struck by the idea of the invisible *woman*: Rosa arriving at the pub – early, soaked from cycling in the pouring rain – and being signalled upstairs, as usual, by Don, the landlord. Rosa, opening the rehearsal room door to be confronted by an apparition of me and Kim in translucent fuck.

If you stared at the graffiti long enough, you began to unravel words from the gore of incoherence. From the cyrillic script of spraypaint, from the very colours. And the words that *were* words – the names, slogans, messages – became mere shapes, merging into meaninglessness. Hieroglyphics on the once white door to No. 37. And the walls, daubed. Stained and flaking and mottled with urban rash; strung as before with slung bicycles on posts and pipes. The litter. The disproportionate angles of the roofs of buildings of ill-matched height, like men and women and stooped old folk standing in two lines so you were a child between them, looking up at a template of asymmetrical blue sky that revolved, when you did. And the windows, of No. 37, opaque with grime or with rectangles of reflection or just plain black.

These windows, knowing what was inside but keeping it from you. People went by, on foot and on bikes, but I didn't pay them any attention nor notice whether they paid me any. The intercom. The panel of buzzers, pertinent to each room of an interior so unknown to me that it was a warren.

Rosa. Rosa Kelly, née Houlihan.

Her rings and her bright green nails pick pick picking at the label on a bottle of Belgian lager. Her hands. The door would open any minute – any second – now and she would be there, taking my hand and kissing me, her lips moist with mine. *Hiya.* Taking my hand and walking with me to the bar at the end of the alley where we would sit and drink and smoke, her green nails shredding the label. And the barman, the men, looking at her. Her neck, her throat, her sarcophagus – not sarcophagus, oesophagus, as she tipped her head back to swallow the beer.

Beer. Cum. Smoke. Air. All swallowed by that same throat.

She would come out, any second, through that graffitied door, her head, intact, unimpacted with track chippings, or strobe-lit, flailing long black hair and sweat on a dance-floor or in the breeze on her bike. *Look no hands!* No lights. Her laughter. Her voice, talking like a Kerrywoman altogether ya bollix. And there's me. If you're good you can make me a giraffe out of balloons.

The ash. Her palm. Her tongue, streaked.

We wouldn't. She wouldn't. The door was closed and would not open and was not her and was not concealing her any more, only fragments of her past, like a blue plaque . . . Rosa Kelly Lived Here.

Rosa Kelly lived.

Go 'way'n' fick yeself ya ficken great gobshite.

Her inhalations of smoke and catfood, she loved the smell of Kerrygold/Merlin's food. Having recently fucked, you walk together along a riverbank aromatic with wild garlic . . . *Shoite* . . . Smoking with her fingers her cut finger her rings her hands on the handlebars as she cycled away. *Seeya* and turning cards of the tricks you taught her.

Her.

Me hole. Her, whole.

Herself.

I leaned my face against the cold metal of the intercom, pressing my ear against its perforations in expectation of nothing at all and for no reason. I could hear nothing. I could feel only metal and the moisture caused by my own touch. I laid the palm of my hand flat on the door, the wood made matt with old paint. No more pressure than that required to sustain contact between two surfaces, mine and its. If the building had been alive, I would've been able to detect the rhythms and warmth of its vitality.

Your furniture could do with a good scratching. She would, would not, would not appear at that window above me and smile and wave *down in a minute.* Falling at my feet and, as if by magic, passing from one place or condition to another.

'Mr Fletcher Brandon.'

I stepped back abruptly from the door, wheeling round in self-confession of my proper name to discover who had addressed me by it.

'Mr Fletcher Brandon,' the voice said again.

Inspector Oosterling smiled. He had shaved off his moustache, the bald pink expanse of upper lip disconcerting me more than the suddenness of him, of his words. He had taken his suit jacket off and wore it over his shoulders like a cape. There were two other policemen, standing apart and watching me.

'So. You wish to go inside? Or you wait for some persons to come out?'

I shook my head. I closed my eyes, and when I opened them he was still there.

We don't sit together, we sit so's we can see each other along the aisle. I've got a seat with a table and I'm playing patience, only two of the cards are stuck together with sugar from where Carole-Ann spilt some in the cafe while we were waiting. I pick it off, crusty bits of it. She kept going on about Red so I got the cards out to shut her up cos she'd play rummy for a week without sleeping if you let her. She beat me both times. Red this Red that. I mean, fuck sake. But I can't tell her. She's got this notion of him in her head like a dog with a stick it won't let go of no matter what, like you could lift it off the ground by its fucking teeth. She's reading now. Some book. And I'm shagged on a black ten. Your man next to me has this lap-top and a mobile that goes off every two minutes. I'm feeling the bag between my feet all the time, like anyone's going to nick it when it's there between my feet, only with what's inside it's like you want it chained to your wrist or something and even then you wouldn't stop touching it to make sure it's still there.

Didcot. Not far from his brother's place. Red on the doorstep and me going 'Seeya' and I didn't even look round when I said it. Seeya. I pick up, shuffle and deal out again.

There's a trolley going through with food and drinks. In the seats after Carole-Anne's, a guy's trying to buy something, but your trolley woman says she's away up the end of the train first and he's to wait till she comes back this way. He tells her, 'I've never heard anything so ridiculous in all my life.' I'm watching all this. When the trolley moves off, there's a guy – sitting opposite the one who's complaining – and he's gawping at me. Right at me. My hair, probably, where it's all shaved short. People stare all the time like you're a fucking freak show or something. Only I'm looking at him looking at me and he's got this sort of smile and then I see him, his face. Jesus fuck. Jesus fucking jesus fuck. The bag. The bag's still there between my feet, I can feel it. I can feel it. He's staring straight at me and I have to make Carole-Ann know without him seeing or we're fucked. She's reading her book still and I'm

296

turning cards over and laying them down like the guy's just some guy giving the lech only he's seen me see him and I can feel his eyes on me. What he mustn't do is find the bag under the table. Fuck this.

I look at my watch. We'll be coming into Reading soon and I've got to make it happen so even if they get me they don't get the passport cos as soon as they know it's Charity . . . So I stand up, like I'm off to the loo. And I'm walking along the aisle, towards Carole-Ann and towards him, but I don't look at them, not at all, not even a glance or nothing though I can tell she's watching me and wondering where I'm off to without the bag. The train's jolting and when I'm right by her I have to put out a hand on her table to steady myself and then I'm OK and I'm off again down the aisle, except what I've left on her table is the queen of spades. So now she knows we've to pull the plug. The number of times we've been through this, and now it's actually happening and my shit's gone jelly and I don't know if I can lead him away while she sees to the bag. Or if she'll fuck it up somehow. I caught her face for a second when she saw the card and jesus christ. And in my head I'm going: Do it girl. Do it.

I go past him. I don't look, but I can tell the way he sits he's going to follow, like he's bracing himself to get up once I've gone by. There's an old boy getting his suitcase down off the shelf and I have to push. The door opens and I'm through it and into the place where the toilets are. I could lock myself in but they're both engaged and I'm thinking shit shit shit when I see number two, standing there like he's been expecting me. Max van Dis. Jesus I'm fucked. I'm fucked. Fucking Max van Dis. He goes to say something only I'm moving towards the door. Houses out there, through the window, back gardens right up to the track and we're going slowly now, not fast at all and if I'm out the door and away I could make it to the fence, the fence is nothing, I could be over the fence and into the gardens and maybe they wouldn't follow cos they'd be so fucking surprised to see me jump but even if they did I could be away into the gardens and the houses so they wouldn't find me.

It's like he knows what I'm thinking, van Dis, like he knows what I'm going to do, cos he's moving to stop me and I hear the door go behind me with number one so it's him and me and him and I'm turning the handle it won't turn turning the it won't jesus fuck turning the *handle and it turns and the door's heavy but it swings open and I'm away out and jumping jumping jumping and the train's hardly moving at all and it's breezy I can feel the air on my skin and this is OK cos I land crunch with both feet on the gravel and I'm away but my knees give my knees give and I'm on my face on the gravel and there's metal the rail the rail and I'm thinking fuck it's electric but it isn't my hands and knees hurt and I'm winded but I'm off the train and there's track and grass and fence and a house with washing on the line in the breeze and I'm OK I'm OK cos I have the strength to lift myself.*

Everyone can be deceived. Whatever we desire, any area in which we seek to have control but don't, is a perfect place to hook any human being. Figure out what makes someone human and that's what you catch them with. The only defence is to trust no one, cut yourself off from any human interaction. Better to be deceived than live life like that.

— Ricky Jay, magician

Merlin and I are reunited. He no longer mopes about the house in expectation of Rosa, and holidaying with the Fievre family has also cured him of his predilection for butter and random violence. The twins cried the day I came to take him home.

'How are we fixed, you and me?' I asked Paul, when we were alone. 'Do I still have a friend and agent?'

'There's the possibility of a residency, if you're interested.'

'Yeah?'

'Cruise ship. Antarctic. Two years, no trips home.'

Strudwick and Crookes don't much like me either, nor does Oosterling; tired of my company after so many hours' interrogation – my role in the liaison between Dutch and British police resulted in a trip to Amsterdam for the officers from Oxford. A file on *my* offences is with the CPS, decision pending. Taaffe, at least, isn't pressing charges, though that may change when he receives his next credit-card statement.

Rosa remains dead.

I'm better. There was a time, here and in Amsterdam – especially in Amsterdam – when I was literally mad about her; mad with grief, guilt and remorse, mad with confusion and frustration. I am still all of those, but I'm better now; better than I was. I can be rational about her and myself in relation to her, about what I did. I cope. I function. Yet there isn't a day goes by when I don't think of her. Not a day. How long will that continue? Six months, a year? A lifetime? I don't think so, not a lifetime; already there is an alteration, a subtle transition, from thinking of her to not thinking of her. In the immediate aftermath of Rosa's death I couldn't get through an hour without unbidden thoughts of her; now, the measure of missing her is the day. Is it callousness, this slow, subliminal forgetting? I don't know. There are so many things I don't know.

Insp. Oosterling asked what I had hoped to achieve by coming to Amsterdam.

I told him, 'I wanted to understand the methodology of her womanhood.'

C'mere Red, you know what you're full of?

That's what I mean about madness: saying things so you hear her voice in your head afterwards, putting you straight. I don't do that any more.

A few days after my return, the doorbell rang. I'd just finished talking to Denis Huting and I had the idea that this was a spoof – he was in Oxford, not Amsterdam, had called from a payphone and was now at my door, in chicken costume. His way of apologizing for betraying me to Oosterling. But it wasn't Denis, it was a woman. It took a moment to recognize her; my shock transmitted itself, dissolving her already uncertain smile.

'Is it safe for you to be here?' I asked.

'I had to see you.'

Her hair was longer than I recalled from the CCTV picture and from the night of the stigmata, but the face – and the voice, from our one brief phone conversation on the eve of my departure to Holland – were unmistakably hers. Carole-Ann.

'When I heard she'd died, right, first thing I did was go out and score. I mean, I'd been clean for months but I just wanted to blank it. You know? I cooked up and everything, I had the strap on and the vein was tapped up and the syringe, the needle . . . I was that close. And then I heard Rosa's voice, in my head.'

'You stopped yourself, because of her?'

'No, man, I shot up. Fucking twenty quid, that gear cost!'

Carole-Ann laughed so long and hard I thought she wouldn't stop. She had me going as well, and it felt good. The first time I'd laughed – really laughed – in weeks; her too, I suspected. There were tears in our eyes. Then the tears in hers became real and she sobbed and I reached across to place my palm on her bowed head like a faith healer until she ceased of her own accord. She raised her streaked face.

'Did you stop at one shot?' I asked.

'Aye.' She nodded. 'Miracle, that.'

I looked at her.

'You know, a couple.' She sniffed. 'I'm OK, I'm getting there. I was out of it when I sent you the bag, actually. Didn't know what the fuck I was doing.'

We were in sunshine on the back patio, using the white plastic chairs and table Rosa had stolen from the pub. I told Carole-Ann about that and was surprised at how disapproving she seemed. Her accent was broad Geordie, though when I asked if she was from Newcastle she replied indignantly: *Sunderland*.

'Why do southerners always have to know where you come from?'

Daylight etched the cushions of discoloured flesh beneath her eyes. The sleeves of her denim jacket were too long. She matched me cigarette for cigarette, fidgety in her seat, hooking wayward locks of dark brown hair behind her ears now and then in a mannerism I'd seen captured on film on a congested railway platform.

'How did you find out she'd died?'

'I got off the train, right. Cacking myself. I've got her bag and I haven't a clue where she's at or what's going on but I'm – in my head – I'm going over what I have to do. I mustn't go back, I must hole up somewhere and ring them.'

'Ring who?'

'The refuge. I'm in this dump of a B&B in Reading and when I ring they don't know shite, so I've to wait and ring again.' She paused, composing herself. 'I saw it in the paper the day after. "A woman in her twenties" was all it said.'

'Did you go back to the refuge?'

'Nap. Unsafe. If they'd got that close to Rosa – if they knew what fucking *train* she was on . . . you know? I went to a friend's. That's when I sent you the bag.'

'What was I supposed to do with it?'

'I was hoping you'd go to the police, actually.'

'Fucked up there, didn't I?'

'Aye.' She smiled. 'Me an' all. They went ape. Police start

poking around, the whole thing's blown.' She faked posh: '*The integrity of the operation.* Yeah, right.'

Carole-Ann took her jacket off. She wore a black sleeveless T-shirt. Her right upper arm was tattooed with small dots and hexagons, in alternating green and violet, encircling her bicep like a bracelet. She didn't shave her armpits.

'Rosa fetched me back from Amsterdam.' She finished her cigarette and lit another, the sunlight making gauze of the smoke. 'She got me off smack.'

'Was that where she used to go, Thursdays and Fridays – to see you?'

Her eyes filled up again. 'I loved her, right.'

I didn't say anything. Carole-Ann began chewing her thumbnail, the cigarette, wedged between first and second finger, close enough to singe her hair. She sniffed.

'D'you believe in heaven?' she said.

'No.'

'I do.'

I got her to talk about Rosa's last day: the game of gin rummy in the café (*I beat her, I'd never beaten her before!* as though this in itself was an omen); the train journey. I asked how she'd been, her mood, her conversation. *You mean did she talk about you?* I shook my head. *Well, she didn't, right.* And I knew, then, that Carole-Ann knew.

'Why are you here?' I asked.

And she came out with it at last, the unasked question that had been nagging at us since her arrival. 'Were you screwing around?'

'Did she tell you that?'

'Were you?'

I hesitated. 'I was unfaithful, yes. Once, with one woman.'

'Rosa never told me.'

'She . . . I think she saw us together.'

She nodded. 'You look like the sort of bloke who'd do that.'

The phone rang. The answering machine was on, but I went inside to intercept. It was my niece, Gemma, asking if I was going to prison and if I was could she stay in the cell for a night to see what it was like and what would they give me to eat and was there telly? I talked to her, we swapped silly jokes. When I returned to the garden, Carole-Ann was standing at the end of the lawn, flicking ash on to the flowerbed.

'Was that her?' she asked, not turning round.

'No.'

I stood beside her, using her cigarette to relight mine then handing it back. Her hands were cold, the hairs on her forearm pronounced against the pale, blemished skin.

Things Carole-Ann told me that I already knew:

1) Rosa deliberately sat opposite me in the pub on the evening of the stigmata illusion, with the intention of letting me seduce her.

Things Carole-Ann told me that I didn't already know:

1) Vicky was a nickname, a throwback to Carole-Ann's days on the game in London, when she used to tout for business by Victoria station.

2) 'Charity Jackson' was sprung from No. 37 Pijlsteeg and brought back to the refuge. The escape plan, devised in the wake of Rosa's death, was entirely unconnected to the one I'd been led to believe I was involved in. Different name, different passport. At Nikolaas's instigation, Lena had misdirected me while the real rescue was effected.

'*Why?*'

She shrugged. 'In case you fucked things up.'

They knew I'd lied to Lena about the police and my brush with the men from No. 37. I couldn't be trusted; also, I couldn't be trusted not to be reckless. When I kept on asking questions, Carole-Ann lost patience. This wasn't about *me*, this visit, or about Amsterdam, or the refuge, or Charity Jackson – it was about her. She needed to talk about Rosa, because she missed the woman like fuck. *I need to have her alive in my head.* For two hours, beneath a receding sun, we talked of nothing else.

★

'Did you love her, Red?'
  'Yes.'
  'You couldn't of.'
  'I did.'
  'You couldn't of.'

It's more than a week since the visit. I don't expect to see her
or hear from her again, but you never know. You never know.
On her way out, she asked if I had a spare photo of Rosa, as she
had none; I gave her the last one, the one of Rosa pruning roses.

Now I too have received a gift, though not from Carole-Ann.

Today, a large package came, with Dutch stamps; flat, rectangular and heavy, enclosed in brown padded paper. It was
addressed to 'Mr Red'. I took it through to the kitchen, setting
it down on the table where I had once arranged Rosa's belongings.
The parcel was bound with twine. I cut it open. A large framed
picture lay face down on the splayed wrappings; there was no
accompanying note. Even before I turned it over, I knew what
it was: the portrait of Rosa I'd seen at Lena's apartment, stored
among others on the top shelf of a wardrobe. Black-and-white,
capturing Rosa in half-profile from head to waist, a breast laid
bare by the cleft in her gown; face, free from cosmetics, her dark
hair damp and tousled as though from a shower; she holds a mug
in one hand, rings on fingers and thumb. She isn't striking a
pose, she doesn't even know her picture is being taken – her
eyes, focused on something or someone out of shot, or maybe
not looking at anything at all. Rosa is smiling. She is at the refuge
and she is smiling with unaffected abandon. Regardless, in that
instant, of her impact on others and indifferent to their attention.
Not even having to assert *This is me*; content merely to be *Me*,
to sing *Me* to herself. For all the abuse, for all the physical,
emotional and sexual exploitation, for all the violation . . . Rosa
possessed, possesses, an essence of inviolability. *You can't touch
me*. And I see now that I wasn't big enough to contain her in
my life, nor strong enough to lift her higher than she could lift
herself. She was beyond me. I was the last in a long line of those
who deflected her from the one true source of her release: herself.

Despite the protective packaging, the photograph has been damaged in transit between Amsterdam and Oxford. The glass is cracked right across in a neat and almost horizontal fracture that divides the picture unequally in two. A straightforward repair job, this, to take the frame apart and reassemble it with a new pane of glass so you'd never be able to tell it had been broken.

Acknowledgements

My heartfelt thanks to my wife, Damaris, and to my friend, Phil Whitaker, for their love, support, criticism and encouragement.

In researching this novel I found the following books an invaluable help: *The Encyclopedia of Magic and Magicians* by T. A. Waters (Facts on File Publications, New York, 1988); *Telling Lies: Clues to Deceit in the Marketplace, Politics and Marriage* by Paul Ekman (W. W. Norton, New York, 1991); *The Moral Animal* by Robert Wright (Pantheon Books, New York, 1994); *Our Magic* by Nevil Maskelyne and David Devant (George Routledge & Sons, London, 1911); *Teach Yourself Magic Tricks* by John Wade (Hodder & Stoughton, London, 1992); *The Great Illusionists* by Edwin A. Dawes (David & Charles, Newton Abbot, 1979); *Working Girls and Their Men* by Sheron Boyle (Smith Gryphon, London, 1994); *Amsterdam – The Rough Guide* by Martin Dunford and Jack Holland (Rough Guides/Penguin, London, 1997); *Berlitz Pocket Guide – Amsterdam* (Berlitz Publishing Co., 1996); *Essential Amsterdam* by Michael Leech (AA Publishing, 1997); and *Act Normal! 99 Tips for Dealing with the Dutch* by Hans Kaldenbach, trans. J. G. Knecht (Prometheus, Amsterdam, 1996).

Numerous articles and letters in the *Guardian* and *Observer* were very useful, as were the following television programmes: *Liar* (*Horizon*, BBC2, 30/10/95); *The Lie Detectors* (*Witness*, Channel 4, 19/11/95); *No Child of Mine* (ITV, 25/2/97); and *Close Up North* on child prostitution (BBC2, 27/2/97).

I am grateful, too, to staff at the excellent Ramesis computing centre at Bradford Central Library for access to the Internet.

Almost all of the stage illusions featured in *The Houdini Girl* are based on actual feats performed by professional magicians down the years. In common with anyone who customizes the work of others to produce something new, I am indebted to the original artists. So, my thanks to the following for their inventions: Robert Harbin (1908–78), 'Zigzag Girl' and 'Assistant's Revenge'; Dante, The Mormon Wizard (1869–99), 'Backstage Illusion'; Herr Boelke, 'Creo', or 'Living Doll' as I call it; Oswald Williams, 'Dizzy Limit'; Leon (1876–1951), 'Fire and Water'; Guy Jarrett (1881–1972), 'Bangkok Bungalow'; Chuck Jones (b. 1942), 'Mismade Girl'; Frederick Culpitt (d. 1944), 'Bathing Beauty'; Cyril Yettmah and David Bamberg (1904–74), 'Light Cabinet'. The 'Basket Trick', aka 'Hindu Basket Trick', is an ancient illusion from India. The origins of the 'Lost Princess' (properly known as the 'Princess of Bakhten') are obscure, but the illusion derives its principle from 'Pepper's Ghost', invented by Henry Dircks and first demonstrated by Dr John Henry Pepper.

Finally, many thanks to Janet, who performed the stigmata illusion on a mate of mine one boozy night in a pub in Tooting – thereby giving me the idea for the opening scene of this novel.

M.B.